His gaze didn't
She was embarr

"Oh, I have no one to
she said wistfully.

"I may not be an expert on babies, but I do know how they're made. And I'm fairly certain there has to be a partner." It was his turn to shoot her a confused look.

"Adoption," she said.

And then he gave her another.

"Surely you've heard of adopting a baby before," she said with an exasperated look.

"Of course I have. I just didn't know that was your circumstance," he said stupidly.

Looking closer at the baby, Dallas couldn't help but notice the boy had dark curly hair.

Not unlike his own.

STOCKYARD
SNATCHING

BY
BARB HAN

First Published in Great Britain 2016
By Mills & Boon, an imprint of HarperCollins*Publishers*
1 London Bridge Street, London, SE1 9GF

© 2016 Barb Han

ISBN: 978-0-263-91913-4

46-0816

Our policy is to use papers that are natural, renewable and recyclable products and made from wood grown in sustainable forests. The logging and manufacturing processes conform to the legal environmental regulations of the country of origin.

Printed and bound in Spain
by CPI, Barcelona

USA TODAY bestselling author **Barb Han** lives in north Texas with her very own hero-worthy husband, three beautiful children, a spunky golden retriever/standard poodle mix and too many books in her to-read pile. In her downtime, she plays video games and spends much of her time on or around a basketball court. She loves interacting with readers and is grateful for their support. You can reach her at www.barbhan.com.

My deepest thanks to Allison Lyons. It's hard to believe this is already our 10th book together! Working with you is a dream come true and I'm so very grateful. Special nod to Jill Marsal for your unwavering support and guidance (and brilliance!).

My love to Brandon, Jacob and Tori. I'm so proud of each one of you. You're bright, talented and have the best quirks!

To Amelia Rae, you stole our hearts a year ago. Happy 1st Birthday!

And to you, Babe. I can't even imagine being on this journey without you. All my love. All my life.

Chapter One

It was a bitterly cold early October morning. The temperature gauge on Dallas O'Brien's dashboard read 17 degrees, beneath a gray sky thick with clouds.

As it turned out, the Lone Star State had a temper and its tantrums came in the form of cold snaps that made him miss having a winter beard. Dallas hated cold.

Yesterday, the sun had been out and he had been in short sleeves. Texas weather—like life—could turn on a dime.

Another frigid breeze blasted through Dallas, piercing his coat as he slid out of the driver's seat and then closed the door of his pickup. He flipped up the corners of his collar. Since there was no traffic, he'd made it to the supply store in record time. Normally the place would be open, but Jessie had been running late ever since his wife gave birth to twins early last month.

A car tooled around the back of the building and across the parking lot. Was that Kate Williams, the proud owner of the soup kitchen, The Food Project? Dallas hadn't had a chance to meet her yet, with everything going on at the ranch after his parents' deaths.

A female came out of the driver's side, rounded the car and moved to the rear passenger door. From this distance, Dallas estimated she wasn't an inch more than

five and a half feet tall. He couldn't see much of her figure through her thick, buttoned-to-the-collar, navy blue
peacoat. Her cable-knit scarf looked more like an afghan
wrapped around her neck. He suppressed a laugh. Apparently, she didn't do cold any better than Dallas.

From what little he could see of her legs, she had on
blue jeans. Furry brown boots rose above her calves. She
wore expensive clothing for someone who owned a soup
kitchen. And apparently—Dallas glanced at his watch—
that process began at five thirty in the morning.

This had to be her, he reasoned, as she pulled a baby
out of the backseat, bundled from head to toe in what
looked like a fitted blue quilt. Blue.

A boy?

Didn't that twist up Dallas's insides?

First, his ex Susan Hanover had dropped the bomb that
he was going to be a father. Then she'd pulled a disappearing act. And even the best private investigator money
could buy hadn't been able to locate her or the baby since.

Knowing Susan, she'd been lying to trap him into a
wedding ring. Dallas's finger itched thinking about it.

With her and the baby gone, all he had left were questions—questions that kept him tossing and turning most
nights.

What if she'd been lying? What if she hadn't? What
if Dallas had a child out there somewhere? What if his
child needed him?

Dallas would never be able to rest until he had answers.

Walking away from a child wasn't something an
O'Brien could ever do. Dallas had already lost his parents, and family meant everything to him.

As Ms. Williams closed the door to her vehicle, shivering in the cold, a male figure emerged from around

the side of her building. The guy had on a hoodie and his face was angled toward the ground. His clothes were dirty, dark and layered. He was either homeless or trying to look the part.

The guy glanced around nervously as he approached Ms. Williams.

Didn't that get Dallas's radar jacked up to full alert? He strained to get a better view. *Come on. Look up.*

All this guy would have to do would be ask Ms. Williams a question to distract her—say, what time the place opened. She would answer; he would rob her and then run. There were plenty of places to disappear downtown or in the neighborhood near the stockyard.

It would be a perfect crime, because not only was she holding a baby, but her thick clothing would weigh her down, making it impossible for her to catch him.

Well, a perfect crime if Dallas wasn't right there watching.

Then again, this really could be a man in need of a meal. Experience had taught Dallas not to jump the gun when it came to people. There was no shortage of homeless, even in a small town like Bluff, Texas.

The times he had driven by this location early in the morning and found the line of needy individuals stretched around the block were too many to count. He was pretty certain Ms. Williams's neighbors on Main Street didn't appreciate her clientele. None of them would be wandering through the stores after a meal to buy handmade jewelry or quaint Texas souvenirs. These businesses were important to the local economy.

Just then, the hooded figure lifted his head and made a grab for the baby.

This wasn't a robbery; it was a kidnapping.

Dallas spewed curse words as he ran full throttle toward them. "Stop right there!" he shouted.

Ms. Williams fought back and her attacker shifted position, ensuring she was between him and Dallas.

The baby cried, which seemed to agitate the attacker. Ms. Williams kicked the guy where no man wanted the tip of a boot. He coughed, then cursed as he seemed to catch sight of Dallas out of the corner of his eye.

The man shouted as he struggled to take the baby out of Ms. Williams's arms. "Don't come any closer!" His voice was agitated and Dallas didn't recognize it. Must not be someone local. The guy forced the woman back a few steps with him, a knife to her throat. "I didn't want to do it like this, but now she's coming with me."

The baby wailed and Dallas came to a stop.

This situation had gone sour in a heartbeat.

To make matters worse, all Dallas could see clearly of Ms. Williams was a set of terrified blue eyes staring at him. She had that desperate-mother look that said she'd do anything to save her son. Dallas's heart squeezed as she held tight to her baby with the determination only a loving mom could possess.

He hoped like hell she wouldn't do anything stupid.

Tires squealed from behind the building and Dallas instantly wished it would be his best friend, Sheriff Tommy Johnson. No way would Tommy be dumb enough to come roaring up, however. His friend was smarter than that and a better lawman.

A vehicle rounded the corner and lurched to a stop nearby. The white minivan's sliding door opened.

The attacker broke eye contact to look. If Dallas had a shot at taking the guy down, he'd grab it.

"Toss your keys to me," the kidnapper shouted to him.

Dallas dug a set from his pocket and pitched them forward.

If he didn't make a move soon, this jerk would disappear into that van with mother and baby. She'd most likely be killed and her body dumped before they left the county. Dallas had read about vicious illegal adoption rings in the area and stories of mothers being killed for their infants.

Between the hoodie pulled over the thug's forehead and the turtleneck covering his jaw, Dallas couldn't get a good look at his face. The guy glanced away again, as if calculating the odds of getting inside the vehicle before Dallas could catch him. Then he bent to grab the keys.

It was now or never.

Dallas lunged toward his target and knocked the guy's arm away from Kate's throat. The sheer amount of fabric she had wrapped around her neck made certain the blade wouldn't get anywhere near her skin. For the first time in his life, Dallas thanked the cold weather.

Breaking free, Ms. Williams bolted toward her car, while trying to soothe the crying infant.

In the bustle, the attacker broke out of Dallas's grip and darted toward the vehicle. Damn. No plates.

"The sheriff is on his way," Dallas said in desperation, knowing full well his target was about to hop into that van and disappear.

Just as expected, the guy hurled himself in the open door and, without waiting for it to close, shouted at the driver to go. On cue, the van swerved, then sped away.

Dallas muttered a curse. Pulling out his cell, he told Ms. Williams to stay put. Even though his pickup wasn't far, he couldn't leave her to give chase. No way would he risk this guy circling back or sending others to finish the job. Dallas would have to stay with her to ensure her safety.

At least this morning wasn't a total bust. The baby was safe in his mother's arms. Dallas could call his friend the sheriff, who would track down the minivan while Dallas guarded Ms. Williams.

"Where are you?" he asked as soon as Tommy picked up.

"A couple of blocks from Main Street," the lawman replied. "Why? You okay?"

"I'm in the back parking lot of the soup kitchen and a man just tried to abduct Ms. Williams's baby. There's a white Mazda minivan heading in your direction. He hopped inside it before I could get to him. No tags in front," Dallas reported, noticing for the first time that he was practically panting from adrenaline. He took a deep breath and then finished relaying the details of what had just gone down.

"Is there a high point you can get to for a visual on the minivan?" Tommy asked.

Dallas kept an eye on Ms. Williams as he climbed on top of the closed Dumpster to see if he could spot the vehicle. She had managed to settle the baby. Dallas was certain her hands would be shaking from her own adrenaline, and he was grateful for the few extra minutes he'd get while she fumbled with securing her son in the car seat. The panicked look on her face said she'd get as far away as possible the second she could.

"No. I don't see him," Dallas said.

"I'm on Main now. A couple of blocks from your location, but I don't see anyone on the street." Tommy asked Dallas to stand by while he gave his deputies a description of the vehicle. "I'm sending someone over to you just in case the guy is on his way back or sends someone else."

"Call me back when you know anything. I have to check on Ms. Williams and make sure she doesn't do anything stupid," Dallas said, knowing full well that her eyes would haunt him if he didn't ensure she was okay. It would be a long time before he shook off the image of those frightened sky blues, and he had to admit to being a little interested to see what the rest of her face looked like. He told himself it was protective instinct mixed with curiosity and nothing more.

Besides, she'd been as blindsided by all this as he had. He hopped down and jogged toward her sedan. "Ma'am."

She spun around with a gasp. "Kate. It's Kate."

He brought his hand up, palm out, to help communicate the idea that he wasn't there to hurt her.

"I'm Dallas O'Brien." He offered a handshake. She was most likely still in shock, and from the look of her wild eyes, she was in full get-the-heck-out-of-Dodge mode. "The sheriff is sending someone over to talk to us."

She stood there, frozen, for several seconds, as if her mind might be clicking through options. She didn't seem to realize there was only one: talk to Dallas.

"Do you know who that was?" he asked, figuring he already knew the answer. But he wanted to get her talking.

"No. I've never seen him before in my life." Her breath was visible in the cold air as she spoke, and even though she had on a thick layer of clothes, she was shivering. That, too, was most likely caused by residual adrenaline.

"First of all, I want to make sure you and your baby are safe. Can we go inside the building?" Dallas's own adrenaline surge was wearing off and he was starting to feel the biting wind again. He'd stay with her until law enforcement arrived and then he'd get supplies and head back to the ranch.

"Okay. Yes. Sure. I was going in anyway before—" She stopped midsentence, as if she couldn't bring herself to finish.

Then another round of panic seemed to set in.

"No. Never mind. We have to go somewhere else," she insisted, her gaze darting from left to right.

"He's gone. They won't be back, especially not while I'm here," Dallas stated.

"You can't know that for certain," she said quickly.

"Kate, I can assure you—"

"No. You can't. We can talk, but we have to do it somewhere else." She glanced about, her terror and desperation mounting.

Dallas's cell phone buzzed. He fished it from his coat pocket and checked the screen. "This call is from the sheriff. I need to answer."

She nodded.

"Give me some good news," Dallas said into the phone.

"Wish I could. Seems your white Mazda minivan is just as slippery as your suspect. There's no sign of either anywhere. We have no plans to give up searching. You'll be the first to know when we locate him," Tommy said with a frustrated sigh.

Dallas thanked his friend for the update and then ended the call, cursing under his breath.

An expectant victim stared at him, needing reassurance.

He shook his head.

"I have to get out of here before they come back," she said, making a move toward the driver's side of her sedan.

"Hold on," Dallas cautioned. "What makes you so sure he'll try again?"

Chapter Two

"I feel too exposed here. Can we go somewhere besides my soup kitchen? I need to get away from this place," Kate blurted out. It was then she realized that she'd been holding her breath. She exhaled, trying to calm her rapid pulse.

"A deputy is on his way," the handsome cowboy said, and his name finally sank in. Dallas O'Brien. She knew that name from somewhere. But where?

Her mind raced. She was still shocked that anyone would try to rip her baby from her arms in the middle of town. She'd waited so long for him, had been through hell and back. What kind of horrible person would try to take him away?

Tears threatened, but Kate forced herself to hold them at bay.

"My son will need to eat soon and I'd rather not feed him in the parking lot, whether a deputy is coming or not," she said, glancing from Dallas to Jackson.

The cowboy looked around and then checked his watch. "Fine. We're going to the sheriff's office to give statements, then," he said.

Jackson would be safe there, so she nodded.

"I don't have a child safety seat in my truck, so we'll have to take your car," he added, his voice sturdy as steel.

As calming as his presence was, her body still shook from fear of that man coming back and the horror of him trying to pry Jackson out of her arms.

"You gave him your keys," she reminded Dallas, wasting no time slipping into the driver's seat, while he took the passenger side of her sedan.

"Those? That'll get him into my old post office box," he said with a wry grin. It was the first time she really noticed Dallas's good looks. He had a strong, square jaw and intelligent dark eyes.

"I'd like to go home," Kate said as she turned the ignition. "Can the deputy meet us there?"

"Too risky," Dallas said.

It took a second for her to realize that he meant the men might know where she lived.

Could they?

Being single and living alone, she'd taken great pains to ensure her personal information remained private. Then again, with the internet these days, it seemed there was no real privacy left, and most people in the small town knew each other anyway. All a determined bad guy would have to do was ask around and he'd be able to figure out where she lived.

"All of Jackson's supplies are there, except what's inside the diaper bag in the backseat," she said as she pulled onto Main from the alley.

Dallas surveyed the area and she realized that with her driving, he would be able to keep watch for the minivan in case it returned. She racked her brain, trying to figure out how she knew him.

"We can pick up new diapers if need be. I don't want to go to your place until we know it's safe. For now, take a right at the next stoplight," Dallas said. He sent a text and she assumed he was telling the sheriff about their change in plans.

Normally, being told what to do was like fingernails on a chalkboard to Kate. In this case, she decided it was better to do as Dallas said. At least he was strong and capable. She already knew he could handle himself in a fight, and he had just saved her and Jackson, so she knew she could trust him.

"Three blocks ahead, take another right, then a left at the stop sign," he instructed.

She did. The horror of what had just happened was finally sinking in and it dawned on her how lucky she'd been that someone was there to help.

"I owe you an apology for being rude to you. Thank you for stepping in to save my son," she said. "You didn't have to get involved."

"You're welcome," Dallas replied. "I'm just glad I was there to help. I don't normally go to the supply store on Wednesdays."

"Your change of plans probably just saved Jackson's life." She shivered at the thought of what might've happened if this cowboy hadn't been there to intervene. "I know it saved mine."

Reality was setting in, which also made her realize there was no one to open the kitchen this morning. She needed to call her assistant director or dozens of people would go hungry.

"I have to make sure the kitchen opens on time. Is it okay if I make a quick call before we go inside?" She parked in the lot of the sheriff's office and gripped the steering wheel. "A lot of people are counting on me for a meal."

Dallas nodded, while staring at the screen of his cell. "Make an excuse as to why you can't do it yourself, and put the call on speaker. I don't want you to give away what happened yet. Got it?"

She shot him a sideways glance. "Why?"

"That was a planned attack. Those men knew exactly when and where you'd be alone. The sheriff will want to know if someone close to you gave them that information, and we have to assume it could've been anyone, even people you trust."

An icy chill ran down her spine. "You think one of my employees might've supplied that?" she asked, not bothering to mask her shock. Who would want to hurt Jackson or her? He was just a baby. Her mind could scarcely wrap around the fact that someone had tried to take him in the first place. Panic flooded her at the memory. "Who would plan something like this?"

"The sheriff will help find the answer to that question," Dallas said, his voice a study in composure, whereas she was falling apart.

"None of this seems real," she said, bile rising, burning her throat. "I think I might be sick."

"Take a few deep breaths." His voice was like calm, soothing water pouring over her.

She did as he suggested.

"Better?" he asked.

"Yes." She apologized again.

"Don't be sorry for wanting to protect your child," Dallas said. And there was an underlying note in his tone she couldn't easily identify. Was he a father?

"You have every right to be upset," he said.

"It's just that I moved here for a safe environment." And now it felt as if everything in her life was unraveling. Again.

"Who are you going to call to open the kitchen?" Dallas asked.

Oh, right. She'd gotten distracted once more. Her mind was spinning in a thousand directions. "Allen Lentz. He's my second in command and my right hand."

Her phone weighed almost nothing and yet shook as she held it. She paused. "You don't think…?"

"Get him on speaker." There was a low rumble to Dallas O'Brien's voice now, a deep baritone that sent a different kind of shiver racing down her spine—one that was unwelcome and inappropriate given the circumstances.

Her rescuer's name seemed so familiar and she couldn't figure out why. Wait a minute. Didn't his family own the Cattlemen Crime Club? She'd received an invitation to a Halloween Bash in a few weeks, which was a charity fund-raiser, and realized that she'd seen his family name on the invite.

In fact, her kitchen was one of the beneficiaries of his family's generosity. She hadn't met any of the O'Briens yet. She'd read that they'd lost their parents in an accident a few weeks ago.

So far, she'd dealt with office staff, even though she'd been told that the O'Briens personally visited every one of the charities they supported.

She hadn't expected Dallas O'Brien to be this intense, down-to-earth or staggeringly handsome. Not that she could think of a good reason why not. Maybe since he'd grown up with money she'd expected someone entitled or spoiled.

And yet now wasn't the time to think about how off her perception had been or that her pulse kicked up a few notches when he was close. She chalked her adrenaline rush up to the morning's events and closed the door on that topic.

Lack of sleep was beginning to distort her brain. No one had prepared her for the fact that she'd worry so much or rest so little once the baby arrived. No way would she admit defeat to her parents, either. They'd been clear about how much disdain they had for her decision to have a baby alone. Her mother had been mortified when she found out Kate was getting a divorce, so adopting a baby by herself was right up there on the list of ways she'd let her mother down.

Kate had expected her mom to come around once she met Jackson, but was still waiting for that day to happen.

This battle was hers to fight alone.

And none of that mattered when she held her little guy in her arms. No matter how tired she might be or how distanced she was from her family, she wouldn't trade the world for the baby of her heart.

"Hey, what's going on?" Allen asked, sounding surprisingly alert for five fifty in the morning. The phone must've startled him.

"I need your help. Can you open the kitchen for me?" she asked, trying to think up a reasonable excuse to sell him. Then she went with the tried-and-true. "Jackson kept me up all night again."

"Oh, poor baby. And I'm talking about you," Allen said with a laugh. He yawned, and she heard the sound clearly through the phone. "His days and nights still confused?"

"Yes, and I have the bags under my eyes to prove it," she said, hating that she had to lie to cover what had really happened. Allen had been nothing but a good employee and friend, and she hated deception.

"No problem. I'll throw on some clothes and head over," he said.

"You're a lifesaver, Allen."

"Don't I know it," he quipped. There was a rustling

noise as if he was tossing off his covers and getting out of bed.

"I'll owe you big-time for this one," Kate said.

"Good. Then get a babysitter for Friday night and let me take you out to dinner." He didn't miss a beat.

Out of the corner of her eye, Kate saw Dallas's jaw muscle clench. She couldn't tell if his reaction was good or bad.

"I don't know if I'll be in today," Kate said awkwardly. She quickly glanced at Dallas, realizing that she needed to redirect the conversation with Allen. "The Patsy family's donation should hit the bank today. Would you mind watching for it and letting me know when it arrives?"

"Got it," he said. "And don't think I didn't notice that you changed the subject."

"We've already gone over this, Allen. He's too little to leave with a sitter," Kate said quietly into the phone. Her cheeks heated as she talked about her lack of a life in front of a complete stranger, and especially one as good-looking as Dallas.

"That excuse doesn't fly with me and you know it," Allen said flatly.

Kate had no response.

"Fine. At least take me as your date to the Hackney party next weekend," he offered.

"I'm skipping that one, too. Can we talk about it later? I'm too tired to think beyond today," she said, then managed to end the call without any more embarrassing revelations about her life. The truth was her perspective had changed the instant Jackson had been placed in her arms. There was no man worth leaving her baby for, even for a night.

"Is he usually so…friendly?" Dallas asked.

"I stay out of my employees' personal lives," she said,

hating the suspicion in Dallas's voice. "There's no way Allen would do anything to hurt me or Jackson."

"I take it there's no Mr. Williams to notify?" Dallas asked.

Clearly, he'd picked up on the fact that she was single. She'd listened intently for condemnation in his tone and was surprised she didn't find a hint. She'd expected to and more after cashing out her interests in the tech company she and her brother had started together and moving to a small town. If her own family couldn't get behind her choices, how could strangers?

"No. There isn't. Is that a problem?" she asked a little too sharply. Missing sleep didn't bring out the best in her, and she'd been only half lying about not sleeping last night due to Jackson's schedule or lack thereof. At his age, he took a bottle every four hours, day and night.

"Not for me personally. The sheriff will want to know, and I'm taking notes to speed along the process once we go inside." Dallas motioned toward the small notepad he'd taken out of his pocket.

"Oh. Right." As soon as Jackson was old enough to take care of himself—like, age eighteen—Kate planned to stay in bed an entire weekend. Maybe then she'd think clearly again. Heck, give her a hotel and room service and she'd stay there a whole week.

"Where's the father?" Dallas asked, still with no hint of disapproval in his voice.

"Out of the picture."

There was a beat of silence. "Ready to go inside and talk?" he asked at last, his brow arched.

"Yes. I'll just get Jackson from the backseat," she said defensively. There was no reason to be on guard, she reminded herself. Besides, what would she care if a stranger judged her?

Dallas stood next to her, holding the car door open. She thanked him as she pulled Jackson close to her chest. Just the thought of anything happening to her son…

She couldn't even go there.

"Can I help with the diaper bag?" Dallas held out his hand, still no hint of condemnation in his tone.

"You must have children." Kate managed to ease it off her shoulder without disturbing the baby, who was thankfully asleep again. Her nerves were settling down enough for her hands to finally stop shaking.

"Not me," he said, sounding a little defensive. What was that all about?

Kate figured the man's family status was none of her business. She was just grateful that Jackson was still asleep.

Thank the stars for car rides. They were the only way she could get her son down for a nap some days. It probably didn't hurt that he'd been awake most of the night. He'd been born with his days and nights mixed up.

Family man or not, Kate's life would be very different right now if Dallas hadn't been there. Tears threatened to release along with all the emotions she'd been holding in.

Or maybe it was the fact that she felt safe with Dallas, which was a curious thought given that he was a stranger.

This wasn't the time or place to worry about either. Kate needed to pull on all the strength she had for Jackson. He needed his mother to keep it together.

"I can't thank you enough," she said, knowing that she wouldn't be holding her baby right now if not for this man. "Not just for carrying a diaper bag, but for everything you did for us this morning."

Dallas nodded. He was tall, easily more than six foot. Maybe six foot two? He had enough muscles for her to know he put in serious time at the gym or on the ranch owned by him and his family. His hair was blacker than the sky on any clear night she'd seen. There was an intensity to him, too, and she had no doubt the man was good at whatever he put his mind to.

She told herself that the only reason she noticed was because they'd been in danger and he'd just saved her son's life.

DALLAS WALKED KATE into the sheriff's office and instructed her to take a seat anywhere she'd be comfortable.

Looking at the baby stirred up all kinds of feelings in him that he wasn't ready to deal with. Not until he knew for sure one way or the other about his own parenthood status. Being in limbo was the absolute worst feeling, apart from knowing that he was in no way ready to be a father.

And yet a part of him wondered what it would be like to have a little rug rat running around the ranch. He chalked the feeling up to missing his parents. Losing them so unexpectedly had delivered a blow to the family and left a hole that couldn't be filled. And then there was Dallas's guilt over not being available to help them out when they'd called. He'd been halfway to New Mexico with an unexpected problem in one of his warehouses.

His gut twisted as he thought about it. If he'd turned around his truck and come back like they'd asked, they'd still be alive.

Dallas needed to redirect his thoughts or his guilt would consume him again. An update from his private investigator, Wayne Morton, was overdue. When Morton had last made contact, three days ago, he'd believed he was on a trail that might lead to Susan's whereabouts. He'd been plenty busy at the ranch, trying to get his arms around the family business.

"Can I get anything for you or the baby?" Dallas asked Kate, needing a strong cup of coffee.

"Something warm would be nice," she said, wedging the sleeping baby safely in a chair.

Dallas nodded before making his exit as she began peeling off her scarf and layers of outerwear.

A few minutes later he returned with two steaming cups of brew. He hesitated at the door once he got a good look at her, and his pulse thumped. Calling her five and a half feet tall earlier had been generous. The only reason she seemed that height was the heeled boots she wore. Without them, she'd be five foot three at the most. She had on fitted jeans that hugged her curves and a deep blue sweater that highlighted her eyes—eyes that would challenge even the perfect blue sky of a gorgeous spring day. Her shiny blond hair was pulled off her face into a ponytail.

"Wasn't sure how you took yours, so I brought cream and sugar," he said, setting both cups on the side table near where she stood. He emptied his coat pocket of cream and sugar packets, ignoring his rapid heartbeat.

She thanked him before mixing the condiments into her cup.

The baby moved as she sat down next to him and she immediately scooped him up and brought him to her chest.

The infant wound up for a good cry, unleashed one, and Kate's stress levels appeared to hit the roof.

"He's got a healthy set of lungs," Dallas offered, trying to ease her tension.

"He's probably hungry. Is there a place where I can warm a bottle?" she asked, distress written in the wrinkle across her forehead.

Abigail, Tommy's secretary, appeared in the doorway

before Dallas could answer. She'd been with the sheriff's office long before Tommy arrived and had become invaluable to him in the five years since he'd taken the job. She threatened to retire every year, and every year he made an offer she couldn't refuse.

"I can take care of that for you," she said. "Where's the bottle?"

"In there," Kate said, attempting to handle the baby and make a move for the diaper bag next to her. She couldn't quite manage it and started to tear up as Abigail shooed her away, scooping the bag off the floor.

"Thank you," Kate said, glancing from Abigail to Dallas.

"Don't be silly." The older woman just smiled. "You've been through a lot this morning." She motioned toward Jackson. "It'll get easier with him. The first few months are always the most difficult with a new baby."

Dallas felt as out of place in the conversation as catfish bait in a tilapia pond. And then a thought struck him. If he was a father—and he wasn't anywhere near ready to admit to the possibility just yet—he'd need to learn about diaper bags and 3:00 a.m. feedings. Kate's employee had taken her up-all-night excuse far too easily, which meant it happened enough for her to be able to know using it wouldn't be questioned.

Speaking of which, Allen seemed to know way too much about Kate's personal life, which could mean that the office employees were close, and it was clear he wanted more than a professional relationship with her. The guy was a little too cozy with his boss and Dallas didn't like it. She obviously refused his advances. A thought struck. Could that be enough for him to want to punish her by removing the only obstacle between them—her child?

He was probably reaching for a simple explanation. Even so, it was a question Dallas intended to bounce around with Tommy.

Dallas made a mental note to ask Kate more about her relationship with Allen as soon as the baby was calm again, which happened a few seconds after Abigail returned with a warmed bottle and he began feeding.

The look of panic didn't leave Kate's face entirely during the baby's meal, but she gazed lovingly at her son.

Dallas had questions and needed answers, the quicker the better. However, it didn't feel right interrupting mother and son during what looked to be a bonding moment.

But then, not being a father himself, what the hell did he know about it?

Sipping his coffee, he waited for Kate to speak first. It didn't take long. Another few minutes and she finally said, "I want to apologize about my behavior this morning. I'm not normally so…frazzled."

"You're doing better than you think," he said, offering reassurance.

"Am I?" she asked. "Because I feel like I'm all over the place emotionally."

"Trust me. You're doing fine."

Her shoulders relaxed a little and that made Dallas smile.

"I do have a question for you, though," he said.

She nodded.

"How well do you know your employees?" he asked, ignoring the most probable reason Allen's attraction grated on him so much. Dallas liked her, too.

"Some more than others, I guess." She shrugged. "We're a small office, so we talk."

The baby finished his bottle and she placed a cloth

napkin over her shoulder before laying him across it and patting his back.

"What does that do?" Dallas's curiosity about babies was getting the best of him. His stress was also growing with every passing day that Morton didn't return his texts.

"Gets the gas out of his stomach. Believe me, you want it out. If you don't he can cramp up and become miserable." She frowned.

"And when he's miserable, you're miserable."

"Exactly," she said, her tone wistful. A tear escaped, rolling down her cheek. She wiped it away and quickly apologized. "This whole parenting thing has been much harder than I expected."

"Whoever did this to you and left should be castrated," Dallas said. And he figured he was a hypocrite with that coming out of his mouth, given that he might have done the same to another woman. However, he had very strong feelings about the kind of man who didn't mind making a baby, but couldn't be bothered to stick around to be a father to the child. The operative word in his situation was that he might have *unwittingly* done that to someone. And he had no proof that Susan had actually been pregnant with his child, given that she'd disappeared when he'd offered to bring up the baby separately, instead of agreeing to her suggestion that they immediately marry. Her call had come out of the blue, months after they'd parted ways.

His gaze didn't budge from Kate. He expected some kind of reaction from her. All he saw was genuine embarrassment.

"Oh, I have no one to blame. I did it to myself," she said.

"I may not be an expert on babies, but I do know how

they're made. And I'm fairly certain there has to be a partner." It was Dallas's turn to shoot her a confused look.

"Adoption," she said.

He gave her another.

"Surely you've heard of adopting a baby?" she asked tartly.

"Of course I have. I just didn't know that was your circumstance," he said stupidly.

Looking closer at the baby, Dallas couldn't help but notice the boy had dark curly hair.

Not unlike his own.

Chapter Three

Kate recognized the sheriff as soon as he stepped inside his office. Not only had she seen him around town, he'd stopped by the kitchen to welcome her when she'd first opened her doors.

He was close to Dallas O'Brien's height, so at least six feet tall. His hair was light brown and his eyes matched the shade almost perfectly.

She was relieved for the interruption, after sharing the news about Jackson being adopted, and especially after Dallas's reaction, which made no sense to her. He seemed fine with her being a single parent, but lost his ability to speak once she'd mentioned the adoption. What was up with that?

The sheriff acknowledged Dallas first and then offered a handshake to Kate.

Dallas relayed the morning's events succinctly and Kate's heart squeezed at hearing the words, knowing how close she'd been to losing her son. She reminded herself that she had Dallas to thank for thwarting the kidnapping attempt.

If he hadn't been there...

She shivered, deflecting the chill gripping her spine. "Most kidnappings involve family. Sounds like that isn't the case here," the sheriff said. "We can't rule out the birth parents. What's your relationship with them?"

"None," Kate responded. She hadn't thought about the possibility that Jackson's biological parents could've changed their minds. "The adoption was closed, records sealed, based on the mother's request."

"I'll make contact with the agency to see if I can get any additional information from them. I wouldn't count on it without a court order, though," Tommy warned. "What's the name?"

"Safe Haven," she stated.

Tommy nodded. "Good. I know who they are."

Kate held tighter to Jackson. Could the kidnapper have been the birth father? If an investigation was opened, could the birth mother change her mind and take her son away?

"Can you give a description of the man from this morning?" Tommy asked.

"Everything happened so fast. All I can remember is that he was wearing a hoodie and a high turtleneck. He was medium height and had these beady dark eyes against olive skin. It didn't look like he'd shaved in a few days. That's about all I can remember," she said.

"It's a start," Tommy said, and his words were reassuring.

He turned to Dallas with that same questioning look.

"He was young and I didn't recognize his voice, so I don't think he's from around here," Dallas added.

"Is it possible that he's the father? If he's not local, then maybe he just found out about the baby and tracked us down," Kate said, fear racing through her at the thought.

"We can't rule it out, but that's just one of many possibilities," Tommy said. "What about your neighbors on

Main? I heard some of them weren't too thrilled when you moved in."

"That's the truth," she said.

"Someone might have tried to scare you enough to get you to close shop and leave town. That's a best-case scenario, as far as I'm concerned, because it would mean they never intended to hurt you or the baby. I need a list of names of family, friends, anyone who you've had a disagreement with, and your employees."

The last part caught her off guard. *Employees?*

That had been Dallas's first suspicion, too.

"Sheriff Johnson, you don't seriously think one of my people could be involved, do you?" she asked, not able to fathom the possibility that one of her own could've turned on her.

"Please, call me Tommy," he said. "And I have to search for all possible connections to the guy we're looking for. You'd be surprised what you find out about the people you think you know best."

In his line of work, she could only imagine how true that statement was. How horrible that anyone she trusted might've been involved.

No, it had to be a stranger.

"I have received threats from some of my business neighbors," she said.

"Tell me more about those," Tommy said, leaning forward.

"A few of the other tenants got together to file a complaint with my landlord. They said they didn't think Main was the appropriate place for a soup kitchen," she explained.

"And what was his response?" Tommy asked.

"He didn't do anything. Said as long as my rent was

paid on time and I wasn't doing anything illegal, it wasn't anyone else's concern," she said.

"I'll send one of my deputies to canvass the other tenants and see what he can find out. We'll cover all bases with our investigation." Tommy glanced up from his pad. "How long ago did they make the complaint?"

"Right after we first moved in, so about six months ago," she said.

"Anyone make a formal complaint since?"

She shook her head.

"What about direct threats?" Tommy asked.

"Walter Higgins threatened to force me out of town," she said. "But that was a while ago."

"The town needs your services," Dallas said through clenched teeth. "What kind of jerks complain about a person doing something good for others?"

Jackson stirred at the sound of the loud voice and Kate had to find his binky to pacify him. She shuffled through the diaper bag and came up with it. Jackson settled down as soon as the offering was in his mouth.

"Sorry," Dallas said with an apologetic glance.

"It takes all kinds," Tommy agreed. "I'm guessing they figured it would hurt their business. We'll know more once my deputy speaks to them."

"It's not like people hang around after they eat. There's no loitering allowed downtown," Kate said.

"It's a big escalation to go from complaining to your landlord to a personal attack like this on your son." Based on the sheriff's tone, her neighbors weren't serious suspects. Tommy fired off a text before returning his gaze to Kate. "Now tell me more about your people."

"We have a small office staff," she conceded. "Allen Lentz is my second in command and takes care of everything when I'm not around. Other than that, there are about a dozen cooks and food service workers. Only one is on payroll. The others are volunteers."

Dallas's posture tensed when she mentioned Allen.

Kate registered the subtle change and moved on. She rattled off a few more names and job descriptions.

The sheriff nodded and jotted a few notes on his palm-sized notebook.

"And then there's Randy Ruiz. He keeps the place running on our tight budget. He's our general handyman, muscle and overall miracle worker. Anything heavy needs lifting, he's our guy. He's been especially helpful and dependable in the six months he's been with us." Despite Randy's past, she knew full well that he would never hurt her or Jackson.

Dallas seemed to perk up and she was afraid she'd tried to sell Randy a little too hard. True, she could be a little overprotective of him. He'd had a hard road and she wanted to see him succeed.

"Tabitha Farmer does all our administrative work," Kate added quickly, to keep the conversation moving. "Her official title is volunteer coordinator."

"How close are you with donors?" Tommy asked.

Thinking about the possibility that anyone in her circle could have arranged to have her child kidnapped was enough to turn Kate's stomach. She clasped him closer.

For Jackson's sake, she had to consider what Dallas and the sheriff were saying no matter how much she hated to view her friends and acquaintances with a new lens.

Maybe she was being naive, but she'd been careful to fill her life with genuine people since moving to Bluff from the city. "I maintain a professional distance. However, I do get invited to personal events like weddings and lake house parties."

"And what do you do with your son during these outings?" Dallas interjected, no doubt remembering her conversation with Allen earlier.

"I don't usually go. But I used Allen once," she replied.

"Allen?" Dallas looked up from intensely staring into his cup of coffee.

"We're like a family at the kitchen, and we take care of each other," she said defensively.

Dallas's cocked eyebrow didn't sit well with her. She could feel herself getting more and more defensive.

"Despite what you may be thinking about my employees, they really are a group of decent people," she stated, making eye contact with him—a mistake she was going to regret, given how much her body reacted to the handsome cowboy.

"In my experience, that doesn't always prove the truth," he said, holding her gaze. "When did Allen babysit for you?"

"It's been a while. I used Tabitha one other time recently."

"There a reason for that?" Dallas asked, lifting one dark eyebrow.

"Yes, but it doesn't mean anything," she said quickly. Then she sighed. "Okay, I thought Allen was getting a little too…involved with me and Jackson, so I thought it would be best to use Tabitha instead. He's made it clear that he'd like to date." She involuntarily shivered at the thought of going out with anyone, much less someone from work. "And I'm just not ready for that."

She'd probably emphasized that last bit a little too much, but what did she care if they knew she wasn't in the mood to spend time with a man, any man.

"How old is your son?" Tommy asked, after a few uncomfortable seconds had passed.

"Jackson? He's almost three months old." Kate gently

patted her baby on the back, noticing something stir in Dallas's eyes.

"What about friends and family?" Tommy asked, his gaze moving from her to his friend. "Anyone in the area?"

"I didn't know anyone when I moved here, and everything about preparing for the baby was harder than I expected, so, yes, I bonded with my employees."

"You don't have family in this part of Texas?" Tommy asked.

"It's just me and Jackson." She shook her head. "My brother and I are close, but he lives in Richardson, which is a suburb of Dallas. He works nonstop. We started a tech company together after college and made enough to do okay. I sold my interest in the business to have a baby, and now he's running it alone."

"Forgive this question…" Tommy hesitated before continuing, "But how did your brother take the news about you leaving the business the two of you started?"

"Carter? He was fine with my decision. He knew how much I wanted to start a family," she said defensively, a red rash crawling up her neck. And if he hadn't been the most enthusiastic about her choice at first, he'd come around.

"Again, I'm sorry. I had to ask," the sheriff murmured, taking a seat across from her in the sitting area of the office.

"Mind if I ask why you decided to move to Bluff?" Dallas asked.

"There was a need for a soup kitchen, and it's one of the most family-friendly towns in Texas three years running, according to the internet," she said with a shrug. "I thought it would be a good place to bring up a baby."

"Even without family here?" Tommy asked.

"My parents didn't approve of my decision to have a

child alone." She didn't really want to go down that road again, explaining the quirks of her family to a stranger. The one where her mother had flipped out and pretended to have a heart attack in order to alter Kate's course.

She glanced at Dallas, ready to defend herself to him, and was surprised by the look of sympathy she got instead.

"I guess I don't understand that particular brand of thinking. It's my personal belief that families should stick together even if they don't agree with each other's decisions," Dallas said, his steely voice sliding right through her.

The sincerity in those words nearly brought her to tears.

Why did it suddenly matter so much what a stranger thought about her or her family?

DALLAS NOTICED KATE's emotional reaction to what he'd said about family. If she really was at odds with hers then they couldn't rule them out as suspects.

"If you'll excuse us, I'd like to speak to the sheriff in the hallway for a minute," he said to her.

"Do we have to wait around? Can we go home now?" she asked, clearly rattled from their conversation.

"I don't think it's safe," Dallas said, before Tommy could answer. "This attack was ambush-style and planned."

His friend was already nodding in agreement. "The kidnapper had a knife and a getaway vehicle," he added. "This indicates premeditation. I'll need to run this scenario through the database and see if there are similar incidents out there. In the meantime, I'd like to send a deputy to your house to take a look around."

Kate gasped and the baby stirred. She immediately

went into action, soothing the infant in her arms. He was such a tiny thing and looked so fragile.

"You think they know where I live?" she asked when the baby had settled into the crook of her arm.

"It's a possibility we can't ignore, and I'd rather be safe than sorry," Tommy said.

"Can I see you in the hallway?" Dallas asked Tommy as his friend rose to his feet. Dallas's protective instincts were kicking into high gear.

"If you're going into the hall to discuss my case, I have a right to know what's being said." Kate's gaze held steady with determination.

Dallas paused at the doorjamb. He couldn't deny that she was right, and yet he wanted to protect her and the baby from hearing what he needed to ask Tommy next.

"Whatever it is, I deserve to hear it," she insisted.

A deep sigh pushed out of his lungs as he turned toward her and stepped back inside, motioning for Tommy to do the same. "The person who did this could be someone who sees Jackson as in the way of being with you," Dallas said, and it seemed to dawn on her that he was talking about Allen.

"Is that why you zeroed in on Allen when I called him earlier?" she asked Dallas pointedly.

"Yes," he answered truthfully.

"We won't stop searching for whoever is behind this," Tommy interjected. "And we're considering all possibilities."

She sat there for a long moment. "What about those other possibilities, Sheriff?" she finally asked.

"It could be that someone wants revenge against you. It's obvious that your child is very important to you and that snatching him would be one way to hurt you," Tommy said. "Or a teen mom has changed her mind about giving up her child. She might've figured out who you were and told the father."

"The adoption was sealed based on the mother's request. However, I made sure of it to avoid that very circumstance. How on earth would she know where Jackson is?" Kate asked.

"You can find out anything with enough money or computer hacking skills," Dallas answered, even though he knew firsthand either option could take time. And in this case, maybe it had. Jackson was nearly three months old, so that would give someone plenty of time to find the two of them. Grease the right wheels and boom.

"I have to think that if this was a teen mother, then she'd be destitute. Wouldn't she? If she had money or family support, would she really be giving up her baby in the first place?" Kate asked.

Good points.

"How well did you vet this adoption agency before you used them?" Dallas asked.

"They're legitimate, from everything I could tell. I hired a lawyer to oversee things on my end and make sure everything was legal," Kate stated.

"I'll need the name of your lawyer," Tommy said.

"William Seaver."

"Is he someone you knew or was that the first time you'd dealt with him?" Tommy asked.

"My brother connected us. He'd heard of Seaver through a mutual friend. I'm sure he checked him out first," Kate replied.

"I'll run his name and see if we come up with anything in the database," Tommy offered. "We'll be able to narrow down the possibilities once I get all this information into the system and talk to a few people. Also, I'd like to send someone to take a look at your work computers. I need permission from you in order to do that."

Kate gave her consent even though she seemed reluctant. Her reaction was understandable given the circumstances. Dallas would feel the same way if someone wanted to dig around in the ranch's books.

Tommy called for Abigail.

The older woman appeared a moment later and he asked her to send someone to Kate's house to look for anything suspicious, and after that to run information through the database to see if she got a hit on any similar crimes.

As soon as she left, Dallas turned to Kate. "That's everything I wanted to ask or say about your case. If you'll excuse us, I need to discuss a personal matter with the sheriff."

Dallas motioned for his friend to follow him down the hall and into the kitchenette.

"I'm sorry we lost the guy earlier," Tommy said once they were out of earshot. "If we'd caught him, this nightmare could be over for her."

"Whoever it was seems to know how to disappear pretty darn quick," Dallas commented.

"It's difficult to hide something that weighs more than four thousand pounds," Tommy agreed, obviously referring to the minivan.

"You think this whole thing might've been a setup to scare her out of town?" Dallas asked, unsure of how to approach the subject of his possible fatherhood to his friend.

"I thought about that, as well," he admitted. "It's too early to rule anything out even though it's not likely. I'm anxious to see if we find similar crimes in the database. And, of course, we'll look at her personal circles."

Dallas leaned against the counter and folded his arms across his chest. "I've been looking into adoption agencies myself lately."

"Come again?" Tommy's eyebrows arched and Dallas couldn't blame his friend for the surprised glance he shot him. "I know you're not looking to adopt."

"You remember Susan," Dallas began, uneasy about bringing this up. Susan had grown up in Bluff, so Tommy knew her well.

"So glad you finally saw through her and moved on." His friend rolled his eyes. "She was a head case."

Dallas couldn't argue. His judgment had slipped on that one. As soon as he'd figured her out, he'd broken it off. "She might be more than that. She might be the mother of my child."

The possibility that Dallas could be that careless had never occurred to his friend, a fact made clear by the shock on his face. "There's no way you could've done that!" he declared. "Have you considered the possibility that she's lying?"

"Of course I have," Dallas retorted.

"If this is true, and I'm not convinced it is, where is she? And why didn't you come to me before?" Tommy asked.

"Those are good questions," Dallas admitted. "As far as where she went, I'm looking to find an answer. She disappeared from New Mexico and not even her family here in Bluff has seen her since. We both know that she loved it here. Why wouldn't she come back?"

"She didn't say anything to you before she left?" Tommy folded his arms, his forehead wrinkled in disbelief.

"And I didn't get a chance to ask where she was headed before she disappeared."

"What makes you think she used an adoption agency?" Tommy said, after carefully considering the bomb that had just been dropped. "And why *didn't* you come to me sooner?"

"She told me she was pregnant and said we should get married right away," Dallas said. "I told her to hold on. That I would be there for my child, but that didn't mean we needed to make a mistake."

"That probably went over as well as a cow patty in the pool." His friend grunted. "She seemed bent on signing her name 'O'Brien' from when we were kids."

Dallas had been an idiot not to see through her quicker.

"But that still doesn't answer my question of why you didn't come to me right away," Tommy said.

"I needed answers. You have to follow the letter of the law," Dallas said honestly. "I wanted someone who could see those lines as blurry."

Tommy took a sip of his coffee. "That the only reason?"

"I knew you'd want to help, and you have a lot of restrictions. I wanted fast answers and I wasn't even sure there'd be anything to discuss," Dallas said. "Plus I didn't want to tell anyone until I was sure."

"Didn't you suspect she was seeing someone else?" his friend asked.

Dallas nodded. "I'm certain she was. I figured she was making a bid for my money when she played the pregnancy card with me."

"She probably was." Tommy grimaced. "Which was a good reason for her to disappear when you refused to marry her. She couldn't get caught in her lies."

"I thought of that, too. There's another thing. I used protection, but it's more than that. We didn't exactly... It's not like..." Hell, this was awkward. Dallas didn't make a habit out of talking about his sex life with anyone, not even his best friend. "There was only the one time with Susan and me. Afterward, she got clingy and tried to move into my place. Started trying to rearrange furniture. I caught her in lie after lie and broke it off clean after I witnessed her in the parking lot with that other guy, looking cozy. I'd suspected she was seeing someone else and she got all cagey when I confronted her and asked her to leave. I couldn't prove my suspicion, though. But when she called a few months later and said she was pregnant with my child, I didn't believe her."

"I can't blame you there," Tommy said. "I wouldn't have bought it, either."

"But I can't turn my back until I know for sure." If what Susan said was true, then he'd already messed up what he considered to be the most important job in life—fatherhood.

Dallas had known Susan could be dishonest, and that was the reason he'd broken it off with her. He couldn't love someone he couldn't trust. But he never imagined she'd lie about something this important.

"If there was another guy involved, and I believe you when you say there was, then he could be the father of her child." Tommy sipped his coffee, contemplating what he had just learned.

"You know I can't walk away until I know one way or the other," Dallas said. "This isn't something I can leave to chance."

"And there was that one time," his friend finally said, his forehead pinched with concentration. "So, there is a possibility."

"If I'm honest…yes."

"But it's next to impossible. I know you. There's no way you would risk a pregnancy unless you were one hundred percent sure about a relationship staying together," he stated.

Dallas nodded.

And then it seemed to dawn on Tommy. "But she could've sabotaged your efforts."

"Right."

"Well, damn." His friend's expression changed to one of pity. "I'm sorry to hear this might've happened. Any idea how old the baby would be now?"

"According to my calculations…about three months old." And that was most likely the reason Kate's case hit him so hard. If he had a son, the boy would be around the same age as Jackson.

"Any idea where Susan and the baby may be? It'd be easy enough to get a paternity test once you find them."

Tommy said the exact thing Dallas was thinking.

"I don't know. Neither does the man I hired to find them. She literally disappeared." Ever since hearing about a possible pregnancy with Susan, Dallas had found his world tipped on its axis and he didn't exactly feel like himself.

"There might not even be a baby," Tommy said.

Dallas's phone buzzed. He fished it out of his pocket and then checked the screen. "Susan had a boy," he said, focusing on the message from his private investigator's assistant, Stacy Miller. "And Morton was able to link her to an adoption agency."

Tommy rubbed his chin, deep in thought.

Yeah, Dallas felt the same way right about now. Especially when the next text came through, and he learned the adoption agency was named Safe Haven.

Chapter Four

"I'd say that's a strange coincidence, but I know Safe Haven is the biggest agency in the area, so I guess I'm not too surprised to hear their name again," Tommy said. "And just because Susan had a baby doesn't mean it's yours."

"That kid in there is around the age Susan's baby would be," Dallas supplied.

"Doesn't mean he's Susan's," Tommy said. "Odds are against it."

"I know." Dallas nodded, still trying to digest the news. His plans to help Kate Williams get settled with the sheriff and then head back to the ranch to start a busy day exploded. They had a record number of bred heifers and there'd be a calf-boom early next year that everyone was preparing for. But nothing was more important than this investigation.

"In fact, I'm inclined to think that's the closest thing we have to proof that the baby isn't yours."

Dallas made a move to speak, but his friend raised his hand to stop him. "Hear me out. If Susan was telling the truth and the baby was yours, she would stick around for a DNA test. If she couldn't have your last name, then at least her son would, and he'd have everything that comes with being an O'Brien, which is what we all know she's always wanted anyway."

Dallas thought about those words for a long moment. "I see your point."

"And I'm right."

"Either way, if she used Safe Haven, then everything should be legit, right?" Dallas asked, hoping he'd be able to gain traction and get answers now that a child had been confirmed and he had the name of an adoption agency. His investigator was making good progress.

"They've been investigated before and came up clean." Tommy took another sip of his coffee. "That doesn't mean they are. They could be running an off-the-books program for nontraditional families. Kate's case gives me reason to dig into their records. I'll make a request for access to their files and see how willing they are to cooperate."

"Will you keep me posted on your progress?" Dallas asked, knowing he was asking a lot of his friend.

Tommy nodded. "I'll give you as much information as I legally can."

"As far as Susan goes, you're the only one who knows, and I'd appreciate keeping it between us for now."

"You haven't told anyone in the family?" Tommy asked in surprise.

"Everyone's had enough to deal with since Mom and Pop…" Dallas didn't finish his sentence. He didn't have to. Tommy knew.

"If you have a child, and I'd bet my life you don't, we'll find him," Tommy said, and his words were meant to be reassuring.

He was the only person apart from Dallas's brothers who would know just how much the prospect would gnaw at him. And if his brothers knew, they'd all want to be involved, but Dallas didn't want to sound the alarm just yet. There might not be anything to discuss, and he didn't like getting everyone riled up without cause.

Another text came through on his phone.

"Looks like my guy left to investigate Safe Haven last night and hasn't checked in for work this morning," Dallas murmured. "His assistant said he's always the first one in the office. She's been texting and calling him and he isn't responding."

"We need to talk to her," Tommy said. "You know I'm going to offer my help investigating Susan's disappearance. She's originally from here and that makes her my business."

"And I'll take it," Dallas declared. He wouldn't rely solely on Tommy, because his friend was bound by laws. Dallas saw them more as guidelines when it came to finding out the truth. "We can work both cases and share information. As far as Kate's goes, I'm not sure I like Allen Lentz."

The sheriff leaned against the counter with a questioning look on his face.

"He sounded possessive of her when she called him this morning, and I got the impression he sees the kid as an obstacle to dating her," Dallas explained. The news that Susan had had a boy was still spinning around in the back of his mind.

"I'll have one of my deputies bring him in for questioning this morning," Tommy said. "See if I can get a feel for the guy."

"I'd be interested to hear your take on him," Dallas stated. "I told her not to clue him in to what had happened this morning when she phoned him to open the kitchen for her. And I asked her to put him on speaker so I could hear his voice."

"What was your impression of how he sounded?"

"I didn't like the guy one bit." Dallas would keep the part about feeling a twinge of jealousy to himself.

"Wanting the kid out of the way would give him motive," Tommy said. "I'll run a background check on him when I bring him in. See if there's anything there."

Tommy's phone buzzed. "This is my deputy," he said, after glancing at the screen.

Dallas motioned for them to return to Kate as his friend answered the call.

She was cradling the baby and Dallas got another glimpse of the little boy's black curly hair—hair that looked a lot like his own—as they walked into the office. Dallas wasn't quite ready to accept that possibility completely as he moved closer to get a better look at Jackson. There was no way that Kate's son could be Susan's baby.

Right?

Tommy was right. All of this would be way too much of a coincidence. The adoption agency was large and there had to be dozens of dark-haired baby boys who had been adopted around the same time. Not that logic mattered at a time like this.

Plus, Dallas hadn't considered the fact that if Susan had had his baby, then wouldn't she sue him for support? Or blackmail him to keep the news out of the press?

Until he could be certain, would Dallas look at every boy around Jackson's age with the same question: Could the child be his?

Not knowing would be mental torture at its worst. Every dark-haired boy he came across would get Dallas's mind spinning with possibilities. What-ifs. Was he getting a glimpse of the torment he'd endure for the rest of his life if he couldn't find Susan?

Morton had confirmed there'd been a child, which

didn't necessarily mean Dallas was a father. And Morton had been able to link Susan to Safe Haven Adoption Agency. Dallas had every reason to believe that his PI would figure out the rest and Dallas would get his answers very soon. Being in limbo, not knowing, would eat what was left of his stomach lining.

Kate was watching him with a keen eye as Tommy entered the room.

"Can I go home now?" she asked, cradling Jackson tighter.

"This might sound like an odd question, but do you close and lock your doors when you leave your house?" Tommy asked.

"Yes. Of course. I'm a single woman who lives alone with a baby, and I wouldn't dream of leaving myself vulnerable like that," she said, and her cheeks flushed.

Embarrassment?

Dallas noted the emotion as his friend moved on. "Well, then, your place has been broken into," Tommy said.

"What happened?" Kate's face paled.

Dallas's first thought was Allen. But wouldn't he already have access to her house?

Not if she never let him inside. Maybe the date bit was a ruse to get into her home.

"The back door was ajar and the lock had been tampered with. My deputy on the scene said that nothing obvious is missing inside. All the pictures are on the walls and the place is neat." Tommy listened and then said a few "uh-huh"s into the phone.

"Do you have a home computer?" he asked Kate.

"A laptop on my desk," she answered.

Tommy repeated the information to his deputy and then frowned.

So, someone took her laptop?

"Are you sure it was on your desk the last time you saw it?" Tommy asked.

"Certain. Why? Is it gone?"

He nodded. "The cable is still there."

That same look of fear and disbelief filled her blue eyes.

"Can you think of anything on your hard drive someone would want?" Tommy asked. He also asked about work files, but Dallas figured whoever broke into her house wasn't going after those. This had to be personal, especially after the failed kidnapping attempt.

If someone was trying to scare her, then he was doing a great job of it, based on her expression.

"No. Nothing. I keep all my work stuff at the office. I vowed not to work at home ever again once I left the corporate scene. I have a manila file folder in the drawer, right-hand side, about Jackson's adoption," she added, holding tighter to her baby. "Is it missing?"

Once again Tommy relayed the information and then waited. "There's nothing labeled Safe Haven or Adoption," he said at last.

"Then that's it," she murmured, almost too quietly to hear.

Tommy thanked his deputy and ended the call. "How did you get connected with Safe Haven?"

"Through my lawyer. He was the one who arranged everything," she said, and based on her expression, Dallas figured her brain was most likely clicking through possibilities.

He made a mental note that they needed to speak to her brother, and the rest of her family, as well. Dallas didn't like to think that her family wouldn't be 100 percent supportive of her choices, but he wasn't stupid. He couldn't fathom it, but if her mother was really against the adoption, then she could be trying to interfere by shaking Kate up. Maybe even hoping that she'd realize she'd made a mistake.

If that were true, then Kate's mother hadn't seen the woman holding Jackson.

A family intervention, albeit misguided, would be so much better than the other options Kate faced. Such as an employee's fixation or the fact that this could've been a shady adoption gone bad for Safe Haven.

KATE HELD ON to Jackson as if he'd drop off a canyon wall if she let go. She'd walked away from the only life she'd ever known to have a chance at a family. Her husband, Robert Bass, had filed for divorce within weeks of learning that she had a 4 percent chance of ever getting pregnant. Four percent.

Half the reason she'd worked so hard at the start-up was so she could sell her interests when she became pregnant and be home with the baby. And then suddenly that wasn't going to be an option, ever.

At thirty-three, she'd had everything she thought she wanted, a nice house, a Suburban and a husband. She'd believed she was on the track to happiness, and it was easy to ignore shortcomings in her marriage to Robert considering how much time she spent at the office. He worked all the time, too.

Within weeks of learning the devastating news, her entire life had turned upside down, and all she could do was kick herself for not seeing it coming earlier. All those times Robert had decided to stay late at the office even when she'd made special arrangements to leave early… And she'd been too busy to really notice how frequent his ski trips had become—ski trips she later realized hadn't been with his best friend, but with his coworker Olivia Gail.

In fact, he'd been on the road more than he was home and Kate felt like an idiot for thinking he was working hard to secure a future for their family, too.

Whatever love had been between them had died long before she'd been willing to acknowledge it. Or had she kept herself too busy to notice? Too busy to face the reality of the loneliness that had become her life?

She'd been trapped with a husband who cared for her but didn't love her. And the worst part was that she'd kept convincing herself that they'd be able to get back what they'd had in the early days of their relationship as soon as she had more time or had a baby. How crazy was it to think a child would somehow make things better, make them a family?

To make matters worse, Kate Williams didn't give up. Hard work and staying the course had made her business a success. It had gotten her through a difficult childhood with a mother who was bent on controlling her. Was her mother's lack of real love the reason Kate had fallen for Robert in the first place? Was she seeking approval from someone who would never give it?

Robert had been all about keeping his tee time and staying on track with his future career plans. He even seemed content to have a family with Kate though he no longer loved her.

And then when the disappointing news had come that having a baby would be next to impossible, he'd started traveling even more. He'd lost interest in her sexually.

Kate had reasoned that he needed time to process the news, as she did. It was a bomb she'd never expected to be dropped on her, especially not when her biological clock wouldn't expire for years.

Robert's decision to give up on the marriage shouldn't have come as a complete shock. Except that she'd ignored or made excuses for every single one of the signs that it was coming.

Given the amount of time he had spent calculating return on investment with his stock portfolio, she should've realized he'd cut his losses with her when she was no longer a good deal. Apparently, she hadn't been worth the risk. It had taken Robert about six weeks to divest himself of her.

Kate had signed the divorce papers and then made a life-changing decision.

She was going to have a family anyway.

When she'd told Carter, her brother, he'd scoffed at the idea, initially telling her to take a long vacation instead. Then he'd reminded her how much she'd be hurting their mother, as if Charlotte Williams hadn't already made her position clear throughout the whole divorce. Chip and Charlotte had been the perfect parents, to hear her mother talk about their life.

Kate had been clear on what she wanted, and being a mother had more to do with love than DNA, so she'd decided to adopt.

Carter came to his senses, apologized and then located the best adoption attorney he could find.

Not long after, Kate had sold her interests in the company and moved to Bluff.

Life might have thrown her a twist, but that didn't mean she had to roll over and take it.

The move had given her a new lease on life. Becoming Jackson's mother was the greatest joy she'd experienced. And, dammit, no one would take that or him away from her.

A voice she immediately recognized as Allen's boomed from the other room.

Kate popped to her feet. "Why's he here?" she asked, glancing from Tommy to Dallas.

"I'll be interviewing everyone on your staff," the sheriff said, drawing her gaze back to him. "Would your family members be willing to come down and speak to us, as well?"

"My family?" she echoed, as Allen walked into the office.

"What's going on?" he asked, concern widening his eyes as he zeroed in on Kate and the baby.

Dallas stepped in front of her, blocking his path.

"Did something happen?" Allen shouted over him. "Are you okay?"

"I'm fine now," she said, hating that her employees would be worried.

"Will someone please tell me what's going on?" Allen begged, and there was desperation in his voice as he was being hauled away.

DALLAS POSITIONED HIMSELF near the two-way mirror on the other side of the interview room. His cup of coffee had long ago gone cold, but holding on to it gave him something to do with his hands.

"Miss Williams authorized my department to take a look at your computer," Tommy said to Allen.

"So what?" The confusion on the guy's face was either an award-worthy acting job or he really didn't have a clue.

"Would you agree to give one of my deputies access to your house?" Tommy asked. He knew full well that an innocent guy would have nothing to hide.

"Not until you tell me what this is about," Allen retorted.

Fair enough.

"We're looking for information that will aid an ongoing investigation," Tommy hedged.

"One that involves my boss." It wasn't a question.

The lawman nodded.

"Look, I would do anything to help Kate. She's like family to me," Allen said. "But I have no idea what's going on."

So asking out a family member was okay in Allen's book? Dallas covered up his cough.

"And I'm not sure how invading my privacy will accomplish your mission, so I'm afraid you'll have to tell me a little bit more about what you think you'll find," Allen added.

Dallas had been sure this guy was guilty as sin, but something was gnawing at him and he couldn't figure out what. He might be covering for a crush he had on his boss and didn't want to be embarrassed any further.

Based on his actions so far, Allen was coming across as a concerned friend. But then, he might just be that good at acting.

Dallas returned to Tommy's office, where Kate waited.

"How long has Allen worked for you?" he asked.

"He was my first hire," she said, looking as if she was about to be sick. "So, about six months now."

"Do want water or something else to drink?" Dallas asked.

She shook her head and mumbled that she was fine.

Tommy walked in.

"How would you characterize your relationship with Allen Lentz?" he asked Kate.

"Professional," she retorted.

"I had to ask." Tommy brought his hand up defensively.

"But he wasn't kidding about our office being like a family. Do you really think he broke into my house and stole my laptop and adoption files?" she asked Tommy, looking as if she was trying to let that possibility sink in.

"Not completely, no," he answered. "It doesn't mean he's not involved, though. The kidnapping attempt could've been a distraction while the burglar got what he really wanted."

Kate pinched the bridge of her nose as though staving off a headache.

Tommy's cell buzzed. He glanced at the screen. "If you'll excuse me."

Kate nodded as Tommy hurried out of the room.

Dallas didn't say that none of this added up quite in the way he wanted it to. All her employees would know that she was already at the soup kitchen. If someone wanted her laptop and adoption files, all he had to do was break in while she was gone. But it was clear that her adoption was at the center of the kidnapping attempt. Could someone be trying to erase the paperwork trail? "Do you ever go back to your place after leaving for work?"

"Not unless I've forgotten something for Jackson," she said.

"Do you normally take him to work with you?" Dallas asked.

"Yes. And then Mrs. Zilker picks him up, although sometimes she sticks around the office for a while," Kate stated. "Oh, no. I forgot to let her know I don't need her today."

"Then someone could've been trying to make sure you didn't go back home," Dallas said.

"I hope that's all it is and not the fact that someone wants to take Jackson away from me." Kate clutched him closer, as if daring anyone to try.

"If Allen will agree to let a deputy search his house, then that'll go a long way toward clearing him," Dallas said.

"I hope he does so we can cross him off the suspect list," she said, and she sounded as if she really didn't want her friend to be involved, more than that she was convinced he wasn't.

Tommy entered the room with a stark expression.

Dallas didn't like the look on his friend's face.

"What is it?" he asked.

"A vehicle registered to Wayne Morton was found abandoned off of Farm Road 23," Tommy said, a look of apology in his eyes. "They found blood spatter but no sign of a body."

"I'm guessing there's no other indication of Morton anywhere?" Dallas asked. But he already knew the answer to that question and an ominous feeling settled over him. Between the blood spatter and the fact that Morton hadn't checked in with his assistant this morning, Dallas feared the worst. "We need to talk to Stacy to find out what she knows about his itinerary."

"No. I need to talk to his assistant," Tommy said. "I can send a deputy to Morton's office."

"Might be best if I speak to her personally. She might open up to me more than a stranger," Dallas suggested. He felt guilt settle heavy on his shoulders, knowing that if anything had happened to Morton it could be his fault. History would be repeating itself. He muttered a curse too low for anyone else to hear.

"Does this have anything to do with my case?" Kate asked. "Because if it does, I'd like to go with you."

"No," Dallas said. "You should stay here in the sheriff's office just to be safe."

He hadn't anticipated the uncomfortable feeling he

got in his gut at the thought of leaving her. She'd be in good hands with Tommy and yet he felt the need to stick around and watch over her. He told himself that it was all protective instinct and had nothing to do with the sizzle of attraction he felt when she was near.

"Hold on a sec. Did Lentz give you permission to search his place?" Dallas asked Tommy, figuring it would be good to rule out one suspect.

His friend said, "No."

"Are you done questioning him?" Dallas pressed.

Tommy frowned. "He lawyered up."

Chapter Five

"Deputy Lopez just briefed me on the computer search at the soup kitchen," Tommy said to Dallas. "Turns out that Allen Lentz has an unusual amount of pictures of Ms. Williams on cloud storage that we accessed via his computer."

Dallas didn't like the sound of that.

"He takes all the office party photos." Kate jumped to Lentz's defense.

Abigail knocked on the door to Tommy's office and all eyes focused on her. "There have been six other kidnappings in the past three weeks in Texas, all boys, all adopted and all at gunpoint."

"He used a knife with me," Kate stated, shivering at the thought that it could've been worse.

"The first infant was found three days later in a car seat on the steps of his day care center," she said. "The second and third were found several days after their disappearances, under similar circumstances."

"Three are still missing?" Tommy asked.

His secretary nodded. "The three most recent ones."

"Was there a ransom demand in any of the cases?" Tommy asked.

"Not once," she stated.

"Have Deputy Solomon check into the incidences to see if we can find a link to Safe Haven," Tommy said.

Kate perked up. "That means Allen is innocent, right?"

The sheriff looked from Dallas to her apologetically. "Not necessarily. He could be mimicking other kidnappings to distract attention away from him. The MO was different with you and I can't rule anyone out until I know why."

"To be clear, someone is taking babies who are the same sex and around the same age with no ransom demand and then making sure they're found a couple of days later?" Dallas asked Tommy.

"I'm inclined to draw the same conclusion," Tommy said. "The kidnappers are looking for a specific child."

Abigail moved to Kate, motioning toward Jackson. "Let me take him in the other room where he can sleep peacefully."

Kate stilled.

"I'll take good care of him. Don't you worry," Abigail assured her. "He's in good hands with me."

"Thank you." She handed over her sleeping baby. "So the pictures you found on Allen's computer aren't office pictures, are they?" she said, sinking back into the chair.

"No, ma'am." Tommy waved her and Dallas over to his desk and then pulled up a file on his computer, positioning the monitor for all three of them to see.

One by one, pictures of Kate filled the screen.

"These were taken in my house," she said, shock evident in her voice.

"Actually, from outside your house, like through a window," Dallas observed.

"He's been watching me?" Her hand covered her mouth as she gasped. "Pictures of me sleeping?"

The questions were rhetorical, and the hurt and disbelief audible in them was like a punch to Dallas's gut.

He reached out to comfort her, not expecting her to spin around into his arms and bury her face in his chest.

This close, he felt her body trembling. A curse tore from his lips as he pulled her nearer, ignoring how soft her skin was or how well she fitted in his arms. His attraction to her was going to be a problem if he didn't keep it in check.

"Sheriff, can I see you in the hallway for a moment?" Deputy Lopez peeked inside the door.

Tommy agreed and then shot a warning look toward Dallas. He was telling him not to get too close to the victim, and Dallas couldn't ignore the fact that it was sound advice.

He had moved past logic and gone straight to primal instinct the second her body pressed to his.

But he wasn't stupid enough to confuse this for anything more than what it was for her—comfort from a stranger.

The sudden urge to lift her chin and capture her mouth with his wasn't logical, either. But Dallas couldn't regret it the instant her pink lips pressed against his.

Her arms came up to his chest, her palms flat against his pecs.

As if they both suddenly realized where they were and that someone could walk through that door at any second, they pulled back, hearts pounding in rhythm.

Chemistry sizzled between them, charging the air.

Tommy walked in and his tense expression signaled more bad news.

"Two things," he stated. "First, Morton's body has been found floating in the lake on the Hatches' property.

He'd been fatally shot, but the perp tied a bag of heavy rocks around his midsection."

"Amateurs?" Dallas asked.

"It would appear so," Tommy agreed. "And it looks like they did this on the spur of the moment, using whatever they could find."

"What else?" Dallas was trying to digest this news. He was the one who'd gotten Morton involved in this case and now the PI was dead. Guilt sat heavy on his chest as he tried to take a breath.

"The other news—" he glanced from Dallas to Kate "—is that more pictures were found at Lentz's place. A lot of them."

"And that would confirm his fixation on Kate," Dallas said, which was the logical assumption. But he had a gnawing feeling that the guy was innocent. Dallas wanted him to be guilty. That would tie this whole troubling case up with a bow. Lentz would be arrested. Kate and Jackson would be safe. Problem solved.

And yet Dallas worried this was more complicated.

Babies were going missing. Investigating Safe Haven had most likely cost Morton his life. Anger pierced Dallas, leaving a huge hole in his chest.

Kate took a step back, grabbing the desk to steady herself. "What kind of pictures?"

"Just like the ones you saw earlier," Tommy said. "And there were ones with markings across Jackson's face."

Kate gasped again, looking stunned. "I can't believe Allen would do something like that. I know I saw the photos with my own eyes, but it doesn't make any sense."

As much as Dallas didn't like the guy, part of him agreed with Kate. This was too easy. "Does Allen have any enemies? Did he get into a fight with anyone lately?"

Someone could be setting up Lentz. But who? And why?

Her lips pressed together and Dallas forced himself not to stare. Thinking about that kiss was inappropriate as hell and yet there it was anyway.

"The baby keeps me busy. I don't really socialize with anyone outside of work, so I couldn't say for sure about his personal life." She shot an apologetic look toward Tommy. "He didn't talk about having any arguments and no one's been around the soup kitchen."

"Kate!" The anguish in Allen's voice shattered the silence in the hallway. "Let me talk to Kate. Those aren't my pictures. I don't know where they came from. I'm being set up."

Dallas heard one of the deputies shuffling Lentz down the hall, most likely to a jail cell.

"I would never do something like this. I love Jackson," the man shouted, and it visibly shook Kate.

She glanced around the room. "I honestly don't know what to say. I have no idea who would do this to him, and even though those pictures completely creep me out, I still can't believe he would do something like this."

Dallas rubbed his chin. "It would have to be someone with access to his computer at work and at his home."

Kate gripped the desk. "There's one person I can think of who would have access to both, but there's no way he would do anything like this."

Dallas nodded, urging her to keep talking.

"My handyman, Randy Ruiz," she finally said and then bit her bottom lip.

"I'll check him out." Tommy typed the name into the system. "We ran Lentz earlier and his background check came up clean, by the way."

"And Ruiz?" Dallas asked.

"He has a record," Tommy noted, staring at his computer screen.

"I know. I knew that when I hired him. But that was a long time ago, and good people deserve a second chance," Kate said. "He's never been so much as late to work, let alone missed a day. He has a wonderful family."

And a rap sheet, Dallas thought.

Tommy locked gazes with him. "Ruiz has a history of burglary."

"So he would know how to get in and out of a house without anyone seeing him," Dallas confirmed.

"He wouldn't have had to. Allen gave him a copy of his keys so he could fix a leaky pipe in his downstairs bathroom," Kate declared.

Dallas could only imagine how difficult it must be to have to think about the possibility that people she trusted would do something to hurt her. The employees at the ranch were more family than most of Dallas's cousins.

"We need to bring in Ruiz for questioning," Tommy said.

"I'M SO SORRY this is happening, Randy," Kate said to her employee as he was led into the sheriff's office.

"Someone tried to hurt you and little Jackson?" Randy asked, concern lines bracketing his mouth.

"Yes. This morning," she said.

"That's why you weren't at work today?"

She nodded.

"Mrs. Zilker was worried. Allen told her everything was fine and to take the day off," Randy said.

Dallas couldn't help but notice the prison tattoos on the handyman's arms when he took off his jacket. The guy was a five-foot-nine wall of solid muscle. He had clean-cut dark hair and a trim mustache. His genuine worry made him seem far less threatening. And even though his job could have him snaking out a toilet at a moment's notice, his jeans looked new and had been pressed. He definitely fit the bill of someone who cared about doing a good job.

Kate nodded. "I told the sheriff how much you love your job and what an exemplary employee you are," she said to Randy. "I'm so sorry you have to come here and answer questions."

"I'm not," he said emphatically. "If this helps them find the guy who tried to kidnap Jackson, then I want to do everything I can to help."

Kate thanked him.

Based on his serious expression, he meant every word. And that pretty much ruled him out as a suspect, because with his record, Dallas would've thought he'd be offended. His genuine lack of self-concern said he would jump through any hoop if it meant figuring out who was trying to hurt Kate.

But the interview wasn't a total loss. They'd ruled someone out and it was possible that Randy had seen or heard something that could help them figure out if anyone else in the office was involved.

Tommy shot a sideways glance toward Dallas and he immediately knew that his friend thought the same thing.

"I heard about what happened to Allen," Randy said, shaking his head, his slight Hispanic accent barely noticeable.

Interesting word choices, Dallas noted.

"I made mistakes in the past, but I'm a family man now," he said to the sheriff. "Don't waste your time looking at me."

"All I need is for you to answer a few questions so we can figure out who did this," Tommy replied, a hint of admiration in his eyes.

"Allen's a good guy," Randy said. "He would never do anything to hurt Miss Kate or her baby."

Dallas believed that to be true, too. It was almost too easy to pin this on Lentz. And that made Dallas believe that the guy might have been set up.

"How long did it take Deputy Lopez to find the pictures on Lentz's computer?" Dallas asked Tommy.

"Not long. Why?" his friend asked.

"How good is Allen with computers?" Dallas asked Randy, and Tommy's nod of approval said he'd figured out where Dallas was going with this.

"That man knows his way around them for sure. He helps me all the time with the one I have at home for my kids," the handyman said.

Dallas turned to Kate. He needed a reason to rule out Lentz. "How would you classify Allen's computer skills?"

"Very competent," she said, and then it must've dawned on her. "And you're thinking why wouldn't he have password protected those files, aren't you?"

"That's exactly what I'm thinking," he agreed. "I'm sure the deputies could've gotten to those files, given enough time, even if they'd been buried. But it was easy."

"Too easy," Tommy said, "because they weren't hidden at all."

"And then at Allen's house they happen to find even more damning evidence," Dallas said.

Kate was already rocking her head. "The black bars across Jackson's face."

"Let's take a closer look at some of those pics and see if we can get a clue." Tommy moved to his computer and his fingers went to work on the keyboard.

"If not Allen, then who took the pictures?" she wondered.

"Great question," Dallas said.

Tommy clicked through the pictures once again, slowly this time.

"What are you looking for?" Dallas asked.

"Clues to when these pictures were taken. I'm trying to piece together a timeline. It'll take a while to have all the evidence analyzed, but maybe we can figure out a window and then narrow down the possibilities. Kate, can you identify when you wore those pajamas?"

"Hard to tell. I wear something like those most nights." A red blush crawled up her neck to her cheeks.

Randy's gaze immediately dropped to the floor, as if to spare her further embarrassment.

"I can clear the room if you'd be more comfortable doing this alone," Tommy said to her.

"No. It's fine," she said. The red blush on her cheeks belied her words. "I always wear an oversize T-shirt. I rotate between a couple, so that could be any night."

She studied the new picture on the screen. "This one was recent." She pointed to a mug on the side table next to her bed. "I just started drinking tea within the last two weeks."

"Good," Tommy said. "Could most of these pictures have been taken within that time frame?"

"Let's see," she said, studying each one as more flashed across the screen. "Yes. All of them could."

"So, someone gets happy with a camera in the past two weeks and then tries to snatch Jackson, all while pointing the finger at Allen to distract attention from the real person behind this." Dallas summed it up. On a larger scale, baby boys around Jackson's age were being kidnapped and released.

"And then we have the issue of Kate's kidnapping attempt being slightly different than the others," Tommy said, and that was exactly Dallas's next thought. Jackson's kidnapper had used a knife. And someone had broken into her house and stolen her adoption files.

"Were there break-ins at the other houses?" Dallas asked.

Tommy said there weren't.

"I should go." He needed to get over and talk to Stacy, to see what else she knew about Morton.

"I know what you're thinking. I'm coming with you," Tommy said.

"I might get more out of Stacy if I'm on my own," Dallas pointed out. "And I need to follow up with Safe Haven."

"This is a murder investigation, Dallas. I'm going with you or you're not going at all." The lawman's tone left no room for argument.

"I'm coming, too," Kate said. Her eyes fixed on Dallas and all he could see was that same determination he'd noted earlier when someone had been trying to snatch her baby from her arms.

"Absolutely not." He didn't have to think about the answer to that one.

"If this involves Jackson, then I'm coming, and you can't stop me," she said emphatically.

"I don't know if it does or not yet." If someone at the adoption agency was involved in Morton's murder and that same person was after Jackson, the last thing Dallas intended to do was put Kate in harm's way.

"That's the place I adopted him and my files are missing from home," she said. "I have to believe that's not a coincidence."

Maybe not.

"It might be best for you to stay put," Dallas countered. The thought that this could be one of her neighbors died on the vine.

"I don't have to ask your permission. I can go with or without you." She stood her ground. "I have a relationship with them and I have every right to request my file and talk to the people there who were involved in my case."

Dallas blew out a frustrated breath, suspecting that if she went in alone she could be walking into danger. A perp could be watching the place, seeing who came and went to get information.

"Both of you need to calm down," Tommy said. "I don't want either one of you going without me, especially if they're responsible for a murder. You'd be putting yourself in unnecessary danger."

Tommy was right about one thing. Kate had no business investigating Safe Haven, given what had happened to Morton after he'd started going down that route.

"A man is dead because of me," Dallas said to his friend.

"He was a professional and he knew the risks his job carried," the lawman said soberly.

"I hired him and he was there because of me. I'm responsible for him," Dallas countered, realizing he was arguing with the one man who'd understand taking risks on his job.

"Does this mean Allen is in the clear?" Randy asked.

"It does for now," the sheriff said.

"Good. Then I can give him a ride home."

"Not yet," Tommy said. "I have a few more questions for him, so I want him to stick around."

Dallas stood and thanked the handyman, offering a handshake.

"I know this is asking a lot," Kate interjected, "but could you go back to the office? I have no idea when I'll be able to return, and I want to make sure people are being fed."

"Of course," Randy said. "We'll keep things running until you can come back."

"Thank you!" Kate rose to her feet and gave him a hug. "I'm so sorry that this is happening and I hope you know how much I trust you and the rest of the staff."

"Don't worry about us or the soup kitchen." Randy looked her in the eye. "We're all adults. We can handle this. Just take care of yourself and little Jackson and leave the rest up to us."

Dallas could feel the sense of family in the room. He would know, because he had five brothers who would be saying the same things had they known what was going on.

Which reminded him that he needed to fill them in on his situation with Susan. Just not yet.

With Morton's death, Dallas also realized that Susan could have gotten involved with the wrong people and ended up in over her head. The two of them as a couple didn't work, but he had some residual feelings for her. She was someone he'd dated and at one time had wanted to get to know better. They'd grown up in the same town and had known each other for years. Dallas didn't wish this on anyone and especially not Susan. Baby drama aside, he hoped that she hadn't done something to put herself at risk.

For her sake as much as his, Dallas needed to know what had happened to her and the baby she'd given birth to.

As he started toward the door, he realized that he had no means of transportation. He also realized he had a shadow. Kate was buttoning up her coat as she followed him.

He stopped and she had to put on the brakes in order

to avoid walking straight into him. Her flat palms on his back brought a jolt of electricity.

Dallas turned around quickly and Kate took a step back. "My pickup is at the supply store parking lot. Can you take me to it?"

"For the record, I don't like either one of you anywhere near the attempted kidnapping site or Safe Haven," Tommy interjected.

Dallas shot his friend a telling look. "I'm going to talk to Stacy first."

"While you do that, I'll investigate the crime scene," the sheriff conceded. "Keep me posted on what you find out from her and let her know that I'll be stopping by her office for a statement later today."

KATE HATED THE thought of being separated from Jackson, to the point her heart hurt. If leaving to find answers wasn't a trade-off for his ultimate safety, then she wouldn't be able to go, not even knowing he'd be with someone as competent as Abigail. His security had to be the priority.

For a second, Kate considered calling her babysitter, but after this morning's kidnapping attempt there was no way she would risk putting Mrs. Zilker in danger.

Abigail stopped at the doorway, Jackson resting peacefully in her arms. "Walter Higgins is refusing to answer questions without an attorney present."

"He's always been a stubborn one." Tommy shook his head and shrugged. "We'll give it to him his way. Send Deputy Lopez to pick him up and bring him in. I doubt he'll be useful given the turn of events, but I'd like him to know that we're aware of his antics with Ms. Williams."

"Yes, sir."

"Any news about the other incidences?" the sheriff asked.

Her gaze bounced from Kate to him, making the hair on Kate's arms stand on end. "So far, we've been able to make contact with one of the families."

"And?" Tommy asked.

"They adopted their son from Safe Haven almost three months ago," Abigail stated, with an apologetic glance toward Kate.

Kate struggled to breathe as anxiety caused her chest to squeeze.

"Any other obvious connections to our current case?" he continued.

"Other than the fact they've all occurred between Houston and San Antonio?" Abigail asked.

Tommy nodded.

"That's all I have so far," she replied. "We'll know more as we hear back from the other families."

Kate stepped forward and kissed Jackson, praying this would not be the last time she saw him. Then she walked out the door and toward her car.

"We need to switch to my pickup at some point today," Dallas said, once they were in the parking lot.

"Hold on a second. I have a few questions before we leave." She stopped cold. She'd been so distracted by her own problems, she hadn't stopped to really think about everything she'd heard at the sheriff's office.

Dallas turned around and faced her.

"What is your connection to Safe Haven?" she asked.

"I've been helping a close friend figure out if he's a father or not," he said, and something told her there was more to that story than he was sharing. "He wants to keep his identity out of the papers, so he asked me to help. I hired Morton to investigate and you know the rest from there."

Kate tossed him her keys. No way could she concentrate on driving in her current state.

"My adoption was legal," she said, once she was buckled in. "I followed all the right channels."

Kate pressed her fingers to her temples to stave off the headache threatening.

Dallas glanced at her and then quickly focused on the road again. "When was the last time you ate?"

"Last night, I think," she said. "Guess I shouldn't have had that cup of coffee on an empty stomach. I feel nauseous."

Dallas cut right.

"Where are you going?" she asked.

"Somewhere I can get you something to eat," he said in a don't-argue-with-me tone.

So she didn't. There wouldn't be a point, and Kate didn't have the energy anyway. She'd drained herself putting up enough of a fight to go with him.

"What about your truck?"

"We'll swing by and pick it up after I get food in you."

She expected Dallas to pull into the first fast-food drive-through they saw, but there were none on the route he chose. After a good twenty minutes, she started to ask where he was taking her and then saw the sign for his family's ranch, Cattlemen Crime Club.

"Why are we here?" she asked. Wasn't this too far out of the way?

"Because I need to know that you'll be safe while I feed you," Dallas said, pulling up to the first gate and entering a code. A security officer waved as Dallas passed through the second checkpoint.

"I still think these guys are after Jackson, not me," she countered. "But I won't argue, since we're already here."

Kate didn't want to admit to being curious about Dallas. In fact, she wanted to know more about him, and that was a surprise given that she didn't think it would be possible for her to be interested in another man so soon after Robert.

Interest wasn't necessarily the word she'd use to describe what she was feeling for Dallas. Attraction? Sizzle? She felt those in spades. Neither seemed appropriate under the circumstances. But there was something about the strong cowboy that pulled her toward him. Something she'd felt with another man. Not even with Robert. And she wasn't sure how to begin to process that. Kate had loved Robert...hadn't she?

She'd been married to the man and yet she hadn't felt this strong of a pull toward him. There was something about the cowboy that caused goose bumps on her arms every time he was near. So much more than sexual attraction.

And even in all the craziness, she couldn't ignore the heat of that kiss.

Chapter Six

To say the ranch was impressive was like saying Bill Gates had done okay for himself.

The land itself was stunning even though the cold front had stripped trees of their foliage, scattering orange and brown leaves across the front lawn.

The main building was especially striking. It was an imposing two stories with white siding and black shutters bracketing the windows. Grand white columns with orange and black ribbons adorned the expansive porch filled with black, orange and white pumpkins. Large pots of yellow and orange gerbera daisies led up the couple of stairs to the veranda, where pairs of white rocking chairs grouped together on both sides. The dark silhouette of a witch loomed in the top right window. Kate counted fourteen in all, including a set of French doors on the second floor complete with a quaint terrace. When she thought of a Texas ranch, this was exactly the kind of picture that would've come to mind.

The place was alive with charm and a very big part of her wished this for Jackson. Given the strain on her family since the divorce and the adoption, she didn't expect to go home for the holidays this year.

In fact, that was the last fight she and her mother had had.

If her mom couldn't support her decision and accept Jackson, then Kate had no intention of visiting at Halloween, Thanksgiving or anytime. Jackson was just as much a part of the family as she was, so rejecting him was no different than rejecting her.

Thinking about the fight still made her sad and she wished her mother understood. But her mom had been clear. Kate had been clear. And neither seemed ready to budge.

And right now, Kate had bigger problems than disagreeing with her mother over her adoption.

"Do you live here?" Kate asked, wiping away a sneaky tear while trying to take in all the warmth and grandeur of the place.

"I do now but not in this building. This was my parents' home. They opened up a wing for club guests and there are offices on the other side. My brothers and I each have our own hacienda at various places on the land," he said. "Our parents built them in hopes we'd stay on after college."

"Your parents don't live here anymore?" she asked, unable to imagine leaving such a beautiful home.

Dallas shook his head, and seeing the look on his face, a mix of sorrow and reverence, she regretted the question.

"They died a few weeks ago." He said the words quietly, but the anguish in his voice nearly robbed her of breath.

She exhaled and said, "I'm so sorry."

He put the car in Park, cut the engine and stared out the front window for a few seconds. "Let's get some food in you," he finally said. Then he opened the door and exited the car.

Before she could get her seat belt off, Dallas was opening her door and holding out his hand. She was greeted by a chocolate Lab.

"Who's this guy?" she asked, patting him on the head.

"That's Denali. Been in the family fourteen years," Dallas said.

"He's beautiful." She took his outstretched hand, ignoring the sensual shivers vibrating up her arm from the point of contact. What could she say? Dallas was strong, handsome. The cowboy had shown up just in time to save her and her son from a terrible fate. So she couldn't deny a powerful attraction.

He was also a complete stranger, a little voice reminded her—a voice that repeated those words louder, a warning from the logical side of her brain.

Maybe if she had taken more time to get to know Robert before she'd jumped into a relationship and marriage, things might've turned out differently, that same annoying voice warned.

Instead, she'd allowed herself to be influenced by his easy charm and good looks. She'd gone against her better judgment after a couple of months of dating when he'd handed her a glass of wine and asked if she wanted to "get hitched and make babies."

Looking back, a piece of her, the logical side, had known all along that she didn't know Robert well enough to make a lifelong commitment. She'd been young and had given in to impulse.

And when things didn't go as planned, he'd bolted.

Not that she could really blame him for wanting out when she couldn't make the last part happen. He'd been clear that babies had been part of the deal all along. And his attention had wandered after that. Or maybe even before. Kate couldn't be sure. All she knew for certain was the information in the texts that she'd seen once she'd figured out he was having an affair. Even though she should've read the signs long before, and maybe a little part of her knew, there was still something about discovering proof of his lies—seeing them right there in front of her—that had knocked the wind out of her.

Logically, she knew all men were not Robert. But her heart, the part of her that withstood reason, knew she'd never be able to completely trust a man or a relationship again. She'd always question her judgment when it came to them now.

Dallas held the front door open for her as she forced her thoughts to the present. One step at a time, she entered the O'Brien home. The inside was even more breathtaking than the outside, if that was possible.

"Did you grow up here?" She imagined him and his brothers chasing each other up one side and down the other of the twin staircases in the foyer.

"Yes, ma'am," Dallas said, and there was something about his deep baritone that sent sensual shivers racing down her back.

"It must've been a wonderful childhood," she said and then chided herself for saying it out loud. She, of all people, should know that looks could be deceiving when it came to families. Maybe her perfect-on-the-outside relationship with Robert had been easy to fake, given that she'd grown up in a similar situation. Oh, the holiday cards her mother had insisted on posing for and sending out had painted a different picture. In those, they'd looked like the ideal family, complete with the requisite perfect boy and girl. What couldn't be seen in those paper faces and forced smiles was the constant bickering between her parents. Or how much her mom had needed both her children to be perfect in every way.

Kate could still see the disappointment in her mother's eyes when she'd brought home a C in Lit or when her SAT scores didn't quite measure up to expectations.

Their relationship had really started to fragment when Kate left for college and declared that she wanted to study computers instead of interior design. Her mom had thrown another fit, saying that career field was unfeminine.

Even when Kate and Carter had created a successful tech business together, their mother hadn't changed her position. She'd mostly been impressed with Carter and had insinuated that he'd carried Kate.

In selling her share, she'd done well enough to buy a house in Bluff, finance an adoption and provide the seed money to start The Food Project. And she'd still managed to save enough money for Jackson to study whatever he wanted in college.

"It was," Dallas said, bringing her out of her reverie. And she realized he'd been studying her reaction all along.

"So you spent your whole life here?" Kate asked, following him down the hall and into an impressive kitchen, the chocolate Lab at her heels.

There were batches of cookies in various stages of cooking. The place smelled like warmth and fall and everything wonderful. "Is that hot apple cider mulling on the stove?"

Dallas nodded and gave a half smile. "Janis goes all out this time of year through New Year's. She keeps this place running and has been helping my family most of my life. Would you like some cider?"

An older woman padded in from the hallway. "Dallas O'Brien, what are you doing in my kitchen this late? I expected you two hours ago for lunch," she said.

"Janis, I'd like you to meet Kate." He motioned toward her.

Janis wasn't tall, had to be right at five foot or a little more. She was round and grandmotherly with soft features.

Kate held out her hand. "Nice to meet you."

"My apologies for being so rude. I didn't realize Dallas had company," Janis said, shaking Kate's hand heartily. She had on a witch hat and her face was painted green.

Janis must've caught Kate's once-over because she added, "And forgive this old outfit. I just delivered cookies to The Learning Bridge Preschool for Special Children."

"You look—"

"Silly to anyone standing over three feet tall," Janis said drolly, cutting Kate off.

"I was going to say 'as adorable as a witch.'"

The woman grinned from ear to ear.

Kate wasn't trying to score brownie points with the comment, but it seemed that she had.

"Well, then, can I get you something to eat? I made a special Italian sausage soup this morning," Janis said. "Can't believe how cold it is this early in the season. Then again, I shouldn't be surprised given how unpredictable Texas weather can be."

"That sounds like heaven." Kate smiled. She couldn't help but like pretty much everything about the O'Brien house. She could imagine the look on Jackson's face when he was older, running through halls like these, surrounded by family.

Her heart squeezed, because Jackson would never have that. But he had her and Carter, and they would have to be enough, she told herself. Or maybe just her, that irritating little voice said, because Carter hadn't been out to meet his nephew yet, either.

"There's a formal eating space in the other room, but this is where my brothers and I prefer to hang out." Dallas motioned toward the oversize wood table in the kitchen. "Janis would tease us and say it's because we weren't taught enough manners to sit in the other room."

"This is perfect. Closer to the source," Kate said.

"Where is everybody?" Dallas inquired.

"After lunch, they all took off outside. A few of the boys headed to the barn. Austin said he would be running fences if anyone needed him," Janis added, bringing two steaming bowls of soup to the table.

"He's been doing that a lot lately," Dallas noted thoughtfully, almost as if talking to himself. "I'll check on him later." He walked over to the stove.

"Running fences?" Kate asked.

"We have livestock on the property, so every foot of fence has to be routinely checked," he explained.

The hearty soup smelled amazing and Kate figured it was about the only thing she would be able to get down. Even though she knew she should eat, it was the last thing on her mind, since her nerves were fried and her stomach was tied in knots.

Dallas brought her a cup of apple cider and it smelled even more delicious. But nothing was as appealing as Dallas when he hesitated near her. His scent was a powerful mix of virile male and the great outdoors, and it affected her in ways she didn't want to think about right then.

"This food is amazing." She couldn't allow herself to get too carried away in the moment because the horrible events of the day were constant in her thoughts, and being separated from Jackson even though he was safe at the sheriff's office was another reminder of their present danger. Her son being secure was the most important thing, and she needed to get back to him as soon as possible.

The best way to do that would be to figure out what was going on and stop it, she reminded herself.

"Janis is the best cook in Collier County," Dallas was saying, and the older woman smiled.

"Did you make contact with Stacy to let her know we're coming?" Kate asked a moment later, focusing on the problem at hand.

"I'll do that now." Dallas took a seat across the table from her, fished his phone from his front pocket and then sent a text.

The soup tasted every bit as good as it smelled and eased her queasy stomach instantly.

Janis brought over a plate of fresh bread before asking Dallas to keep an eye on the timer for the latest batch of cookies while she changed into regular clothes.

"Earlier, you gave the impression you'd moved back to the ranch. Where did you live before?" Kate asked him.

"I had a logistics business based in New Mexico," he explained.

"I've been to Taos to ski," she offered.

"Up the mountain is too cold for my blood." Dallas laughed and the sound of his voice filled the room. "But then, I figure you know a thing or two about that, given the way you were dressed this morning."

"There's no substitute for sunshine and Texas summers," Kate said. "Why did you move back?"

"There were a lot of reasons to come home, but the main one was to run the ranch with my brothers," Dallas said. His business in New Mexico was booming and he'd built a life there, but no sacrifice was too great for his family, and he'd always known that he'd return to the ranch full-time at some point. This land was where his heart belonged.

"I'm sorry again about your parents." Kate must've realized the real reason he'd returned.

"We inherited the place along with an aunt and uncle, and I guess it just felt right to keep ownership in the family. Between the cattle ranch and rifle club, this place is more than a full-time job and it takes all of us pitching in to keep it going. Especially now. We're still getting our arms around the business, while a few of us are in the process of selling off our other interests."

"How many brothers did you say you have?" Kate asked, taking another spoonful of soup. The little moan of pleasure in her throat made him think of their kiss— a kiss that wasn't far from his thoughts, no matter how little business it had being there.

"Five, so there are six of us total. One is still living in Colorado, but the others are settling their affairs and/or living here. The youngest two are twins," he said. Dallas wasn't much of a talker usually, but conversation with Kate came easy.

"Twins?" she gasped. "My hands are full with one baby."

Dallas couldn't hold back a chuckle. "Tommy practically grew up in this house, too. He came to live with his uncle, Chill Johnson, who's been a ranch hand since longer than I can remember. So he makes a solid seven boys."

The bewildered look in Kate's eyes was amusing. "I can't even imagine having that many kids around. Taking care of Jackson is keeping me busier than I ever thought possible." She glanced about. "Then again, it's just me and Jackson."

Something flashed in her eyes that Dallas couldn't quite put his finger on.

"Despite having plenty of help around, Mom insisted on taking care of us herself," he said. "She was an original DIY type."

"Then she really was an amazing woman," Kate declared.

"Pop helped out a lot," Dallas added. "Being the oldest, so did I. They were forced to hire more help around the ranch, especially as they got older and we moved on to make our own way in life."

The look of admiration in Kate's eyes shouldn't make Dallas feel proud. But he didn't want to spend any more time talking about himself.

He wanted to learn more about Kate Williams.

Before he could ask a question, she'd devoured the contents of her bowl, drained her cider and made a move to stand.

"We should head to your detective agency," she said, and that look of determination was back. That was most likely a good thing, because Dallas didn't need to go down that path, didn't need to go to the place where he was getting to know her better and learning about all the little ticks that made her unique. Especially if Susan's baby turned out to be Jackson.

As he walked her to the front door, Janis met them in the hallway.

"I almost forgot to tell you that your uncle Ezra was around looking for you this morning," she said. "He and his sister are at it again, and I think Ezra was jockeying for support. He said that he didn't want to trouble you, but when one of your brothers shot down his idea he felt he needed to get another opinion."

"If he's still angling to get an invite for the McCabe

family to the bash then he's barking up the wrong tree." Hollister McCabe and Dallas's father had been at odds for years. McCabe had been trying to buy fifty acres from Pop, and when Dallas's dad had refused, the other rancher had tried to strong-arm a local politician to force the issue. That hadn't gone over well with the self-made, independent-minded senior O'Brien.

And Dallas had never trusted the McCabe family. Especially since Faith McCabe was one of Susan's best friends. That should've been enough of a red flag for him. Maybe it was the fact that he'd missed home that had drawn him to date Susan in the first place. Susan had always loved Bluff, so it was even more of a surprise that she'd come to New Mexico. Tommy had balked when Dallas had told his friend about who had shown up to a job interview at D.O. Logistics, the successful company Dallas had founded. He'd said that he shouldn't be too surprised given how much she'd been talking about missing Dallas around town.

"I believe that was one of Ezra's complaints," Janis said, snapping his mind to the current conversation. "But he's always got something up his sleeve."

Knowing Ezra, that was the tip of the iceberg. He'd been making a play for more control over the family business since before Pop's death—a business Pop had begun and made a success on his own. In the weeks since his death, Ezra's efforts had doubled.

Pop had included his siblings, giving them a combined 5 percent of the company in order to help them be more independent in their older years. Pop was a tough businessman, but his heart was gold, and even though he'd disagreed with his brother and sister on most counts, he'd felt a responsibility to take care of family.

Dallas could relate to the emotion, being the oldest of

the O'Brien siblings, and was grateful that his brothers shared the same work ethic as he did and he wouldn't have to carry them.

"Gearing up for the holiday season always brings out the best in those two, doesn't it," he said to Janis, shaking his head.

"I don't know why they have to act up around the biggest parties of the year." She nodded and took in a slow breath.

"How's planning going for the Halloween Bash?" Dallas asked.

"Good. Busy. You know how it is around this time. You'd think with all we have going on that he'd relax." She paused and then added, "But no. He's always scheming. Families can be *interesting* sometimes."

"That's a good word for it," Dallas agreed. Janis had become as much a part of the O'Brien clan as anyone in her decades of service.

"Will you be back in time for supper?" she asked.

"Not exactly sure. Don't hold it up on my account, though. Also, I need to let the others know I have a situation to deal with and I might need their assistance. Do you mind helping with that?" Dallas asked.

"Consider it done."

"Hold on." He moved to his father's gun cabinet and pulled out his favorite, a .25 caliber, put on a shoulder holster and secured the weapon underneath his coat.

He returned, thanked Janis and then placed his hand on the small of Kate's back to usher her out the front door. It was too much to ignore the heat rippling through him from the contact, even though she wore a coat, so he accepted it.

There was no use denying the fact that Kate was a beautiful woman. Dallas needed to leave it at that. Because not keeping his feelings in check would just complicate an already crazy situation. Hormones had no place in the equation. He'd already decided to offer her and Jackson a place to stay on the ranch. There was plenty of room in his hacienda, and Tommy would be hard-pressed to find anywhere for them with better security.

And Dallas didn't need to create an unnecessary distraction because of the feelings he was developing for Kate. *Feelings? This soon?*

He wasn't going to touch that one.

Besides, having her and the baby stay with him had everything to do with offering a safe place for the mother and child. State-of-the-art security was a necessity on the ranch, given that this part of south-central Texas was known for poachers. Other than being some of the worst scum on earth, poachers presented a danger to their clients and the hunting expeditions offered by the Cattlemen Crime Club.

KATE WAS QUIET on the ride over. Dallas exited the sedan and she followed suit. He'd caught a glimpse of her, of the questions she had. At least for now she seemed to think better of asking.

"Mr. O'Brien, how can I help you?" Stacy peeked out the door. The petite brunette wore business attire that highlighted her curves. Based on her puffy eyes, Dallas guessed she'd been crying all day.

"I'm here to talk to you about Wayne and the case he was investigating," Dallas said.

"Of course you are. Come in. I'm sorry. My mind's not right. Not since learning about Wayne this morning from the deputy." She froze, embarrassment crossing her features, and then corrected herself. "Mr. Morton. It's all such a shock."

Based on the woman's general demeanor, it occurred to Dallas that she and Morton might have had more than a working relationship. Given the circumstances, he wasn't surprised that she looked in such bad shape.

"This is my friend Kate Williams," Dallas said.

"Please, come in," Stacy said. "It's nice to meet you." She and Kate shook hands as she invited them inside.

"Has anyone else been here to speak to you?" Dallas asked, instinctively positioning himself between Kate and the door.

"Just the appointments Wayne—Mr. Morton—already had on the books," Stacy said, blowing her nose into a wrinkled handkerchief. "Excuse me. I'm sorry, but I'm just a mess. He was a good guy, you know, and I can't believe he's gone."

"No need to apologize," Dallas said quickly, guilt settling on his shoulders yet again. He knew full well that Morton would still be alive were it not for Safe Haven and Dallas's case. "I couldn't be sorrier this happened."

"It's not like his job doesn't bring with it a certain amount of danger," she continued, as more tears rolled down her cheeks. "He's licensed to carry."

Dallas knew that meant Morton had been armed.

"And he went to the gun range all the time to keep his skills sharp," she said with a hiccup. "I just can't believe someone would get to him first like that."

"It shouldn't have happened. Other than working on my case, has there been anything unusual going on lately with Wayne? Has he been keeping any late nights or other appointments off the books?" Dallas asked, knowing Safe Haven was the reason Morton was dead, but wishing for another explanation.

"No. Not that I can think of, anyway, but then, you know Wayne." She seemed to drop the front of being strictly professional with her boss. "He took on extra assignments all the time, which didn't mean I'd know about them."

Any hope, however small, that this wasn't Dallas's fault was slowly dying.

More tears spilled out of Stacy's eyes and she looked like she needed to sit down.

Dallas urged her toward one of the seats in the lounge area of Morton's expansive office. She perched on the arm of a leather chair as Kate took a seat near her on the matching sofa.

"First of all, I want to say that I'm really sorry about Wayne," Kate said sympathetically, leaning toward her. "I can only imagine the pain you must be feeling right now."

The gesture must've created an intimacy between the two because Stacy leaned forward, too, and her tense shoulders relaxed a bit.

"I just keep expecting him to walk through that door," she said, looking away. "It hasn't really hit yet that he's not going to, ever again."

"It's unfair to have something unthinkable happen to someone you love," Kate continued. "My son was almost abducted this morning and we're here because we think the cases might be connected."

Kate was taking a long shot, but Dallas understood why she'd need to try.

"Where are my manners?" the other woman asked, looking noticeably uncomfortable. "Can I get either of you something to drink?"

"No, thank you," Kate said.

"Can you tell me what's been going on the past few days? Maybe a timeline of his activities would help," Dallas said.

"He's been acting weird ever since he started investigating that adoption agency for—" Stacy glanced from Dallas to Kate "—you."

"How long ago did he fit the pieces together of Susan and Safe Haven?" he asked, as Kate crossed her legs and folded her arms. Everything about her body language said she was closing up on him.

He shouldn't be surprised. They knew very little about each other aside from facts pertaining to her case. Circumstances had thrown them together and they'd been through more this morning than most people would in a year. There was an undeniable pull, an attraction, between them, but that was where it ended. Where it had to end. As soon as she and Jackson were safe, Kate and Dallas would return to their respective lives.

"Let's see…" Stacy leaned back and thrummed her manicured fingernails on her thigh. "It had to be recently, because he decided to make an official visit this morning and he never does that before he thoroughly checks out a place. Normally, he gives me names—" she paused long enough to glance between Kate and Dallas "—just in case things go sour. This time, he only gave me the address where he was going. He didn't even tell me the name of the agency. I had to look it up on the internet when he didn't come home after checking the place out last night. Then I called the sheriff's office and spoke to a deputy. Not long after, they found his car."

Dallas figured all the secrecy was due to the fact he'd paid Morton extra in order to keep the information private. The last thing Dallas needed was for a news outlet to get wind of what was going on. Not that he gave a damn about his own reputation. People had a way of making up their own minds with or without actual facts. He was trying to keep Susan's name out of the papers, as well as that of the family business. The amount of false leads news like this could generate would make it next to impossible for Tommy to sort out fact from fiction and would add too much weight to the investigation. A whole lot of people would likely come out of the woodwork to get their hands on O'Brien money if they thought a reward was involved.

"Any idea about the trail leading up to Safe Haven? Who Wayne might have contacted in order to get that information in the first place?" Dallas asked, hoping for a miracle.

"Those are great questions," Stacy said, looking flustered. "He usually runs everything past me, but he was keeping this one close to the vest. He does that with special clients, so I didn't think to ask more. Believe me, I've been kicking myself all day over it."

"You couldn't have known this would happen," Kate said sympathetically.

The woman smiled weakly.

"Does he keep a file on his more discreet clients in the office anywhere?" Dallas pressed. Tommy wouldn't like that he had asked the question, but this was starting to feel like a complete dead end. For the sheriff to get the records, he'd have to get a court order, which would take time. Dallas didn't have that luxury. He had a woman and child being targeted, no answers, and his own personal agenda to explore. If investigating Safe Haven was responsible for Morton's murder, then they could also be the reason Susan hadn't turned up.

Dallas was still trying to figure out why the kidnappers would change their MO, using a knife instead of a gun when they'd targeted Jackson. If it was the same group, that didn't make sense.

Stacy was too distraught to think clearly, which was understandable under the circumstances.

And now Kate had locked up on him, too.

Dallas was cursing under his breath just as the door to Morton's office flew open and two men burst in.

Stacy jumped to her feet and ran toward them, blocking Dallas's view. "The office is closed. You need an appointment to come in here."

The entrance to the private bathroom was about six steps away. If he could get Kate inside and lock the door, then he could face down the pair of men threatening Stacy.

Just as Dallas made it to the door, Stacy shouted, *"Go!"*

Chapter Seven

Before Dallas could react, a bullet cracked through the air, and a split second later Stacy let out a yelp. Another bullet pinged into the wood not a foot from Dallas's head. He ducked and shoved Kate into the bathroom, falling on top of her. He performed a quick check to see if either one of them had been hit, needing to get her to safety so he could return to Stacy.

The guys in the other room had no intention of allowing him or Kate to walk out of here alive. They hadn't come for Stacy, so her best chance at survival was if he and Kate got the hell out of Dodge.

Dallas closed and locked the door.

The office was on the second floor, which could present a problem getting out the window. Land the wrong way, break an ankle and it was game over.

"Where is he?" one of the men asked.

"I don't see him," the other replied.

The first man cursed.

As Dallas moved to the small box window, he quickly scanned himself and Kate again for signs of blood, relieved when he saw none. From his experience with guns, he knew that bullets didn't travel in a straight line. They rose after exiting the barrel and then started dropping.

Aiming a fraction of an inch off could make a decent marksman miss his target even at fairly close range.

Dallas opened the window and checked below. A row of bushes would help break Kate's fall.

He stepped aside, allowing her enough room to climb into the small space. She'd fit through it just fine, but Dallas was much bulkier. He'd have a difficult time getting through that tiny opening.

"Take your coat off," he said.

She pushed it through the window and let it drop to the ground.

"Run as soon as you get down there. Don't wait for me, okay?" he said, boosting her up to the window ledge.

She hesitated, which meant she must've realized what he already knew—he'd be trapped if he couldn't squeeze through. He knew she was about to put up an argument. He couldn't let her. She had a child depending on her and she had to make it to safety.

So he hoisted her up and through before she could protest, hoping that she'd call Tommy as soon as she was in the clear.

On closer inspection, the window was definitely too small for him to climb through, so he decided to create a diversion to keep the men engaged upstairs while Kate escaped.

The knob jiggled and then it sounded like someone was taking a hammer to the door followed by a male-sounding grunt.

"We're coming out. Get down on the floor," he shouted, pulling the .25 caliber from his holster. He fired a shot at the panel.

A few bullets pinged around him, so he dropped to the tiles. Scuffling noises in the other room gave him the impression the guys might be leaving. That couldn't be good. Then again, it could be a ploy to draw him out.

"Stacy," he shouted and then quickly changed position so they couldn't target him based on his voice.

Dallas palmed his phone and dialed 911. He immediately requested police and an ambulance and then ended the call.

Next, he moved to the window to check on Kate. His chest almost went into spasm as he realized what could've happened to her. He pushed his head through the opening and scanned the row of boxwoods below, releasing a relieved breath when he didn't see her.

Surveying the area between buildings revealed no signs of her, either.

Good.

He'd have to take a risk in order to check on Stacy. She might be hurt and there was no way he'd leave her bleeding out when he could help.

Dallas listened at the door for what felt an eternity, but was more likely a minute. There were no sounds coming from the other room. He muttered a string of swearwords, took a deep breath and then opened the door a crack.

He couldn't get a visual on anyone, so he opened the door a little more.

Footsteps shuffled on the wooden stairs leading down to the street.

As soon as he realized the men were gone, Dallas bolted toward Stacy, who was on the floor curled in a ball. Not moving.

"Stacy." He repeated her name as he dropped to his knees beside her. Red soaked her shirt by her right shoulder. He felt for a pulse and got one.

"Hang in there, Stacy," he said. "Help is on the way."

Dallas could already hear sirens, and relief washed over him when her eyes fluttered open.

More footsteps sounded, growing louder. Could the men be returning to finish the job with Dallas?

They'd been looking for someone. A man?

He pointed his gun at the door, with every intention of firing on anyone who walked through it. He couldn't leave Stacy alone, especially when she gripped his hand. He was her lifeline right now and he knew it.

The door burst open as Dallas's finger hovered over the trigger, ready to fire.

"Dallas," Kate said, her chest heaving from running. "Oh, my gosh. Is she okay?"

"Get inside and shut the door behind you," Dallas growled, lowering his pistol. He knew the door locked from prior visits to Morton's office. "Shove the back of that chair against the knob. Let only the law or an EMT cross that threshold."

Kate did.

Dallas cradled the wounded woman's head and neck in his free hand. "Stay with me, Stacy," he said. "Help is almost here."

"I loved him," she said, and the words were difficult to make out.

"I know you did. And he loved you, too," Dallas replied, trying to comfort her. He was never more thankful than when an emergency team showed up and went to work on her.

The gunshot wound in her shoulder was deep and she'd lost a lot of blood. As the EMT strapped her to a gurney and another placed an oxygen mask over her nose and mouth, Dallas heard them reassure her that she was going to be fine.

And Dallas finally exhaled. He palmed his phone and

called Tommy with a quick explanation of what had just gone down.

The lawman agreed to take their statements personally and said he'd let the deputy who was about to arrive on the scene know the details. "Do not visit Safe Haven."

Dallas contemplated his friend's suggestion. Tommy was right. "I won't. I'm bringing Kate to the station."

"Good," Tommy said, ending the call.

"Let's get out of here," Dallas said to Kate.

She didn't utter a word as they made their way back to her vehicle, and he suspected she was in shock.

"I'm driving to my truck first," he stated, as he fired up the engine. "And then I'm going to drop you off at the sheriff's office, where you'll be safe."

"That was horrible," Kate murmured, obviously still stunned and trying to process everything that had just happened.

"I'm sorry. I shouldn't have brought you here." Dallas half expected her to curse him out for putting her in danger.

"It's not your fault, and I can't go back to the station until we figure this out," she said. "So where are we heading next?"

"We have no idea where those men could be or why they left," he said. "You're going back to the sheriff's office."

Gripping the steering wheel, Dallas noticed the blood on his hands. Anger surged through him that he hadn't been able to stop Stacy from being shot. No way would he put Kate in further danger. She could argue all she wanted, but he was taking her back to Tommy.

Then Dallas had to fill his brothers in on the situation, so he could hide her at the ranch.

He had every intention of helping Kate and Jackson,

so he needed to have a family meeting to figure out how best to proceed. It wouldn't be fair to put at risk anyone who wasn't comfortable with that.

And Dallas might have a target on his own back now that he'd stirred up an investigation into Safe Haven. That would bring more heat to the ranch—heat that he had no doubt they'd be able to handle.

His cell buzzed. Dallas took one hand off the wheel to fish it out of his pocket.

"Would you mind answering that and putting the call on speaker?" He handed his phone to Kate.

She took it and did as he asked.

"This is Dallas and you're on speaker with me and Kate," he said.

"Where are you?" Tommy asked, and Dallas immediately picked up on the underlying panic in his friend's calm tone.

"Heading toward Main to get my pickup. Why?" Dallas asked, an ominous feeling settling over him.

"Someone just tried to break into my office," the sheriff said. "Jackson is okay. He didn't get to him."

Kate gasped. Dallas didn't need to look at her to know her eyes were wild, just like they'd been earlier that morning.

"What happened?" he asked, glancing at her before making the next left. His pickup could wait. Based on Kate's tense expression, she needed to get to her son and see for herself that he wasn't harmed.

"He's safe," Tommy reiterated. "I have him in protective custody and I promise no one will get to him on my watch."

The desperate look Kate gave Dallas sent a lead fireball swirling through him.

"WE'RE ON OUR WAY," Dallas said. "Did you find anything at the Morton crime scene?"

"Nothing yet. It'll take a while to process and it could be days or weeks before we get anything back from analysis," Tommy said truthfully.

Kate had had so many other questions—questions about the man sitting in the driver's seat beside her—all of which died on her tongue the second she'd heard that Jackson was in danger.

Dallas couldn't drive fast enough to get her to the station so she could see her son. Her brain was spinning and her heart beat furiously, but more than anything her body ached to hold her baby.

Dallas thanked the sheriff and asked her to end the call.

Whoever was after them had proved at Morton's office just how dangerous they could be. People were being shot right before her eyes, not to mention turning up dead. She and Dallas had barely survived another blitz-like attack, this time with guns.

The thought of men like that being after her baby was almost too much to process at once. It was surreal.

She remembered them asking if "he" was there. Did they mean Jackson? If so, they must've realized he wasn't with her.

Nothing could happen to her little boy. He was more than her son; he'd been her heart from the moment the adoption liaison had placed him in her arms. The thought of anyone trying to take him away from her, especially after how hard she'd fought to get him, was enough to boil her blood.

"Why would they want to harm an innocent little baby?" she fumed.

"They don't. I know how bad things look right now,

but even if they got to Jackson, and they won't, they wouldn't hurt him."

"How can you be so sure? People are being shot, killed," she countered.

"Think about it. Hurting him doesn't make sense. A few of the other babies have been returned. My guess is that someone is looking for their child, a child they very much want," Dallas said.

He was right.

Logic was beginning to take hold.

And yet that didn't stop her blood from scorching.

"A stray bullet could've killed him," she said.

Dallas agreed.

"How much longer until we get there?" She didn't recognize any of the streets yet. Not that she'd been anywhere aside from home and downtown at the soup kitchen in the six months she'd been in Bluff. There had been a couple of donor parties, but most of them were lined up in the future. The Halloween Bash at the ranch that she'd been invited to was next on the agenda, but the last thing she could think about was a party.

"I'm taking a back road, so I can make sure we aren't being followed, and because this should shave off a few minutes." He floored the gas pedal, pushing her car to its limit. "We'll be there in five."

"I'm scared," she said, hating how weak her voice sounded.

"I know," he murmured—all he had to say to make her feel she wasn't alone. "Jackson is in good hands."

"They tried to…"

She couldn't finish, couldn't face the harsh reality that someone was this determined to find her son and take him away from her.

"We know whoever is behind this is capable of horrendous acts," Dallas said. "But they wouldn't hurt Jackson even if they could get to him, which they can't and they won't."

"You said it before and you're right," she admitted, and it brought a little relief. Still, the idea that Jackson could be taken away and she might never see him again, when he was the very thing that had breathed life into her, was unthinkable.

Kate might not have been deemed "medically desirable" by nature—wasn't that the phrase the infertility specialist had used?—but she was born to be a mother. She'd stayed awake the entire first night with Jackson while he'd slept in her arms. And it hadn't mattered to her heart one bit that she hadn't been the one to deliver him—Jackson was her son in every way that mattered.

Being a mother was the greatest joy.

And no one—no one—got to take that away from her.

Dallas pulled into the parking lot of the sheriff's office. His set jaw said he was on a mission, too. And it was so nice that someone had her back for a change. Carter had been her lifeline before, but even he'd had his doubts about her plans, and she never saw her brother since leaving the business.

She also knew that Dallas had questions of his own about Safe Haven. Supposedly for a friend but she wondered if that was true. No matter how many times she'd thought about the kiss they'd shared this morning, she was keenly aware of the fact that this man had secrets.

As soon as the car stopped, Kate unbuckled her seat belt.

"Hold on there," Dallas warned. "Someone might be waiting out here."

That could very well be true, but she was determined to see her son.

She practically flew through the door, Dallas was a step behind, and all eyes jumped to her.

"I'm sorry." She held up a hand. "I didn't mean to startle anyone. I'm looking for my son."

At that moment, she heard Jackson cry from somewhere down the hall and she moved toward the sweet sound of her baby.

Abigail met her halfway and handed Jackson over, and then Dallas was suddenly by her side, just as Tommy appeared from his office.

"Hold on. I need to call my brothers," he said, stepping inside a room while digging out his cell.

He returned a few minutes later with a nod.

"I need to get him out of here," Kate said. "And to someplace safe."

"You can't take him home." The sheriff didn't sound like he was disagreeing so much as ruling out possibilities.

"She can take him to my place," Dallas said. "I just had a quick conversation with my brothers about it. They don't have a problem with the arrangement."

Tommy looked to be seriously contemplating the idea.

"I don't want to put your family at risk," Kate argued.

"I can put you in a safe house but it might take a little time," the lawman said. "You'd be welcome to stay here in the office in the meantime."

"My place is better," Dallas protested as he shifted his weight. "You already know how tight security is."

"I advised you on every aspect of it," Tommy agreed. "But—"

Dallas's hand came up. "It's perfect and you know it. There's no safer place in Bluff right now. My family is fine with the risk."

Kate hesitated, trying to think if she had another option. She could go to her brother's house, but it was nearly a four-hour drive and he had no security. Also, she might be placing him in danger. Ditto for her parents' home. She couldn't risk her family, and honestly, she'd have so much explaining to do it wasn't worth the effort.

No, if these guys were bold enough to strike at the sheriff's office, then they would stop at nothing to get to Jackson.

At least for now, she had no other options but to stay with Dallas until a proper safe house could be set up. Jackson's security was the most important thing to her and had to take precedence over her internal battle about whether or not spending time with the strong and secretive cowboy was a good idea for her personally.

"I'm all for any place we can keep Jackson safe," she said to the sheriff. "If you think this is a good idea."

Tommy nodded.

"Then let's go back to the ranch," she said.

The sheriff shot a look toward Dallas that Kate couldn't get a good read on. What was up with that?

She didn't care. The only thing she was focused on at this point was her son. And ensuring that he didn't end up in the hands of very bad men. She held him tighter to her chest and he quieted at the sound of her voice as she whispered comforting words.

"Allen can go now, right?" she asked Tommy. "If the attacks are still happening while he's locked up, then he can't be involved."

"A deputy is already processing his paperwork," the sheriff said.

"It's been a very long day and I'd like to get out of here," she said to Dallas. Then she turned toward Tommy. "Are you okay with us leaving?"

"Go. Get some rest. We're trying to track down your

lawyer to bring him in for questioning. So far, he isn't answering our calls." Tommy paused. "Also, you should know that we're planning to send a deputy to talk to your family members."

"My family?" she echoed, not able to hide her shock.

"It's routine in cases like this," he said. "We take the 'no stone left unturned' approach to investigations."

Oh. Kate tried to process that, but it was all too much and she was experiencing information overload. She needed a few quiet hours to focus on feeding Jackson and allow everything that had happened that day to sink in. Even though it was only four o'clock in the afternoon, she was exhausted. A warm shower and comfortable pajamas sounded like pure heaven to her right then.

"And it might be better if they don't know we're coming," Tommy said, and the implication hit her square in the chest.

"Surely you don't think…" No way could her family be involved. She held on to Jackson tighter. They had their differences about the adoption, but they were still family.

"I won't take anything for granted," the lawman said.

Dallas's strong hand closed around her bent elbow, sending all kinds of heat through her arm. Heat that had no business fizzing through her body and settling between her thighs.

Dallas O'Brien was a complete stranger, and since that scenario had worked out so well the first time she'd broken her rules for someone, she decided no amount of chemistry was worth falling down another rabbit hole like that. But she wasn't fool enough to refuse his help.

He urged her toward the door and then to the car, surveying the area as they walked out.

She buckled Jackson into his seat and slid next to him in the back.

A few seconds later they were on the road again, but this time Dallas drove the speed limit and she appreciated the extra care he was taking with her son in the car.

If Dallas O'Brien was a father, and she figured that had to be the real reason he was investigating Safe Haven, then he was going to be a great one. He already had all the protective instincts down.

She could only imagine what horrible circumstance had brought him the need to hire a private investigator, but decided not to let her imagination run wild. Especially when she kept circling back to that kiss and the fizz of chemistry that continued to crackle between them.

Because another thought quickly followed. How could a man who obviously loved his family so much allow his own child to be adopted? The question helped her see how precious little she knew about the magnetic cowboy. And even if she could risk the attraction on her own behalf, she'd never be able to go down that road now that she had a baby.

"Is there anything Tommy should know about your family?" Dallas asked, his voice a low rumble that set butterflies free in her stomach.

"You already know they don't support my decision to bring up a child alone," she said softly. "Our relationship has been strained since my divorce, and my mother sees *this*—" she motioned toward Jackson "—as me adding insult to injury."

In the rearview mirror, she could see Dallas's eyebrows spike. She could also see how his thick dark eyelashes framed his dark brown eyes, and her heart stirred in a way she'd never experienced.

She ignored that, too.

Besides, they'd dodged bullets and he'd saved her son. Of course she'd feel a certain amount of admiration and respect because of that, and a draw to his strength. That was normal in such a situation, right?

"I'm sorry about your folks. Everyone should have love and support from their family, even if they don't agree with your choices."

"My mom has never been the type to give up that kind of control," Kate said, trying to make a joke, but recognizing that the words came out carrying the pain she felt instead. "Sorry—you don't want to hear about this."

"I do," Dallas said so quickly she thought he meant it.

Why would he care about her family drama?

Kate didn't talk about it with anyone. She figured she'd have to explain to Jackson one day why he didn't have grandparents, but life for her was a "take one day at a time" commitment at the moment.

"That must be hard," Dallas said.

And lonely, she added in her head. Thank the stars for the relationship she had with Carter, barren as it was now that she didn't see him on a daily basis.

Speaking of which, she needed to call her brother as soon as Tommy gave her clearance.

Carter and she had forged a tight bond that had felt strained since Kate had said she was leaving the business they'd started. He had said he understood, but she knew down deep he'd been hurt by her decision.

"My brother and I were close growing up, and that helped," she said, trying to gain control of her emotions before she started crying. Even though she knew that her mother's rejection wasn't her fault, it still stung.

"Brothers can be a blessing and a curse," Dallas said, sounding like he was half joking.

She was grateful he seemed to take the cue that she

needed a lighter mood. There was so much going on around them and she felt so out of control that she needed levity to help her get a handle on her emotions.

"That's the truth," she agreed, thinking about all those times her younger brother had annoyed her over the years.

She glanced down at Jackson. He was her sanity in this crazy, mixed-up world. He made her see that life was bigger than just her and her problems.

"I used to be so angry at my parents," she said, finding love refilling her well, as it did every time she looked at her son.

"What changed?"

"Him."

The surprised look on Dallas's face caught her off guard. Because there was something else there in his expression. It was so familiar and yet she couldn't quite put it into words. "Can I ask a personal question?" Kate murmured.

He nodded.

"Was Susan your girlfriend?"

"Yes. A while back," he admitted. He took a hard right turn and there was a security gate with a guard.

"And the baby you're investigating… Is that for you or a friend?" Kate didn't look at him.

"Me," he said so quietly that she almost didn't hear him.

"Where are we?" she asked, not recognizing the wooded area. Hadn't there been another layer of security earlier?

"This is the west end of the ranch property," he answered, as he was waved in by security.

When Dallas had told her he owned a hacienda on the ranch, she wasn't sure what she'd expected. A large shed? A tiny log cabin?

Certainly not this.

The gorgeous Spanish-style architecture was about the last thing she would have imagined.

He'd explained that each of his brothers had a place on various sites on the land. His sat near the west end so he could take advantage of the sunset.

"This whole property must be enormous," she said, eyes wide.

"Pop added acreage over the years," Dallas said as he parked in the three-car garage.

There was a vintage El Camino, completely restored, in the second.

"That belong to you, as well?" She hadn't thought about the fact that Dallas might not live alone.

"I like to work on cars in my spare time," he said, holding her door open. "That is, I did when I *used* to have free time."

She let him take the diaper bag as she unhooked Jackson, and then she followed Dallas into the house.

The kitchen was massive and had all gourmet appliances. There was an island in the center with enough room for four bar chairs.

"Is the ranch keeping you too busy to pursue your hobbies?" she asked.

"That and trying to transition my old business to the new owner," he said.

"Why sell? Why not hire someone to run the other business for you and keep it?" she asked.

"Didn't think I could do justice to either place that way." Dallas's tone was matter-of-fact. "If I'm involved in something then that's what I want to be able to put all my attention into, and not just write my name on an office door for show. A man's name, his reputation and his word are all he really has in life."

"Powerful thought," she said, trying not to admire this handsome stranger any more than she already did. Those were the kinds of principles she hoped to instill in her son.

Dallas stood there, his gaze meeting hers, and it felt like the world stopped for just that brief moment.

And that was dangerous.

Kate threw her shoulders back. "Is there somewhere I can give Jackson a bath?"

"Let me give you a quick tour so you'll know where everything is," he said. "My brothers arranged for you to have supplies waiting."

She nodded, afraid to speak. Afraid her voice would give away her emotions.

The rest of the house's decor was simple, clean and comfortable looking.

"A crib was delivered from the main house. They keep a few on hand up there for overnight guests." He stopped in the middle of the living room. "If you need to reach out to your employees, I'd rather not alert anyone to the fact that you're here. The fewer people who know where you and Jackson are, the better."

"I know I already asked, but are you sure this is a good idea?"

"The security staff knows we have a special guest and that you're staying at my place. They'll tell maintenance what they need to know to stay safe, so no one's in the dark. But it'll be best to keep your identity as quiet as possible," Dallas said, showing her the bathroom attached to her guest suite. "Is there anything else I can do?"

"Once I'm able to put Jackson down, I'd love clean clothes to change into after a hot shower."

A dark shadow passed through Dallas's eyes.

"What's wrong?"

"I don't want to think about you naked in the shower," he grumbled. Then he said something about making a fresh pot of coffee and walked out of the room.

Kate smiled in spite of herself. She didn't want to like the handsome cowboy any more than she already did. Her heart still hadn't recovered from its last disappointment.

And an attraction like the one she felt for the cowboy could be far more threatening than anything she'd experienced with Robert.

Adding to her confusion was the fact that Dallas O'Brien had secrets.

... and there, ...

Chapter Eight

He had tried not to watch too intently as Kate fed Jackson his bottle. But Dallas couldn't help his natural curiosity now that the seal had been broken on that subject and the possibility he was a father grew a fraction of an inch.

"Mind keeping an eye on him while I clean up?" Kate asked and then laughed at Dallas's startled reaction.

Dallas couldn't say he'd had a stunning track record watching his brothers. Colin had broken his arm twice in one year on the tire swing Pop had set up on the old oak in the yard. Both the twins, Ryder and Joshua, had endured broken bones more than once on Dallas's watch, while climbing trees, and then there was the time Tyler had rolled around in poison ivy. And forget about Austin. That kid had had Pop joking that he needed a physician on staff for all the sprained ankles and banged-up body parts over the years.

"You sure about this? I'm not exactly qualified to take care of a baby," Dallas said, eyeing the sleeping infant.

The little boy looked so peaceful and innocent.

And Dallas figured that would last until Kate turned on the water in the shower.

"I think you'll be okay while he's out. He's a heavy sleeper," she said. "Or I could just take him in the bathroom with me and open the shower curtain to keep an eye on him, if you're not comfortable."

"No, don't do that," Dallas said, figuring he might need to know how to take care of a baby sooner than he'd anticipated. If Susan's child was his, these were skills he was going to need. And Jackson really did seem like a good baby. "I'll be okay."

"Are you sure?"

"Positive," Dallas said with more confidence than he felt.

"I'm just in the next room showering if you need me," she said, and he shot her a warning look about mentioning the shower again.

The last thing he needed while he was caring for a baby was the image of her naked in his mind.

His nerves were already on edge and even seeing the baby sleeping so peacefully in his Pack 'n Play didn't help settle them.

"Just go before you put any more images in my mind I can't erase," Dallas said to Kate.

One corner of her lip turned up in a smile and it was sexy as hell.

Watching a sleeping baby had to be the easiest gig ever, he told himself. And yet he could feel his own heartbeat pounding at the base of his throat. His mouth was dry, too. He hadn't felt this awkward and out of place since he'd asked Miranda Sabot to be his girlfriend in seventh grade.

Jackson half smiled in his sleep and it nearly melted Dallas's heart. There was a whole lot of cuteness going on in that baby basket.

There was a knock at the door. Thankfully, the disturbance didn't wake the baby.

Dallas welcomed the delivery from Sawyer Miles, one

of the security team members who worked for Gideon Fisher. He thanked him and brought the box into the kitchen.

The pj's were folded on top, so he took those and placed them on the bed in the guest room. Next, he put the food containers in the fridge for later. Dallas returned to the living room and eased onto the chair next to the little boy.

All Jackson had to do was fist his little hand or make a sucking noise for Dallas to jump to attention. Was this what parenting was like all the time? He felt like someone had set his nervous system on high alert. It was fine for a few minutes, but this would be exhausting day and night.

He'd seen that same look of panic on Kate's face more than once in the past twelve hours, and for good reason.

Being alone with a baby was scarier than coming face-to-face with a rabid dog in a dark alley.

Jackson made a noise and Dallas jumped to his feet. He stared down at the Pack 'n Play with more intensity than if there was a bomb ready to explode inside.

The little guy must be dreaming, because he was making faces. Cute faces. And they spread warmth all through Dallas, which caught him completely off guard. He didn't expect to feel so much for a baby that probably wasn't even his.

The door to the guest room opened and Dallas heard Kate padding down the hall.

He swallowed his emotions.

"Going outside to get some fresh air. Jackson's fine," he said, before she entered the room.

Dallas moved to the back door and walked outside.

The past half hour had been nerve-racking, to say the least. A whole host of emotions Dallas wasn't ready to acknowledge had flooded him. If he was a father, would he be awful at it?

He told himself that knowing Kate was in the shower had him on edge. But it was more than that and he knew it. Being on the ranch had always centered him, no matter how crazy the world around him became. Not this time. His life had spun out of control fast. And he felt nothing but restless.

Distancing himself from Kate and the baby would provide much-needed perspective, he told himself as he tried to regain footing on that slippery slope.

The truth was he liked having Kate and Jackson in his home, way more than he'd expected or should allow. And that caught him off guard. He chalked the sentiment up to facing the first holiday season without his parents.

Then there was the issue of what had happened to Susan and her baby. Dallas hoped both were doing fine. He hadn't thought about babies much before being told that he might be a father. He'd been too focused on making a name for himself, striking out on his own. Not that his last name was a curse, by any means; Dallas had never thought of "O'Brien" as anything but a blessing.

But being a man, he'd needed to make his own mark on the world. Having come from a close family with a man like Pop at the helm had made Dallas want to do his father and himself proud.

Instead, he'd let him down in the worst possible way.

Dallas had always known he'd eventually come back to the land he loved so much and step into his legacy. That was all supposed to happen far off in the future, however.

His parents weren't supposed to die. And it sure as hell wasn't supposed to be his fault.

If they'd only listened to him when he'd said he could arrange to have the unsold art pieces taken back to the art gallery in the morning, instead of insisting on returning them that evening. Then Pop wouldn't have had that heart attack while driving, and both would still be alive.

He couldn't help but wonder if his father would think of him as a disappointment now. Sure, Dallas had been successful in business, but his personal life had always been more important to Pop. Dallas had failed his parents. And he couldn't help but think he'd failed Susan in some way, too.

Not knowing what had happened to her and her baby gnawed at him.

Then there was the news about Morton's death. So much was going on, and Dallas decided that half the reason his attraction to Kate was so strong was that, on a primal level, he needed comfort, proof life could still be good.

He tapped his boot on the paved patio as he gripped the railing. Even the evening chill couldn't snap him out of the dark mood he was in.

He could blame his missteps on working too much, or on his emotional state, but the truth of the matter was he should've known better.

Now Susan might be dead, and he couldn't ignore the weight of that thought or how awful it made him feel.

If he'd told her they could get married, would she be okay?

Maybe he should've strung her along until the baby was born, and all he'd have had to do was swipe a pacifier and send it to the lab for DNA testing. Susan would have never had to know and wouldn't have been in such a desperate state.

Then he'd know for certain if the child was his. He could've arranged help for Susan, and not just with the baby. She needed counseling or something to help get her mind straight.

Dallas stabbed his fingers in his hair as the wind blew a chill right through him.

So many mistakes. So many questions. So many lives hanging in the balance.

He caught a glimpse of one of his brothers out of the corner of his eye.

"Hey," Tyler said. A shotgun rested on his forearm as he approached.

"What are you doing out here?" Dallas asked, before he hugged him.

"We're taking voluntary shifts, walking sections of the property," Tyler replied. "Haven't seen anything suspicious so far."

"Thank you for everything," Dallas said.

"What are you doing out here all by yourself?" Tyler asked.

"Thinking."

"You figure anything out yet?" he said with a half smile. He always knew when to make a joke to lighten the tension.

"Pie is better in my mouth than on paper," Dallas quipped.

"A math joke." Tyler chuckled. "I like it." His expression became solemn. "Seriously, is there something on your mind you want to talk about?"

"Nah. I got this under control," Dallas said. He did want to talk, but surprisingly, not with one of his brothers. He wanted to talk to Kate.

"You always did carry the weight of the world on your shoulders, big brother," Tyler said. "We're here to help if you want to spread some of that around."

"And you know how much I appreciate it," Dallas answered.

They stood in comfortable silence for a little while longer, neither feeling the need to fill the air between them.

"It's going to be different this year," Tyler finally said with a sigh. He didn't need to elaborate for Dallas to know he was talking about the upcoming holidays.

"Yeah."

"Won't be the same without her holiday goose and all the trimmings at Christmas supper," Tyler murmured.

"Nope." None of the boys had accused Dallas of being responsible for their parents' deaths and none would. He held on to that guilt all on his own.

"You heard anything from Tommy lately about possible involvement from another vehicle?" Tyler asked.

"Nothing new." Dallas rubbed his chin and looked toward the setting sun.

"I get angry thinking about it," his brother admitted.

Dallas nodded and patted him on the shoulder. "Heard Uncle Ezra has been talking to the rest of the family about letting him take over the gala," he said at last.

"You know him—always blowing smoke," Tyler said. "He couldn't handle it alone anyway, and I don't know why he wants his hand in everything."

"Have you spoken to Aunt Bea lately?"

"Heard it through the grapevine that Uncle Ezra has been trying to get her to sell her interests in the ranch to him," Tyler said. "And he's been cozying up with the McCabes, which I don't like one bit."

"Neither do I. That family has been nothing but trouble over the years, and just because Pop is gone doesn't mean I'd betray his memory by bringing them anywhere near the ranch, let alone the gala." Dallas swung his right

leg up and placed his foot on the wooden rail off the deck-
ing, then rested his elbow on his knee.

"Isn't that the truth," Tyler said. "Uncle Ezra needs
to check his loyalty. He wouldn't have anything without
Pop's goodwill."

"Unfortunately, not everyone is as grateful as Aunt
Bea," Dallas said. "Plus, together they only own five
percent of the company. What does he hope to gain by
forcing her out?"

Tyler shrugged. "He's making a move for something.
We'd better keep an eye on him. Harmless as he seems,
we don't know what he's really up to, and I just don't trust
him. I don't think Mom ever did, either."

"Good point. She was adept at covering up in front of
Pop, but I saw it, too."

The back door opened as the sun disappeared on the
horizon.

"Everything okay out here?" Kate asked.

"I better get back to the main house," Tyler said to
Dallas.

"Check in if anything changes," he replied, then introduced his brother to Kate.

"Evening, ma'am." Tyler tipped his gray Stetson before disappearing the way he'd come.

"I didn't mean to make your brother feel like he had
to leave," Kate said.

"You didn't," Dallas assured her.

"I made coffee in case you want more," she told him,
stepping onto the patio and shivering.

"It's cold out here. We can talk without freezing inside." Dallas glanced around, aware that there could be
eyes watching them from anywhere in the trees.

This time of year, the sun went down before six
o'clock.

"Where's Jackson?" he asked.

"Sleeping in the other room." As Kate walked past him, Dallas could smell the wild cherry blossom shampoo Janis kept stocked, and it reminded him of a warm, sunny Texas afternoon. There wasn't much better than that. "It's been a long day and I'm glad he doesn't realize what's going on."

She'd showered and had changed into the pajamas that had been brought over for her. They'd been pulled from a stash of extra supplies in case guests forgot something at home.

"Good. You found them." The all-white cotton pajama pants and simple matching V-neck button-down shirt fitted her as if they were hand-tailored, highlighting her soft curves.

Dallas forced himself to look away after he caught himself watching a bead of water roll down her neck and disappear into her shirt.

Coffee.

He poured a cup, black, and then paused.

"Think you can sleep?" he asked.

"Probably not," she said with a sigh.

"Coffee sound good? Because I can have some tea they serve at the main house delivered if you'd prefer," he said.

"Coffee's fine. Maybe just half a cup."

"Cream's in the fridge." He pulled out a jar of sugar and set it on the counter.

She thanked him.

"Can I ask you a question?" Kate perched on the countertop and took a sip of her coffee.

He nodded.

"What's your actual connection to Safe Haven?" Her eyes studied him.

"I already told you that I was investigating them."

Not a total lie, but not the truth, either. Dallas drummed his fingers on the counter. "I was in a relationship with someone."

"Susan." Kate's gaze didn't falter. "And you had a baby?"

"There's where everything gets dicey." He paused long enough to see the confusion on her face. "She had a baby. Said it was mine. I'm not so sure."

"You didn't get along with her?" Kate asked, with more of that shock in her voice.

"It's more complicated than that, but the answer would be no."

"What happened?" Those blue eyes stared at him and he wanted to be honest with her.

"I thought she was seeing someone else, and it would have been next to impossible for me to have fathered a child with her," he said. This was awkward, but not as strange as talking to Tommy or the thought of opening up about this to one of his brothers. Why was that? Dallas had known Tommy since they were three years old. And he and his brothers couldn't be closer.

Being the oldest, Dallas had always felt a certain responsibility for taking care of the others. Was he afraid he'd somehow be letting them down by admitting his mistakes?

"Why did she go to Safe Haven?" Kate asked.

"That's a good question. I don't have the answer to it. I had others, so I hired a PI to investigate," Dallas said.

"Wayne Morton," she said.

"That's right. He started digging around. Told me that she'd had a baby and there's a tie to Safe Haven, but I have no idea if the baby was put up for adoption or not."

"I can't even imagine," Kate said, and there was

agony in her voice. "That must be the worst feeling in the world."

"Hell can't possibly be worse," he admitted. "Even though I know there's barely a chance I could have a son out there, I can't sleep at night."

"It was a boy?" Kate said, glancing at Jackson's blanket on the couch. "Do you have any idea how old the baby would be now?"

"Maybe three months old," Dallas said, eyeing her reaction.

She glanced at the blanket again and then her gaze fixed on him with a look of sheer panic.

Yeah, he'd noticed the slight resemblance between him and Jackson, but that didn't mean... Did it?

That look of determination came back as Kate squared her shoulders and took a sip of coffee.

"He's not mine," Dallas said, trying to convince both of them. "All we have to do is swab us both if you want proof."

"I don't need it. Jackson is my son until someone proves otherwise," she said defensively. She hopped off the counter and then walked to the sliding glass door.

It was dark outside, so she wouldn't be able to see a thing. "Don't do that, Kate," he said.

"What?"

"Close up like that." He should know that was what she was doing. He was the king of shutting people out.

She whirled around and there was fire in her glare. "Is that why you've been so nice to us? Because you think Jackson is your son?"

"Hell, no," Dallas said, closing the distance between them in a couple of strides. "And for the record, I *don't* think he's mine. I have more questions than answers, and to say my relationship with Susan was brief puts it lightly."

Kate was too stubborn or too daring to look away, even with him standing toe to toe with her.

And Dallas noticed the second her anger turned to awareness. He could see her pulse beating at the base of her throat, her uneven breathing.

If she planned to walk away, then she needed to do it soon, because he'd made an enormous mistake in getting so close. Close enough that her scent filled his senses and he couldn't think straight anymore.

Before he could overanalyze it, he dipped his head and kissed her.

Her flat palms moved down his chest until her hands stopped at his waist. She gripped the hem of his T-shirt and he helped her pull it up, over his head and onto the floor.

Dallas spread his feet in an athletic stance, preparing himself to call on all his strength and tell her that this would be a very bad idea. One look in those hungry blue eyes and he faltered.

That was all it took? *Seriously, O'Brien? Way to be strong.*

He brought his lips down on hers with bruising need and delved his tongue inside.

She tasted like a mix of the peppermint toothpaste he kept in the guest room and coffee.

Dallas stopped long enough to close the blinds behind them.

Kate wound her arms around his neck and he caught her legs as she wrapped them around his midsection, their bodies perfectly flush, and then he carried her to the kitchen island.

There wasn't a whole lot of cloth between them as he

positioned her on the granite, and he could feel her heart-beat against his bare chest.

Need overtook logic when her fingers dug into his shoulders, pressing him against her full breasts.

Dallas took one in his palm and his erection strained when she arched her back.

He groaned, which came out more like a growl, and felt himself surrender to the moment. He'd never felt so out of control and yet so in the right place in his life. Sex with Kate was going to blow his mind.

An annoying little voice asked if this was a good idea under the circumstances. And he'd be damned if that unwelcome little voice didn't make a second round, louder this time.

Nothing inside him wanted to stop this runaway train, so he needed Kate to.

He pulled back enough to press his forehead to hers and force his hands on the countertop beside her thighs.

"Tell me this is a good idea," he said, and his breathing was ragged.

Her fingers trailed down his back, stopping at the waistband of his jeans.

"I want it, too," she said, breathless. "But it's a terrible idea."

He sucked in a breath and made a halfhearted attempt to step back.

Sure, he could back off if he wanted to, but the problem was he didn't. He wanted to nestle himself between those silky thighs of hers, free his straining erection and bury himself inside her.

Dallas trailed his finger along the collar of her cotton shirt and down the V. So far, he was the only one with any clothes off. That was about to change. He undid the first pair of buttons on her nightshirt.

Her chest moved up and down rapidly, matching the pace of his own breathing, as he reached up and freed her right shoulder.

Dallas bent low enough to brush a kiss there and then one on her collarbone.

Kate was perfection.

"You're beautiful," he whispered, drawing his lips across the base of her neck, pausing long enough to kiss her there, too.

She made a move to touch him, but he caught her hands in his. He kissed the fingertips of both before placing them on either side of her.

"No. I get to touch you first."

Her breath caught.

He slicked his tongue in a line down to her breast and gently captured her nipple between his teeth.

"Dallas," she started, her body rigid with tension.

He stopped long enough to catch her eye. "You can tell me to stop at any time and I will. It won't be easy but I won't force this."

"Oh, no. I want you to move faster."

"I can't do that, either," he said. "I move too fast and this will be over before it gets good. And I'm a hell of a lot better than that in bed."

He ran his tongue across her nipple one more time before taking her fully into his mouth, his own body humming with need.

KATE DIDN'T GIVE up control to anyone. Ever. Except for reasons she couldn't explain, she felt completely safe with Dallas O'Brien.

His hot breath on her skin sent shivers up and down her body and caused desire to engulf her. Maybe that was what she needed to clear her head…a night of hot sex with a handsome cowboy.

In some strange way, it felt like she'd known Dallas for more than just a day. But she didn't. He was practically a stranger.

That thought put the brakes on.

She froze and he reacted immediately by pulling back.

"I want to do this, believe me, but I can't." She buttoned the top buttons of her shirt, still trying to convince herself that stopping was a good idea. She had never felt such a strong pull toward someone she didn't know or allowed a situation to get out of control so fast. "I'm sorry."

Chapter Nine

"Tommy just called," Dallas said to Kate as he walked into the living room, thoughts of last night and their almost tryst still a little too fresh in his mind. He figured their emotions were heightened from one seriously crazy day and that was half the reason their hormones got the best of them.

"What did he say?" She was on the couch feeding her son a bottle.

Dallas knew she didn't get a whole lot of sleep last night because Jackson had cried at 10:00 p.m. and then again this morning at three. It was just before eight and he was eating again. Three feedings in ten hours?

For someone who didn't sleep a lot, Kate looked damn good.

"He was able to reach your lawyer," Dallas said.

"What did Seaver say?"

"He made an appointment to drop by Tommy's office today at noon." Dallas crossed the room into the open-concept kitchen.

"I'd like to be there to hear what he has to say."

Dallas nodded. "You want a cup of coffee?"

"That sounds like heaven right now," she said, trying to suppress a yawn. "I usually don't sleep this late."

"This is late for you?" Dallas asked from the kitchen,

where he'd started making a fresh pot. Eight in the morning was late for him, too. Work on the ranch began at five in the morning. He hadn't wanted to make noise, so he'd spent the morning recapping the prior day's events.

"I've always been a morning person," she said. "And since Jackson has me up anyway, I'm usually the first one at the soup kitchen. That reminds me. I need to check in at work. I'm sure yesterday has everyone on edge and I still feel horrible about what happened to Allen."

Dallas poured two mugs and brought one to Kate. "You need to keep an eye on his relationship with you."

She thanked him and immediately took a sip. Based on her expression, she wasn't ready to have that conversation.

"Do you really want to work with someone who is fixated on you?" Dallas continued. Knowing he should leave the topic alone didn't stop him from pressing the issue. He was man enough to admit to himself that he was jealous.

"Honestly, work is the last thing on my mind right now," she said, and she sounded defeated.

"You want me to finish that?" he asked, gesturing to Jackson and his bottle.

A moment of hesitation was followed by "No, thanks."

Did she still think he believed Jackson might be his son?

"Last night, about him…" Dallas said. "Well, I just want to reiterate that the probability he's mine is low. I'm offering to help right now so you can have a cup of coffee, not so I can see if there's some parental-child bond between us. Truth is, I'm more than a little uneasy at the thought of holding something that tiny."

The tension in her shoulders relaxed a little as she smiled. "I thought about it all night and maybe we should have a DNA test done today. If your—" she glanced at him "—Susan's child was adopted out through Safe Haven, then we can't ignore the possibility that Jackson *could* be yours."

"It's not impossible but that would be a huge coincidence." Dallas took a sip, enjoying the burn on his throat and the strong taste on his tongue. He thought about the way Kate's kisses had tasted last night. She was temptation he didn't need to focus on.

"Questions are bound to come up and we'll have the answer ready this way."

True. She put up a good argument.

"Chances are strong that I don't have a child at all," he said. "I'm almost certain that Susan was close to someone else at the time we were going out. He may have been the real reason she'd relocated to New Mexico and not to be close to me."

"You didn't confront her about it?" Kate asked.

"Honestly, no. I probably should have but I figured she could see whoever she wanted, given that we weren't exclusive."

"Your girlfriend seeing another man while the two of you were dating was okay with you?" Kate balked.

Dallas couldn't help but chuckle at her reaction. "We weren't serious at the time," he said. "She wanted more and I couldn't give it, at least not then. I thought we could take it slow. Apparently, she had other ideas."

"You didn't break it off?"

"I did," he said. "And then she called a few months later saying she was pregnant and that we should get married."

"Wow. That seems awfully presumptuous. If she was seeing another man, there was no way you could've known for sure the baby was yours." Kate set the empty bottle down and then placed the baby over her shoulder in a fluid motion. She might not have been a mother for long, but she seemed to have the hang of it.

"I'm not making excuses, but when I asked to slow things down until we could get a paternity test, she disappeared," he said.

"Sounds suspicious if you ask me," Kate muttered, bouncing Jackson gently.

"Either way, I need to know." Even if Susan had lied, she sure didn't deserve to be killed, and he hoped that wasn't the case.

"Did you know the guy?" Kate asked.

"No. Didn't want to."

"I can understand that. What about her friends? Think they might know?"

"We don't run in the same circles." She was onto something. If Susan's friends knew who else she'd been dating then they might be able to give them a name, except that his PI had been killed digging around. Maybe he shouldn't involve anyone else.

The baby hiccuped and then burped.

"He's a hearty eater." Dallas changed the subject, eyeing the little boy.

"That's what his doctor says." Kate beamed.

Motherhood looked good on her.

"I called the hospital this morning to check on Stacy, by the way," Dallas said. "She had to have surgery on her shoulder yesterday to remove the bullet. All went well and the doctor is expecting a full recovery."

"That's great news," Kate exclaimed. "And such a relief."

"I had flowers sent over and I thought we could stop by and check on her later."

"I'd like that very much." Kate held Jackson in her arms, looking like she never wanted to let go of him.

Dallas filed that away. There was no way they could bring the baby with them today. It was too dangerous. When he really thought about it, it was too dangerous for Kate, too. She'd been adamant about going yesterday, but after that close call she might change her mind. If Dallas had anything to say about it then she'd stay right where she was. But knowing her, she wouldn't dream of being left out.

"Maybe we could make a detour on the way to the sheriff's office," he said.

"Great."

"Hungry?" Dallas asked.

"Breakfast would be nice."

"I'm not much of a cook, so I had one of my brothers bring over some of Janis's homemade muffins this morning," he said, setting his mug on the side table and moving toward the kitchen.

"Is that what smells so amazing?" she asked, propping Jackson up on a pillow next to her.

Dallas brought in the basket filled with blueberry and banana nut muffins.

"Janis makes them fresh every morning."

"She could run her own bakery, based on the smell alone," Kate said between bites.

"Don't tell her that or we might lose her," Dallas teased.

"Must be hard to find good help," Kate said with a smile.

"My brothers and I kicked in and gave her a share of the ranch. She's worked just as hard as the rest of us in making the place a success." They had figured that she deserved a cut far more than their aunt and uncle, who hadn't put in an honest day's work in their lives.

"That was really nice of you guys." Kate looked impressed.

"It was the right thing to do."

Unfamiliar ringtones sounded, breaking the morning quiet. Dallas quickly realized they were coming from her diaper bag.

She looked around, panicked, and Dallas realized she was trying to figure out how to get to her phone across the room without leaving Jackson alone on a pillow.

"You want me to get that for you?" Dallas asked.

"Would you mind?"

He retrieved her cell and handed it to her. The ringtones were pulsing loudly, but he felt more than their vibration shoot through him when their fingers grazed.

"It's my brother." She looked up at Dallas. "What should I do?"

"Answer it."

KATE TOOK A deep breath and answered.

"What's going on with you?" Carter was frantic. "I've been trying to call and you haven't been answering. A deputy showed up at my house and at Mom's, asking questions."

"We had an incident yesterday morning, but the baby and I are fine."

"Why didn't you call me immediately?" he asked, and she hated the worry in his voice. She still felt like she'd let him down by leaving the business they'd created, and this didn't help.

"I'm sorry, Carter. Yesterday was a whirlwind and I was exhausted." It was partially true. That wasn't the reason she hadn't called, but she didn't want to say that the sheriff had asked her not to.

"Mom is a wreck," Carter said.

"You talked to her?"

"What choice did I have when a deputy knocked on both of our doors? You could've given me a heads-up, Kate." Carter still sounded concerned, but there was something else in his voice she couldn't quite put her finger on. Anger? Frustration? Hurt?

"What did they say?"

"No one told us a thing. They just started asking all these questions about you and Jackson," he said.

What could she tell him? The last thing she wanted to do was lie to her brother.

"Is Mom okay?" she asked.

"After popping a pill and having a glass of chardonnay, yeah. This came as a shock. I mean, you'd think if something happened to you that you'd be the one to let us know," Carter said, and there was a snide quality to his tone.

Was he upset? Concerned?

Maybe that was what was bugging Kate. He seemed more distraught that he and their mother had been surprised than worried about her or Jackson being hurt.

"We were shaken up yesterday, but we're fine now. Thanks for asking," she retorted.

"I figured you were okay, since you answered the phone," Carter snapped.

"What has you so upset? If you're worried about Jackson, he's fine, too," she stated. She didn't like where this was headed one bit.

Had she overestimated her brother's love for her? At the moment, he seemed more concerned with being surprised by a deputy. Then there were his overprotective feelings for their mother.

That stung.

It had always been she and Carter against the world during their childhood and they'd been thick as thieves.

Then again, maybe he resented her more than she realized for leaving the business. She'd sold her shares to him and he'd seemed to be on board with her plan once he got used to the idea.

The times they'd talked, he seemed to be handling work stress fine. He had a lot on his plate, though, and she figured some of that was her fault.

"Everything okay, Carter?" she asked when he didn't respond, that same old guilt creeping in. Normally, it was reserved for conversations with her mother.

"Sorry, Kate. Mother is just freaking out and I haven't slept in days. We have a new program going live next month at work and I found a hiccup in the code," he said. Now he was beginning to sound like the old Carter. "I've been working twenty-four/seven for a solid week."

Once again she felt bad for leaving him holding the bag even though she'd prepped him far in advance. Still, she knew the stresses of running a business better than most, and of the two of them, she was better at dealing with it.

While she didn't miss the day-to-day operations or the stress, she did miss seeing her brother. Now that they didn't work together and she'd been busy with Jackson, she and Carter had practically become strangers.

"How is the little rug rat who stole you from me?" he finally asked.

"Growing bigger every day."

"Is he allowing you to get any sleep yet?"

"It's better. They don't stay little forever," she said, ignoring Dallas's raised eyebrow.

Their relationship probably did seem odd to an outsider.

"Tell him to hurry up and get big enough to work at the business so his uncle can finally get some sleep," Carter said.

"Sorry. He already said he's going to be a fireman and has no plans to spend his life at a keyboard." Kate could only imagine how this conversation sounded to Dallas, coming from such a close-knit family. *Odd* would most likely be an understatement.

"Mom will be fine," Carter said. "You know her. Breaking a nail is cause for a red alert."

Sadly, that wasn't too much of an exaggeration.

"Have you been spending more time with her lately?" Kate asked, hoping to ease some of her own guilt.

"Not really. Work has been holding me hostage. She'd like to see you, though." Was he trying to make her feel worse about her non-relationship with their mom? Since when was he taking up Mother's cause? "In fact, I better head to the office."

"Oh, where are you now?" Kate asked.

"Nothing. Nowhere. Just out and about," Carter said, and she picked up on the same tone he'd used when he was trying to hide the last candy bar from her when they were kids.

Maybe Mother and Carter were becoming closer now that she was at odds with Kate.

Kate decided not to press the issue, but it ate at her anyway. She should be glad her mom had someone to talk to, since she and Kate's dad hardly ever spoke about anything important. So why did it gnaw at Kate that her mother and brother were on good terms?

Other than the fact that protecting Carter had been half the reason she and her mother had been at odds most of Kate's life?

This suddenly close relationship felt a little like betrayal. Because when Carter had wanted to quit the soccer team at twelve, it had been Kate who'd fought that battle for him, taking on both their parents.

It had been unthinkable for them that Carter wouldn't want to play sports at all. In fact, he'd pretty much hated anything that required him to compete physically. He'd never been the tall, masculine child with a solid throwing arm his father had hoped for and had tried to make him be. Carter had topped out at five foot nine, which pretty much ruled out basketball, a sport their dad had played.

Carter had been great at math, so their parents decided he should be a doctor. That idea fell apart when he couldn't stop vomiting in his high school anatomy class.

It had been Kate who'd stood up to them time and time again on his behalf. She'd let him talk her into the start-up, had worked crazy hours and had sacrificed any kind of social life. Not that she regretted it one bit. She and her brother had been able to do something together that hopefully would last for many years.

"I better go," she said to him now.

"Be careful," he said.

She ended the call, deciding she hadn't had nearly enough rest lately, because she was reading too much into the phone conversation with her brother.

"I've been thinking that maybe you should stay here with Jackson today," Dallas said.

He'd been watching her reactions on the phone and she figured he'd have questions about her family.

"Believe me when I say that I seriously considered it.

In fact, that's just about all I've been thinking about for the past few hours," she said.

"It's risky for you to leave the ranch. And there's no way we can take Jackson with us," he added.

"Both good points," she agreed. Those had been her top two after tossing and turning for a few hours last night.

Jackson started fussing. She picked up her son and cradled him in her arms.

"It would be nice if I had more of his toys here," she said, wishing this whole nightmare was over. "You can't imagine how helpful it is to be able to set him down once in a while."

"I'd be happy to hold him," Dallas offered, and there was just a hint of insecurity in his voice. "On the off chance that I am a father, I probably need to start getting my arms around taking care of a baby, because I have no clue what to do with them."

Actually, he was making a lot of sense.

"It's best if you try this for the first time while sitting down." She stood and walked over to him.

He held out his arms and she placed Jackson in them.

Wow, did that kick-start her pulse.

There was something about seeing such a strong man be gentle with such a tiny baby that hit her square in the chest like a burst of stray voltage. She hadn't thought much about Jackson missing out on having a father before. It struck her now.

Maybe it was the lack of sleep or the thought that it might actually be nice to have a partner around to help raise her son.

Ever since that little angel had come into her life, she questioned pretty much all her decisions. It would be nice to be able to talk her ideas through or just bounce them off someone else for a change.

Why did all that suddenly flood her thoughts now? She and Jackson had been doing just fine before. Hadn't they?

Wishing for something that wasn't going to happen was about as productive as sucking on a rose petal when she was thirsty.

It didn't change a thing and she'd end up with thorns on her face.

"I hear what you were saying about me sticking around the ranch for safety's sake today. I'd like to be there when the sheriff questions Seaver and I want to visit Stacy in the hospital. It might be nice for her to have another woman around. I didn't get the impression she had anyone to talk to," Kate said.

"Same here," Dallas said.

"Plus, I feel guilty that those men showed up at her office to begin with. I'm worried that my car drew them to her," she said.

"When they didn't find Jackson with us, they disappeared." Dallas looked down at the baby. He was beginning to look more at ease.

Her son being in the cowboy's arms filled her with warmth.

"I'll need to figure out something to do with him while we're gone," she said, chalking her emotions up to missing her brother.

"Janis offered her assistance when I asked for baby supplies," Dallas said. "She doesn't know who's here, but I'm sure she suspects it's you, since she met you yesterday."

"She's one of the few people I would actually trust with my son," Kate said, and she meant it. Plus, there was the fact that she was already at the ranch and the security here was top-notch. Dallas had given Kate the rundown. There were armed guards at all three entrances and cameras covering most other areas, especially near the houses.

Although the entire acreage couldn't realistically be completely monitored, and there were plenty of blind spots, no one would get anywhere near the houses without being detected.

That thought would've let her sleep peacefully if the handsome cowboy hadn't been in the bed right down the hall.

Chapter Ten

"I meant what I said earlier." Dallas shifted the baby fidgeting in his arms. Was the child just as uncomfortable as him? Was that why the little guy was squirming?

Sure, holding Jackson felt good in a lot of ways. But he was so little that Dallas was afraid he'd break him without realizing it. Could he break a baby?

This felt like middle school all over again, when he'd had to carry that egg around for a week. Dallas had broken his on the first day. And he'd already seen how many broken bones his brothers had endured while playing with him.

Jackson started winding up to cry and Dallas's shoulders tightened to steel. "I'm afraid I'm not very good at this." He motioned toward the baby with his head. He was afraid to move anything from the neck down.

And it didn't help that Kate was cracking a smile as she walked toward them.

"You think this is funny?"

"It's just a relief to know I'm not the only one who was nervous when I held him those first few times. I thought it would feel so natural to hold a baby, but it didn't." She reached his side, but instead of offering to take her son, she perched on the arm of the leather chair.

"I'm glad my pain bolsters your self-image," Dallas quipped, feeling even more tense as the first whimpers came.

"Sorry. It just reminds me how hard it actually was for me in those early days and how far I've come since then." She placed her hand on his shoulder. "I'm convinced babies can read our emotions. The more we relax, the more they do."

Relaxed wasn't the first word that would come to mind if Dallas was trying to describe himself.

Jackson wound up and then released a wail. Dallas felt a little better knowing that Kate's presence had done little to calm the child.

"And then sometimes he just needs a good cry," she said, finally taking him from Dallas.

As she did, he got a whiff of something awful smelling. She must have, as well, because her nose wrinkled in the cutest way.

"I think someone needs a diaper change," she said as she moved Jackson to the couch and placed him on his back.

"You need help with that?" Dallas asked.

She waved him off and went to work.

"Have you ever done this before?" she asked.

"Nope." He was mildly curious and figured he'd need to know all about it at some point when he became a father.

"Me, either. Well, not until Jackson." She finished taping the sides of the fresh diaper and then tucked his little legs inside his footed pajamas. "I put the first one on backward and didn't realize it until he had a leak. I'd also bought a size too big."

"Sounds complicated."

"You get the hang of it," she reassured Dallas, neatly

folding the used diaper. "We may not want to keep this inside the house."

He held out his hand.

"You sure about that?" she asked.

"I'll have to get used to it at some point in my life, right?"

She nodded.

When he returned from taking it to the garbage out back, she was pacing. "When should we go?"

"Anytime you're ready, if you're certain you want to leave the property."

"Part of me wants to stay right here and never leave," she said, pensive. "I feel safe here and I don't want to let go of that feeling. But whoever is trying to take Jackson away from me is still out there and I need to do everything I can to find him or my son will never be safe."

Dallas understood that logic. He could see all her emotions in her determined blue eyes.

And he tried not to focus on the other things he saw there…

DALLAS'S BOOTS CLICKED against the tiled floors of the hospital wing. The nurse had said Stacy was doing fine when he'd called to check on her last night. He needed to see for himself.

There was a secondary reason for his visit. Maybe there was additional information he could get out of her. Yesterday had felt like a waste of time and he wanted to do everything he could to help locate Morton's killer. Adding to Dallas's guilt was the feeling that he'd put Stacy in harm's way by showing up at her office with Kate.

Stacy was sitting up when he and Kate reached the opened door.

"Come in," she said. Her eyes were puffy from crying and she had a wad of tissues balled in her right fist. Her hair was piled high on her head and she wore a blue hospital gown.

The room was standard, two beds with a cloth curtain in between. It was opened, since the second bed was empty. Stacy's was closest to the window.

"How are you feeling today?" Kate asked, making it to her side in a beat. She had a way with people that made even the worst situation feel like everything would work out all right.

He chalked it up to motherhood. Kate had the mothering gene. Not everyone did. He couldn't imagine that Susan would have that same effect on people. She had good qualities, but was more the invite-to-happy-hour personality than the soothing type.

Of course, being close to Kate brought up all kinds of other feelings Dallas didn't want to think about. And the sexual chemistry between them was off the charts.

He mentally shook off the thought, focusing on Stacy instead.

"Thank you so much for the beautiful flowers." She motioned toward the bouquet on the side table.

Dallas nodded and smiled.

"Did they catch those guys?" she asked.

"Afraid not," he said. Tommy had promised to call or text the moment they were in custody, and so far, Dallas hadn't heard anything. Whoever was behind this had sophisticated ways to disappear when they needed to and that set off all kinds of warning bells for Dallas.

It had also occurred to him that Susan could've gotten herself into some kind of serious trouble. Now that his investigator was dead, there was no one chasing her trail aside from Tommy. And the problem with that was the fact that his friend wouldn't be able to share a whole lot of information about a murder investigation in progress.

So Dallas needed to come up with a plan of his own without stepping on the sheriff's toes.

"Did you get a look at the men?" Dallas asked. He'd been able to give a basic description to law enforcement of dark hair and medium build, before Stacy had blocked his view, which didn't rule out a lot of people in Bluff.

"No, it was a blur," she said. "Everything happened so fast. All I remember seeing was the end of a gun and then a blast of fire, followed by a burning sensation in my shoulder. Once I put two and two together, I honestly thought I was going to die."

Dallas could see why she'd focus on the barrel, given that the gun was fired at her a moment later. "I want to catch these bastards but I need your help," he told her.

"What can I do?" Her gaze bounced from him to Kate and back.

"I'd asked about secret files before. I know you'd never want to betray Wayne's trust, but I need to see mine and any others he has."

"If he had files like that, I didn't know about them." She glanced down, which usually meant a person was lying or covering.

"What about his laptop?" Dallas asked.

"It was in his car," Stacy said, which meant Tommy or one of his deputies was already tearing it apart.

Dallas paced, trying to think of another way to come at this, because he was fairly certain Stacy was holding back. Since his straightforward approach was bringing up an empty net, he needed to take another tack.

"It's okay if you don't know," Kate assured her. "He just wants to find the guy who did this to Wayne."

Stacy glanced at Kate and the softer approach seemed

to be baiting her. "Isn't the sheriff already working on it?" she asked.

"Yes, he is. And we would never do anything to get in the way of that. But these guys are dangerous and they might come back for you if they think you know something," Kate said calmly. "And I think we can help with the investigation."

Stacy stared at the door.

Dallas turned to look out the window, because whatever Kate was doing seemed to be working.

"They have his laptop from the office," Stacy finally started, "but that's not where he would keep a secret file, because it would be the first place people would look if he was subpoenaed."

"He's smarter than that, isn't he," Dallas said, turning toward her.

Stacy half smiled and a deep sadness settled in her hazel eyes. "Yes. He was."

Dallas gave her a minute to recover. "I lost someone very important to me a few months ago," he finally said. "Actually, two people."

"I remember reading about your parents in the newspaper and thinking it was a tragic accident," Stacy said wistfully. "I'm real sorry about that, because I'd always heard they were fine folks. Real down-to-earth types. It must've been hard to lose both of your parents like that and especially…"

She glanced up at him with an apologetic look on her face but couldn't seem to finish her sentence without breaking down.

"Thank you," he said. "I know what it's like to have people taken away before their time. And, yes, the upcoming holidays make it worse. Believe me, very soon, once the initial shock wears off, you're going to be angry."

Stacy nodded, blowing her nose into a wadded-up tissue.

"You already want answers and so do we," Dallas said. She was getting close to trusting him; he could tell by the change in her demeanor. "You already know that I could have a child, a son. And I need to know if Wayne found something that got him in trouble while working on my case."

Shock registered on her face, but to her credit she recovered quickly.

"Family has always been important to an O'Brien, and I'm no different. Losing my parents makes me value it even more," he said. "I have selfish reasons for wanting to get that file. Wayne was most likely killed because of my case…because of something he found. If I know what that is, I have a chance at finding out if I have a son and nailing Wayne's killer. Plus, the whereabouts of my son's mother is unknown. She might be in trouble. You and I both know the sheriff may never figure it out since he has to work within the law. And even if he does, it might be too late."

Dallas believed Tommy could dissect pretty much anything given enough time. But that was one luxury they didn't have. As sheriff, he would have to go through proper channels and file paperwork that could take days, weeks or months to process.

"I hired Wayne," Dallas said. "His death is on me. And I need to find out what he knew."

A tear rolled down Kate's cheek. She quickly wiped it away.

Stacy was already blowing her nose again. "He spoke very highly of you," she said. "I didn't know at the time that it was *you*. He referred to your case as Baby Brian. Now I realize it was because of O'Brien."

"Help me find the jerks who did this to him, who shot him in cold blood," Dallas said. "You have my word you'll be the first to know when I do."

Stacy sat there for a long moment, her gaze fixed out the window.

"Will you hand me my purse? It's in the bottom drawer over there," she finally said, motioning toward the night-stand near the bed. "The deputy brought it to me last night when he stopped by."

Kate retrieved the Coach handbag and Dallas noted the designer brand.

Stacy glanced up at Kate and then Dallas as she reached for it. "This was a gift from Wayne." She finally dropped the pretense that the two of them had had a strictly professional relationship.

Kate reached over and hugged her, and the woman sagged onto her shoulder.

"He was all I had," Stacy said. "I never really had a family. He took a chance when he hired me five years ago, because I was nothing. I didn't know a laptop from a desktop. He said he could send me to training for that. Loyalty was the most important thing to him. I could do that. Our relationship was a professional one for the first three years and then, boom, something happened."

"You fell in love," Kate whispered.

"It was like a lightning bolt struck one day and there was no going back," she agreed. "We kept things a se-cret because Wayne was afraid of someone using me against him."

Kate touched her hand and Stacy looked up with glassy, tearful eyes.

"I'm sure he wanted to do whatever was necessary in order to protect you. He must've loved you very much," Kate said with calm reassurance.

More tears flowed, and even though Dallas was in a hurry to get information, he didn't want to rush out of the room. He was glad that he and Kate could be there for Stacy, and especially since she'd lost her entire support system in one blow.

"I don't know what I'm going to do now," she said. "I don't have a job or a purpose. Wayne showed me his will last year. He left everything to me, but what do I do when I leave here without him?"

There was a lost quality to her voice that seared right through Dallas.

"If you ever want to work again, there'll be a job waiting for you at the ranch," he said. "Once you get your bearings."

"You would hire me without knowing anything about me?" Stacy looked almost dumbfounded.

"Wayne was a good man. I trust his judgment," Dallas said. "Call my cell whenever you're ready and let me know what you decide."

He pulled out a business card and dropped it on the nightstand.

"And the soup kitchen always needs good people," Kate offered.

"That means a lot," she said. "I'm not sure what I'll do at this point, but this gives me options."

Loyalty was important to Dallas, too. And Wayne was right. An employee could be trained for pretty much everything else.

Stacy rummaged around in her purse until a set of keys jingled. She pulled them out and held them on her left palm. With her right hand, she picked through them until she stopped on one.

"This is the key to our house," she said, locking eyes with Dallas. "I'll write down the address for you."

He nodded before she returned her attention to the keys and thumbed through a few more.

"I kept all the keys on one ring, but I also made a duplicate just in case." She pulled out a piece of paper and pen, and then she scribbled the address.

"This little baby right here opens his office door at home," she stated. "There's a house alarm. I'll give you the code. And another one for his office."

Dallas would expect nothing less from an investigator of Morton's caliber.

Next, she dumped the contents of her purse onto the bed. She had a matching wallet, a pair of Ray-Ban sunglasses, a pack of gum and sundry items like safety pins and paper clips.

As she turned the bag inside out, Dallas saw a glint of something shiny inside. Metal? A zipper?

"This purse was made special," she said, unzipping it.

She shook the bag and a key fell out.

Chapter Eleven

"This one unlocks a compartment in a book called *Save for Retirement*. It's on the bookshelf behind his desk in his office, on the second shelf. It should be the second volume from the right. It works like a diary," Stacy said, motioning toward the key. "There'll be a flash drive inside. I never looked at it, wasn't supposed to, so I didn't. I can't tell you what's on that drive for certain. But whatever he found out about your case, I'd bet my life it would be there."

She held out the keys toward Dallas.

"Thank you," he said as he took them.

Kate hugged Stacy again and he could plainly see that she didn't want to leave the woman alone.

"Mind if I send someone over to keep an eye on you while you rest?" Dallas asked. "I don't like you being here without protection."

"Guess I didn't think about it, but you're right. I'd appreciate that very much," Stacy said.

Dallas made a quick call to Gideon Fisher to put the wheels in motion and then settled in to wait for backup to arrive. Fisher said he'd send Reece Wilcox.

Stacy was on medication, and even though she seemed wide-awake and alert, he didn't want to risk her falling asleep and being vulnerable until Reece arrived.

Kate retrieved the remote and put on one of those home decorating shows to provide a distraction for Stacy. Mindless TV was the best medicine sometimes.

"Can I get you anything from downstairs?" Kate asked. "Or order out?"

"No, thanks. I'm fine. The food here isn't horrible." Stacy paused long enough to wipe at a tear. "You can't know how much I appreciate you both."

For the next twenty minutes, they all sat and watched a kitchen makeover in comfortable silence.

By the time Reece showed up, Dallas and Kate were due at the sheriff's office.

They said their goodbyes to Stacy and promised to visit again as soon as they could.

In the parking lot, Kate put her hand on Dallas's arm.

He stopped and turned to face her, but before he could speak, she pushed up on her tiptoes, wrapped her arms around his neck and kissed him. Hard.

KATE HAD MEANT to brush a quick "thank you" kiss on Dallas's lips, but her body took over instead and she planted one on him.

His arms looped around her and dropped to her waist, pressing her to his muscled chest.

Dallas O'Brien was the very definition of *hot*. But he was also intelligent, kind and compassionate. Traits she didn't normally associate with a rich cowboy. He also had a down-to-earth quality that was refreshing. Her body seemed to take notice of all Dallas's good qualities because heat flooded through her even though it couldn't be much more than thirty degrees outside.

When he deepened the kiss, she surrendered.

Instead of fighting her feelings, she tightened her arms around his neck and braided her fingers together. The motion pressed her breasts against his chest even more and her nipples beaded inside her lacy bra.

Neither made a move to break apart when he pulled back a little and locked his gaze with hers.

They stood there, only vaguely aware that it was frigid outside, because inside their little circle was enough warmth to heat a room, and Kate's heart filled with it.

She'd never known this kind of appreciation and acceptance from anyone.

Certainly not from her mother or father. During her childhood, when the two spent time with her, it had felt sometimes as if they were ticking off boxes on a duty list rather than spending real time with her. And then there was her failed marriage to Robert. He'd been handsome and they'd been attracted to one another, but she'd never felt…this, whatever *this* was. More than anything, he just seemed ready to take the next step when the time came. Had their relationship, too, been a box he'd needed to tick off at that point in his life?

Gazing into Dallas's dark, glowing eyes, she saw something she'd never seen when looking into another man's. Rather than analyze it, she kissed him again, because Dallas O'Brien stirred up emotions she didn't even know how to begin to deal with.

And she lost herself in that kiss.

Dallas pulled back enough to whisper in her ear, "You're beautiful, Kate."

She loved the sound of her name on his lips. "So are you."

He laughed at being called beautiful. But he was, inside and out.

His phone dinged, and he checked the screen and then showed it to her.

William Seaver had just checked in at the sheriff's office.

"This is to be continued later," Dallas said, taking her hand in his, lacing their fingers together. He led her to his truck, which had been retrieved by a member of security last night, his gaze sweeping the area as they walked.

Ten minutes later, he parked in the lot at the sheriff's office.

"I hope we didn't miss anything," she said.

"If I know Tommy, he'll hold off the interview until we get inside." Dallas surveyed the lot before ushering her into the office, a reminder of how dangerous their situation still was.

Tommy greeted them in the hall before leading them to his office. "I spoke to Mrs. Hanover last night."

"What did Susan's mother say?" Dallas asked.

"That the last time she heard from her daughter was three months ago," Tommy said.

"What did she remember about their conversation?" Dallas perked up. He seemed very interested in what Tommy had to say and who could blame him?

"She told her mother that she was going out of the country for a while and not to worry about her," he said. "Told her she'd get back in touch when she could."

"That makes me think she planned to disappear," Dallas said. "She knew that she was in trouble."

"That's my guess," Tommy stated.

"This is the first positive sign we have so far that Susan could still be alive," Dallas said.

"Would she just give up her baby and take off?" Kate asked. Those actions were inconceivable to someone like her, but Dallas didn't seem surprised.

"If her child really had been mine, it seems out of character that she'd give up so easily on proving it to me," Dallas said after a thoughtful pause.

"She would've had the paternity test done, the results made into a necklace, and then worn them on a chain around her neck," Tommy stated.

Dallas nodded. "Gives me a lot to think about."

"Sure does," Tommy said. "Let's see what Kate's lawyer has to say."

Tommy urged them into his office. Then he brought in the attorney.

"You already know Kate Williams," Tommy began, "and this is Dallas O'Brien."

Seaver barely acknowledged Kate. What was up with that?

He looked guilty about something, but Kate couldn't pinpoint the exact reason.

Her lawyer's eyes widened when he heard the O'Brien name, a common reaction she'd noticed and figured was due to the status of Dallas's family. Even she'd heard the name before she moved to Bluff, albeit briefly, and that was saying something.

"You represented Miss Williams in her adoption from the Safe Haven Adoption Agency, correct?" Tommy asked.

"Yes, I did." Seaver's eyebrows arched. "Why am I being asked about that? Miss Williams is right there and she can tell you everything."

"We appreciate your patience with the question," Tommy said, redirecting the conversation. Seaver was midfifties and wore a suit. His round stomach and ruddy cheeks didn't exactly create the picture of health.

"Did you know that Miss Williams's home was broken into yesterday?" Tommy pressed.

Seaver seemed genuinely shocked. "Why would I

know that?" he asked, crossing his right leg over his left. "I don't live around here, Sheriff. Have you looked at anyone locally?"

"Whoever did this walked straight to her desk. Isn't that strange?" Tommy continued.

"I guess so. Maybe they were looking to steal her identity," Seaver guessed but he seemed tense.

"People usually search the trash for that information," Tommy said.

"What does any of this have to do with me?" Seaver asked.

"Nothing, I hope," Tommy quipped. "But on that file, the stolen one, was her adoption records. Now, why would anyone want those?"

"Good question. And one that I don't have an answer to," Seaver said, but his eyes told a different story.

It struck Kate as odd because he was practiced at presenting his side of an argument and maintaining a blank face, having done so a million times in court. And yet he seemed unnerved.

"A man tried to abduct Miss Williams's son yesterday, as well. Guess you don't know anything about that, either," Tommy murmured.

Pure shock and concern crossed Seaver's features. His top button was undone and his tie was loose around his neck. He leaned forward. "Look, I never dealt with the guy, but this sounds like the work of Harold Matthews. I've heard rumors about him setting up adoptions and then staging abductions. He works for Safe Haven and that's the reason I specifically requested Don Radcliffe. I don't know if any of the rumors are true, mind you. But that's where I'd look first."

"Could Radcliffe and Matthews be working together?" Tommy asked.

Seaver took a second to mull it over. "It can't be ruled out. I've placed a dozen babies through Radcliffe and this is the first time anything like this has happened."

Tommy asked a few more routine-sounding questions before asking for the list of clients with whom he'd placed babies from Safe Haven.

"I can't do that without a court order," Seaver said, tiny beads of sweat forming at his hairline.

"I'm asking for your cooperation, Mr. Seaver," Tommy countered.

"Look, I don't mean any disrespect, but I'm not about to expose clients who have requested and paid for private adoptions to anyone, not without a signed order from a judge," he said, folding his arms and then leaning back in his chair. "And especially not for a failed abduction attempt and a break-in."

"Then you must not have read today's paper," Tommy said.

Seaver blew out a frustrated breath. "Where is this going, Sheriff?"

"A man was murdered yesterday in connection with investigating Safe Haven Adoption Agency," Tommy said matter-of-factly.

A startled look crossed Seaver's features before he quickly regained his casual demeanor. "I've already told you everything I know. But for my money, I'd locate Harold Matthews." The lawyer pushed himself to his feet. "And if there are no more questions, I have other appointments to attend to today."

"I'll be in touch," Tommy said, also standing.

"I have no doubt you will, but you want to talk to Matthews, not me," he said as he walked out the door.

"I think he's lying," Dallas said when he'd left.

"What makes you say that?" Kate asked.

Before Dallas could answer, Tommy called Abigail into the room. "See if we can get a subpoena for William Seaver's client list as it relates to Safe Haven," he said.

"The judge has been downright cranky lately," she said. "I'll do my best to convince him."

Tommy thanked her. "Another thing before you go. I need everything you can get me on Harold Matthews. Search Don Radcliffe, too. If either one of those men have had so much as a parking ticket in the past year, I want to know about it."

"Will do," she said, before padding out the door and then disappearing down the hall.

"There's another way to go about this," Tommy said, turning to Dallas. "We need to step up our efforts on connecting the existing kidnappings to Seaver. It might take some time. If there's a link, we'll find it. Don't leave until I get back."

"I have a new theory," Dallas said, stopping his friend at the door. "What if Seaver is the kidnapper? He was a little too quick to pass the blame and give names. And he sure as hell seemed nervous to me."

Tommy leaned against the jamb, folding his arms. "I noticed that, as well."

"Has he been to the soup kitchen?" Dallas asked Kate.

"Yes. That's where we met right after the adoption," she said, still stunned at the thought.

"Was Allen around?" Dallas asked and she immediately knew what he was thinking. Seaver might've set up Allen as cover. But why would the lawyer try to take Jackson?

"As a matter of fact, yes," she responded. "But how would he know about Allen's feelings for me?"

"It's obvious to everyone," Dallas said quickly, and there was a hint of something in his voice. Jealousy?

"Seaver knew you and could have easily arranged to set up Allen with the pictures," he added.

"I'm still missing motive," Tommy said.

"He might not be the one pulling the strings," Dallas said.

Tommy was already rocking his head. "If whoever was behind the kidnappings thinks Seaver arranged an adoption they didn't want to happen, then they could be pressuring him to find the infant."

"Exactly what I was thinking," Dallas said.

"Which would confirm our earlier thoughts that someone wants their son back and they're willing to do whatever it takes to find him," Kate said. An icy chill ran up her arms.

Deputy Lopez's voice boomed from the hallway.

Tommy ushered him inside his office.

"Three more of the adoptions shared the same lawyer," Lopez said.

"Let me guess… Seaver?" the sheriff asked.

Lopez nodded. "But here's something you don't know. Two of the babies were found today…"

Kate cringed, waiting to hear the next part as she prayed for good news.

"Both alive," Lopez said.

"Where?" Tommy demanded, before anyone else could.

"One was left at a baby furniture store two towns over, in one of the cribs for sale. An employee discovered the sleeping infant an hour after she opened, and called local police, who were able to make the match," the deputy stated.

"And what about the other one?" Tommy asked.

"He was left at a church, discovered before service

began. Pastor said he'd been in the chapel half an hour before and there was no baby."

"Neither boy was hurt?" Tommy asked, with what could only be described as a relieved sigh.

"Not a hair on their bald heads," Lopez quipped with a smile.

"How long were they missing?" Tommy asked.

"A few days."

"Enough time for a proper DNA test," he mused.

This was good news for everyone except Kate. Some kidnapper was trying to find his own son and checking DNA of all the possibilities before giving them back. And that was fantastic for all the mothers of those babies, because it meant they were in the clear. Jackson, however, was still in question. There was a scrap of hope to hold on to, since the babies were being found alive. Extreme care was being taken to ensure that the infant boys were being located quickly.

Except what if Jackson was the one they were searching for...?

Kate closed her eyes, refusing to accept the possibility.

Tommy excused himself and the deputy followed.

"Seaver lied about not knowing the other family whose baby was abducted," Kate said.

Dallas nodded. "I picked up on that, too."

"What do we do now?" she asked. Dallas hadn't told his friend about the keys from Stacy and Kate hadn't expected him to, given that they'd received them in confidence.

"We have to wait for dark for our next move," he stated, with a look that said he knew exactly what she was asking.

Which meant they'd spend at least another whole day together.

"It's only a few weeks until Halloween. You have a party to help plan. I don't want to get in the way of your family," she said. All she had in the house was a three-foot fake ghost that said "Happy Halloween" and then giggled every time it detected movement. She'd nicknamed him Ghost Buddy and he was all she'd had time to put out. Even though she knew Jackson wouldn't remember his first Halloween, she wanted to find a way to make it special. Ghost Buddy was her first real decoration and she figured that she could build her collection from there.

The thought of going home scared her because the more they dug into this case, the less she liked what they found and the more afraid she felt.

The only bright spot was that a couple more of the babies had turned up and they were fine.

Tommy returned a moment later. "I agree with you, by the way. I think Seaver's lying."

"Which means he's either involved or covering for someone who is," Dallas said.

"He gave us a name," Kate offered.

"That might have been meant to throw us off the real trail, buy some time or take himself off the suspect list," the sheriff said.

"Or dodge suspicion," Dallas added. "He seemed awfully uncomfortable."

"I noticed. I wanted to keep him here but he knew better than anyone that I had nothing to hold him on." Tommy nodded. "At least we have a few leads to chase down now. In the meantime, I think it's safer for the two of you on the ranch."

"You have my word that we won't leave unless we have to," Dallas said. "What did you learn when you interviewed Stacy last night?"

"Not much," Tommy said with a sigh. "She didn't recognize the guys and couldn't give much of a description other than what the gun looked like."

"Sorry that we couldn't help with that, either," Dallas said. "Unfortunately, my back was turned for the few seconds we were in the room, and Stacy blocked my only view of their faces, brief as it was."

"She's going to be okay," Kate interjected. "She's strong."

"I sent over security," Dallas said. "Wasn't sure if the guys would come back and I didn't want to take any chances, just in case someone got worried she could testify against them."

Tommy thanked him. "I'll let you know if we get the subpoena or any hits on linked cases," he added.

"What can you tell me about the murder scene yesterday?" Dallas asked.

"Nothing stood out. It will take time to process the site, but it looks like a standard forced-off-the-road-and-then-shot scenario."

Kate winced. How could any of that be run-of-the-mill?

And then it dawned on her why the voice at Stacy's office sounded familiar. "It was him. The other day at Morton's office. The guy who tried to take Jackson."

Dallas's head was rocking. "I couldn't put my finger on what was bugging me before. That's it."

Tommy added the notation to the file.

Dallas's phone vibrated. He checked the screen and the brief flicker of panic on his face sent her pulse racing.

He muttered a few "uh-huh"s before saying they were on their way and clicking off.

She was already to her feet before he could make a move. "What's going on?" she asked.

"There was a disturbance on the east side of the property. A motorcycle tried to run through the gate," he said, quickly reassuring her that no one got through and everyone was just fine.

She wished that reassurance calmed her fast-beating heart. It didn't.

"You want me to send a deputy?" Tommy called, as they broke into a run.

"I could use an escort," Dallas shouted back.

Kate's chest squeezed and she couldn't breathe.

No way could she allow those men to get near her son.

Chapter Twelve

Dallas raced through the city with a law-enforcement escort clearing the path. He'd enter the property on the west side near his place, because there was more security at that checkpoint. The earlier ruckus had been on the opposite side, miles away, and if he was lucky, he and Kate would be able to slip in from the west before anyone else could realize what he'd done.

Things were escalating and the kidnappers seemed to be zeroing in.

The thought did occur to Dallas that the attempted breach could be a distraction meant to get him and Kate out in the open. Or someone inside, if he took another vantage point. The latter wouldn't succeed, because there was plenty of security at all the weak spots on the ranch. If the former was the case, then it was working, and he had to consider the possibility that he was playing right into their opponents' hands.

Still, he had to take the chance. One look at Kate and he knew she needed to hold her baby in her arms after the disturbing news about Seaver.

He had her pull out his cell and call his head of security. "Put the call on speaker," he instructed.

She did and he could hear the line ringing almost immediately.

"We're close, about five minutes out," Dallas said to Gideon Fisher, his security chief, when he answered.

"I'll be at the gate and ready, sir," Fisher responded. "Ryder and Austin are here, with a team of my men."

"Excellent." Dallas knew all the extra security at the gate would alert anyone watching to the possibility they'd be coming in that way, but his brothers knew how to handle a rifle and Dallas wanted the extra firepower in case anything went down. "Where's everyone else?"

"Tyler's up front. Colin's roaming."

It sounded like his brothers were ready to go, in addition to the staff of eight...well, seven, since Reece stood vigil in Stacy's hospital room.

A sport-utility vehicle with blacked-out windows roared up from behind.

Dallas's truck was sandwiched between the deputy in front and the SUV barreling toward their bumper.

"Hold on," Dallas told Kate, just as the SUV rammed into them, causing their heads to jolt forward.

"Sir?" Gideon said.

"We have company and we just took a hit," Dallas replied.

"Roger that, sir."

Dallas could see the entrance to the ranch in the distance. Once inside, they'd be safe, but it was dicey whether or not they could get there.

He flashed the high beams to alert their escort to the trouble brewing behind him. The deputy must've noticed because he turned on his flashing lights. "Black SUV, stop your vehicle," the officer called out over his loudspeaker.

The SUV rammed them once more, again throwing their heads forward.

"Change of plans." Dallas gunned the engine and

popped over into the other lane of the narrow country road. He was lucky that there was so little traffic in the area and this stretch of road was straight and flat, so there'd be no surprises.

The deputy slowed to allow Dallas safe passage, but the SUV whipped into the left lane, as well, maintaining close proximity to Dallas's bumper.

Even repeating the message over the bullhorn didn't work. The other driver persisted.

Dallas got a good look at him in the rearview and he wore similar clothes to the kidnapper at the soup kitchen. He'd bet money it was the same person.

Worse yet, when Dallas moved into the right lane again the SUV pulled up beside him, blocking his turn.

Austin stepped onto the road and aimed his rifle directly at the oncoming vehicle. Dallas pointed and the driver must've noticed, because he hit the brakes. Before the deputy could respond, the SUV had made a U-turn and was speeding off in the opposite direction.

The deputy followed in pursuit, lights flashing.

Dallas turned onto his property, and that was when he finally glanced at Kate, whose face had gone bleached-sheet white.

She didn't speak and he didn't force the issue.

As soon as he parked in front of his house, she practically flew out of the truck. "Is Jackson in there?"

"Yes." Dallas followed her inside as she ran to her infant son.

Janis met her in the living room, a sleeping Jackson in her arms, and immediately handed him over. She seemed to know that Kate wouldn't care if the baby woke. She had to hold him.

The look on Kate's face, the same damn expression from yesterday morning, cut a hole in Dallas's heart.

Jackson wound up to cry, then belted out a good one. The boy had strong lungs.

Kate cradled her son while Janis excused herself.

The crying abated a few minutes later as Kate soothed her baby, and the sight of the two of them together like that stirred something in Dallas's heart.

He didn't want to have feelings for anyone right now.

The timing was completely off, now that he was chasing down what had happened to Susan. Besides, he was busier than ever, between the ranch and the business. He was helping Kate and didn't need to confuse his feelings for more than that.

Dallas excused himself to work in his home office.

He hadn't turned on his computer in a few days and that would mean an out-of-control inbox. He'd seen the emails rolling in on his smartphone, but he'd been too busy to give them much thought.

Then there was the ranch to run, and Halloween Bash just around the corner.

After answering emails until his eyes blurred, he stretched out his sore limbs while seated in his office chair.

The stress of the past few days was catching up with him and at some point he'd need to sleep. There wasn't much chance of that as long as Kate was in the house. His mind kept wandering to her silky body curled up on the bed in the guest room, her soft skin...

Just thinking about it started stirring places that didn't need to be riled up. Especially since there was no chance for release.

So he focused on his inbox again, wishing he'd receive an email or text from Tommy stating that they got the guys in the SUV.

The next time he glanced at the clock, it was three

o'clock in the afternoon. The house was quiet. He'd worked through lunch, which wasn't unusual for him. His stomach decided it was time to eat.

Work might have distracted him for a little while, but more and more he wondered what had happened to Susan. Given Morton's death and both their associations with Safe Haven, Dallas feared the worst.

There were 437 messages in his spam folder and he checked each one to see if Susan had tried to contact him but her note had gotten hung up in his filter.

Nothing.

He pulled the set of keys Stacy had given him from his pocket, set them on his desk and lazily ran his fingers along them.

Granted, he and Susan had no business being a couple, but he still felt angry at the possibility of something bad happening to her.

Was she in trouble when she'd called him and told him about the baby? Had she been hoping for his protection? He'd assumed all along that she was trying to trap him into marriage, and she had been, but now that he'd seen the look on Kate's face when it came to a threat to her son, another reality set in. Susan might have been desperate and looking for protection. Marriage to Dallas might've been a way for her to secure her son's future.

She had to know that Dallas would've figured out the truth at some point if the child hadn't been his. Then again, if her life had been in danger, she might have figured she'd tell him after the deal was sealed.

Saying he was the father could've been the equivalent of a Hail Mary pass in football, a last-ditch effort to save the game.

Frustration nipped at his heels like a determined predator. Dallas searched his memory for anything he could remember about the last conversation they'd had before she'd gone missing, and he came up empty.

His cell phone buzzed. The call was from Tommy, so Dallas immediately answered.

"I have news," his friend said.

"What did you learn?"

"We got a few hits today. Of the six abductions that we know about so far, four of them used Seaver," Tommy related.

"So most likely he was involved in the others," Dallas reasoned.

"True. And there's something else."

"Okay," Dallas said.

"Don Radcliffe was found dead in his apartment in Houston."

"Isn't that who Seaver worked with at Safe Haven?" Dallas asked.

"It was."

"Any word on Harold Matthews?"

"We can't locate him. But he's roughly the size and shape of the man you described as the kidnapper from yesterday morning," Tommy replied, then paused for a beat. "Are you alone?"

"Yeah. Why?"

"I have personal news." The ominous tone in his friend's voice sat heavy in Dallas's thoughts.

"What is it?" he asked.

"At first I thought I should wait until all this is over, but I figured you'd want to know the minute I found out. It's about your parents. I got a report from the coroner a couple of days ago that indicated your mother had a heart attack," Tommy said quietly.

"What are the chances of both my parents having a heart attack on the same day?" Dallas asked.

"It made me suspicious, too, so I requested a lab workup. The toxicology report came back showing cyanide in both of their systems. Enough to cause heart attacks," Tommy said.

"What does that mean, exactly?" Dallas was too stunned to form a coherent thought beyond that question.

"I'm opening a formal investigation into their deaths and I wanted you to be the first to know."

Those words were like a punch to Dallas's gut.

"I know it's a lot to process right now, and I may not find anything, because ingestion could've been accidental," Tommy added. "But I'm not leaving any stone unturned when it comes to your parents."

Dallas sat there. He couldn't even begin to digest the thought that anyone could've harmed his parents.

"Dallas, are you still with me?" his friend asked.

He grunted an affirmation, then drew a deep, rasping breath. "Is it possible that their accident might have been staged?"

"Yes, but I'm not ready to jump to any conclusions just yet."

The line went quiet again. Because the implication sitting between them was murder.

"You know I'm here for you anytime you want to talk," Tommy said at last.

Dallas realized he was gripping his cell phone tight enough to make his fingers hurt. "Any word on the SUV? Because the driver easily could've been the kidnapper from yesterday."

"It disappeared and we lost the trail."

THE NIGHT WAS pitch-black and the temperature had dipped below freezing. The wind howled. At least Jackson was with Janis, in a cozy bed sound asleep.

Kate's teeth chattered even though she wore two layers of clothing underneath her coat.

She and Dallas had decided to wait until after dark to go to Wayne's house, reasoning that if they left too late, then dogs in the neighborhood might give them away. He'd parked four blocks over.

Ever since she woke from her nap, she'd noticed something was different about Dallas. His mood had darkened and he'd closed up.

Was he preparing himself for the news as to whether or not he was a father?

He had to have considered the possibility that if he'd had a son, the boy could've been targeted in the kidnappings, as well.

At nine o'clock, lights were still on and households busy with activity. Dallas put his arm around Kate's waist and even through the thick layers she felt a sizzle of heat on her skin.

Wayne Morton's house was on a quiet lane in a family neighborhood. Smoke billowed from chimneys on the tree-lined street of half-acre lots. The crisp air smelled of smoke from logs crackling in fireplaces. Halloween lights and decorations filled front yards.

There were enough neighbors about that she and Dallas could slip in and out of Morton's house without drawing attention.

As Kate walked down the sidewalk, tucked under Dallas's arm, she could see kids in the front rooms watching TV or reading on couches, their mother's arms curled around them.

Someone whistled and then called out, "Here, Dutch. Come on, boy."

A tear escaped before Kate could sniff it away. She turned her face so Dallas wouldn't see her emotions, while wondering what it must be like to have a mother's unconditional love and acceptance. She wished that for her and Carter.

Another person half a block down was rolling a trash can onto the front sidewalk for weekly garbage pickup.

"Morton's place is on the next street," Dallas said in a low voice, interrupting her thoughts.

When she didn't respond, he glanced at her.

A second, longer look caused him to stop walking. He turned until they were face-to-face.

Another errant tear escaped and he thumbed it away.

"Are you okay?" He spoke and she could see his breath in the cold air.

Instead of speaking, she nodded.

Dallas's thumb trailed across her bottom lip and then her jawline. Kate had never known a light touch could be so sweet, so comforting.

A set of porch lights turned off across the street and they both pulled back.

Dallas laced their fingers together as they strolled down the lane.

As Morton's house came into view, Kate couldn't help but notice it was the only one on the street that was completely blacked out. That image was sobering and a sad feeling settled over her, making walking even more difficult.

Thinking of Stacy in the hospital, how sad she'd been, made Kate feel awful. Would she come home to an empty, dark house in a few days when she recovered? How would she get past this? Wayne, her job, seemed to be her life. She'd said they were all she had. Before Jackson had come into Kate's life, she could relate to feeling empty inside. And now with Dallas in the picture, she'd never been more aware of how alone she'd been when she was married to Robert.

Dallas stopped at the bottom of the stairs, clearly as affected by the scene as Kate was. She could see guilt so clearly written in his expression. There was something else in his eyes when she really looked closer. It dawned on her what: he might be about to find out if he was a father.

Worse yet, if his child had been adopted out to a stranger, then Dallas might never find the little boy. Given the nature of closed adoptions and the privacy of all involved, it would take moving heaven and earth to locate the baby, and Dallas O'Brien didn't strike her as the kind of man who could live with himself if he had a child out there somewhere and didn't know him.

"Are you ready for this?" she asked.

A car turned onto the street two blocks down.

Dallas glanced around. "As ready as I'll ever be."

The layout was just as Stacy had described. Dallas ushered Kate inside, closing and locking the front door behind them as she disarmed the alarm. The office was to the left of the foyer and had double French doors with glass panels.

There was enough light coming from the surrounding houses with the Halloween lights on for them to see large objects like furniture.

Dallas slid the office key into the lock and then paused to take a fortifying breath.

Here went nothing…

Chapter Thirteen

Dallas stepped through the door and quickly found the next keypad, to punch in the code for the office.

They kept the lights off so as not to alert anyone who might be driving by or watching the place that they were there.

Inside the office, Dallas located a few books and brought them to the window. Stacy had said the volume they wanted would be on the second shelf, two books from the right. She hadn't told them there would be a wall of bookcases to choose from.

A beam of light flashed from outside. A cop?

That would so not be good. Kate froze and held her breath until the beam moved across another window.

What the heck was that?

She didn't know and didn't want to ask questions. Fear assaulted her as memories from yesterday invaded her thoughts. The men, the guns…

She took a deep breath to calm her frazzled nerves. Getting worked up wouldn't change a thing. They'd still be in a dead man's house going through his things. And even that didn't matter as much as getting back to Jackson safely. Janis had taken him to the main house to sleep tonight, and Kate's heart ached being away from him.

Even though she wouldn't see him until morning, being back on the ranch would calm her racing pulse.

She moved to another bookshelf and pulled out a couple of volumes, making her best guess where the right one would be. Then she stepped next to Dallas at the window, where there was more light. One of the books was definitely less heavy than the others. She'd noticed the instant she'd slid it from the shelf.

Disappointment filled her when she opened the lighter book. Nothing.

She and Dallas moved on to other bookcases and flipped open more volumes, placing them back as closely as possible to their original spots.

"I think I have it," he said at last, making tracks to the window to get a better look. He held his offering up to the light. "Yep. This is it."

A noise from the alley caught their attention. Dallas grabbed her hand and moved toward the door in double time.

"It's probably just a cat, but we don't want to stick around and find out," he said.

"What if someone's watching the house?" she asked, ignoring the sinking feeling in the pit of her stomach. Adrenaline had kicked in and her flight response was triggered. She needed to get the heck out of there more than she needed to breathe.

"STAY CALM AND pretend like we're supposed to be here." Dallas checked the peephole before opening the door. So far, the way looked clear, but he couldn't be certain no one was out there. He tucked the book under his coat, thinking about the meeting he needed to set up with his brothers in the morning to deliver Tommy's news about their parents.

Right now, he needed to get Kate and himself the hell out of there and back to the ranch.

After locking the door behind them, he led Kate down the few steps to the porch. That was when he heard the telltale click of a shell being engaged in the chamber of a shotgun.

"Where do you think you're going?" a stern male voice said. "Turn around and put your hands where I can see them."

"Don't panic," Dallas whispered. "Do as he says and we'll be fine."

Dallas turned slowly to find himself staring down the barrel of a shotgun. Behind it was a man in his late sixties with white hair and a stout build. Dallas had spent enough time around law-enforcement officers to know that this guy had been on the job. He wore pajama bottoms, slippers and an overcoat.

"What are you doing here?" the man asked.

"We just stopped by to check on the place for a friend," Dallas said, figuring this was more a friendly neighborhood-watch situation than a real threat. He couldn't relax, though. This guy looked like he meant business.

"Does this friend have a name?" the man asked, business end of the shotgun still trained on Dallas.

"Wayne Morton," Dallas replied, hoping that would be enough. "He and Stacy are out of town and asked us to keep an eye on the house."

"That right?" The guy eyed them up and down suspiciously.

Kate stepped closer to Dallas and put her arm around him. "They're friends of ours and I'd appreciate it if you wouldn't point that thing at us."

The man lowered the barrel, much to Dallas's relief. It was too early to exhale, however.

"You should turn on the porch light," the man said. "And it's dark in the alley. There's a light back there, too."

"Will do," Dallas said, although he'd pretty much agree to anything to walk away from this guy without raising suspicion.

"Honey, we have to go. Babysitter's waiting," Kate said, twining her fingers in his.

"Thanks for the tip," Dallas said with a nod. His chin tucked close to his chest, staving off the cold. He decided keeping it there would shield his face. A man who used to be paid to notice things wasn't a good one to have around.

"When's Morton coming back?" the guy asked.

"In a few days," Dallas said, praying he hadn't read today's newspaper.

That seemed to satisfy the neighbor. Dallas could hear his feet shuffling in the opposite direction. He glanced back just in case and was relieved to confirm the man was heading home.

If this guy was watching the PI's house, then others could be, too. And that got Dallas's boots moving a little faster.

Another sobering reality struck him.

The data on the thumb drive tucked away in the book he held on to could change his life forever.

The weight of that thought pressed heavy on his shoulders as he drove back to the ranch.

"I don't think Stacy should go home until we figure all this out," Kate said, breaking the silence between them as he pulled onto the ranch property.

"Agreed," Dallas said, thankful to focus on something else for a minute. Another thought had occurred to him. The information on that drive might tell him what had happened to Susan. And at least one area of his life could have resolution, even as more questions arose in others.

Whatever was there might be valuable to someone. Morton could be dead because of the information gained since he was on an investigation for Dallas when he was killed.

And then there could be nothing relevant on it, too. Dallas was just guessing at this point, his guilt kicking into high gear again. There were so many emotions pinging through him at what he might find on that zip drive.

Dallas gripped the steering wheel tighter as he navigated his truck into his garage.

"I doubt I'll be able to sleep without Jackson here," Kate said, and he could hear the anguish in her voice.

"You want me to have him brought over from the main house?" Dallas asked. "I can make a call and he'll be here in ten minutes."

"No. I don't want to wake Janis after she was nice enough to help care for him in the first place." Kate sighed wistfully. "He's probably asleep anyway, and waking him up just so I can look at him seems selfish."

"I can send a text to have her bring him over first thing in the morning, as soon as they wake," Dallas offered, turning off the engine. "In fact, she probably left a message already, letting us know how the night went. I silenced my cell phone before we left."

He fished the device from his front pocket and then checked the screen as he walked in the door to the kitchen. "Yep. Here it is," he said, showing it to Kate.

Her eyes lit up and they felt like a beacon to Dallas. Everything inside him was churning in a storm.

There was a picture of her sleeping baby, with one word underneath: *angel*.

"Thank you," Kate said, tears welling.

"I didn't mean to make you cry." Dallas held the phone

out to her. "You can hang on to that if you want. I need to check the contents of this drive."

"Mind if I come with you?" she asked. "Or I can stay out here if you'd like some privacy."

Normally, that was exactly what he would want.

"I'd rather you be with me when I take a look," he said, and he surprised himself by meaning it. As crazy as everything had been in the past few days, and as much as his own life had been turned upside down even more in a matter of minutes, being with Kate was the only thing that made sense to him.

She set his cell phone on the counter, took his hand and once again laced their fingers together. Rockets exploded inside his chest with her touch.

"Ready?" she asked.

"As much as I can be," he said, and the look she shot him said she knew exactly what he was talking about.

They walked into his office hand in hand and Dallas couldn't ignore how right this whole scenario felt. It seemed so natural to have her in his home, which was a dangerous thought, most likely due to an overload of emotions.

Dallas sat in his office chair and Kate perched on one of his knees. He had to wrap his arms around her to turn on his computer, and that felt so good. A big part of him wanted to lose himself in her and block out everything else.

Another side of him needed to see what was on that flash drive.

His computer booted up quickly and he mentally prepared himself for what he would find. There could be nothing at all, and that would bring a disappointment all its own.

Dallas needed answers and yet there was a healthy dose of fear exploding inside him at finding the truth.

He plugged in the device and a few seconds later a file popped up in the center of the screen.

Dallas clicked on the icon with a foreboding feeling. He scanned a couple of documents.

"Okay, from what I can tell so far, Wayne tracked a baby to Safe Haven and that's where the trail ends," Kate said. "Which is what we already knew."

That about summed up what Dallas had seen, as well. And, no, it wasn't helpful.

"Here's the odd thing. Once the baby was born, Morton seems to think Susan disappeared," Dallas noted. He also realized that the dates didn't rule out the possibility that Jackson was his son.

"And, like, seriously vanished," Kate mused. "No more records of her exist anywhere. I mean, I guess I can see that she might have had a closed adoption, and the agency would have coded her file so as not to give her identity away. That happened with mine. The birth mother wanted a sealed adoption and I was in no position to argue. Plus, I thought it would be better anyway. But there should be some trail of her somewhere—an address, credit card, cell-phone record."

"Her bank account has been closed. There's no record of her existence."

"It's almost like she died," Kate said.

"But then, wouldn't there be a record of that?" Dallas shoved aside the thought that Kate's baby could actually be Susan's.

This was not the time for that discussion. First things first, and that meant Dallas needed to figure out if he was a father.

He opened the other documents one by one, scanning each for any link to his and Susan's baby. If there was one.

There was nothing.

Morton had been thorough and yet... Dallas opened the last file. It was labeled WS.

"Morton questioned your attorney the day before he was killed," Dallas said.

Kate's eyes were wide. He could see them clearly in the reflection from the computer screen.

She opened her mouth to speak but no words came.

"We need to have that DNA test. It's the only way we'll know for sure that you're not Jackson's father," she said.

"If that's what you want. I can arrange one in the morning," Dallas told her.

She muttered something under her breath. She'd spoken so low, Dallas wasn't sure he heard right.

Should he be offended?

"I hope you know that I'd make one hell of a fine father someday," he said, a little indignant. His emotions were getting the best of him.

Kate turned those blue eyes on him and his chest clutched.

"I didn't mean to insinuate that you wouldn't be a good father. You would." Her eyes were filled with tears now. "It's just Jackson's all I have. My relationship with my parents is practically nonexistent. My brother and I used to be close and now he's siding with my mother, which stinks, considering how little she supported either one of us growing up."

Dallas's arms tightened around Kate's waist, and that was a bad idea given the mix of emotions stirring inside him. A very bad idea.

Tears streamed down her beautiful face. Dallas wanted

to say something to make it better, and yet all he could manage was "I'm sorry."

"No. I don't expect you to understand, and I'm embarrassed to say anything. I have Jackson now and he's my world," she said.

"I can see that he is," Dallas assured her.

"And he's enough. All I ever wanted was to have a family. Is that too much to ask?" She buried her face in her hands and released a sob.

"It's not," Dallas said. "And I understand more than you know. Because I have an amazing family, I know exactly how much we build each other up, rely on each other. I can't imagine where I'd be if I didn't have my brothers by my side, and especially since we lost our parents."

He lifted her chin until her gaze met his, ignoring the rush of electricity coursing through his body. It took heroic effort to turn away from the pulse throbbing at the base of her throat.

"You're an amazing mother," he stated, and she immediately made a move to protest. "Don't do that to yourself. You are. Jackson is lucky to have you and you're doing a great job. Don't doubt that for a second."

"I'm scared," she admitted, and it looked like it took a lot to say those words. Someone as strong as she was wouldn't want to concede to a weakness. Dallas knew all about that, too.

"It's okay," he said reassuringly.

"What if I lose him? What if my adoption turns out to be illegal and someone has a claim on my son? I've read stories like that." She stopped to let out another sob.

"It won't happen."

"That's impossible to say right now," she said. "I could lose him and that would destroy me. He's all I have."

"You might not have had friends when you came to town and you might've been too busy to make any since. But you have me now. And any one of my brothers would stand behind you, as well. Plus you've found a friend in Stacy."

"You're kind to say that, but we've only just met," she said, her gaze searching his to find out if there was any truth to what he was saying.

"We may have known each other for just a few days, but that doesn't mean I don't *know* you," Dallas said calmly. He considered himself a good judge of character and any woman this devoted to her child couldn't be a bad person. She put Jackson first every time. Period.

In some deep and unexplainable part of his heart, he knew Kate.

THERE WAS SOMETHING about Dallas O'Brien's quiet masculinity and deep voice that soothed Kate's frazzled nerves. It shouldn't. She shouldn't allow it. But *shouldn't* walked right out the door with self-control as she leaned forward and kissed him.

The instant her lips touched his, Kate knew she was in serious trouble, and not just because she might be sitting across a courtroom from this man someday fighting for custody of her son. Everything in her body wanted to be with Dallas, and that should stop her.

He deepened the kiss and his hands came up to cup her face.

And there wasn't anything she could do to resist what her body craved. With him so close, his scent filled her senses and her heat pooled between her thighs. It had been a very long time since she'd had good sex and her body craved release that only Dallas could give. Normally, it took time to get to know a man before she'd let her guard down and allow him to get this close. But she'd never been *this* attracted to anyone. With Dallas, it felt right, and her brain argued that there was no reason to stop. From a physical sense, her brain was right: she was an adult; he was an adult. They could do whatever they wanted. Her heart was the holdout.

Except that the logical voice that generally stopped her from making life-changing mistakes was annoyingly quiet.

And she wanted Dallas O'Brien with her entire being.

Her hands tugged at the hem of his gray V-neck shirt. The cotton was smooth in her hands as she pulled it over his head and dropped it onto the floor.

This time, there was no hesitation on either of their parts. No stopping to make sure this was right.

Her shirt joined his a moment later and the growl that ripped from his throat sent heat swirling.

"You're incredible," he said, his hands roaming across her bare stomach.

And then he cupped her breast and it was her turn to moan. His lips closed on hers as though he was swallowing the sound.

His hands on her caused her breasts to swell and her nipples to bead into tiny buds. Her back arched involuntarily and she wanted more…more of his hands on her… more of his touch…more of his clothes off.

Kate stood, unbuttoned her jeans and shimmied out of them, kicking off her shoes in the process. Her bra and panties joined them on the floor.

And then she stood in front of Dallas naked.

His hands came up to rest on her hips and he pressed his forehead against her stomach.

One second was all it took for him to decide. No words were needed.

And then in a flash he was standing and she was helping him out of his jeans and boxers.

He lifted her onto the desk and rolled his thumb skillfully across her slick heat.

"I'm ready." It was all she needed to say before the tip of his erection was there, teasing her.

She clasped her legs around his midsection as he drove himself inside her. She threw her head back and rocked against his erection until he filled her. She stretched around his thick length.

"You're insanely gorgeous," Dallas groaned, pulling halfway out and then driving deep inside her again. She met him stroke for stroke as he stroked her nipple between his thumb and forefinger, rocketing her to the edge.

She grabbed on to his shoulders, her fingers digging into his muscles to gain purchase.

Stride for stride, she matched his pace, until it became dizzying and she was on the brink of ecstasy with no chance of returning.

The explosion shattered her, inside and out, and she could feel his erection pulsing as he gave in to his own release. He stayed inside her as she collapsed on the desk, bringing him with her, over her.

He brushed kisses up her neck, across her jawline, her chin.

And then he pulled back and locked eyes with her.

"You know one time isn't going to be enough, right?" And the sexy little smile curving his lips released a thousand butterflies in her stomach.

Chapter Fourteen

Dallas woke at five o'clock the next morning, an hour before his alarm was set to go off. Kate's warm, naked body against his in his bed made it next to impossible to force to get up.

The moment he eased from beneath the covers, he regretted it. He walked lightly to his office so he wouldn't disturb her sleep. He needed to make a call to Tommy and fill him in on what they'd found out last night. And there was so much information making the rounds in his head after learning the news about his parents. He was doing his level best not to jump the gun straight to murder when it came to them, knowing he might be grasping at straws to shift the blame away from himself.

He threw on a fresh pair of boxers and jeans and then moved into the kitchen to make coffee.

"Seaver's involved up to his eyeballs," Dallas said to Tommy over the phone, taking his first sip of fresh brew. His friend had always been an early riser, awake and on the job by five.

"Do I want to know how you know this?" his friend asked, and there was more than a hint of frustration in his voice.

"Morton visited him the day before his death," Dallas insisted, not really wanting to go there with the lawman.

"That's not exactly an answer."

"Just talk to him again. Believe me when I say it'll pay off," Dallas said.

"I'd love to. The problem is I have to walk a fine line with him," Tommy stated. "And it takes time to pull together evidence."

"He killed Morton to silence him. I'm sure he did." Dallas knew full well his words weren't enough to go on. They required proof.

"That may be true, but I need more than your hunch to get a search warrant for his house or his bank accounts," Tommy said. He blew out a frustrated breath.

Dallas knew his friend was upset at the situation and not at him. He shared the sentiment 100 percent.

"I hear what you're saying and I know you have to do this the right way to make it stick, but trust me when I say he knows more than he's telling." Could he share what he'd found on the data drive? He hadn't obtained it illegally, and yet he felt Stacy should be the one to make the call.

"I can put a tail on him. That's about the best I can do under the circumstances." Tommy blew out another frustrated breath.

Speaking of Stacy, did Seaver know about her and Wayne? Dallas wondered.

"I'm probably going to regret this, but what makes you think he shot Wayne Morton?" Tommy asked.

"Believe me when I say it's more than a hunch. Can you check his tire treads to see if they match the ones at the scene?" Dallas asked.

"Already getting someone on it," Tommy said, sounding like his coffee hadn't quite kicked in yet. "Did you get any word on Susan?"

"As a matter of fact, I did." He could share that, since,

technically, he'd paid for that information and part of the data belonged to him. "Here's the thing with her. When she disappeared from New Mexico, it's like she vanished. No more paper. One day she was there and then it was like she never existed."

"She get involved with a criminal who made her go away?" Tommy asked, his interest piqued.

"Wouldn't there be a paper trail? Apartment lease? Something?" Dallas asked. "I mean even in the worst-case scenario there'd be a death certificate."

"True." Tommy got quiet. "Not to mention the fact that she was living in New Mexico. Why use a Texas adoption agency?"

"I'm figuring that she was hoping her child would grow up close to home," Dallas said. "I'd have to think there'd be a missing person's report on her somewhere, right? But you checked and there isn't."

"Where'd you get your information?" His friend clicked keys on his computer. "Never mind. Don't tell me. I don't want to know."

"Is there anything you can use to link Seaver to Morton's murder?" Dallas asked. "Any evidence that might've been overlooked?"

"Tire tracks are iffy, at best. I doubt I could convince a judge to give me what I want based on just that little bit of evidence, so even if they match he'll say so do the tracks of a hundred other vehicles," Tommy muttered. "I'll check to see if Seaver owns a gun. Might get lucky there and get a caliber match from ballistics."

"I've been thinking a lot about Allen Lentz," Dallas said. "About him being set up. Seaver met him, and my instincts say he decided to take advantage of that crush Lentz has on Kate."

"Given his computer skills, Lentz should've been able

to cover his tracks better," Tommy agreed. "Maybe I can find a link there."

"We know the kidnapper didn't act alone. If this was a crime of passion, then Allen would've acted on his own, wouldn't he?" Dallas asked, ignoring the knot in his gut as he thought of another man making a pass at Kate.

"That's a safe bet. Allen seemed to think there was still a chance with Kate. If all hope had been lost then he might be motivated to do something more extreme. She seemed to be dodging his advances without outright rejecting him," Tommy said.

"The guy attempting the kidnapping was fairly young. I'm just trying to cover all the bases, but is there any chance Allen could've hired someone?" Dallas asked.

"Nothing from his bank account gives me that impression. No large withdrawals in the past few months."

"What about neighbors?"

"Everyone alibied," Tommy stated.

"Seems like Lentz can be safely ruled out as a suspect," Dallas said.

"That's where I'm at with him," Tommy confirmed. "Good to look at this from all angles, though."

That gave Dallas another thought. "Could someone else be pulling the strings with Seaver?"

"That's a good question," his friend said. "One I hope to answer very soon. So, yes, it's a definite possibility."

Dallas hoped to have an answer, too. Because Kate's future was hanging in the balance.

"I'll do my best to track down Susan using my means," the lawman told him.

"I'd like that very much," Dallas said. "And thank you for looking into my parents' situation. I'll tell the family this morning."

"I'm not making any promises, but if there's something foul, I'll figure it out," Tommy said.

Dallas thanked his friend again, ended the call and then checked the clock. It was almost five thirty. He'd received a text from Janis. She and Jackson were up and she was about to give him his bottle. She said they'd be there around six.

He could wake Kate up for another round of the best sex of his life before the baby showed up. Or he could fix another cup of coffee.

He stood up and turned toward his bedroom.

KATE ON HIS BED, in his bed, had Dallas wanting more than just a night or two with her. But what else? When this was all over, he needed to sort out his emotions and figure out exactly where he saw this relationship fitting into his already overcrowded life.

Relationship? Was that what was happening between them? Something was different, because for the first time in his life, Dallas had no clue what his next move was going to be.

She stirred and they made love slowly this time.

"I'll grab you a cup of coffee," he said, kissing her one last time before leaving the bed.

"Really?" She stretched and the move caused her breasts to thrust forward. The sheet fell to her waist as she sat up, and all he could see was her silky skin. "'Cause I could get used to this."

"Good," he said, thinking the same thing as he forced his gaze away from that hot body and walked toward the hallway.

By the time he fixed her coffee, Kate was dressed and Jackson was coming through the front door in Janis's arms. Dallas couldn't help but notice that the older woman was beaming.

"Thank you for taking care of him," Kate said, reaching for the baby.

He smiled and that was all it took for her to beam, too.

"It was truly my pleasure. I married young, but we never were able to have children," the older woman said wistfully. "Lost my Alvin to the war and never found anyone I could love as much."

She waved her hand in the air and sniffed back a tear. "No need to get sentimental before coffee. I enjoyed every minute spent with this little man and I hope you'll let me watch him again real soon."

Janis cooed at Jackson, who smiled as Dallas grasped two mugs of coffee.

"You staying?" he asked Janis, gesturing with a cup.

She was already waving him off. "No. I better get back to the main house. There's been a lot of excitement lately and it's best if everyone feels like it's still business as usual."

"You sure? I make the best coffee on the ranch," he said persuasively.

She held out a hand and pretended to let it shake. "Already had half a pot. If I drink any more we'll have an earthquake going."

"Keep me posted if anything happens at the main house," Dallas said.

"I have a few appointments scheduled, planning for the Halloween Bash. Should I have them rescheduled, or plan to meet those individuals for lunch in town?" she asked.

"Off property might be best for now," he agreed. "Until we can sort out everything that's happening and be sure everyone's safe."

"I thought you'd say that," she added, as she excused herself and moved to the front door and then looked at

Kate again. "He's an awfully gorgeous baby. Don't you think so, Dallas?"

"As far as babies go, this one's all right," he said with a wink to Kate. He set her coffee mug next to her and looked at mother and child.

Could the three of them, and possibly four, if he was a father, ever be a family?

He'd known Kate Williams for just a few days and was already thinking about a future with her?

That made about as much sense as salting a glass of tea.

Dallas mentally shook off the thought. He'd gone without sleep for two nights and it had him off balance. Plus there were the holidays and the recent news about his parents. He was grateful his ringtone sounded, providing a much-needed distraction.

It was Tommy.

Dallas answered. "I'm putting the call on speaker so Kate can hear."

She looked up from where she sat on the floor playing with Jackson.

"I have news about Susan," his friend said.

"What did you find out?" Dallas moved closer to Kate.

"Your guy was right. She disappeared. As in cleaned out from the system," Tommy revealed.

"What does that mean? A person can't just vanish, can they?" Kate asked, astonished.

"There's only one way I can think of," Dallas said. "Could she have been placed in a witness protection program?"

"It's the only thing that makes sense," Tommy agreed. "I should be able to pull up some record on her, but they just stopped right around the time her baby would have been born. And there's no report of her hospitalization."

"So she knew she'd be going into the program during the pregnancy," Dallas said, realizing that was most likely why she'd wanted to get married. She wanted the baby to have a normal life, and Dallas was the only person capable of protecting her son. Which brought him back to his initial question... Was he the father?

"Seaver's missing. We'll bring him in for more questions as soon as we locate him," Tommy added.

"Wait a minute. I thought you put a tail on him." Dallas took a sip of coffee, needing the jolt of caffeine. If he understood things correctly, finding Susan was a complete dead end. People in the witness protection program didn't randomly show up again. The only way to figure out if he was the father of her child would be a DNA test of the baby, but he had no idea where the little tyke was or whom he was with.

Speaking of Susan, she'd said a few things to him that made Dallas think she must've wanted a normal life for her child, and that was why she'd given him up for adoption. Dallas would bet money that she'd used Harold Matthews at Safe Haven to handle the paperwork for her or handle the adoption without paperwork. Even if Tommy could get a subpoena for Safe Haven's records, which was highly doubtful, that paperwork most likely wouldn't exist. The agency administrators would be smart enough not to keep records for an under-the-table adoption, especially if the Feds were somehow involved.

Seaver must know something about Susan, and that was why he was involved.

Pieces started clicking together in Dallas's mind.

"I have a theory about what might've happened," he said. "Susan was in over her head with someone. This person was involved in illegal activities and she decided to turn state's evidence against him, putting her and her baby's lives in danger. She didn't want that for her son, so she arranged an adoption through Safe Haven."

"Why Safe Haven?" Kate asked. "Why not somewhere far away?"

"She loved this area, grew up here. When she asked me to marry her, she wanted to move back home with the baby. I'm guessing she wanted her son close to her home-town so she could keep an eye on him when she returned at some point later down the road," Dallas theorized.

"Makes sense," Tommy agreed. "She might've given the stipulation to her handler that her son would be al-lowed to grow up in or near Bluff, Texas. If the guy she was involved with found out about the adoption, he could be targeting babies here."

"To get back at her or draw her out of hiding," Dallas finished. The one bright spot in this crazy scenario would be that Susan was alive and doing well in the program.

"There's another possibility worth considering. The bad guy might be the father, and he found out about the baby," Tommy said. "The recent spate of kidnappings could be him or his henchmen looking for his son. There was a child discovered in his carrier in the baby-food aisle of a Piggly Wiggly last night. A DNA test this morning confirmed he was one of the boys abducted from an ad-opted family."

"Which means that all the boys who were kidnapped have been returned home safely?" Dallas said, glanc-ing at Kate.

He wasn't quite ready to let himself off the hook with Susan just yet. Sure, she might've been grasping at straws in telling him he was the father, but there was still a slight chance that it was true. He hoped that she was alive, thriving somewhere else, and that her baby was safe.

"Until we know for sure, I'm going to stay with the assumption that the boy could be mine."

"I understand your position," Tommy said. "And that's fine to think that way. I'm looking at the facts and I have to disagree."

"What's the next step?" Dallas asked. He appreciated his friend's perspective, hoped he was right.

"Locate Seaver. Get him in for questioning and try to trip him up," Tommy replied. "I already sent someone to pick up Harold Matthews. You mentioned before that you knew Susan was seeing someone else when you two dated. Think you can work with a sketch artist to give me a visual of the guy?"

"Yeah, sure."

"I don't like you leaving the ranch, so I'd rather send someone to you with a deputy escort."

"What time do you think you can have someone sent over?" Dallas asked. He had a few things he needed to take care of in the meantime. Top of the list was calling his brothers together for a family meeting.

"I can probably have someone over by lunch," Tommy said.

"Let me know if you get Seaver in for questioning between now and then. I'd like to be on the other side of the glass when he's in the interview room," Dallas said.

Tommy agreed and they ended the call.

"I'd like to go see myself what Seaver has to say," Kate said, holding Jackson. "I just wish there was something to identify him at the scene of Wayne's murder or connect him in some way."

"So do I. Speaking of which, I want to check on Stacy this morning." Something was gnawing at the back of Dallas's mind.

Kate nodded. "I need to check in at work afterward.

Make sure everything's going smoothly at the kitchen. I can't relax, because I have the feeling that I'm dropping the ball somewhere."

"The curse of leading a busy life. It's hard to slow down long enough to notice the roses, let alone stop long enough to smell them," Dallas agreed.

"Do you work all the time when you're not helping strangers?" she asked with a half smile.

Kate was beautiful and her looks had certainly made an impression on Dallas. There was so much more to her. She was kind, genuine and honest to a fault. Intelligent.

There wasn't much she couldn't accomplish if she set her mind to something.

"Do you have any idea how amazing you are?" He kissed her forehead, wishing he could whisk her into the bedroom again. Not an option with the little guy around. Besides, Dallas needed to get his brothers together and then work until the sketch artist arrived.

She rolled her eyes and smiled up at him. "I doubt it."

She'd built a successful company from the ground up. She ran a successful nonprofit while taking care of one of the cutest darn kids Dallas had ever set eyes on.

He had a hard time believing that she could feel inadequate in any way.

If he had to describe her in one word it would be… *remarkable.*

"You're kidding me, right?" he asked.

"Growing up in my childhood home didn't inspire a lot of confidence." She rolled her shoulders in a shrug.

"Then I wish you could see the person I see when I look at you." And Dallas needed to figure out how she fit into his life when this was all over.

Chapter Fifteen

Kate made a few calls to check on work and then spent the balance of the morning playing with her son. She had always believed that she needed work to keep her busy, to feel fulfilled, and was surprised to realize that being with Jackson was enough.

Maybe once she got her donor base full, she'd consider cutting back to working half-time. She couldn't imagine stopping altogether. Being a mother was incredibly rewarding, but feeding people filled another part of her heart.

The one thing she'd realized when she'd cashed out of her start-up was that wearing the best clothes or paying two hundred dollars to have her hair colored and cut did nothing to refill the well. Did she enjoy looking good? Of course. She still thought it was important to feel great in what she wore and how she took care of herself. But she'd figured out that she could still look pretty amazing with just the right color sweater. And a ponytail and pair of sweats were all she needed to impress the little man she was holding. Jackson didn't even care if her socks matched, which some days they probably didn't since he'd come into her life.

Her work at the kitchen was important. It felt good to

make sure people were fed, to know she was making a difference for others on a most basic level.

Then there were other feelings she was having a harder time getting under control, feelings for Dallas O'Brien.

The rich cowboy was smart, handsome and successful. And he did things to her body that no man before him had come close to achieving.

It was more than great sex with Dallas. There was a closeness she felt with him that she'd never experienced with anyone else.

And yet a nagging question persisted. What did she really know about him?

Like what was his favorite color? Was he a lazy Sunday morning person or did he get up early and go out for a jog? When did he have time to work out between running the ranch and taking care of his business in New Mexico? A body like his said he must put in serious time at the gym. Heck, she didn't even know his favorite meal, dessert or alcoholic beverage.

All the little details about each other that added up to true intimacy were missing.

The one thing she knew for certain was that if she was in trouble, then he was the guy she wanted standing beside her. Dallas O'Brien had her back. And he was capable of handling himself in every situation.

Kate placed Jackson on his belly on the blanket Dallas had spread out on the wood floor. The few toys Janis had brought were keeping her son entertained.

And she wondered how long she could keep him safe like this.

The reality of their situation hit fast and hard, like lightning on a sunny day. They were in hiding in a near stranger's house. Her mind argued that she and Dallas couldn't possibly be strangers anymore, but she pushed logic aside.

She focused on her boy, shuddering at the thought someone could want to take him from her. Rather than give in to that fear, she sipped her coffee.

There were so many facts and theories rolling around in her head. If what they'd talked about earlier was true, then she had to consider the possibility that Jackson's father was a criminal. She wouldn't love her son any less either way, but that would complicate their lives, given that this criminal seemed intent on finding his son.

If he found Jackson, and Jackson turned out to be his, she wouldn't have to worry about courts and judges, because this guy could take Jackson and make a run out of the country. He'd eluded law enforcement so far.

Kate's chest squeezed as she thought about the possibilities.

There was another option. Dallas could be Jackson's biological father. That thought didn't startle her as much as it probably should.

"Don't do that to yourself." Dallas's voice startled her out of the dark place she'd gone.

"You scared me," she said, avoiding the topic.

"Sorry. The deputy and sketch artist are on their way here." He sauntered across the room toward the kitchen with his coffee mug in hand and Kate couldn't help but admire his athletic grace. She also thought about what he looked like naked and that sent a different kind of shiver down her back.

"Don't get tied up with what-ifs," Dallas said, pouring a fresh cup of coffee. He held up the pot. "Want more?"

She shook her head.

"It's hard." She looked at Jackson. He was such a

happy baby and her heart hurt at the thought of him being taken away, let alone never seeing him again.

"My mother used to tell me that it was her job to worry," Dallas said.

"Then I'm overqualified," Kate quipped.

He smiled and it was like a hundred candles lit up inside her.

"It would be impossible not to worry under the circumstances," he conceded. "And I think it comes with the territory of parenting."

She locked on to his gaze. "I can't lose him."

"If I have anything to say about it, you won't." The sincerity in his voice soothed her more than she should allow, because nothing about their current situation said that Dallas could protect them forever.

There was a comfort in being with him that she'd never known with anyone else. "How's work? I can't help but feel we're keeping you from your own life," she said, trying to redirect her thoughts.

Dallas eyed her for a minute before he spoke. "It's no trouble. I have everything covered here and in New Mexico."

"I appreciate all you're doing for us," she said, stiffening her back. "In case I haven't told you that lately."

"Don't do that. Don't bring up a wall between us." Hurt registered in his dark eyes.

"I'm sorry. I just don't know how to deal with this," she said, her gaze focused on the patch of floor in front of her. Feeling a sudden chill, she rubbed her arms.

"How about we take it one day at a time," he suggested. He covered well, but she detected a note of disappointment in his voice.

The last thing Kate wanted to do was hurt the one man helping her. The emotions she felt for Dallas confused her, and even though it made no sense, they felt far more dangerous than anything else they faced.

"I don't know if I can do that," she admitted.

"Will you at least tell me why not?"

"I'm scared."

"Then let's not overthink whatever's happening between us," Dallas said, moving to her and then kissing her forehead.

She smiled up at him, which wasn't the same as agreement, and his heart stuttered.

His cell phone buzzed. He fished it out of his pocket and answered, deciding the two of them needed to have a sit-down when this mess was all over to talk about a future. Dallas had no idea what that meant exactly, but he wanted Kate and Jackson in his life.

After saying a few "uh-huh"s into the phone, he ended the call.

"Doc's here," he said, moving to the front door.

He opened it before she could knock. Dallas was ready to get an answer to at least one of his questions.

After introductions were made, he asked, "What do you need from me to get the ball rolling?"

Dr. McConnell smiled, winked and set down her bag. "A swab on the inside of your cheek should do the trick."

Kate brought Jackson over, sat on the couch and then put him on her lap for easier access. She dropped his toy at least three times before the doctor managed to obtain his swab.

"How long before you'll get the results?" Dallas asked, mostly wanting to ease Kate's concern.

"I'll walk this into the lab myself as soon as I leave here," Dr. McConnell said as she secured the samples. "So I should have news tomorrow around this time."

Kate's eyes grew wide and then she refocused on her son. Dallas could almost feel the panic welling inside her.

"Thank you for taking care of this personally," he said, standing to offer a handshake.

"You're not getting away that easily," Dr. McConnell said, pulling him in for a hug. She and his mother had been close friends. "I said it before, but I'm sorry about your folks. I miss my friends every day."

"Same here," Dallas said, appreciating the sentiment. "There's something I need to tell you before you go."

She looked up at him.

"It'll be in the news soon enough, even though Tommy is doing his level best to suppress the story, and I told my brothers this morning," Dallas said. "I thought you should know before everyone else."

"What is it, Dallas?"

"The toxicology results came back with a suspicious substance, cyanide. Mother and Pop were poisoned," he said.

It looked as though the doctor needed a minute to let that information sink in.

"That would explain your father's heart attack. He was in excellent physical condition and I couldn't shake the feeling that something was off about him having a heart attack while driving." Dr. McConnell touched his arm and drew in a deep breath. "I'm so sorry."

"Me, too."

"Why? How?" Her voice was soft. Tears streamed down her face. "They were such good people. I can't imagine anyone wanting to hurt your parents. Is there any chance the substance was accidentally ingested?"

"That's the question of the day." Dallas brought her in for another hug. "No matter what, I pledge to get to the bottom of this. If someone killed my parents, then I won't rest until they pay for what they did."

"I'd like to have the poison expert at my hospital take a look at the report. Give another opinion." Dr. McConnell wiped away her tears and straightened her rounded shoulders.

"Any additional eyes we can get on the case, the better," Dallas said. "Any help you can give is much appreciated."

"This happened the day after the art auction," she said. "So they were around a lot of people that night and the next day."

"If they were murdered, we'll find the SOB," he said, his mind already clicking through possibilities. He'd have Tommy request all the pictures taken that night so he could figure out exactly who had attended the party. The guest list would be easy enough to locate and there'd be dozens of others—waiters, bartenders and cooks.

There was a professional photographer hired for the party, as well as Harper Smith from the society page of the local newspaper.

"I can't think of one person who would want to hurt your parents," Dr. McConnell said, still in disbelief.

"Me, either," Dallas stated.

She took a breath, pursed her lips and nodded. "If I can be of any help, you know my number."

"I won't hesitate," Dallas said.

She hugged him again before taking up her bag and saying goodbye to Kate. Stopped at the door, she shifted her gaze from Kate to Dallas. "I hope everything works out the way it's supposed to."

Dallas saw the doctor out, then turned to Kate. "Are you doing okay?"

Her shoulders sagged and sadness was written in the lines of her face. "I didn't know about your parents."

"I just found out yesterday. I'm still trying to process the news."

"From Tommy?" Kate seemed hurt that he hadn't shared the information with her sooner.

Dallas moved to her side and sat down next to her, ignoring the heat where his thigh pressed against hers. "The only reason I didn't bring it up last night was because there was so much else going on."

"It's okay, Dallas. You don't have to tell me anything," she said, trying to mask her pain and put on a brave face.

"I'd planned to tell you, but with everything else happening I was trying to process the news myself and then tell my brothers. I overloaded last night, and being with you was the only thing keeping me sane."

He leaned forward and pressed his forehead to hers. "I just hope you can understand."

She didn't say anything right away. She just breathed.

"I do," she murmured at last, and Dallas finally exhaled.

The deputy and sketch artist stopped by next. It took Dallas only fifteen minutes with the artist for him to capture the image in Dallas's mind. He thanked them before walking them both out.

For the next hour, Dallas played with Jackson on the floor alongside Kate. He sensed that her nerves were on edge.

"I wasn't expecting to feel this stressed about the test," she finally admitted.

"One phone call is all it takes to make it go away, if you don't want this to go any further," Dallas said.

"Between you and some random criminal being Jackson's father, I'm hoping it's you," she said.

"That's quite an endorsement," he responded, and he couldn't help but laugh despite all the heaviness inside him.

Kate joined him, a much-needed release of nervous tension for both of them, despite the tragic circumstances.

"Well, if I have to have a child out there, this little guy isn't a bad one to have," Dallas said. "You hungry?"

"Starving," she said. "I need to feed Jackson and put him down for a nap first."

"What sounds good?" Dallas asked, ignoring her comment. He might not be able to take care of Jackson on his own, but he could order lunch.

"A hamburger and fries," she said, making a little mewling sound.

Dallas remembered hearing a similar one earlier that morning while they'd made love. He cracked a smile, thinking how much he'd like to hear it again.

EARLY THE NEXT MORNING, the door to the guest room opened a crack. Kate pushed up to a sitting position, careful not to wake Jackson.

"Thought you'd want to know that Stacy's going home this morning," he said in a whisper.

"That's great news," Kate said. "Or maybe not. I'm worried about her being home alone."

"I'm sending Reece to stay with her just until this case is resolved," he said, and then his expression sobered. "I got a text from Tommy that Seaver has been picked up and is being brought into the station. From what I've been told, he's not real happy about it. Janis is on her way over to stay with the baby. I'll put on a pot of coffee."

Kate kissed her son, got dressed and met Dallas in the kitchen.

He walked up to her, gaze locked on hers, cradled her neck with his right hand and pressed a kiss to her lips.

"There," he said, after pulling back. "That's a better way to start the day."

"I couldn't agree more," she said, smiling. "I missed you last night."

He kissed the corners of her mouth as a soft knock sounded at the door.

"I'll get the coffee." Kate had already noticed the travel mugs on the counter.

Dallas opened the door for Janis.

"Is my baby sleeping?" she asked.

"Yes. But probably not for much longer." Kate filled mugs and brought them with her into the living room.

"Then I'll read quietly. Is he in the guest room?"

Dallas nodded as he took his mug from Kate. "Ready?"

"Let's do this," she said.

"We'll take my brother's Jeep. Colin drove it over this morning for us," Dallas said.

He had a big family. She'd met Tyler so far. She wanted to get to know the others, too.

As she said goodbye to her son and hauled herself into the Jeep, Kate wondered what it must've been like growing up in such a large family. It had been only she and Carter as children. Maybe that was why his recent closeness with their mother seemed like such a betrayal.

Dust kicked up on the road, which was barely visible in the predawn light.

"We're going to exit on the east side of the ranch, near Colin's place. He's similar in height and build, so I'm hoping no one will recognize me. You might want to get in the backseat and lie on your side until we clear the area safely."

Kate unbuckled her seat belt and climbed into the rear. "Tell me when to duck."

...Susan's child."...

Chapter Sixteen

The ride to the sheriff's office went off without a hitch. Dallas's plan to throw off whoever might be watching by switching vehicles seemed to be working, and Kate finally breathed a sigh of relief when they pulled into the parking lot.

Facing Seaver had her nerves on edge, knowing he was somehow involved if not completely behind the abduction attempt.

Tommy met them as soon as they walked through the door. "He's confessed to everything," he said.

"What?" Kate could hardly believe what she was hearing.

"We're making arrangements for Seaver to turn state's evidence against Raphael Manuel," the lawman added, ushering them into his office. "Manuel was Susan's boyfriend. We connected him using the sketch you gave us yesterday.

"The man you identified is a known criminal who's wanted for murder in New Mexico and Texas. And Seaver confessed that he happens to be the father of Susan's child."

Kate's head spun as she tried to wrap her mind around the information coming at her at what felt like a hundred miles an hour. It occurred to her that while Dallas was in the clear, her son's situation still hung in the balance. Susan and this man could be Jackson's parents.

"You know this for certain?" Dallas asked.

"One hundred percent," his friend declared. "There's no way you fathered Susan's child."

The paternity-test results would prove that, but Dallas was relieved not to have to wait. "What about Susan?"

"Found out from the marshal who will handle Seaver that she is safe and tucked far away until the trial," Tommy said. "She broke off her relationship with Manuel after she caught him engaging in criminal activity, and made a desperate call to you. The Feds have been building a case ever since. With her and Seaver's testimony, Manuel will go away for a long time."

"How is Seaver involved?" Dallas asked.

"Manuel had his henchmen kidnap babies, but he learned from Harold Matthews that some of the adoptions were kept off the books at Safe Haven. Manuel tracked several to Seaver and threatened to kill the lawyer's family if he didn't help locate his son."

"And he had worked with me and Jackson," Kate said quietly.

Both men nodded.

"Which accounts for the change in MO," Dallas said.

"Seaver is deathly afraid of guns and he didn't want to take the chance that someone would get killed. The assignment was to take the babies and test them, not hurt them or their mothers," Tommy explained.

"So, Seaver arranged Jackson's abduction," Dallas said.

"And admitted to setting up Allen to throw us off the trail," Tommy stated.

"Which almost worked," Kate mused.

"Where's Manuel?" Dallas asked.

"We don't know. The marshal is processing a warrant right now so they can pick him up."

"They have to locate him first," Dallas said.

Tommy's cell buzzed. "Hold on. I need to take this."

Dallas's arms were around Kate, and for the first time in a long time, she felt a glimmer of hope.

And then Tommy looked at her with an apologetic expression. Her stomach dropped.

"Manuel must've followed Seaver's trail to your brother. Carter has been abducted."

"What?" Kate's heart sank. This could not be happening. She'd spoken to him just yesterday. Carter had to be fine.

The only thing keeping her upright was Dallas's arms around her. Her head spun and she could barely hear the quiet reassurances he whispered in her ear.

"We have to find him," she said, her knees almost giving out.

"They want Jackson," Dallas said, holding her tight. "They won't hurt Carter." His words wrapped around her, kept her from succumbing to the absolute panic threatening to take her under.

She gasped. "My phone. What if Carter tried to call? I have to get to my phone."

"Where is it?" Dallas asked.

"In the diaper bag at the ranch." Hold on. She could check her messages from anywhere.

Dallas must've realized what she was thinking, because he made a move for his own cell. "Try this."

She put the call on speaker.

Carter's voice boomed into the room. "Kate, don't do anything rash. He wants Jackson."

A male voice she didn't recognize urged Carter to tell the truth.

Her brother hesitated. "He says he'll kill me if you don't deliver Jackson to one of his men."

The line went dead.

The automatic message system indicated that the call had come in at four o'clock that morning.

"Can you trace it?" Kate asked Tommy.

"We'll do our best. Manuel most likely has a program to scramble his signal, though," the lawman conceded.

"They're somewhere local," Dallas said. "Manuel would have brought Carter here."

"What makes you so sure?" Tommy asked.

"This guy is desperate to find his son and he's narrowed his search down to this area. I'm sure Morton told him about the other local adoptions," Dallas said. "A man who goes to these lengths to find his boy would want to be right here."

Tommy nodded. "Good point. I'll check in with local motels."

Dallas held his hand up. "I might already know where he'll be."

"Morton's house." Kate gasped. "Stacy."

"Reece is with her. He's very good at his job. She'll be fine," Dallas said, his thumbs moving on the keyboard of his phone. "I just asked him to call me."

Kate immediately realized that Dallas wouldn't want Reece's cell tones to give him away, or he would have phoned the security agent himself.

Her heart pounded against her ribs.

Dallas pointed toward the landline. "Call your mother. Tell her to get out of the house and not come back until we say it's safe."

Kate did, unsure what kind of reception she'd get.

Her mother picked up on the first ring.

"Mom, it's Kate. I need you to listen carefully. Go next door and stay there until I call."

Her mother must have grasped the panic in Kate's tone because she stuttered an agreement. "What is it, Kate? What's going on?" she finally asked.

"I need you to go now. I'll explain later."

"All right," she said tentatively. "I'll wait next door until I hear from you."

"Tell Dad to be careful, too. He should stay at the office until I give the all clear."

"I'm worried. Are you and the baby okay?" It was the first time her mother had asked about Jackson.

"We're good, Mom. I'll explain everything when I can. Just go, and be careful, okay?" Tears streamed down Kate's face. She and her mother had had their difficulties, but she couldn't stand to think of anything awful happening to her.

"I will. I love you, Kate. And I'm sorry. If anything happens to me I need you to know that."

"Me, too, Mom. And I love you." Kate held in a sob, promising herself that she'd stay strong. "Call my cell when you get to the neighbor's and leave a message. Let me know you got there safely."

Kate's cell was at the ranch, but she could check the message when she retrieved it or call voice mail again using Dallas's cell.

"Okay. Take care of yourself." Her mother paused. "And give Jackson a kiss from Grandma."

Kate had wanted to hear those words from her mother for months. She promised she would do as asked, then ended the call.

Thankfully, her parents were safe. At least for now.

Dallas was urging her toward the exit as soon as she hung up.

"Any chance I can talk you out of walking through that door?" Tommy asked.

Dallas stopped at the jamb and turned.

"I didn't think so," his friend said. "Okay, fine. But we're going in with my tactical unit."

"I'm dropping Kate off at the ranch first," Dallas stated.

"They might hurt her brother if they don't see her." Tommy looked from Dallas to Kate.

"You can't take me back there. Not when my brother needs me," she declared.

Dallas's jaw clenched and every muscle in his body was obviously strung tight. "They're going to want to see a baby."

Tommy called down the hall and a deputy showed up a few seconds later cradling something in his arms.

The plastic baby looked real from a distance. Kate took it from the deputy. "He sees me with this and he'll assume it's Jackson."

"I won't use you as bait," Dallas muttered.

"Neither will I, but I want her in the car nearby," Tommy said, before she could argue.

"We brought Colin's Jeep. I'll let my brothers know what's going on," Dallas said.

"This one needs to stay quiet," Tommy said. "There's no one I trust more than your family, but we're taking enough of a risk as it is."

Tommy called in his unit. "Kate will be in the Jeep with Dallas, here." He pointed to a spot on the Google map he'd pulled up on his computer screen. "We'll come in from around the sides while she makes contact. Our perp will be watching the front and back doors, so we're looking at side windows."

Kate glanced at Dallas, not bothering to hide her panic. "We have to get there before Stacy and Reece do."

"I know." But the expression in Dallas's eyes said it was probably already too late.

Very little was said between Dallas and Kate on the ride over. He had agreed to give Tommy's men a ten-minute head start, which wasn't much time.

Kate regretted having this go down on such a quiet suburban street. It was afternoon, but thankfully a weekend, and she hoped the cold and nearness to the holiday would keep everyone inside.

The sun peeked out from battleship-gray clouds as they approached.

"That's Reece's car," Dallas said. "But this is good. If they surprised him then we'll have someone on the inside. If I know Reece, he's already planning an escape route, and he'll keep Stacy safe."

"She's been through so much already," Kate said under her breath, hating that so much bad could strike such a good person all at once. Stacy must be terrified.

Kate cradled the pretend baby in her arms, making sure anyone watching could see. The look of panic on her face was real.

Dallas eased down the quiet road and then parked across the street from Morton's house, just as they'd planned.

The porch light flickered on and off a couple of times.

"They're signaling," Dallas said.

"What do we do now?" Kate asked.

"We wait."

But they didn't have to sit for long. There was a loud boom inside the house and smoke billowed out one of the windows.

"Stacy's in there," Kate said, her hand already on the door release.

Dallas stopped her. "We have to let Tommy do his job."

"We can't just sit here," she argued.

Dallas's door opened just then and the barrel of a gun was pressed to the back of his head.

The noise inside the house, the smoke, must have been meant to be a distraction while Manuel grabbed his son.

"I'll take that baby," a male voice said, and it had to be Manuel, based on the sketch Dallas had provided.

Kate pulled the plastic baby to her chest to shield its face from the man. If he got a good look, he'd shoot. "I'll come with you."

She made a move toward the door handle, and at the same time, Dallas jerked the guy's arm in front of him, pinning it against the steering wheel. A shot sounded and Kate's heart lurched.

"Run, Kate," Dallas cried, wrestling the gun out of Manuel's hand.

Dallas must've been putting a ton of pressure on the guy's arm, based on the look on his face.

Kate bolted. She ran straight to the house, flung open the door and shouted, "He's out front!"

Another crack of gunfire sent her stomach swirling. *Dallas.*

Tommy ran out the door toward her.

By the time the two of them reached Dallas, he had Manuel facedown and was sitting on his back while twisting his right arm behind him.

The criminal was spewing curse words.

Tommy dropped his knee into Manuel's back as he wrangled with flex-cuffs. Kate frantically searched for the gun and noticed, as Dallas turned, that he had blood on his stomach.

"Dallas," she cried with a shocked sob.

His gaze followed hers and he pressed his hand against his abdomen.

Tommy was already calling for an ambulance as Dallas lost consciousness. He slumped over onto his side as Kate dropped to her knees, unaware that she was still clutching the plastic doll.

It took ten minutes for the EMTs to arrive. Kate was vaguely aware of Stacy and Reece comforting her.

Reece drove her to the hospital behind the ambulance in his SUV. Being told that the kidnappers had been arrested did nothing to settle Kate's nerves, not while Dallas was in trouble.

She could see the gurney Dallas was on as it rolled into the emergency entrance. She asked Reece to stop, bolted out of the SUV and rushed forward.

One of the EMTs turned around. "Are you Kate Williams?"

Her heart clutched. "Yes."

"Good. Will you come see this guy? He hasn't stopped talking about you since he opened his eyes in the ambulance."

Kate nodded, tears streaming down her cheeks as she ran toward Dallas.

She had never been so happy as when he looked at her and said, "We did it. Jackson's safe."

"I love you!" It was all she could manage to say before he squeezed her hand and was wheeled away.

"TEST RESULTS ARE IN," Dallas said as he entered the room, his hand fisted around something that Kate couldn't readily make out.

"You shouldn't be out of bed," she fussed. "The doctor won't be happy when she hears about this."

He'd been a trying patient at best since Dr. McConnell agreed to let him recuperate at home.

"Well, if you aren't the least bit curious, then I'll head back to our room," he said, turning.

"Dallas O'Brien, you better stop where you are," Kate muttered.

He did. "Good to know you have that 'mom voice' perfected," he teased. "We already knew I wasn't Jackson's biological father," he continued. "Manuel is."

"Which means he's Susan's child," Kate said. "What if she wants him back now that this is all over?"

"She doesn't," Dallas said. "Said he would remind her too much of her mistakes. All she ever wanted was for him to be brought up in Bluff by a loving family. He's your son and Susan has no intention of trying to change that."

Relief flooded Kate hearing those words. The child of her heart was hers to keep.

"I heard you on the phone earlier with your mother," Dallas said.

"She's making a real effort," Kate said, beaming up at him. "Once you're well, I'd like to invite her and Dad over for dinner."

"I think that's a great idea," he said. "And what about Carter?"

"It'll be tough to drag him away from his company, but I'm determined to spend more time with family."

"About that." Dallas kissed Kate as he struggled to bend forward. He set a small package next to her. "Christmas is a couple of months away."

"The doctor said to take it easy," she warned.

"And what's my punishment if I don't?" He winked.

"An even longer wait before we resume any more adult-only playtime," she teased.

Dallas laughed it off and grunted as he managed to sit down next to her. He made a face at Jackson, who cooed in response, causing her heart to swell.

Kate stared at the roughly two-by-two-inch Tiffany Blue Box beside her.

She opened her mouth to speak, but was hushed by Dallas.

"I know what you're thinking. You don't want to rush, because you think we need to get to know each other better," he said. "I disagree, because I know everything I need to know about you. I intend to spend the rest of our lives together bringing up this boy, our boy. I don't need a test to prove he's my son. He's yours and that's good enough for me."

Tears welled in Kate's eyes. More than anything, she wanted to say yes. Everything in her heart said this was right. "So before you say anything, here's the deal. I love you, Kate. I want to spend the rest of my life with you and Jackson. And that's all I need you to know for now. Sometime before the end of next year, I plan to ask a very important question, but the only thing I'm asking today is…will a year be enough time for you to feel like you really know me?"

"Yes." Happy tears streamed down her cheeks.

"Then hold on to that box as a promise from me," Dallas said. "When you finally do feel like you know me well enough, I want the three of us to be a family. I love you, Kate. And I want you to be my wife."

All Kate could do in answer was kiss the man she loved.

* * * * *

Kendall's scream pierced the still night and turned the blood in Coop's veins to ice.

Coop had already been making his way back down the drive when he'd heard Kendall's truck coming back to the house. Now his boots grappled for purchase against the soggy leaves on the walkway as he ran toward Kendall.

"What is it? What's wrong?" By the time he reached her, he was panting as if he'd just run a marathon.

She'd stumbled back from the truck and stood staring at the tailgate with wide, glassy eyes. Raising her arm, she pointed to the truck with her cell phone. She worked her jaw but couldn't form any words—no coherent words, anyway.

He pried the phone from her stiff fingers, aimed the light at the truck bed and jumped onto the bumper. The phone illuminated a light-colored tarp with something rolled up in it.

"I-it's a body."

SINGLE FATHER SHERIFF

BY
CAROL ERICSON

First Published in Great Britain 2016
By Mills & Boon, an imprint of HarperCollins*Publishers*
1 London Bridge Street, London, SE1 9GF

© 2016 Carol Ericson

ISBN: 978-0-263-91913-4

46-0816

Our policy is to use papers that are natural, renewable and recyclable products and made from wood grown in sustainable forests. The logging and manufacturing processes conform to the legal environmental regulations of the country of origin.

Printed and bound in Spain
by CPI, Barcelona

Carol Ericson is a bestselling, award-winning author of more than forty books. She has an eerie fascination for true-crime stories, a love of film noir and a weakness for reality TV, all of which fuel her imagination to create her own tales of murder, mayhem and mystery. To find out more about Carol and her current projects, please visit her website at www.carolericson.com, "where romance flirts with danger."

To my sister Janice, my cheerleader

Chapter One

"Let go of my sister." The little girl with the dark pigtails scrunched up her face and stomped on the masked stranger's foot.

He reached out one hand and squeezed her shoulder, but she twisted out of his grasp and renewed her assault on him, pummeling his thigh with her tiny fists.

The monster growled and swatted at the little girl, knocking her to the floor. "You're too much damned trouble."

As he backed up toward the door, carrying her sleeping twin over one shoulder, the girl lunged at his legs. "Put her down!"

With his free hand, the stranger clamped down on the top of her head, digging his fingers into her scalp, holding her at bay. As he gave one last push, he yanked off the pink ribbon tied around one of her pigtails and left her sprawled on the floor.

She scrambled to her knees, rubbing the back of her head. Whatever happened, she couldn't let the man take Kayla out that door. She crawled toward his legs once more.

"Your parents are gonna wish I took you instead of this one." Then he kicked her in the face and everything went black.

KENDALL RAN A HAND across her jaw as she dropped to her knees in front of the door. "I'm sorry, Kayla. I'm sorry I couldn't save you."

Common sense and her therapist's assertion that a five-year-old couldn't have done much against a full-grown man intent on kidnapping her twin were no match for twenty-five years of guilt.

Kendall leaned forward, touching her forehead to the hardwood floor. She'd relegated the trauma of that event to her past, stuffed it down, shoved it into the dark corner where it belonged. Now someone in Timberline was bringing it all back and that sheriff expected her to help in the investigation of a new set of kidnappings.

If she could help, she would've done something twenty-five years ago to bring her sister home. Her heart broke for the two families torn apart by the same torment that destroyed her own family but she couldn't save them, and that sheriff would have to look elsewhere for help solving the crimes.

She'd come back to Timberline to sell her aunt's house—nothing more, nothing less. It just so happened that her aunt's house was the same house where she'd spent many days as a child, the same house from which someone abducted her twin sister and had knocked her out cold.

Raising her head, she zeroed in on the front door. She could picture it all again—the stranger with the ski mask, her sleeping sister thrown over one of his shoulders. Much of what followed had been a blur of hysterical parents, soft-spoken police officers, sleepless nights and bad dreams.

She still had the bad dreams.

Someone knocked on the door, and her muscles tensed as she wedged her fingers against the wood floor like a runner ready to shoot out of the blocks.

"Who's there?"

"It's Wyatt, Wyatt Carson."

Her thundering heartbeat slowed only a fraction when she heard Wyatt's voice. If she was looking for someone to bring her out of the throes of these unpleasant memories, it wasn't Wyatt.

Clearing her throat, she lumbered to her feet. "Hold on, Wyatt."

She brushed the dust from her knees and pushed the hair back from her face. Squaring her shoulders, she pasted on a smile. Then she swung open the door to greet the last man she wanted to see right now.

"Hey, Wyatt. How'd you know I was back?"

"Kendall." He swooped in for a hug, engulfing her in flannel and the tingly scent of pine. "You know Timberline. Word travels fast."

"Supersonic." She mumbled her words into his shoulder since he still held her fast. She stiffened, arching her back, and he got the hint.

When he released her, she shoved her hands in her pockets and smiled up at him. "I just arrived yesterday and took one trip to the grocery store."

He snapped his fingers. "That must've been it. I heard you were back when I was getting coffee at Common Grounds this morning."

"Come on in." She stepped back from the door. "How have you been? Still the town's best plumber?"

"One of the town's only plumbers." He puffed up his chest anyway.

"Do you want something to drink?" She held her breath, hoping he'd say no.

"Sure, a can of pop if you have it."

"I do." She moved past him to go into the kitchen. She ducked into the refrigerator and grabbed a can of soda. "Do you want a glass?"

She cocked her head, waiting for an answer from the other room. "Wyatt?"

"Yeah?"

She jumped, the wet can slipping from her hand and bouncing on the linoleum floor. Wyatt moved silently for a big man.

"Sorry." He pushed off of the doorjamb and crowded into the small kitchen space.

Before she could recover her breath, he crouched down and snagged the can. "Do you have another? I don't want to spray the kitchen with pop."

She tugged on the fridge door and swept another can from the shelf.

He exchanged cans with her. "You're jumpy. Is it this house?"

Her gaze met his dark brown eyes, luminous in the pasty pallor of his face—a sure sign of a Timberline native.

Ducking back into the fridge, she shoved the dented can toward the back of the shelf.

"You just startled me, Wyatt. I'm not reliving any memories." She waved her arm around the kitchen to deflect attention from her lie. "This is just a house, not a living, breathing entity."

"I'm surprised you'd have that outlook, Kendall." He snapped the tab on his can of soda and slurped the fizzy liquid from the rim. "I mean, since you're a psychiatrist."

"I'm a psychologist, not a psychiatrist."

"Whatever. Don't you dig into people's memories? Pick their brains? Find out what makes them tick?"

"It doesn't work that way, Wyatt. You get out of therapy what you put into it. My clients pick their own brains. I'm just there to facilitate."

"Wish plumbing worked that way." He slapped the thigh of his denims and took another gulp of his soda. "Seriously, if you ever want to talk about what happened twenty-five years ago, I'm your man."

"I think we've talked it all out by now, don't you?"

"But you and me—" he wagged his finger back and forth between them "—never really talked about it—not when we were kids right after it happened and not as adults."

Folding her arms, she leaned against the kitchen counter. "Do you need to talk about it? Have you ever seen a therapist?"

He held up his hands, his callous palms facing her. "I'm not asking for a freebie or anything, Kendall."

A warm flush invaded her cheeks, and she swiped a damp sponge across the countertop. "I didn't think you were, but if you're interested in seeing someone I can do a little research and find a good therapist in the area for you."

"Nah, I'm good. I just thought..." He shrugged his shoulders. "You know, you and me, since we both went through the same thing. You lost your sister and I lost my brother to the same kidnapper. We just never really discussed our feelings with each other."

Years ago she'd vomited up these feelings to her own therapist until she'd emptied her gut, and she had no intention of dredging them up again with Wyatt Carson... or with anyone.

"It happened. I was sad, and we all moved on." She brushed her fingertips along the soft flannel of his shirt-sleeve. "If you need—if you want more closure, my offer stands. I can vet some therapists in the area for you."

He downed the rest of his drink and crushed the can in his hand. "Don't tell me you don't know what's going on, Kendall."

"I know." She took a deep breath. "Two children have been kidnapped."

"I moved on, too." He toyed with the tab on his can until he twisted it off. "I had it all packed away—until this. I just figured that's why you came back."

"N-no. Aunt Cass left this house to me when she passed, and I'm here to settle her things and sell the property."

"Aunt Cass passed away ten months ago."

"You know, probate, legal stuff." She flicked her fingers in the air. "All that had to get sorted out, and I had a few work obligations to handle first."

"If you say so." He held up the mangled can. "Trash?"

"Recycle bin in here." She tapped the cupboard under the sink with her toe.

He tossed the can into the plastic bin and shoved his hands into his pockets. "You know, you might not be able to slip in and out of Timberline so easy."

"What does that mean?"

"There's a new sheriff in town—literally, or at least new to you. He's actually been here about five years." Wyatt tapped the side of his head. "He's been picking my brain, and I'm pretty sure he's gonna want to pick yours, too, once he knows you're back."

Her heart flip-flopped. "I'd heard that from someone else—that he wanted to talk to me."

"Timberline's still a small town, even with Evergreen Software going in. Coop must've heard you were back already."

"Coop?"

"Sheriff Cooper Sloane. He moved here about five years ago."

"Yeah, you said that. Isn't the FBI involved?"

"As far as I heard they were. I think they set up operations just outside of Timberline. There are a couple of agents out here poking around, setting up taps on the families' phones, waiting for ransom instructions."

Kendall pressed her spine against the counter, trying to stop the shiver snaking up her back. There had been no ransom demands twenty-five years ago for the Timberline

Trio—the three children who'd been kidnapped. Would there be any now?

"Anything?"

"Not yet and it's already been almost three weeks." Wyatt scratched his chin. "That's one of the reasons Coop's so interested in talking to all the players from the past. He sees some similarities in the cases, but the FBI agents aren't all that interested in what happened twenty-five years ago."

"Well, I'm not going to be much help." She pushed off the counter. "But I do need to get back to work if I hope to get this place on the market."

"Don't worry. I'm outta here." Wyatt exited the small kitchen and stood in the middle of the living room with his hands on his hips, surveying the room as if he could see the ghosts that still lingered. "If you ever want to talk, you know where to find me."

"I appreciate that, Wyatt." She took two steps into the room and gave the big man a hug, assuaging the pangs of guilt she had over her uncharitable thoughts about him. Had he sensed her reluctance to talk to him? She squeezed harder.

"Take care, Wyatt. Maybe we'll catch up a little more over lunch while I'm here."

"I'd like that." He broke their clinch. "Now I'd better head over to the police station."

As much practice as she'd had schooling her face into a bland facade for her clients, she must've revealed her uneasiness to Wyatt.

His dark eyebrows jumped to his hairline. "This is just a plumbing job, not an interrogation."

"Honestly, Wyatt, what you plan to do is your business." She smoothed her hands over her face. "I'd rather leave it in the past."

"I hear ya." He saluted. "Let's have that lunch real soon."

She closed the door behind him and touched her forehead to the doorjamb. Wyatt didn't even have to be an amateur psychologist to figure out she was protesting way too much.

She'd need a supersize session with her own therapist once she left this rain-soaked place and returned to Phoenix.

Taking a deep breath, she brushed her hands together and grabbed an empty box. She stationed herself in front of the cabinet shelf that sported a stack of newspapers.

She dusted each item in her aunt's collection before wrapping it in a scrap of newspaper and placing it in the box. She'd have an estate sale first, maybe sell some of the stuff online and then pack up the rest and take it home with her. She studied a mermaid carved from teak, running her fingertip along the smooth flip of hair. Her nose tingled and she swiped the back of her hand across it.

Kayla had loved playing mermaids, and Kendall had humored her twin by playing with her even though she'd have rather been catching frogs at the river or riding her bike along the dirt paths crisscrossing the forest.

She'd been the tomboy, the tough twin—the twin who'd survived.

She rolled the mermaid into an ad for discount prescription drugs and tucked it into the box at her feet. Thirty minutes later, she sprayed some furniture polish on a rag and swiped it across the empty shelves of the cabinet. One down, two to go.

The round metal handle on the drawer clinked and Kendall groaned. Most likely, Aunt Cass had more stuff crammed into the drawer.

She curled her fingers around the handle and tugged it open. She blew out a breath—papers, not figurines.

Grabbing a handful, she held the papers up to the light. Bills and receipts. Probably of no use to anyone now.

She ducked and grabbed the plastic garbage bag, already half-full of junk she'd pulled from her aunt's desk. She dropped the papers in the bag, without even looking at them, and reached for another batch.

A flash of color amid all the black and white caught her eye, and her fingers scurried to the back of the drawer to retrieve the item. She tugged on a silky piece of material and held it up.

The pink ribbon danced from her fingertips, taunting her. She couldn't scream. She couldn't breathe.

She crumpled the ribbon in her fist and ran blindly for the door.

Chapter Two

Sheriff Cooper Sloane wheeled his patrol SUV onto the gravel driveway of Cass Teagan's place, the damp air tamping down any dust or debris that his tires even considered kicking up.

He owed Wyatt Carson for giving him the heads-up about Kendall Rush's presence at her aunt's house. The plumber hadn't even done it on purpose, just let it slip.

He opened his car door and planted one booted foot on the ground where it crunched the gravel. He clapped his hat on his head and adjusted the equipment on his belt.

As he took one step toward the house, the front door crashed open and a woman flew down the steps, her hair streaming behind her, a pair of dark eyes standing out in her pale face.

She ran right toward him, her gaze fixed on something beyond his shoulder, something only she could see.

"Whoa, whoa." He spread his arms as she barreled into him, staggered back and caught her around the waist so she wouldn't take both of them down.

Her heart thundered against his chest, and her mouth dropped open as one hand clawed at the sleeve of his jacket.

"Ma'am. Ma'am. What's the matter?"

She arched back, and her eyes finally focused on his face, tracked up to his hat and dropped to his badge. She blinked.

"Are you all right?" Her body slumped in his arms, and he placed his hands on her shoulders to steady her.

Then she squared those shoulders, and shoved one hand in the pocket of her jeans. A smile trembled on her lips. "I am so sorry."

"Nothing to be sorry about." He gave her a final squeeze before releasing her. "What happened in the house to send you out here like a bat outta hell?"

She wedged two trembling fingers against her temple and released a shaky laugh. "You're not going to believe it."

Raising one eyebrow, he cocked his head. "Try me."

"S-spider." She waved one arm behind her, the other hand still firmly tucked into her front pocket. "I have an irrational fear of spiders. I know it's ridiculous, but I guess that's why it's irrational. A big, brown one crawled across my hand. Freaked me out. I should've just killed the sucker. Now I don't know where he is. He could be anywhere in there."

As the words tumbled from her lying lips, he narrowed his eyes.

She trailed off and cleared her throat. "Anyway, I told you it was silly."

"We all have our phobias." He lifted one shoulder, and then extended his arms. "After that introduction, we should probably backtrack. I'm Sheriff Sloane."

"Kendall Rush, Sheriff. Nice to meet you. I'm Cass Teagan's niece, and I'm here to sell her place."

"I know. That's why I'm here." He gestured toward the front door, which yawned open behind the screen door that had banged back into place after Kendall's flight from the…spider. "Can I talk to you inside?"

"Of course."

She rubbed her arms as if noticing the chill in the soggy air for the first time.

When she didn't make a move, he said, "After you."

She spun on the toes of her sneakers and scuffed her feet toward the steps with as much enthusiasm as someone going to meet her greatest fear—and it had nothing to do with spiders.

He followed her, the sway of her hips in the tight denim making his mouth water—even though she was a liar.

She opened the screen door and turned suddenly. His gaze jumped to her face.

Her eyes widened for a nanosecond. Had she busted him? He didn't even know if she had a husband waiting on the other side of the threshold. The good citizens of Timberline probably could've told him, but that piece of information hadn't concerned him—before.

Standing against the screen door, she held it wide. "You first."

"Still afraid that spider's going to jump out at you?"

Her nostrils flared. "Better you than me."

Something had her spooked and she hadn't gotten over it yet.

He patted the weapon on his hip. "I got him covered if he does."

"Even I'd consider that overkill for a spider."

He brushed past her into the house, and a warm musky scent seeped into his pores. He had the ridiculous sensation that Kendall Rush was luring him into a trap—like a fly to a spider's web.

The dusty mustiness of the room closed around him, replacing the seductive smell of musk and even overpowering the pine scent from outside. His nose twitched and he sneezed.

"I'm sorry. I haven't had time to clean up ten months' worth of dust in here yet." She plucked a tissue from a box by the window and waved it at him.

"Why don't you open a couple of windows?" He scanned the room, cluttered with boxes of varying degrees of emptiness, his gaze zeroing in on a cabinet with an open drawer, papers scattered around it.

"There was a breeze this morning, and I thought opening the window would stir up the dust and make it worse." She walked backward to the cabinet and leaned against it, shutting the drawer with her hip in the process.

"Hope to trap him in there?"

A quick blush pulsed in her cheeks. "What?"

"The spider." He pointed to the cabinet she seemed to be trying to block with her slight frame. "It looks like you were going through that drawer when you discovered him."

The line of her jaw hardened. "I was going through the drawer, but the spider crawled on my hand while I was carrying one of the boxes."

He looked at the neat row of boxes, not one dropped in haste, and shrugged. If she wanted to continue lying to him about what gave her such a scare that she'd run headlong out of the house and into his arms, he'd leave it to her. He hadn't minded the introduction at all.

"If I happen to see him or any of his brethren, I'll introduce him to the bottom of my boot." He tipped his hat from his head and ran a hand through his hair. "Now, can I ask you a few questions, Ms. Rush?"

"All right, but I can't help you."

"That's a quick judgment when you haven't even heard the questions yet." He put his hat on the top of a box filled with books. "Is there someplace else we can talk so I don't have a sneezing fit?"

"I cleaned up the kitchen pretty thoroughly. Do you want something to drink while we talk?"

"Just water." He followed her into the kitchen, keeping his eyes on the back of her head this time, although the way her dark hair shimmered down her back was just as alluring as her other assets.

She cranked on the faucet and plucked a glass from an

open cupboard. "That's one thing I miss about living in Timberline, maybe the only thing—the tap water. It's as good as anything in a bottle."

"It is." He took the glass from her and held it up to the light from the kitchen window. He then swirled it like a fine wine and took a sip.

She pulled a chair out from the small kitchen table stationed next to a side door that led to a plain cement patio. She perched on the edge, making it clear that she was ready to get this interview over with before it even started.

She kicked out the chair on the other side of the table. "Have a seat."

He placed his glass on the table and sank into the chair, stretched his legs to the side and pulled a notepad from his pocket. "You obviously know I'm interested in asking you questions about the kidnapping of your sister."

She drummed her fingers on the table. "Did Wyatt Carson tell you I was out here?"

"No. I heard you'd arrived yesterday—just local gossip."

She rolled her eyes, apparently not believing his lie any more than he believed hers. "Okay. Ask away, but you're asking me about something that happened a long time ago."

"A traumatic event."

"Exactly, I've squished down a lot of those memories, and I'm not inclined to dredge them up."

"Even if they can help the Keaton and Douglas families today?"

"I don't believe they can." She flattened her hands on the table, her fingers splayed. "You can't seriously believe the two current kidnappings have anything to do with the Timberline Trio disappearances. What, some kidnapper has been lying dormant for twenty-five years and then up and decides to go another round?"

"I think there are some similarities." He hunched forward in his chair. "There are cases where a serial killer is active and then the killings just stop, sometimes because the killer goes to prison for some other crime. Then when he's paroled, he starts killing again."

"So you think the man who kidnapped my sister is on the loose and picking up where he left off over two decades ago?" She folded her hands in front of herself, and his gaze dropped to her white knuckles.

Before his action even registered in his brain, his hand shot out and he covered her clasped hands with one of his. "I'm sorry. I didn't mean to be so blunt."

"I'd rather you be truthful with me, Sheriff Sloane."

"Call me Coop. Everyone does." He slid his hand from hers. "I'd like you to be truthful with me, too, Ms. Rush."

Her eyes flickered. "Call me Kendall, and I'll be as truthful as I can. What do you want to ask me?"

So he wouldn't be tempted to touch her again, he dragged his notebook in front of him and tapped the eraser end of his pencil on the first page. "What do you remember about that night?"

"That's an open-ended question."

"Okay. Why were you and your sister spending the night at your aunt's house instead of your own?"

"If you read the case file, you know the answer to that question."

"You're not going to make this easy, are you?"

Tucking her hair behind one ear, she ran her tongue along her lower lip. "I'm trying to make it easy on you and save some time. A lot of that stuff is in the case file. I don't see the point in rehashing it with me."

"You're the therapist. You understand the importance of reliving memories, of telling someone else your version of events. Isn't that what therapists are supposed to do?" His lip curled despite his best efforts to keep his feelings about therapists on neutral ground.

"You're trying to psychoanalyze me?"

"I'm trying to see if you have anything to offer that doesn't come through on a page written twenty-five years ago." He snorted. "Unless you're trying to tell me talk therapy doesn't work. Does it?"

She studied his face, staring into his eyes, her own dark and fathomless. Could she read the disdain he had for therapy? He'd brought up the therapy angle only to make her feel comfortable.

She tapped the table between them with her index finger. "Therapy is supposed to help the subject. You want me to start spilling my guts to help you, not to help myself."

He closed his eyes and pinched the bridge of his nose. God, he wished he was questioning Wyatt again and not this complicated woman.

The gesture must've elicited her pity because she started talking.

"Kayla and I were at Aunt Cass's that night because my parents were fighting again. Aunt Cass, my mother's sister, felt that my parents needed to work out their differences one-on-one and not in front of the kids."

"The police suspected your father of the kidnapping at first because of the fight."

"I didn't realize that at the time, of course, but that assumption was so ridiculous. I'd given a description of the kidnapper, and I would've recognized my dad, even in a mask. I suppose the police figured I was too traumatized to give an accurate description or I was protecting my father."

"What was your description, since the guy had a ski mask on?" He doodled in his notebook because Kendall had been right. All this info was in the case file.

"He was wearing a mask, gloves, and he was taller and heavier than my dad. That I could give them. Oh, and that he had a gravelly voice."

"He just said a few words, though, right? 'Get off' or 'let go'?"

She shifted her gaze away from him and dropped her lashes. "I'd grabbed on to his leg."

"Brave girl."

"It didn't stop him."

His eye twitched. Did she feel guilty because she didn't stop a grown man from kidnapping her twin?

"No surprise there."

Her dark eyes sparkled and she shrugged her shoulders.

"He took something from you, didn't he?"

"My twin sister. My innocence. My security. My mother's sanity. My family. Yeah, he took a lot."

He wanted to reach for her again and soothe the pain etched on her face, but he tapped his chin with the pencil instead. "Not that it can compare with any of those losses, but he also took a pink ribbon from your hair."

The color drained from Kendall's face, and a muscle quivered at the corner of her mouth.

"Do you want some water?" He pushed back from the table. "You look pale."

"I'm okay." Her chest rose and fell as she pulled in a long breath and released it. "I'd forgotten about that ribbon. Pink was Kayla's favorite color. Mine was green. That night Aunt Cass had put our hair in pigtails, and Kayla had insisted on tying pink ribbons in my hair while she tried the green. I was glad he took that ribbon."

"Why?" He held his breath as Kendall's eyes took on a faraway look.

"I always thought that when Kayla woke up and found herself with this strange man, she'd feel better seeing the pink ribbon. Now…" She covered her eyes with one hand.

"Now?" He almost whispered the word, his throat tight.

"Now I think that he just killed her, that she never saw the ribbon."

When her voice broke, he rose from his chair and crouched beside her. He took the hand she had resting on the table and rubbed it between both of his as if she needed warming up.

"I'm sorry. I'm sorry I'm forcing these memories and thoughts back to the surface."

A misty smile trembled on her lips. "This is exactly what I put my clients through every day."

"And it's supposed to help them. Is it helping you?"

Sniffling, she dabbed the end of her nose with her fingertips. "This is well-traveled territory. It's not like I haven't been through all of this before with my own therapist."

"You see a therapist?" He sat back on his heels.

"All therapists do at the beginning. It's part of our training, and most of us keep it up because it helps our work."

"So I must be a poor substitute." Although he could probably do a better job than half the quacks out there.

She curled her fingers around one of his hands. "She never holds my hand, so you've got her beat there."

He squeezed her fingers and released them as he backed up to his own seat. "Did your therapy ever bring up any memories of that night that you hadn't realized as a child? The man's accent? Someone he reminded you of?"

"Nothing like that." She stretched her arms over her head. "I don't have any repressed memories of the event, if that's what you're driving at, Doctor Sloane."

He stroked his chin, wishing he had a clean shave. "You know, sometimes I feel more like a psychiatrist than a cop when I'm questioning people."

"So tell me." She wedged her elbows on the table and sunk her chin into one cupped palm. "What makes you think these two kidnappings are at all related to the Timberline Trio case? Wyatt mentioned you were working on some theory that the FBI didn't share."

When Kendall mentioned the FBI, he ground his back teeth together. He'd never met a more arrogant bunch, who seemed more interested in dotting *i*'s and crossing *t*'s than doing any real investigative work.

"It's something I'd rather keep to myself."

She swiped his glass from the table and jumped up from her chair. As she sauntered toward the sink, she glanced over her shoulder. "You want me to help you, but you won't share your findings?"

"Can you keep a secret?" He sucked in his bottom lip as he watched her refill his glass with water from the tap. She'd lured him into a comfortable intimacy, making him forget that she'd lied about the spider, but she seemed like someone who could keep secrets because she had plenty of her own.

"Who am I going to tell? I'm only going to be here for a short time anyway. Pack up the house, list it, outta here."

He scooted back his chair and stood up, leaning his hip against the table. "When this guy snatched the two children on separate occasions, he left something behind."

"What?" She placed the glass on the counter and wiped her fingers on the dish towel hanging over the oven's handle.

"When he took the boy, he left a plastic dinosaur. When he took the girl, he left…a pink ribbon."

Chapter Three

The room tilted and Sheriff Sloane's handsome face blurred at the edges. The pink hair ribbon that she'd found in the drawer of the cabinet burned a hole in her pocket where she'd stuffed it.

What did this mean? Who had put the ribbon in the drawer? What was the significance of the ribbon left at the scene of the kidnapping?

She swallowed. "A dinosaur?"

"You didn't know that, did you?" He reached over and took the glass from the counter. "When Stevie Carson was kidnapped, his parents insisted that one of his dinosaurs from his collection was missing. When Harrison Keaton was taken from his bedroom, the same kind of dinosaur as Stevie's was on the floor."

"The boy's parents confirmed the dinosaur didn't belong to him…to Harrison?" She twisted her fingers in front of her.

He gulped down half of the water. "No. That's why the FBI isn't looking at this angle. Harrison's parents can't say whether the dinosaur belongs to him or not."

"And the p-pink ribbon?"

"Same thing. The ribbon was on the little girl's dresser. Cheri Douglas wears ribbons. She likes pink."

Kendall eked out a tiny breath. Sounded like a coincidence to her. Lots of little boys played with plastic dinosaurs. Lots of little girls wore ribbons, especially pink ones, in their hair. Sheriff Sloane was grasping at straws, perhaps trying to stay relevant as the FBI moved into Timberline and took over the investigation.

She hooked her thumb in the front pocket of her jeans, the ribbon tickling the end of her finger. "Your theory is a stretch."

"Could be." He downed the rest of the water. "I'll let you get back to work, Kendall. If anything comes to you while you're still in town, give me a call."

He plucked a white business card from the front pocket of his khaki shirt and held it out between two fingers.

Taking it from him, she glanced at the embossed letters before shoving it in her back pocket. "I'll do that."

"I'd appreciate it if you didn't mention the ribbon or dinosaur to anyone else—just in case they mean something."

"My lips are sealed. As a therapist, I'm good at keeping secrets. It's part of my job description."

"I figured you were, or I wouldn't have told you. I think you're probably very good at keeping secrets." He jerked his thumb toward the living room. "I'm gonna head on out."

She followed him into the other room and then scooted past him to open the front door. "It was nice meeting you, Sheriff Sloane—Coop. I sure hope you can help those families, and I wish I could do more."

"I appreciate your time, Kendall. I'll probably be seeing you around before you leave." He stopped on the porch and did a half turn. "Watch out for those…spiders."

She squinted through the heavy mesh of the screen door at the sheriff as he climbed into his SUV. He beeped his horn once as he backed down the drive.

He hadn't bought her story about the spider. She did hate the creepy crawlies, but that mad flight from the house would've been over-the-top even for her.

Shutting the door, she dug into her pocket, the ribbon twining around her fingers. She pulled it free and dangled it in front of herself.

The soft pink had a slight sheen to it that caught the lamplight. It couldn't be the same one yanked from her pigtail that night or even its companion. A twenty-five-year-old ribbon would be faded and frayed, not buoyantly dancing from her fingertips.

She dropped it on top of the cabinet and shuffled through the drawer where she'd found it. Nothing else jumped out at her, not even a spider.

Although the ribbon had spooked her, there was probably a good, reasonable explanation for its presence in the drawer—not that she could think of one now.

She grabbed another handful of papers and shoved them into the plastic garbage bag. The sooner she got Aunt Cass's place ready, the sooner she could get out of this soggy hellhole.

And the sooner she could escape the tragedies of Harrison and Cheri. Damn Sheriff Sloane for naming them and making them human—a boy who liked dinosaurs and a girl who liked pink hair ribbons.

And damn Sheriff Sloane for peeling back her facade so easily. He'd just given her another reason to run back to Phoenix.

A man like that spelled trouble.

A FEW HOURS LATER, Kendall scrubbed the grit and dust from her skin under the spray of a warm shower—her first since arriving in Timberline because she'd forgotten to contact the gas company until she got here. If she'd known she would be having a meet and greet with the hunky sheriff in town, she would've gotten on that sooner.

She'd been dreading the social engagement tonight but

after finding that ribbon and answering the sheriff's prying questions, she was glad for the distraction.

Melissa Rhodes, a friend of hers from high school, had invited her over for a dinner party. Even if she didn't plan to stay in Timberline longer than she had to, she'd use the time to catch up with some old friends—the few that still remained.

The dinnertime conversation had better not revolve around the current kidnappings or she'd have to cut the evening short.

She stepped into a pair of skinny jeans and pulled some socks over the denim and finished off with knee-high boots. Topped with a sweater, the outfit pretty much defined the casual look for the Washington peninsula.

Her flip-flops and summer skirts called to her, but she hadn't even packed them for this cold climate.

She braided her long hair over one shoulder, brushed on a little makeup, and then yanked a wool shawl off the hook by the door.

Crossing her arms, she faced the living room and took a deep breath without worrying about choking on the dust for the first time since she'd arrived. After Sheriff Sloane had left, she'd gotten down and dirty with a rag and a can of furniture polish. She even took a vacuum to the drapes at the windows.

Rebecca, her Realtor, would be thrilled with the progress.

After locking up, she slid into her aunt's old truck and trundled down the drive to the main road. The lush forest hugged the asphalt on either side, the leaves still dripping moisture from the rain shower an hour ago.

The brakes on the truck had seen better days, and Kendall mentally added the sale of the vehicle to her list of to-do items. There had to be some local kids who wanted to practice their auto shop skills on an old beater.

She drove the few miles on slick roads and pulled behind a line of cars already parked on the street in front of Melissa's house—Melissa and Daryl's house. Daryl had come to Timberline almost two years ago to take a job with Evergreen Software and had fallen for a local girl. Melissa had never left Timberline since she'd had to take care of her mom who'd had Parkinson's disease. She'd found her prince charming anyway, in the form of a software engineer.

As she ground the gear shift into Park, Kendall winced. Anyone interested in this truck had better be a good mechanic.

She jumped from the truck and wrapped her shawl around her body as she headed up the pathway to the house. Warm lights shimmered from the windows and smoke puffed from the chimney.

She knocked on the door, tucking the bottle of cabernet under one arm.

A man—presumably Daryl—opened the front door and broke into an immediate smile. "You must be Kendall."

"I am." She stuck out her hand. "And you must be Daryl."

Taking her hand, he pulled her over the threshold. "Honey, Kendall's here."

Kendall's gaze shifted over his shoulder to the living room, and her fingers tightened around the neck of the bottle as several pairs of eyes focused on her. The few friends Melissa had mentioned looked like a full-scale party, and it seemed like she'd just interrupted their conversation.

She rolled her shoulders. She liked parties. She liked conversations—some topics better than others.

"I brought sustenance." Kendall held up the bottle of wine.

"We can always use more alcohol." Melissa broke away

from a couple and approached Kendall, holding out her hands. "So good to see you, Kendall."

Kendall hooked her friend in a one-armed hug. "Same. You look great."

"And you look—" Melissa held her at arm's length "—tan. I'm so jealous. I'm as pale as ever."

"What do you expect when the sun shines maybe three times a year, if you're lucky?" Kendall jerked her thumb over her shoulder at the damp outdoors.

"She's dissing our lovely, wet, depressing weather." Melissa held up the bottle to read the label. "But she's not snobby enough to dis our local wineries."

As Melissa peeled away from her side to put the wine in the kitchen, Kendall stepped down into the living room. She waved and nodded to a few familiar faces, shrugging off her shawl.

Melissa materialized behind her, a glass of wine in one hand. "This isn't yours. Is merlot okay?"

"Fine. The other stuff's for you and Daryl to drink later."

"Thanks. Let me take your shawl. We keep it warm in here." Daryl joined them, and Melissa patted her husband's arm. "Daryl's a transplant from LA. After two years, he's still not acclimated."

"Has my scatterbrained wife introduced you to everyone?" He went around the room, calling out names Kendall forgot two seconds later, until he named everyone there.

Melissa started carrying dishes to the dining room table, and Kendall broke away from the small talk to help her. The other guests' conversation had seemed guarded, anyway, and she'd bet anything they'd been talking about the kidnappings before her arrival.

Joining Melissa in the kitchen, she tapped a Crock-Pot of bubbling chili sitting on the kitchen counter. "Do you want this on the table, or are you going to leave it here?"

"You can put that on the table next to the grated cheese and diced onions."

Kendall hoisted the pot by its handles and inhaled the spicy aroma. "Mmm, this has to be your mom's recipe."

"It is." She patted the dining room table. "Right here."

Kendall placed the Crock-Pot on the tablecloth and removed the lid. "What else?"

"Can you help me scoop some tapenade and salsa and some other goodies into little serving dishes?"

"Absolutely, as long as I can sample while I'm scooping." Kendall pulled a small bowl toward herself and plopped a spoonful of guacamole in the center. "I like Daryl."

"Yeah, he's an uptight programmer—just perfect for his flaky, artsy-fartsy wife."

"Opposites do attract sometimes. He's a good balance for you."

"And what about you?" Melissa pinched her arm. "Any hot guys in hot Phoenix?"

"Lots, but nobody in particular. You single gals here in Timberline hit the jackpot when Evergreen Software came to town, didn't you?"

"It definitely expanded the dating scene, but a lot of the Evergreen employees came with ready-made families. Came to Washington for clean air, clean living, safety. Or at least it was safe until…" Melissa shoved a tapenade-topped cracker into her mouth.

"I know all about the recent kidnappings, Melissa." She scraped the rest of the guac into the bowl. "Wyatt Carson dropped by today and so did Sheriff Sloane."

"Coop already talked to you?"

"He came by the house this afternoon."

"Talk about your hot property." Melissa licked her fingers.

"He is definitely hot." Kendall elbowed her friend in

the ribs. "I'd like to see him without all that khaki covering everything up."

"Ladies? Need any help?"

Kendall's face burned hotter than the salsa she was dumping into the bowl. She didn't have to turn around to know who'd crept up behind them. She'd been listening to that low-pitched, smooth voice all afternoon.

"Hey, Coop. Glad you could make it." Melissa nudged Kendall's foot with her bare toes. "Have you met Kendall Rush yet?"

Kendall got very busy wiping salsa spills from the counter as she glanced over her shoulder, trying not to zone in on the way the man's waffle knit shirt stretched across his broad chest. "We met this afternoon. Hello again, Sheriff Sloane."

"I thought we were on a first-name basis. Call me Coop."

He entered the kitchen with a few steps and, even though he still must've been yards behind her, it felt like he was breathing down her neck.

"Do you need any help in here, Melissa?"

"I do not. We have it all under control." She tapped Kendall's arm. "My hands are goopy. Can you grab a cold beer for Coop from the fridge?"

Kendall shuffled over a few steps and yanked open the refrigerator. "What kind would you like?"

"Anything in a bottle, not a can. Surprise me."

She studied the bottled beer, grateful for the cool air on her warm cheeks. Had he heard their schoolgirl conversation about him? She grabbed a bottle with a blue label and spun around, holding it up. "How's this?"

He ambled toward her, his eyes, as blue as the label on the bottle, sparkling with humor. He reached for the beer and for an electrifying second his fingertips brushed hers. With his gaze locked on hers, he said, "This'll do."

"Well, then." Melissa grabbed a dish towel and wiped her hands. "Once we get these bowls to the table, dinner will be served."

Coop reached around Kendall, his warm breath brushing her cheek, and pinched the edge of a serving dish between his fingers. "I'll get this one."

Kendall followed him to the dining room while Melissa made wide-eyed faces at her, which she had no idea how to interpret.

"Come and get it," Melissa called out to the group. "Paper plates and bowls on both sides of the table. Nothing but first class around here."

Coop stuck to her side as they both filled up plates and bowls with food.

Stopping at the chili, Kendall spooned some into her bowl and held up the ladle to Coop. "Have you tried Melissa's famous chili yet?"

"Nope. Fill 'er up."

She dipped the spoon into the dark red mixture and ladled it into his bowl. "Another?"

He nodded.

"This stuff only makes it better." She sprinkled some grated cheese, chopped onions and diced avocado on the top.

Holding her plate in one hand and a bowl in the other, her fingers curled around her plastic cutlery, Kendall shuffled into the living room and nabbed a spot at a card table Melissa had set out for her guests. As she placed her food on the plastic tablecloth, Coop joined her.

"You left your wineglass in the kitchen. Do you want a refill?"

"I don't have far to drive, but I'm still driving. I'll take some iced tea. There are some cans in the fridge."

"Responsible driver." He put his fist over his heart. "Just what a man of the law wants to hear."

By the time Coop returned with their drinks, Melissa and Daryl had claimed the other two places at the table, but they didn't last long. One or the other and sometimes both kept hopping up to see to their guests' needs, which left Kendall alone with the sheriff...which suited her just fine.

"Verdict on the chili?" She poked the edge of his empty bowl with her fork.

"Awesome. I'm going to have to ask her for the recipe."

Blinking, she stole a glance at his ring finger, which she hadn't bothered to check before. Bare. She hadn't pegged him as a domestic sort of guy. Maybe he was joking about getting the recipe.

With his face all serious, he took a sip of the beer he'd been nursing all through dinner and started cutting into a piece of barbecued chicken.

"Did you have any more scares cleaning up your aunt's place after I left?"

Knots tightened in her gut, but she didn't know if thinking about the pink ribbon had caused the sensation or the fact that Coop had nailed her as a liar.

"If you don't count the scary dust bunnies, all went smoothly. I'm going to hire a cleaning crew to come in and finish the rest of the house, so I can focus on selling my aunt's things."

"You're not taking any of it back home?"

"Aunt Cass's decorating style and mine clash." She slathered a pat of butter on a corn bread muffin and took a bite.

"She had a lot of collections, didn't she?"

"Mermaids, wood carvings from the old days when Timberline was a lumber town—stuff like that."

"And you're just going to sell that stuff? Might be nice to hand down to the kids one day."

She almost inhaled a few crumbs of corn bread. Kids?

She had no intention of having kids. Ever. She coughed into her napkin. "Maybe."

He reached forward so suddenly, she jerked back, but then he touched his fingertip to the corner of her mouth. "Corn bread."

To quell the tingling sensation his touch had started on her lips, she pressed the napkin to her mouth again. "Great. Do I have chili in my eyebrows, too?"

Taking her chin between his fingers, he looked in her eyes, his own darkening to a deep blue. "Not that I can see."

Laughter burst from the crowd sitting on the floor around the oversize, square coffee table, startling them both. He dropped his hand.

"You heard that story, didn't you, Coop?" A woman from the group called to him.

He eased back into his chair and finished off the last of his beer. "What's that, Jen?"

"Davis Unger, the little boy in Ms. Maynard's class, who announced to everyone that his mom and the mailman were boyfriend and girlfriend."

Coop chuckled. "Out of the mouths of babes. Does Mr. Unger know about that relationship?"

"I think it was all a misunderstanding."

"Riight."

"Doesn't your daughter give you the kindergarten report every day?"

His daughter? Kendall sucked in a quick breath, her gaze darting to that finger on his left hand again.

"Steffi's in her own little world half the time." He stood up and stretched. "When I ask her about school, she tells me bizarre stories about unicorns and fairies. Should I be concerned?"

Jen and a few of the other women laughed. "She just

has an active imagination, and all the kids are crazy about that fairy movie that just came out."

Coop piled up his trash, and his hand hovered over her mostly empty plate. "Are you done?"

"You don't need to wait on me." She pushed back from the table, crumpling her napkin into her plate. "After all that food, I need to move. Let me take your empties, and you can go over there and discuss kindergarten."

A vertical line flashed between his eyes as he handed his paper plate and bowl to her. "I'll do that."

"Another beer?"

"Wouldn't do for the sheriff to set a bad example, would it?"

"Not at all." She meandered back to the kitchen, exchanging a few words here and there with Melissa's guests.

She slipped the trash into a plastic garbage bag in the kitchen and cleaned up some other items from the counter. Maybe Coop was divorced and had joint custody with his ex. Melissa would know. She made it her business to know everyone else's.

But the interrogation would have to wait. Melissa took her hostessing duties very seriously, and Kendall couldn't get one word with her alone.

After chitchatting and helping out with the cleanup duty, Kendall checked the time on her phone and decided to call it a night. She had a meeting with Rebecca tomorrow morning and wanted to check out a few online auction sites to assess Aunt Cass's collections.

She eyed Coop across the room talking with a couple of men and mimicking throwing a football. Thank God she hadn't stuck her foot in her mouth and admitted to never, ever wanting children since Coop had one.

Not that Coop's parenthood, marital status or anything else about his personal life would matter to her one bit once she flew the coop. She grinned at her lame joke and strolled to the den off the foyer to grab her shawl.

She dipped next to Melissa sitting on the couch and whispered in her ear. "I'm going to take off. I'm exhausted."

"Are you sure? There's still dessert."

"I can't handle another bite, but let's try to get together for lunch before I leave."

"Let me see you out." Melissa rocked forward, and Daryl placed a hand on her back to help her up.

"Nice to meet you, Daryl. You and Mel are welcome in Phoenix anytime." She pecked him on the cheek, and he gave her a quick hug around the neck.

Melissa took her arm as they walked to the front door. "Daryl and I are taking off for Seattle for a few days, but we should be back before you leave. Don't be a stranger while you're here and if you need any help with Aunt Cass's house, call me."

"Call *you* for help cleaning a house?"

"Hey." Melissa nipped her side with her fingertips. "I know people."

"I think I know the same people."

Coop materialized behind Melissa. "I'll walk you to your truck."

With her back to Coop, Melissa gave her a broad wink.

"Okay, thanks." Kendall hugged her friend goodbye and stepped out onto the porch with Coop close behind her.

He lifted his face to the mist in the air. "Ahh, refreshing."

"Are you a native of Washington?"

"No, California. I've been here about five years."

"Oh, the reviled California transplant."

He spread his arms. "That's me."

"Well, this is me." She kicked the tire of her aunt's truck.

He took her hand as if to shake it, but he just held it. "Good to talk to you tonight about…other things."

"It's always good to talk about other things." She squeezed his hand and disentangled her fingers from his.

She climbed into the truck and cranked the key twice to get the engine to turn over. Waving, she pulled into the street. As the truck tilted up the slight incline, an object in the truck bed shifted and hit the tailgate.

She drew her brows over her nose. She didn't have anything in the back.

She reversed into her previous parking spot and threw the truck into Park. As she hopped from the seat, Coop turned at the porch.

Using the light on her cell phone, she stood on her tiptoes to peer into the truck bed. She traced the beam along the inside where it picked up a bundle wrapped in a tarp. Then the light picked up one small, pale hand poking from the tarp.

Kendall screamed like she'd never stop.

Chapter Four

Kendall's scream pierced the still night and turned the blood in his veins to ice. Coop had already been making his way back down the drive when he'd heard Kendall's truck coming back to the house. Now his boots grappled for purchase against the soggy leaves on the walkway as he ran toward Kendall.

"What is it? What's wrong?" By the time he reached her, he was panting as if he'd just run a marathon.

She'd stumbled back from the truck and stood staring at the tailgate with wide, glassy eyes. Raising her arm, she pointed to the truck with her cell phone. She worked her jaw but couldn't form any words—no coherent words, anyway.

He pried the phone from her stiff fingers and aiming the light at the truck bed, he jumped on the bumper. The phone illuminated a light-colored tarp with something rolled up in it.

"I-it's a body."

His heart slammed against his rib cage when his gaze stumbled across a hand peeking from the tarp. He leaned in close, aiming the phone's flashlight at the pale appendage, sniffing the air.

He smelled…turpentine. The hard plastic of the hand gleamed under the light and he poked it with the corner of the phone.

Pinching a corner of the tarp between his fingers, he lifted it, exposing the foot of the mannequin.

He blew out a breath and jumped down from the truck. "It's not a body, Kendall. It's a mannequin."

Her eyebrows collided over her nose. "A mannequin?"

"Do you want to have a look?"

She hunched her shoulders and drew her shawl around her body. "No. What's it doing in my truck? I didn't put a mannequin in my truck. I don't even have a mannequin. Why is it wrapped up like that?"

"Beats me, but I'm going to get a few of my guys down here to collect some evidence, and I'd better call the FBI."

"FBI?" Her voice squeaked and she burrowed further into her shawl. "Why would you call the FBI?"

"I'm pretty sure the agents investigating the kidnappings will be interested in this development, or at least they should be."

"Why?" She tilted her head and her long braid almost reached her waist.

"The mannequin?" Coop chewed on his bottom lip before spitting out his next words. "It's a kid."

Kendall choked and swayed on her feet.

He jumped forward to grab her and ended up pulling her against his chest, wrapping his arms tightly around her shaking frame. Beads of moisture trembled in the strands of her hair, and he brushed his hand across the top of her head to sweep them off.

"Let's go inside. I'll make those calls and you can warm up." He rubbed her arms still wrapped in the shawl. "You're shivering."

"Do we have to?" she murmured against his chest. "You can't use your cell phone for those calls?"

"And keep you waiting around outside while I do? No way."

She placed her hands against his chest and leaned back,

looking into his face. "I don't want to go back in there and make a scene. I'm surprised they didn't all come rushing out here when they heard me scream."

"They didn't hear you. I was standing on the porch and the decibel level is high in there. Someone even turned on some music, not to mention the house is set back from the street." He spread his arms. "So, no alarm bells."

"Until we walk into that house. They were already eyeing me in there like I was some kind of black cloud."

Grabbing the edges of her shawl, he tugged. "It's just a mannequin, Kendall, not a dead body. Just some kind of sick trick."

"If you really believe that, why are you calling out your officers, the FBI and God knows who else?"

"Because we've had two kidnappings in this town, and that mannequin was left for you. If there's any kind of forensic evidence in your truck, we need to get our hands on it."

"All right." She rolled back her shoulders. "Let's get this over with."

He ushered Kendall back into the house, but most of the guests were too busy talking, eating and singing karaoke in the corner to notice them.

As one of Daryl's colleagues from Evergreen hit a high note in a 1980s rock song, Coop winced and squeezed Kendall's arm.

She rewarded him with an answering grimace and an eye roll.

"Couldn't stay away from the karaoke?" Melissa sailed forward, snapping her fingers and shaking her hips. Then her eyes widened and the smile dropped from her lips. "What's wrong?"

Coop bent forward until his lips almost grazed Melissa's ear. "Someone pulled a prank on Kendall by leaving a mannequin wrapped in a tarp in the back of her truck."

"Why would someone do that?" Melissa clapped one hand over her mouth. "You think it has something to do with—" she glanced over her shoulder at her guests whooping it up "—the kidnappings?"

"Maybe, maybe not, but if it is just teenagers and we catch them, let's just say this could be a teachable moment for them."

"I'm sure that's all it is." She yanked on Kendall's braid and grabbed a phone from its stand. "You can use our land-line. Our reception is so iffy down here, we can't always depend on our cell phones."

Coop called the station first and asked the sergeant on duty to bring a forensics kit and send a squad car over. Then he plucked Agent Dennis Maxfield's business card from his wallet and punched in his number.

While the phone rang, he covered the mouthpiece and jerked his chin toward an open bottle of wine on the counter. "Have another glass, Kendall. I'll give you a ride home when this is all over."

"Agent Maxfield."

"This is Sheriff Sloane. There was an incident tonight I thought you might want to know about. Someone wrapped a tarp around a child-sized mannequin and put it in a truck bed to make it look like a body."

"Sick SOB. What's that got to do with the kidnappings?"

Coop turned his back to Kendall and Melissa chatting over their wine. "The truck belonged to Kendall Rush."

Silence ticked by for two seconds. "Who?"

"Kendall Rush. Her sister Kayla Rush was one of the Timberline Trio."

"Yeah—twenty-five years ago."

Coop's jaw tightened. "It's a coincidence, don't you think? If the mannequin had appeared in some random employee's truck at Evergreen, I wouldn't be as interested in it as I am."

"Is your department already looking into it, Sheriff?"

"My guys are on the way."

"We'll let you handle…this one. Let us know if you find anything of interest to *our* case."

Coop had a death grip on the phone, but he closed his eyes and relaxed his muscles. "Copy that, Maxfield."

He held out the phone to Melissa. "Thanks."

"Well? Is everyone going to rush out here with their lights spinning and guns blazing?" Kendall swirled the single sip of wine left in her glass before downing it.

"Couple of my guys are going to have a look—fingerprints, fibers, footprints. Then they'll take the mannequin away and we can figure out where it and the tarp came from."

"My guests are going to know, aren't they?" Melissa's gaze slid to the merrymakers in the other room.

Coop snorted. "By the sound of it, they'll be too drunk to notice what's going on. I hope they all have designated drivers."

Ten minutes later, Sergeant Payton called to indicate he and the patrol officer were out front.

Coop popped a mini creampuff in his mouth and charged toward the front door, eager to escape the screeching duo on the makeshift stage.

"Hold your horses." Kendall grabbed on to his belt loop. "I'm coming with you."

"Are you sure?"

She covered her ears. "Even looking into the dead eyes of a mannequin has got to be better than this."

Nodding, he opened the door for her, releasing a breath into the cold night. The wine had done her good, or maybe it was being around people oblivious to her uneasiness. He glanced back into the room, still frothing with hilarity.

That wouldn't last long.

Both officers had double-parked their squad cars, since the party guests had left no room on the street. They broke off their conversation when Coop and Kendall exited the Rhodes' yard.

Sergeant Payton pushed off the door of his car and met them at the truck. "We already took a look. Creepy."

"Did you watch where you were stepping?" Coop pointed at the ground. "Ms. Rush and I already tromped through here before we knew what we had."

The sergeant flicked on a spotlight to flood the truck bed and the area around it with light. "We had a look before, but either the person who planted the mannequin covered up any footprints and disturbances or the wind and rain did it."

Coop crouched next to the back tire and examined the road. It hadn't helped matters that Kendall had driven the truck away and then backed up. The moist dirt bordering the street showed no footprints except theirs.

The patrol officer joined them—a new kid named Quentin Stevens.

He held up a black case. "I have the fingerprint materials. Should I give it a try?"

"Why not? Dust the tailgate and all around the back of the truck."

"Do the homeowners have a surveillance camera, by any chance?" The sergeant poked his head into the yard.

"Not that I know of. Like I said, Ms. Rush and I were both attending a party at the house. The owners are friends of mine. I think they would've told me if they had cameras, but I'll ask."

The front door swung open, and a couple descended the porch steps. As they looked up, they stumbled to a stop.

"What's going on?"

Kendall cleared her throat. "Someone left something in my truck, probably a stupid joke."

The couple, who had two kids at home, picked up their pace and approached the circle of white light. The woman spoke up. "What kind of joke?"

"A stupid mannequin."

The man draped his arm around his wife and forced a laugh. "Teenagers."

Coop shot a glance at his two deputies, willing them to keep quiet about the fact that the mannequin was a child and wrapped up to look like a dead body.

Melissa and Daryl must've ended the party because a steady stream of people started leaving their house, all drawn to the investigation area like lemmings to the sea.

Sergeant Payton and Stevens went about their business as Coop and Kendall fielded questions and kept the looky-loos at bay.

Finally, they all cleared out and when the last one drove off, Melissa and Daryl barreled down the drive.

Melissa took Kendall's hand. "Anything?"

"Nothing yet, but they're about to take the thing out of the truck."

"Maybe we'll find something when we bring it in." Coop opened the back door of the squad car. "Lay it in the backseat."

He turned to Daryl while the sergeant and Stevens wrestled with the mannequin. "Do you guys have a security camera on the house?"

"No, but after this? We're getting one. Tell us the best model to buy and we'll buy it."

"Will do."

"Sweetie, do you want to come inside for a while?" Melissa rubbed a circle on Kendall's back. "You're freezing, and I promise I won't make you help clean up—unless you want to."

"Thanks, Melissa, but I just want to get home."

Coop raised his hand. "I'm taking Kendall home."

"That's okay. I think that second glass of wine has worn off by now."

"Ha! Let me warn you, ma'am, if you attempt to get behind the wheel of this truck, I'm gonna have to arrest you."

Melissa squeezed Kendall's shoulder. "I can pick you up tomorrow, Kendall, to get the truck or if you want to leave the keys, Daryl can take it over in the morning."

"If you don't mind." Kendall dug the keys to the truck out of her purse and dangled them in front of Melissa.

Melissa snatched them from her fingers. "Not at all. Go—warm up, relax. You're in good hands with Sheriff Sloane."

They said their goodbyes and Coop bundled Kendall in the passenger seat of his civilian car—a truck but a newer model than Kendall's old jalopy.

He slid a glance at Kendall's profile, which looked carved from ice. "Are you okay?"

"I'm fine."

"It might just be a joke. There's some pretty sick humor out there, and you know teens."

"You're probably right. Why would the kidnapper want to expose himself to scrutiny before he collects his ransom?"

His hands tightened on the steering wheel in a spasm. She had to know that if the kidnapper hadn't demanded a ransom now, chances are good he never would. None was ever asked for her twin sister.

Spitting angry droplets against his windshield, the rain started up again before he pulled into her driveway. Steffi hated the rain and another pinprick of guilt needled him next to all the others for making her stay in a place she didn't like, a place that never seemed like home even though she was born here. It had seemed like a good idea at the time to stay. Now he wasn't quite so sure.

He parked the truck and killed the engine. He'd at least walk Kendall up to the front door, not that he felt comfortable leaving her here after that stunt.

She swung around. "Do you want to come inside for a minute? I hate the rain."

"Sure. This was supposed to be a relaxing evening for me, a kickoff to a few vacation days, and I spent the second half of it working."

"Sorry."

"I don't blame you—not much, anyway."

A smile quirked her lips, and she grabbed the door handle.

He exited the truck and followed her to the porch, scanning her outdoor lighting and the screens on her windows. She could use a surveillance system here, too.

She unlocked the door and twisted her head over her shoulder. "I think you'll find it a little easier to breathe in here compared to this afternoon."

He stepped across the threshold and took a deep breath. Not only did he not get a lungful of dust, but the sweet scent of a candle or some air freshener tickled his nose. "That's better."

"I can't vouch for the rest of the rooms, but at least this one's clean, and the kitchen and the bedroom where I'm sleeping." She tossed her purse on the nearest chair. "I'm going to admit defeat and get a cleaning crew in to finish the job."

"Probably not a bad idea." He poked the toe of his boot at one of the boxes. "When are you going to have the estate sale?"

"As early as this weekend. You looking for some furniture from the Nixon era?"

"I think I'll pass."

"Would you like something to drink?"

He took a turn around the room, his gaze wandering to the cabinet where the phantom spider had been hiding. "Coffee, if it's not too much trouble."

"None, but do you need to get home to your daughter?"

Ah, he knew that was coming. "She's having a sleepover with her friend, who happens to be the daughter of our receptionist at the station."

"She's five?" She crooked her finger. "Follow me to the kitchen while I make the coffee."

He folded his arms and wedged a shoulder against the doorway into the small kitchen. "Yeah, Steffi's five and a half, as she'll be quick to tell you, and she's in kindergarten at Carver Elementary."

"Good, old Carver." She poured water into the coffeemaker and punched the button to start the brew. "Are you...married?"

Knew that one was coming, too.

He held up his left hand and wiggled his fingers. "Nope."

"Divorced?"

Even though it had been business, he'd poked into her personal life and that intimacy must've given her the impression it was okay for her to return the favor. She probably wouldn't feel the same way if one of her clients turned the tables and started asking her personal questions.

"I'm sorry. I'm prying. Occupational hazard. You can just ignore me, if you like." She turned and grabbed the handle to the refrigerator. "Milk with your coffee? No cream."

"I take it black, and I don't mind the third degree."

"Yes, you do." She pulled a carton of milk from the fridge. "Your face closed down, and your mouth got tight."

"You'd be good interviewing suspects." He took a quick breath and then blurted out, "She's dead."

Her hand jerked and the milk she'd been pouring into a mug sloshed onto the counter. "Excuse me?"

"My wife—she's dead."

"I'm so sorry." She swiped a sponge from the sink and dabbed at the pool of milk.

He pointed to the coffeemaker, the last drips of coffee falling into the pot. "Coffee's done."

Kendall tossed the sponge back into the sink and poured a stream into his cup. Then she added some to the mug with the milk.

Taking the handles of both cups, she said, "Let's go sit in the living room where it's warmer."

He took the mug from her. "Thanks."

They sat in chairs across from each other, and he used the box next to his chair as an end table.

"Do you like Timberline?" She watched him over the rim of her cup and he got the sense that she had the same look in her eye when she was sitting across from a patient or a client or whatever term they used.

"I like it. I'm an outdoorsy kind of guy, so I like the fishing, hiking, rafting."

"You've come to the right place for that." She ran the tip of her finger around the rim of her mug. "Looks like Evergreen Software is making an impact on the area. Young and Sons Lumber had gone out of business before I left for college, and Timberline was in danger of becoming a ghost town."

"Evergreen had already planted stakes by the time I got here, so I don't have the before and after picture, except from the locals' stories of the old days, and Mayor Young is always crowing about how much he's done for development in Timberline."

"Ah, so Jordan Young is mayor now."

"Actually, he stepped down recently, but he's a one-man cheerleading squad."

"Timberline does have a storied history—from silver mining to lumber to high tech. It's nice to see some life in the old place—maybe a little too much life." She wrapped both hands around her mug. "What do you really think about that mannequin?"

He blew the steam from the surface of the coffee in his cup and took a sip. "I don't think it was a coincidence that it was left for you, even if it was a joke. Everyone in town knows your connection to the old kidnappings."

"I wonder if Wyatt got any surprises tonight." She tapped her fingernail against her mug. "I'm not the only one in town connected to the Timberline Trio, although it's just the two of us after Heather Brice's family left the area. I don't suppose her older brother, wherever he is, has been getting these little reminders"

"Good idea. I'll check with Wyatt tomorrow. He's still working on a job at the station for us."

"I have a hard time believing it's the kidnapper who left it. What's the point?"

"He's a kidnapper. Who knows? There could be a million reasons in his deranged mind—if he has a deranged mind."

Her eyes widened. "It's like you just said—he's a kidnapper. Why wouldn't he have a deranged mind? Anyone who kidnaps a child for whatever reason has to be sick."

"These two kidnappings could be for a purpose."

"You mean like some kind of ring?" She laced her fingers around her cup as if trying to draw warmth from the liquid inside. "I can't bear to think about that possibility."

"I know. Believe me, as the father of a young daughter, I can't, either."

"Someone like that wouldn't hang around to plant mannequins in trucks."

"Exactly, so we don't know what we're looking at yet,

but I'm sure that mannequin is connected to the kidnappings, even if it is just a cruel joke on you."

She yawned and covered her mouth. "Sorry. Not even coffee can keep me awake after the day I've had."

"I'll get going. Didn't mean to keep you up all night."

His mind flashed on keeping her up all night another way and as her brows lifted slightly, he had an uneasy feeling the therapist could not only read his face but his mind, too—unless it was all an act. A therapist didn't know much more than a layman or a cop, for that matter.

"I was glad for the company. Having you here in this empty house made my jitters go away." She rose from the chair and held out her hand for his cup.

"Good." He handed her the mug. "Is it okay if I use your restroom before heading out?"

"First door on your right."

After he washed his hands and stepped into the short hallway, he heard clinking glass in the kitchen. He glanced at the cabinet again.

Something had spooked her this afternoon, and then the mannequin had spooked her tonight. Was this a pattern? And didn't he have an obligation to find out if it was?

He crept toward the cabinet and eased open the drawer, his gaze tracking through the contents.

"Shouldn't you get a search warrant before you go snooping through my stuff?"

Her cold voice stopped him in his tracks. Then he plucked the pink ribbon from the drawer and turned, dangling it in front of him.

"Funny-looking spider."

Chapter Five

Heat flashed across her cheeks and she dug her heels into the carpet to keep from launching herself at him and snatching the ribbon from his hand.

"Why are you pawing through my aunt's possessions? You can't wait for the yard sale?"

"Nice try, Kendall." He shook the ribbon at her. "This is what scared you this afternoon, sent you running for the hills."

"So what if it was?" She jutted her chin forward. "You're a cop, not my therapist. I don't have to reveal every facet of my life to you."

"I'd at least appreciate the ones that are pertinent to my case." He dropped the ribbon where it fluttered to the top of the cabinet.

"I didn't know it was."

"C'mon, Kendall, a pink ribbon like the one the kidnapper took from you that night? That's why it freaked you out, isn't it?"

She dropped her chin to her chest and studied his face through lowered lashes. "I'd just met you, so to speak. I felt foolish for taking off like that, for exposing my frailties to a stranger."

He wedged his hands on the cabinet behind him. "I can understand that, but why didn't you tell me about it tonight after you found the mannequin?"

"Not sure." She crossed her arms over her chest, cupping her elbows. "Telling you later would be admitting I lied to you."

"Look, Kendall." He blew out a breath. "You're right. You don't owe me anything. You don't even owe anything to those two grieving families."

She sliced her hand through the air. "It's not that I don't want to help them. God knows I do, but it can't be at the expense of my own mental health, especially if that help doesn't do anything to find their children."

"We don't know that yet. Let's put everything on the table." He launched off the cabinet and took her by the shoulders. "Trust me. Just trust me. Am I that scary? Do I come across as judgmental? I'm not."

She tilted her head back to look into his earnest blue eyes. Was it that important for him that he have her trust?

"You don't. Not at all." She ringed her fingers around his wrists, or at least as far as they would go. "I lied this afternoon because I didn't want you to see how affected I was by the events in my past, and I didn't think the ribbon had any meaning for the current case. I didn't tell you about the ribbon after the mannequin because it would've exposed my earlier lie. Is that plain enough for you?"

"Why try to hide your feelings about the tragedy? Anyone would be traumatized."

Her lips twisted into a smile. "Only the strong survive."

His eyes flickered for a second as they darkened with pain.

Who didn't trust whom here?

"You found the ribbon in the drawer of that cabinet. It can't be the same one." He jerked his thumb over his shoulder. "That's not a twenty-five-year-old ribbon."

She stepped back from his realm. How did he get truths from her so easily? Who was the therapist here?

"I've been thinking about it all day. It could be the original one left in my hair, or another one of Kayla's that my aunt found. If the ribbon hadn't been exposed to the sun, it wouldn't have faded. Or maybe my aunt had bought some new ribbons for some project, and this one happens to be pink."

"Or the same person who left a child-sized mannequin in your truck bed, left the ribbon for you to find knowing the effect it would have on you."

"Which brings us back to square one." She massaged her temples. "Why would the kidnapper, or anyone else for that matter, want to needle me?"

"Not sure, but it's on my list of things to find out." He skimmed a hand over his short hair. "It's late."

Hooking a finger on the edge of the curtain, she peeked outside. "The rain stopped—for now."

He touched her back. "Are you going to be okay?"

Turning, she curled her arm and flexed her biceps. "I'm tough. And, listen, I would've told you about the ribbon... eventually. Especially after finding the mannequin."

"I'm glad to hear that." He grabbed the handle and then turned his head to the side, so that she could see his face in profile only. "You don't have to be so tough, Kendall. I can share some of your burden. Let me."

Then he slipped outside, and she watched him until the darkness swallowed him.

If she transferred some of her pain onto his shoulders, it was only fair that he transfer some of his onto hers.

Because Sheriff Cooper Sloane had pain to spare.

"STOP KNOCKING YOURSELF OUT." Rebecca Geist, her Realtor, held out a card between two perfectly manicured nails. "I've used this cleaning crew before, and they're professional and reasonably priced."

"Thanks. I should've called them sooner." Kendall shoved the card beneath the phone on the kitchen counter. "But I did manage to get Aunt Cass's collections boxed up. I'm going to try to sell some of them at the estate sale, and I'm going to take the rest to one of those places that will list them online for a fee. I've already found a business in Port Angeles that will do that."

"Sounds like a good idea." Rebecca held up the camera hanging around her neck. "If we want to get this place listed, I need to take photos now. I can always replace them with newer photos once you clear out of here."

"This room, the kitchen, the master and the bathroom. Hold off on the other two rooms if you can until I get that cleaning crew out here."

"I think that'll be fine." She winked. "You know those buyers from California. They'll snap up anything in the low threes."

"Three hundred thousand dollars? This dump?" Kendall waved her arms around the small living room.

Rebecca put a finger to her glossed mouth and swiveled her head from side to side as if she suspected a potential buyer was lurking in the corner. "This," she said, spreading her arms, "is a charming cottage in the woods. Don't forget, you've got an acre of land here, and ever since Evergreen planted its corporate headquarters in Timberline the housing market—if not the weather—has been heating up."

"Okay, scratch that. It's a bucolic hideaway, a nature buff's paradise, a forest love nest." She could even half imagine that last one with the carpet stripped away, refinished hardwood floors, a Native American rug before a crackling fire in the grate—and Coop Sloane, half-naked, lounging in front of it.

One corner of Kendall's mouth curled up.

"That's the spirit." Rebecca nudged her side. "Of course, we will have to reveal the history of the house."

Kendall snapped out of her daydream. "History? Like

when it was built and any additions? I can assure you, there have been no additions to this house."

"No, dear." Rebecca had the camera to her face and was aiming it around the room. "The kidnapping."

The daydream completely evaporated.

"Really? We have to reveal something that happened twenty-five years ago? It's not like the house is haunted." Her gaze darted around the room, bouncing over the cabinet with the pink ribbon stashed inside.

"Well, it *was* a crime scene, but I don't think the negative will be too great." Rebecca lowered the camera and chewed on her bottom lip. "Unless…"

"Unless what?"

"Unless the FBI can't solve these two current kidnappings, or God forbid, there's another. Then it might not just be your house, but the whole area that's going to suffer." Rebecca's cheeks flushed beneath her heavy makeup. "And the families. Of course, the housing market is nothing next to the pain of the families."

"That's a given. You don't have to explain yourself, Rebecca." Kendall twirled a lock of hair around her finger. "Hopefully, the FBI, along with Sheriff Sloane, can find the children and stop this guy."

"Mmm." Rebecca smacked her lips. "My money's on Coop. Have you met him yet?"

Kendall shoved a hand in her pocket, trying to look nonchalant. "I did meet him. We were at the Rhodes' party last night."

"Good-looking tough guy but has a sensitive side. How often do you get that combo?" She clicked her nails on the side of the camera. "Now that you brought up Melissa's party, what happened to your truck there? When I went to get coffee this morning at Common Grounds, someone was saying the cops were looking at your truck last night."

"Teenagers playing a prank."

"Little miscreants." She shivered. "Noah wants kids, but I told him I'd only agree if we can give them away before they hit puberty."

"Noah's your husband?" She tried to keep the hopeful note out of her voice, since it really shouldn't matter to her one way or the other if Rebecca Geist had any interest in Coop or not.

"Not yet, but we're working on it." She raised her hand, wiggling her left ring finger. "He'll put a ring on it once we work out some little details."

Kendall raised her brows. "Sounds like a real estate deal instead of a marriage."

"Oh, yeah. That's one of the details. Noah wants me to sign a prenup, and I'm okay with it. He's loaded, already has one ex-wife and doesn't want another bleeding him dry."

"Sounds...reasonable."

"Works for us. I'm done in here." Rebecca pointed to the kitchen. "I'll take a few pics of the kitchen, the master bedroom and the bathroom, and then we'll head outside."

Kendall glanced at Rebecca's high heels. "You are *not* going back there wearing those. I can try to find you a pair of wellies, so you can slog around the moist earth or I can take the pictures for you."

Rebecca wrinkled her nose. "You are kind of rural out here, aren't you? If you wouldn't mind taking some pictures of the property out back, that would be great."

While Rebecca snapped away in the kitchen, Kendall headed to the bedroom and dug a pair of rain boots out of the closet. She toed off her sneakers and pulled the boots on over her bare feet, wiggling her toes.

"Bed made in here?" Rebecca poked her head into the bedroom.

"It's all yours." Kendall scuffed past Rebecca and lifted her jacket from the hook by the front door. She hadn't looked at the property that stretched beyond the patio since she'd been back. A small creek ran through it, but Aunt Cass had never done much with the land.

Rebecca emerged from the back rooms, lifting the camera strap over her head. "I think those will work. Between you and me, if we get one of those California buyers in here with money to burn, they'll probably do a teardown. It's getting more and more common in this area since Evergreen went in. I hope you're not too sentimental about the place."

Sentimental? About a house that had a prominent role in all her nightmares? "Not at all."

"Good. You take this. It's just point and shoot." She snatched the camera back. "Although I should probably make a few adjustments for the outdoors."

"Follow me." Kendall stuffed her arms in the jacket and led the way to the kitchen where a door opened onto the property at the back of the house.

They stepped onto the cement patio, the edge of it dropping off to a small clearing before the trees and brush grew thicker. Kendall tilted her head back and flipped up her hood. "It's drizzling again."

"Big surprise." Rebecca tapped the camera's display screen while aiming it at the forest of trees. "Would be nice if you could get a shot of the creek. I plan on listing this as a waterfront property."

"All of Timberline is waterfront property." Kendall stuck out her tongue and caught a few raindrops in her mouth.

"Your turn." Rebecca thrust the camera at her. "Do you mind if I go back inside and, um, take some more notes."

"Be my guest. I have some sodas, coffee and tea bags in the kitchen. You'll have to warm up the coffee, but it should be fine."

"I still have my latte from Common Grounds, but I'll zap it in your microwave."

"How many pictures do you want?" Kendall ducked her head into the strap of the camera.

"Five or six. Use your judgment." Rebecca slipped back into the house through the door, leaving it open behind her.

Gripping the camera, Kendall crossed the patio and stepped off the cement where her boots squelched against the soggy leaves and saturated dirt. About halfway across the clearing, she turned and took a picture of the back of the house.

When the kidnapper had taken Kayla, he'd left by the front door, which led the police to suspect he wasn't a local, wasn't sure of the terrain back here—not that there weren't a few locals under suspicion.

A drop of rain had found its way into the neck of her jacket and ran down her chest. She shivered and drew the jacket closer. She snapped another photo as she neared the edge of the clearing and approached the dense forest.

The trees and bushes looked as if they presented a solid front, but her father had carved a path for Aunt Cass through the forest to the creek. Kendall parted the branches of some scrubby trees and the path materialized before her, somewhat overgrown, but still distinguishable if you knew where to look.

And she knew where to look.

Whenever her parents had brought her and Kayla to Aunt Cass's, Kendall would escape at the first opportunity to explore. She'd dragged her sister along a few times, but Kayla proved to be more of a hindrance than a companion.

Kendall bit her lip on the guilt. In exchange for having her sister by her side all these years, she would've gladly played with Barbies on the porch every day of her childhood, no matter how much the green mystery of the forest had beckoned.

The wind rustled the wet leaves and they whispered as if Kayla herself stood before her, laughing in disbelief of her twin's vow.

Kendall planted a booted foot on the path and allowed the branches to snap in place behind her. "You're wrong, Kayla. If I could've had you back, I'd gladly have dressed up dolls with you all day long."

Her voice sounded like a shout amid the stillness of the forest. Putting one foot in front of the other along the slick path, Kendall trudged down the slight incline to the creek.

The underbrush thinned out, and the sound of gurgling water broke the silence. She stepped on top of a fallen, rotting log, sending a colony of bugs scurrying out of their home.

She took a deep breath of the pine-scented air, and surveyed the creek. If it had ever run dry, she'd never seen it.

The camera hung heavy around her neck, reminding her of her purpose. She lifted it and positioned the viewfinder to encompass the creek and the big trees that bracketed a stretch of it.

That would be a good place to hang a hammock. Unfortunately, who would want to lounge under perpetually gray skies?

She pressed the button for the picture and scanned to the left. Her brows collided and she zoomed in on a couple of objects sticking up next to the creek bank.

Her heart pounded. Her skin tingled.

She dropped the camera where it banged against her midsection.

As if in a trance, she stumbled over rocks and twigs, her feet making a sucking sound as they met and released the saturated earth beneath them, her eyes focused on the bank of the creek.

When she reached the dreaded destination, that both drew and repelled her at once, she fell to her knees. Her hands shot forward and she traced the outlines of two crosses.

Two small crosses—just the right size for two children.

Chapter Six

"How long has she been out there?" Coop peered around the red-and-white-checked curtain at the kitchen door.

"Longer than I thought she'd be." Rebecca Geist swirled her to-go cup of coffee. "Long enough for me to almost finish my coffee."

"It's starting to come down again." He tapped on the glass of the window installed in the top of the door.

"It's been on and off all morning. I don't think she's going to get swept away by the creek, if that's what you're worried about."

"Maybe not, but that trail down to the water has to be overgrown. She might've tripped over a root or fallen tree." He zipped up his jacket over his khaki uniform. "I'm going to go find her."

"Go ahead, Sir Galahad."

"What?"

Rebecca wiggled her fingers at the door. "Go forth and rescue."

He rolled his eyes and yanked open the kitchen door. A few pieces of patio furniture huddled next to the house, under the eaves, as if trying to stay dry. He marched past them, across the cement patio, and jumped into the dirt at the end of it. This would be a great place for a deck with a fire pit and a gas barbecue.

He slogged through the wet grass of the clearing until

he hit the tree line. With gloved hands, he pawed at the branches bordering the forested area until he found the gap.

Broken twigs and mashed mulch marked Kendall's path down to the creek, and he followed in her footsteps. The silence of the forest closed around him, making him feel like the last man on earth.

"Kendall!" He called her name just to upset the stillness. But she didn't answer.

Unease nibbled at the corners of his mind, and he lengthened his stride in an effort to suppress the worry. The tree stump came out of nowhere and he sprawled forward, the moistness of the dirt soaking into the knees of his pants.

"Damn!"

Staggering to his feet, he brushed the debris from his knees and lunged forward. By the time the world lightened up, his breath was coming in short spurts. He crashed into the clearing fronting the creek, and his mouth dropped open.

"Kendall!"

The frantic creature on the bank of the creek didn't even look up from her task—and her task was digging a hole with her bare hands.

He jogged toward her, tree stumps be damned, and called her name again.

This time she turned her pale face to him, and his heart jumped into his throat as he stumbled to a stop. Her eyes resembled two dark pools, wide and unseeing.

Without saying a word, she resumed her digging.

He rushed to her side and almost bowled her over when he saw the two wooden crosses in front of her.

"Kendall, Kendall, stop." He crouched beside her and grabbed her dirt-caked hands formed into claws.

"Th-they might be here. The children might be here." Her voice broke into a wail.

He pulled her against his chest, and they both fell over, their heads inches from the roiling water of the creek.

"Shh. Kendall, let's get back to the house. Let's get you warmed up." He struggled into a sitting position, dragging her with him. "I'm going to call the FBI to take a look and finish the digging. You don't want to compromise any evidence."

She blinked and a rivulet of water ran down her cheek, and he couldn't tell if it was a tear or just the damned, unstoppable rain.

Hoisting himself to his feet, he hooked an arm around her waist to pull her up with him. "Let's go back."

With one arm around Kendall, Coop fumbled for his cell phone but as soon as the dark canopy of trees sucked them in, he lost reception. "I'll call when we get to the house. How are you holding up?"

Spreading her dirty palms in front of her, she dropped her head. "D-do you think that's where he buried them? Why? Why on my property?"

"We don't know anything yet, Kendall." He brushed a hand across her damp hair, and then flicked up her hood. "Even if the FBI wasn't interested in that mannequin last night, I'm sure Agent Maxfield will be all over this."

They tromped through the dark woods, which had taken on an even more menacing air. When Kendall's sister had been snatched, the FBI must've combed through this area. But they'd never found Kayla, Stevie or Heather. How did children just disappear off the face of the earth? It was every parent's worst nightmare.

The clearing of the house's backyard beckoned beyond the branches crisscrossing over the entrance to the pathway. Coop clawed his way through with one hand, never releasing his hold on Kendall since he still didn't believe her capable of standing on her own.

As they broke free of the underbrush, Rebecca called from the kitchen doorway. "Everything okay?"

Coop pressed his lips together and navigated Kendall to the patio. "Rebecca, can you run a warm bath for Kendall?"

"No!" Kendall dug her fingers into the arm of his jacket. "I want to know what's out there."

Rebecca put a hand to her throat. "What's wrong? What happened out there, Kendall?"

"There are two wooden crosses by the creek, two small crosses."

"You don't think…" Rebecca's eye twitched and she sat down—hard.

"We don't know what to think yet." He reached for the landline. "Did you notice crosses or anything else out there when you looked at the house before?"

"I never actually looked at the property, never went down to the creek. Just looked at the land surveys, property boundaries and some pictures." Rebecca's hand shot out, and she tugged on Kendall's sleeve. "What happened to you? Why are you so filthy?"

He held up his finger as the phone on the other end of the line rang. Agent Maxfield picked up on the third ring. Coop gave all the details to Maxfield and ended the call.

Kendall dragged her sleeve across her nose. "I saw those crosses, and I just started digging."

"Kendall, no." Rebecca jumped from the chair. "I'm going to get you some hot tea. Even if you won't take a bath, why don't you clean up in the bathroom?"

Kendall gazed at her mud-caked hands again as if they belonged to a stranger. "Is Agent Maxfield coming?"

"He's on his way with a team. Wash your face and hands and drink that tea."

Kendall pulled off her muddy boots and lined them up next to the door. Then she slipped the camera from around her neck and placed it on the kitchen table. "I hope I didn't ruin your camera."

"We'll worry about that later." Rebecca held a tea kettle beneath the tap.

When Kendall left the kitchen, Rebecca lifted her eyebrows at him. "Is she okay? It seems like she's in shock—not that I blame her."

"When I found her, she was on her knees digging into the ground with her bare hands." Coop scratched his jaw. "Looked like she'd lost it."

"Yeah, well I would've, too, after what she's been through." Rebecca plucked a tea bag from a tin canister by the stove and swung it around her finger. "If those kids are buried out there, I think we can say goodbye to a sale for a while."

"Really?" Crossing his arms, Coop tilted his head to one side.

"Just thinking ahead. Of course, that's not my only concern or even my primary concern." She dropped the tea bag into the mug and grabbed the handle of the kettle when it started whistling.

Kendall shuffled back into the kitchen in stocking feet, her hands clean, her face still smudged with dirt.

"You look somewhat human—" Rebecca trailed her fingers in the air "—but you really need to get out of those wet clothes."

Kendall took the cup Rebecca extended to her. "I had a jacket on. My clothes are not as wet as they look."

"Sit down, Kendall." Coop shoved out a chair with the toe of his boot. "Agent Maxfield and his guys will be here soon. They're staying one town over."

Her gaze traveled to the window in the back door as she curled her fingers around the mug handle. "I want to be there when they dig."

"Kendall." He pinched the bridge of his nose, squeezing his eyes closed. "I don't think that's necessary."

"It's my property, my…life. I want to be there."

"Do you mind if I don't?" Rebecca hitched her purse over her shoulder and grabbed the camera. "I'm going to get these pictures developed, list the house on MLS and put it up on my website—before anything else happens."

"You might want to tweak a few of those pictures with a photo editor." Kendall dredged the tea bag up and down in the steaming water.

"Why?"

"That's when I first noticed those crosses—through the viewfinder on the camera."

Rebecca gasped. "That's just creepy. Thanks for the heads-up."

"I'm going to want to have a look at your pictures, Rebecca, so send them to me when you upload them to your computer." Coop pushed off the counter. "I'll walk you to your car."

He unfurled one of Kendall's umbrellas stashed in a wicker holder by the front door and held the screen open for Rebecca. Holding the umbrella over Rebecca's head, he accompanied her to her pearl-white caddy and stayed put while she fumbled at the driver's side door.

When she dropped onto the seat, she turned a pale face toward him. "You'll let me know, won't you? What they find?"

"Sure, I'll tell you, but if those kids are there, I won't have to. That news is going to spread around the town like a wildfire."

"I hope to God they're not. For Kendall's sake and the families', I hope to God they're not." Her voice quavered.

And this time, he didn't think Rebecca had the housing market on her mind. He slammed her car door and hustled back to the house.

Kendall was still sipping her tea, staring out the window. Her eyes had lost their vacant look, but he didn't like what had replaced it—fear, sadness.

"Are you okay? I'm going to make a few phone calls to the station."

"I'm fine. Go ahead." She dragged in a deep breath. "I'm not going to fall apart, despite what you witnessed out there."

"There are different ways to fall apart, Kendall."

"You're talking to a therapist here. I realize that. I'm not going to fall apart in any way."

He held up his phone. "I'm going to call the station, even though I don't think we can spare anyone to come out and assist the FBI."

"I thought you were taking a few days off, starting today."

"I have vacation time to burn, but I had to come in today—and now I'm glad I did."

"I know you have a small department, but was this section of the woods searched when the first child went missing?"

"Of course. We searched all along the creeks and rivers."

"So, those crosses are a recent addition to the landscape."

"It would seem so." He placed his cell on the counter and punched in the number to the station on Kendall's landline. The desk sergeant picked up on the first ring. Must be a slow day—in some parts.

"Anyone available to come out here, Sarge?"

"Probably not, Coop. Ever since the kidnappings, the folks want to see the police presence. We've got two guys on patrol right now."

"Okay, just keep everyone apprised of the situation, and I'm going to stay out here to wait for the FBI." He ended the conversation with the sergeant and placed two more calls. By the time he was off the phone, Kendall had finished her tea and had wandered into the living room.

She called out. "I think the FBI's here."

Coop joined her in the other room and looked out the window at the dark sedan pulling into the drive behind Kendall's truck. A white, unmarked van drove up seconds later.

Coop opened the front door and stepped onto the porch.

Maxfield started up the drive toward the house and Coop called out, "We'll meet you around the back. Go through the wooden gate to your right."

He shut the door and turned to Kendall. "You sure you want to do this?"

She answered him by yanking her still-damp jacket from the hook.

She pulled on her rain boots by the door and he followed her out to the cement slab her aunt had called a patio.

Agent Maxfield and another dark-suited agent with a trench coat led a procession of CSI types, two of them carrying shovels.

Coop's gaze dropped to the fibbies' dark wing tips, and he shook his head. At heart the agents were a bunch of city-boy desk jockeys.

"Let's do this, Sheriff Sloane. Lead the way."

After a few brief introductions, Kendall charged ahead. "I'll show you. This way."

The small army crashed through the wooded area, dispelling the aura of mystery and foreboding he'd sensed before.

They swarmed into the clearing by the creek, and Kendall jabbed her finger in the air. "Over there."

As Maxfield drew closer to the crosses, he cursed. "Why is the area disturbed? Is this how you found it, Ms. Rush?"

"I disturbed it. When I saw the crosses, my first instinct was to dig."

"Was it?" Maxfield's nostrils flared. "Did you notice anything on top of the gra…ground?"

"I didn't notice anything."

"Doesn't mean there wasn't something, and you disturbed it."

"Hey." Coop held up his hand. "Kendall was in shock. She reacted. Now let's move forward and make the best of what could be a terrible situation."

Kendall scowled at him for his efforts, and he rolled his shoulders.

"Hendricks, Wong, start digging—very carefully. Chafee, pull up those crosses and wrap them in plastic."

The agents got to work, and with each shovelful of dirt wrenched from the ground, Kendall sidled closer and closer to Coop.

Until her shoulder pressed against his.

The rain had stopped, but the soggy ground made for easy digging, and the agents barely broke a sweat as they piled up mud on the edge of the creek.

After one vigorous plunge into the earth, Kendall jumped. "Be careful, just in case…"

Maxfield responded. "Don't worry, Ms. Rush. They're being as gentle as possible and examining every shovelful of dirt as they dump it out."

Kendall's body grew tauter and tauter with each passing minute. She was practically vibrating beside him, so he draped an arm across her shoulders and pulled her closer until every line of her body pressed against his.

"Maybe it's nothing at all, Kendall. Maybe someone planted two crosses by the river and there's nothing beneath them. Maybe it's a pet."

"Two pets?"

"Hey, hey, I got something." Wong waved his gloved hand in the air.

Kendall sprang from Coop's side as if she'd been poised on coils ready to launch.

Coop followed her with a knot in his stomach and a prayer on his lips.

Maxfield stepped in front of her, his arms spread out to the side. "Hold on, Ms. Rush."

"What is it?" She bobbed her head back and forth like a boxer, trying to see around Mayfield's body.

Coop could see over Maxfield's head, and Wong was plowing through a mound of dirt in his shovel with one hand.

"It's a box, a small, metal box." Wong held it up, and the gray of the legal-envelope-sized box matched the dreary sky.

Kendall let out a sob and stumbled backward, her body going limp.

Coop caught her against his chest and murmured in her ear. "It's a box—a small box. Just a small box."

Not nearly big enough to accommodate a child.

Mayfield held out his hand for the box. "Keep digging, Hendricks."

Wong smacked the box into his boss's palm. "Should I keep digging?"

"You can go a little deeper, but I think this is it."

But both agents had stopped their activity once Maxfield had the box in his hands. He began to pry open the lid carefully with his gloved fingers, and everyone seemed to stop breathing. The air pulsed with expectation.

Maxfield removed the lid. A white rectangle rested at the bottom of the box.

"Is it a note?" Kendall's voice held a hint of dread, and Coop wrapped his arms around her waist, his desire to shield her overpowering.

The object seemed to have mesmerized everyone. Coop cleared his throat. "I think it's a photograph. Maxfield?"

"I think you're right." He withdrew a leather case from his jacket, unzipped the case and selected a pair of tweezers from the felt-lined interior. He pulled off one glove to manipulate the tweezers and pinched the corner of the picture between the pincers and turned it over.

All six of the people in the circle recoiled, and Kendall cried out and dug her fist against her mouth.

"It's the girl, Cherie." Maxfield released the picture so that it dropped back against the metal box. "It's the girl holding a newspaper—proof of life."

"No, no." Kendall raked her fingers through her wet, tangled hair. "It's not proof of life. The newspaper she's holding is from twenty-five years ago. The headline is for the missing Timberline Trio."

Chapter Seven

If Coop, solid as a rock, hadn't been behind her at those mini grave sites, she would've collapsed in the mud.

The other agent, Hendricks, had made a similar discovery under his cross, only the picture in the metal box had been that of the kidnapped boy, Harrison, holding another newspaper from twenty-five years ago with the Timberline Trio story.

The remaining FBI guy in her kitchen, Agent Maxfield, pocketed his phone and placed his coffee cup in the sink. "The parents are going to meet us at our hotel suite to look at the pictures. This development has given them a ray of hope."

Kendall swallowed and exchanged a look with Coop. She wouldn't exactly call finding pictures of the kidnapped children buried in graves with crosses stuck in the ground a ray of hope, but she understood the parents would be grateful for any shred of evidence that their children hadn't been immediately murdered. She hunched her shoulders against the shiver zipping up her spine.

Coop ended his own call to the station and asked, "All the other evidence, including the pictures, is going to a lab?"

"We got this, Sloane."

Coop's jaw tightened. "The guy used a Polaroid camera to avoid having the pictures on his cell phone or having them printed out somewhere, but that in itself is a clue. Who still has a Polaroid camera these days?"

Maxfield shrugged. "Good question. I haven't seen one used in years."

Coop narrowed his eyes. "Now do you believe that mannequin in Kendall's truck is connected to the kidnapper? Those pictures were buried on her property for a reason."

"Maybe, maybe not. Maybe the reason was the soft earth next to the creek, the out-of-the-way location and the fact that the property had been vacant until Ms. Rush arrived yesterday."

Coop opened his mouth, and then shook his head. "Yeah, whatever."

"Thank you for the coffee, Ms. Rush. I know it was a shock for you to find those crosses on your land, but this is a big break for us."

"I—I hope it gives some comfort to the parents, and I hope it means those kids are alive."

She grimaced. But for what purpose if not ransom?

"I'm going to get back to our command center at the hotel and meet with the parents." He thrust out his hand. "Sheriff Sloane, thanks for your assistance. I can see myself out, ma'am."

She walked Agent Maxfield to the door anyway and locked it behind him. Then she turned and pressed her back against it, closing her eyes.

She heard Coop's footfall on the carpet, and her eyelids flew open.

He took her hands. "Are you ready to get cleaned up now?"

She glanced down at her dirty clothes and stringy hair. "I guess so. You'd better head back to the station. You've been camped out here all day."

"For good reason. You heard Captain Obvious there. This is the biggest break they've had in the case yet—the only break. My guys know where I am and how to reach me—and technically I'm on vacation."

"I just hope it means Cheri and Harrison are safe... somewhere." She'd avoided using their names before, but they deserved to be human. Her bottom lip started to quiver and she sucked it in. "Anyway, thanks for all your help today."

"I'm off duty now. Well, I'm never really off duty, but I'm not expected back at the station today." He squeezed her hands once and released them. "You go take that bath that you should've taken about two hours ago, and I'll clean up the mess those fibbies made in your kitchen."

"You don't have to stay, Coop, really. I'm fine." Maybe she would've been more convincing if her voice hadn't wavered on the last word. She cleared her throat. "After seeing those crosses, I understand if you want to see Steffi, give her a hug."

"As a parent, seeing something like that gets you right here." He thumped his chest with his fist. "But somehow, I don't think Steffi would appreciate it if I came by her classroom and gave her a hug. And right after school she has a Brownie meeting."

"Okay, but if you have something to do, I'll be fine."

"I know *you're* fine, but I still need some time to decompress before I see Steffi later, and nothing says decompression like washing dishes."

"Right." She'd put up a fight, but she could tell by the set of his strong jaw that he wasn't about to leave her.

And she didn't want him to.

"The dishes are all yours, but lunch is on me."

He waved her off and strode toward the kitchen—a man on a mission.

She gathered some clean clothes from her bedroom and shut the bathroom door behind her. She turned on the water and shoved the plastic cherry-dotted shower curtain to one side.

The pile of dirty clothes mounted in the corner as she shed one damp layer after another. The clothes didn't even belong in the hamper with her other clothes. She didn't want to contaminate them with creek mud.

She stepped into the tub and faced the spray of water, scrubbing her body hard enough to remove a layer of skin. What was she trying to wash away, the terror of seeing those crosses or the years' old memories that still haunted her?

She poked her head around the shower curtain and grabbed a small brush from the metal caddy hanging above the toilet. She squeezed some soap onto the brush and scrubbed the dirt from her fingernails. She had no idea what she'd been trying to accomplish out there in the rain, on her hands and knees. Instinct had taken over with fear prodding her.

The tap on the bathroom door made her drop the brush.

"You okay in there?"

Coop was really worried about her. What did he think she'd do?

"I'm good. Just trying to get the last bits of dirt from beneath my fingernails." She ducked down to pick up the brush.

"Hurry up. Lunch is getting cold."

She shut off the water. "Lunch? I told you I would make lunch."

"I was too hungry to wait."

She yanked her towel from the rack. That man sure liked to take charge, but right now she didn't mind.

It took her ten minutes tops to dry off, shimmy into a pair of black leggings, a camisole and an oversize red flannel shirt. She stuffed her feet into a pair of fuzzy slippers and scuffed into the living room, still toweling off her hair.

Coop peered around the corner of the kitchen. "It's about time. I thought you'd gone down the drain."

He'd kept his tone light, but it still carried an edge of concern. Did he hover over his daughter, Steffi, like this, too?

"What's for lunch?" She bent over at the waist and wrapped the towel around her head in a turban.

"Get in here and see." He ushered her into the kitchen waving a checkered dish towel and then slung it over his shoulder.

She sniffed the air as she joined him in the kitchen. "Smells good and toasty—and like bacon."

"It's all of the above." He pulled out a chair from the kitchen table. "Grilled cheese with bacon and some tomato soup. You had the can of soup in the cupboard, so I assumed you like tomato soup."

"I do." She sat down and dropped the paper towel that was doubling as a napkin into her lap. "And this sandwich looks yummy. I feel like I'm back in grade school and coming home for lunch. Is this what you feed your daughter?"

"She doesn't like tomato soup, just chicken noodle or excuse me, chicken and stars."

"Sounds like a girl who knows her mind."

He rolled his eyes as he took the seat across from her. "If that's a euphemism for *stubborn*, yeah, she knows her mind."

Coop had even sliced the sandwich diagonally, and she picked up one half and bit off the corner. The melted cheese paired with the crunch of the bread with just a hint of butter fired up memories of warm hugs from Aunt Cass trying to comfort her, trying to make her feel whole again. The kidnapper hadn't just snatched Kayla from the family, he'd destroyed the family. Her father died too early, and her mother had a breakdown. Cass had been there though, maybe to make up for the guilt she'd felt that Kayla had been taken while in her care.

"Bread too soggy?" Coop's eyebrows rose over anxious eyes. "You stopped chewing."

"It's perfect." She dropped the sandwich on the plate and brushed the crumbs from her fingertips. "The cheese is a little hot."

"When you were taking so long in the shower, I zapped everything in the microwave." He dipped his spoon in his bowl. "Are you warm enough? I was going to get a fire going in the fireplace, but I wasn't sure it was safe. If your aunt hadn't used the fireplace in a while, the chimney might need clearing."

"I'm not sure. The furnace works great, though, and I'm plenty warm." She swirled the tip of her spoon in the creamy, red soup, sending rings out to the edge of the bowl. "Do you think this kidnapper is the same guy who took my sister and the other two children?"

He took a big bite of his sandwich and took his time chewing. After he swallowed, he took a sip of soup. "He could be, although the gap in time is unusual."

"At least you're entertaining the thought, unlike the FBI."

"If he's not the same guy, this kidnapper is obviously aware of the Timberline Trio and is playing some kind of game." He tapped his spoon on the side of the bowl. "There might be three perps—the original kidnapper, the current kidnapper and someone else playing games. So, the one playing the games may not even be the kidnapper."

"How could he not be, after those pictures?"

"The pictures do suggest he's the same guy, but I'm not sure why the kidnapper would risk pulling these pranks."

"Didn't you just tell me last night that he was a kidnapper and we couldn't possibly guess his motives?

"I did say that, didn't I? I just can't figure out why this

guy is running around leaving hints that exponentially increase his chances of slipping up and getting caught." He slurped a spoonful of soup, and two red spots that matched the liquid in his bowl stained his cheeks. "Sorry for the noisy eating. That was hotter than I expected. I'm just glad Steffi didn't witness those bad manners since I'm always on her about stuff like that."

"Sounds like you're a good dad—grilled cheese sandwiches and good manners."

"I try."

She broke off a piece of crust from her sandwich. "How old was she when her mom died?"

Coop dropped his spoon in his bowl and took a long drink of water.

Was he going to refuse to answer? He must still be in love with his dead wife since he was so clearly not over the tragedy. She had a client in a similar situation—widowed six years yet had refused to date since. Of course, unless Coop answered, Kendall had no idea when his wife died. It could've been only months ago.

If so, she might have to shelve any designs she'd had on Cooper Sloane's body.

He finished off his water and swiped a paper towel across his mouth. "Steffi's mother died when Steffi was almost two years old."

Kendall was no math genius but she quickly figured three years should be plenty of time to move on, but as a therapist, she knew there was no one-size-fits-all for grief, and leaving a small child behind made healing even more difficult.

"I'm sorry, Coop."

"Thanks." He crumpled the paper towel and tossed it in his plate. "Do you need anything else before I take off?"

Had she driven him off with her questions? Her gaze

darted to the back door. Of course, he had to leave at some point, but she wasn't ready to be in this house alone.

"I'm okay. I'm going to call the cleaning crew Rebecca recommended and post the estate sale online. I might even get ambitious and make a few signs."

"Sounds like you have your work cut out for you. I'm going to swing by the station before I head home." He stood up and took her dishes. "I know you're only going to be here for another week or two, Kendall, but maybe you should set up a security system—at least some cameras on the property. It'll be a good selling point for the house, even if you can't take advantage of it for very long."

"I like that idea. Where would I shop for something like that, a hardware store?"

"I'll help you out with it. I may be able to get it done for free since it could be a police matter."

"Free is good." She joined him at the sink and cinched her fingers around his wrist. "Stop washing. You already cleaned up after the agents and made lunch."

His strong hands stopped their busy work. "Then I'll leave it for you."

She handed him a dish towel to dry his hands. "Thanks for everything today, Coop, not just the cleanup and the lunch. I don't know if I could've handled finding those crosses on my own."

"Anytime." He took her by the shoulders, his touch at once gentle and insistent. "Just promise me one thing, Kendall."

When he looked at her with the intensity of those blue eyes, she'd promise him anything. Her lashes fluttered. "What?"

"If you ever feel scared or upset or…depressed, call me. Can you do that?"

Depressed? Despite the issues she carried with her from childhood, she rarely felt depressed. Had she presented as depressed? "I will. Thanks for the offer, but are you implying that a therapist shouldn't try to heal herself? Because we don't."

"Do therapists really *heal* anyone?" He'd kept his tone light, but something flickered in his eyes.

"*Heal* isn't the right word. I was just playing on the phrase 'Doctor, heal thyself.' As I told you before, a therapist isn't necessarily in therapy because they have issues."

"Do you? Have issues you need to work out, I mean?" He dropped his hands and stepped back. "I'm sorry. All I meant to say is if you need anything don't hesitate to call me. You still have my card?"

"Right by the telephone."

"Put it in your cell, also. Just in case."

"Will do."

He backed out of the small kitchen and threaded his way through the boxes in the living room to the front door. Lifting his jacket from the hook, he turned. "I'll let you know if something comes from the mannequin or the pictures—if the FBI lets me know and it's something we can share."

"That's a lot of ifs, but I'd appreciate it."

She stood at the door watching him saunter to his SUV with his long stride. The attraction between them was undeniable, but did his interest spring from the belief that she could help him with this case?

She slammed the door. It didn't matter anyway. In a few weeks, she'd be putting this case, this house, this town—and Sheriff Cooper Sloane in her rearview mirror.

ALMOST FOUR HOURS LATER, Kendall stepped into the hubbub of Sutter's Restaurant. Standing at the door inhaling the smell of charbroiled burgers, she let the chatter bubble over her.

This was exactly what she needed. After calling the cleaning crew and setting up an appointment, listening to her voice mail, talking to her best friend back home, checking in on a client who was having a minicrisis, and composing an online ad announcing the estate sale, she couldn't sit in that silent house one more minute. Aunt Cass hadn't even had a TV at the end. Her aunt had been quirky, but she'd tried her best to fill in for Kendall's missing-in-action parents, and Kendall had clung to her more than she had her own mother.

As her gaze traveled around the room, she had the distinct feeling people were avoiding her, looking away. Crud. Everyone must've already heard about the pictures buried on her property, and she'd become a walking black cloud. She didn't even have Melissa and Daryl to fall back on since they'd taken off for Seattle for a few days.

Kendall scooped in a big breath and smiled at the hostess. "Table for one, please."

"We have that one in the middle of the room or one by the kitchen."

"I'll take the one in the middle." She had no intention of hiding out by the kitchen, so she followed the hostess to the table set for four, squeezed between a family with two kids and a couple poring over a laptop together. Sutter's was known more for its food than its atmosphere anyway.

When her waitress showed up, Kendall ordered a beer and then snapped open the plastic menu.

"Mind if we join you?"

She edged down the menu and peered over the top at Coop, dressed in a pair of faded jeans and holding hands with an adorable girl with blond ringlets and big eyes as blue as her daddy's.

"Unless you want a quiet dinner by yourself." His mouth quirked into a smile. "But I think you picked the wrong place for that."

"You didn't want the table by the kitchen, either?" She smiled at Steffi. "Pull up a chair."

Coop settled his daughter in her seat, and then took the one across from Kendall. "Steffi, this is Ms. Rush."

Kendall waved. "Hi, Steffi. You can call me Kendall."

The little girl tilted her head to one side. "That's a funny name."

"Steffi, that's not polite," Coop said firmly.

Kendall widened her smile until it hurt. "Well, I like your name."

"It's really Stephanie but Steffi is easier. So everyone calls me Steffi."

"I like Stephanie, too. Are you in kindergarten?"

"Yes. My teacher is Mrs. Bryant and she has a long braid." She eyed Kendall's hair. "Longer than yours and we have a blue rug, but I told her I like pink better and we should have a pink rug instead of a blue rug, and then we read the book with the trains but I don't like the train book because Colby likes the train book and he likes the blue rug."

"Whew, I didn't realize kindergarten was filled with such drama."

Coop chuckled and rolled his eyes. "You had to ask."

Steffi opened her menu and pressed her lips together, ending the conversation.

Kendall let out a long breath between puckered lips when the waitress arrived at the table, tapping her pencil against her order pad. She drew up when she saw Coop and Steffi. "Oh, can I get you something to drink?"

"I'll have a beer." He pointed to Kendall's bottle. "What she's having. And my daughter will have a lemonade."

"Coffee, please." Steffi looked up from her menu and batted her lashes at the waitress.

The waitress raised her brows at Coop.

He shook his head. "Lemonade."

If Kendall had been expecting some shy, sad little girl missing her dead mother, Steffi had just blown that preconception out of the water. If she'd been expecting Coop's daughter to lavish affection on her dad's female friend, Steffi had blown that one out of the water, too.

"She's a pistol, Coop."

"Don't I know it?" He tapped his menu on the table. "Did you get everything done this afternoon?"

"Cleaning crew is coming tomorrow, and I advertised my estate sale. I even managed a telephone session with one of my patients."

"You do that?"

"If it's an emergency."

His eyes narrowed. "Was it an emergency?"

"A minor one." She took a sip of beer through the foam and studied his face. Why did he seem so interested in emergency telephone sessions when he'd given her the impression that he didn't put much stock in therapy? Maybe he could benefit from a little head shrinking.

He buried his un-shrunken head in the menu and gave Steffi some suggestions. "You don't always have to eat chicken nuggets."

"Have you had the hamburgers here yet, Steffi?"

"I like hamburgers, but no onions, no lettuce, no tomatoes, no pickles, no cheese."

"We get it, Steffi." Coop snapped his menu shut. "One burger, ketchup only."

"And onion rings." Kendall winked at Steffi. "We can share some onion rings."

"I don't like onions." Steffi wrinkled her nose.

"You'll like these. They're sort of like chicken nuggets but with onions inside instead of chicken."

Steffi screwed up her face and looked at the ceiling as if trying to picture onion nuggets.

The waitress returned with Coop's and Steffi's drinks and took their order. She jerked her thumb over her shoulder toward the hostess stand. "Do you want me to bring some crayons and a coloring book menu?"

Coop answered, "That would be great, thanks."

He clinked the neck of his bottle against her glass. "Cheers."

"Cheers." She took a sip of beer and dabbed her mouth with a napkin. "Have you heard anything yet from the FBI?"

"Had a conversation with Maxfield." He took the menu and crayons from the waitress, thanked her and put them in front of Steffi. "The parents were both relieved to see the pictures and horrified by the manner in which they were found."

"I can understand that." Kendall took a gulp of beer. "I suppose they haven't found any evidence on the boxes or pictures yet."

"Not yet, and there were no fingerprints or fibers on the mannequin."

Steffi looked up from her coloring. "What's a mannequin?"

Kendall glanced at Coop and put a finger to her lips. Kids tuned in to adult conversations more than the adults realized—at least that's what her clients told her.

Coop tweaked his daughter's nose. "A mannequin is like a big doll. Stores use them to show clothes."

"I know. They don't have any eyes or hair."

A little shiver crept across Kendall's flesh.

They dropped the conversation about mannequins and evidence and Polaroid photos showing kidnapped children. Kendall wasn't sure she could stomach her food if they hadn't.

After several more minutes of talking about the weather, the food at the party last night and the couple that seemed glued to their laptops, the waitress showed up with their food.

"Onion rings for the table, a pepper-jack burger, a house charbroil and a plain with ketchup." The waitress delivered their baskets of food with a flourish. "Anything else? Another round of beers?"

She and Coop both declined a second beer. Then Kendall shoved the basket of onion rings toward Steffi. "Do you want to try one?"

"I guess." Steffi hooked her finger around a ring and dropped it on her plate.

While they fussed with condiments and napkins, Kendall watched the interaction between Coop and his daughter. He seemed to have a good relationship with Steffi—joking and tender with just the right amount of parental sternness.

And for her part, Steffi had dropped the chilly attitude toward the woman who had butted in on the father-daughter dinner, not that the girl had actually warmed toward her. Kendall had always shied away from children, had absolutely refused to see any families or children in therapy. So, the slight chill from Steffi suited her just fine.

After she'd crunched through a few onion rings and had eaten half of her burger, Steffi tugged on her father's sleeve. "Look, Daddy. There's Genevieve. Can I go see her?"

"We don't want to disturb their meal." Coop twisted in his seat and waved at a family of four, the little girl bouncing in her seat in the booth and pointing at Steffi.

The woman cupped her hand and gestured Steffi over.

"Genevieve's mom says it's okay, but as soon as they get their food you need to come back here."

"Okay." Steffi was gone in a flash, squeezing into the booth next to her friend, whispering and giggling.

"Are the children worried about the kidnappings?"

Coop dragged an onion ring through a puddle of ketchup on his plate. "They're aware of the abductions, of course. One of the kids was a first-grader at their school. The other was homeschooled. We parents have warned them about stranger-danger and are much more diligent about keeping tabs on them. But you do know that both children were snatched from their homes, don't you?"

"Yes, just like the Timberline Trio."

He crunched the onion ring and swallowed. "So, the parents are definitely on edge. There was a little of that at the Rhodes party last night, although you might've missed it."

"Yeah, because everyone immediately stops talking about the kidnappings whenever I show up."

"They're just being sensitive."

"Do they have the same consideration for Wyatt?"

"Sort of, but it's different. He still lives here, and he's been doing some work at the police station so it's been kind of unavoidable for him."

"Has anyone started looking funny at Chuck Rawlings yet?"

"Oh, yeah."

"Has the FBI checked him out?"

"FBI checked him out just like the cops checked him out twenty-five years ago."

"Well, he is the only registered sex offender in Timberline."

"Not anymore."

"Really?" She dropped her burger and wiped her hands on the nearest napkin. "Did Evergreen Software bring a few more pervs to town?"

"In an indirect way. The *pervs* in question don't actually work for Evergreen, but the improved economy brought them here."

"That's just great. They all checked out?"

"Yep. Even old Chuck."

"I can't believe Chuck Rawlings had any alibis since he lives in that creepy, old cabin all by himself and rarely goes out. He was the same way when we were kids. We used to dare each other to play ding-dong ditch at his place."

"There's no evidence to connect Rawlings to the kidnappings—now or then." Coop did a quick slice of his finger across his throat, and then smiled. "Hey, Britt, I hope Steffi didn't disturb your family."

"Not at all. Genevieve wouldn't sit still until Steffi came over to the table." The petite blonde put her hands on Steffi's shoulders as her gaze kept shifting to Kendall. "And as soon as our food arrived, she told me she had to go back to your table."

"Good job, kiddo." Coop tugged on one of Steffi's curls. "Britt Fletcher, this is Kendall Rush. Kendall, Britt."

Kendall reached across the table and shook the other woman's hand. "Nice to meet you."

"You, too." Britt acted as if she wanted to say more. In fact, she acted as if she wouldn't mind conducting a thorough interrogation of her.

As if sensing Britt's curiosity, Coop dismissed her. "Thanks for bringing her over. We'll let you get back to your family and your dinner."

Britt held up a hand, wiggled her fingers and returned to her table.

Instead of taking a seat, Steffi hung on the back of her chair. "Daddy, I'm tired. I wanna go home. I don't feel good."

"Really?" Coop's hand shot out to feel Steffi's forehead. "You're a little warm."

"My stomach hurts. I gotta leave *now*."

Coop half rose out of his chair, throwing an apologetic look her way.

"Go." Kendall flicked her hand in the air. "Get Steffi home."

He tucked three twenty-dollar bills beneath the saltshaker on the table. "Dinner's on me. I'll call you tomorrow."

She waved at Steffi whose lips were turned down in a pout. She either really did have a stomachache or she didn't like Daddy's new friend. And that's why Kendall never dated men with kids—one of many reasons.

The waitress returned to the table with the check. "Do you want to take any of this food with you?"

"No, thanks." She handed the waitress the sixty bucks, which was more than enough to cover the bill and the tip, and finished her beer.

Kendall weaved her way through the tables in the dining area and donned her jacket at the hostess stand. She pushed out of the restaurant, flipping up her hood against the drizzle.

The restaurant had been crowded when she'd arrived and all the good parking spots in the front had been taken, but she didn't mind the walk to her truck since it delayed her return to Aunt Cass's house.

She couldn't get the image out of her mind of some sick freak digging those holes by the side of the creek.

Pausing at a gift shop, she cupped her hand around her eyes and peered into the window. She grinned at the stuffed frog sitting on a shelf, its froggy legs dangling in space. Timberline had adopted the Pacific chorus frog as its town mascot years ago, and it appeared that even the high-tech vibe of Evergreen Software hadn't torpedoed the little frog's appeal.

She straightened up and walked past the corner of the shop. Two steps across the entrance of the alley, a whispering sound drew her attention. As she turned her head toward the sound, a strong arm grabbed her around the middle and yanked her into the alley.

Chapter Eight

Just as a scream gathered in her lungs, the vise around her middle dropped.

"Shh. Kendall, it's me, Wyatt."

She stumbled back, her fist pressed against her chest where her heart threatened to escape. "My God, Wyatt. Why did you do that? You scared me half to death."

"I'm sorry." In the shadows of the alley, Wyatt slumped against the wall of the building and covered his face. "I need help, Kendall. I don't want anyone to see me like this."

She licked her dry lips, her heart still pummeling her ribs. "What's wrong?"

He stuffed his hand into his jacket pocket and withdrew it slowly. "I found this on my porch today." He uncurled his fist to reveal a small dark object on the palm of his hand.

"I can't even see what it is." She took his wrist and pulled him closer to the light in the street. And then her stomach sank.

"A dinosaur." She picked up the plastic toy between two fingers as if it could come to life and nip a piece of flesh out of her hand.

"You know what it means, right?" The hand Wyatt still had outstretched trembled.

"The kidnapper left a plastic dinosaur when he took Harrison." Coop had told her not to mention the pink rib-

bon left at the scene of the first kidnapping or the dinosaur, but surely Wyatt knew anyway.

He snatched his hand back and covered his mouth with
it. "What? No, no, no."

"Stop, Wyatt." She tugged on his sleeve.

He jerked away. "I never told you this, Kendall, but
when my brother was kidnapped the guy who took him
also took one of my dinosaurs from my collection."

Kendall crossed her arms. Just like he'd taken the pink
ribbon from her hair. Did Wyatt not know before she'd
told him that the present-day kidnapper had left a plastic
dinosaur when he snatched Harrison?

The chill of the night had seeped into her bones. "Let's
go inside Sutter's and get a beer."

"I can't go in there. Don't you see the way they look at
us? It's almost like they blame us for this second wave of
kidnappings. Heather Brice's family had it right by moving away from all this, away from the memories."

"I—I don't think they blame us." But Wyatt had nailed
it. They were like two bad omens hovering over Timberline bringing bad news, reminding the residents of a past
they'd rather forget, a past that interfered with their bright,
shiny, tech future.

"I don't think you need to worry, Wyatt. You're a big
guy. You can handle yourself, and you can handle a gun,
too. Don't you still hunt?"

"Yeah, but it's not that, Kendall. It's not the physical."
He drove the heels of his hands into his temples. "It's the
memories. I miss my little brother every day. Don't you
miss Kayla?"

"Of course, but we need to move on, Wyatt, or it'll drive
us crazy." She felt for her phone in her pocket. "Give me
your number. I'm going to look up a good therapist in the
area. It can even be someone in the next town, so you don't

run into anyone from Timberline if that's what you're worried about. You really need to get some help."

"I thought I could see you, Kendall. You're the only one who knows what I'm going through. I'll pay you."

"I can't see a friend as a client, Wyatt. It doesn't work that way. Besides, a therapist doesn't have to experience what you're experiencing to be able to help you." She tapped her phone. "Give me your number, so I can call you with a recommendation."

He closed his eyes and recited his number, which she entered into her phone. "You sure you don't want to go into Sutter's and have a beer? Relax a little?"

He grunted. "I already have one DUI on my record. I can't afford another."

"Okay, I don't want to encourage drinking and driving." She patted his arm. "Are you feeling better? You should tell Coop about the dinosaur even though it's probably just someone playing a trick. There's a lot of that going on."

"But nobody knew about the dinosaur he took from me. That wasn't released."

It had been the same with the pink ribbon, but that had been years ago. "Look, Wyatt, those old files have been passed around and seen by hundreds of pairs of eyes by now. Anything could've gotten out about the case."

If she could follow the advice she was dispensing so freely to Wyatt, she'd feel a lot better about going back to Aunt Cass's house by herself. But then therapists were great at dishing out advice to others that they didn't take themselves.

"I guess you're right, but I'll let Coop know. I've been on edge since this whole thing started."

"I think everyone has." She glanced at the sky. "I'm going to head home before the heavens open."

"Do you want me to walk you to your truck?"

She wanted to get away from Wyatt as far and as quickly

as she could. "That's okay. Try to breathe and I'll get back to you with a therapist."

"Thanks, Kendall, and I'm sorry I scared you."

"I'm a little on edge, too, Wyatt."

Grasping the edge of the building, he leaned into the sidewalk and looked both ways. "Be careful, Kendall."

"I'm fine. The truck is close, and there are still lots of people out and about."

She raised her hand in a wave and started down the sidewalk, her boots clicking on the cement. She paused at a few more shop windows and at her second stop, became aware of a figure across the street paralleling her course down the sidewalk.

Flipping up the hood of her jacket, she jerked her head to the side, catching the man across the way illuminated by the light spilling from a candy shop. She sucked in a quick breath.

Chuck Rawlings hadn't changed much in twenty-five years. His long hair had turned silver, but he still carried himself hunched over as if guilty of something. He'd shoved a hand in his pocket and made a half turn toward the display of sweets in the window, but he'd been watching her and maybe even following her since Sutter's.

She lengthened her stride and bypassed the remaining shop windows to reach the truck. As she unlocked the door, she cranked her head over her shoulder. This time she met Chuck's eyes.

He'd stopped and turned toward the street, toward her. He nodded once and continued on his way, his silver ponytail swaying behind him.

Did he want a therapist, too? The man had been the one registered sex offender in town back in the day. As a kid, she'd had no idea what that meant. As an adult, she'd looked him up and discovered he'd had what he'd called consensual sex with a sixteen-year-old and a seventeen-year-old. Creepy, but hardly dangerous—unless you were a sixteen-year-old girl.

As she climbed behind the wheel it occurred to her that Wyatt hadn't even mentioned the pictures of the kidnapped children holding newspapers with the Timberline Trio headlines. He obviously hadn't heard about the discovery, and she was glad she hadn't been the one to tell him.

If a plastic dinosaur had sent him over the edge, what would those pictures have done to him?

She drove back to Aunt Cass's and left the truck in front of the house. Looking left and right, she unlocked the front door and scooted inside. She clicked the dead bolt into place and closed her eyes. First Wyatt and then Rawlings—must be something in the air tonight. She could use that security system Coop had suggested right now. His protectiveness gave her a warm and fuzzy feeling. Well, maybe not fuzzy but definitely warm.

She liked everything about the man. Too bad his daughter didn't like her, not that Kendall was the nurturing, maternal type with kids anyway.

She checked the windows and wandered into the kitchen to make some tea. As the water boiled on the kettle, she peered out the back door toward the creek. A few minutes later, her eyes ached trying to pick out shapes and movement in the forest.

The tea kettle screamed, and Kendall placed her palms against the cold glass of the window. *Please, God. Keep those children safe—even if You couldn't protect Kayla.*

THE FOLLOWING MORNING, Kendall showed the four-woman cleaning crew around the house. "Don't worry about the boxes. Clean around them, and maybe I can have you back out for a once-over with the vacuum and a mop once I get rid of this stuff."

"Do we have to go out there?" Annie, the group's

spokeswoman, a Native American from the local Quileute tribe, jerked her head toward the patio.

"I'm going to hire a landscaping service to clean the patio and trim the bushes bordering it." Crossing her arms, Kendall drummed her fingers against her biceps. "Why?"

Annie placed one hand over her heart. "We heard about the pictures of the children buried by the creek."

"Yes, it was…unnerving. If it was the kidnapper who planted those photos, he's not going to be back here, though. You'll be fine." Kendall added a bright smile to punctuate her words. If she kept telling everyone else how fine they'd be, maybe she could believe it of herself.

While the women hauled their cleaning supplies into the house, Kendall finished tagging the boxes—ones for the Salvation Army, ones to drag outside for the estate sale and ones for the online auction site. None to take home—she didn't need any more reminders of this damp, gloomy place once she'd escaped back to Phoenix. She had fond, warm memories of Aunt Cass. She didn't need her knick-knacks.

Someone tapped on the screen door.

Kendall scribbled on a box with black marker. "No need to stand on ceremony. You can come in and out as you please."

"That's mighty nice of you, ma'am."

She swiveled around at the sound of Coop's low, teasing voice that had started doing funny things to her insides.

"Oh, it's you!" She folded her legs beneath her and leaned against the stack of boxes. "I have some ladies helping me out with the rest of the cleaning today."

"I saw their van—Dreamweavers." He circled his finger in the air. "Is that what they're going to do? Weave dreams with their brooms and mops?"

"I hope so." Her gaze skimmed up and down his body, his long legs in a pair of worn jeans again, topped with a plaid flannel shirt with a blue T-shirt peeking out of the unbuttoned neck. "You're not on duty today? You're finally going to use that vacation time?"

"I'm not officially on duty, but as I mentioned before—small department like this and I'm always on call." He tilted his cell phone back and forth. "I just came out to make sure you were okay and to see if you still wanted me to look into a security system for you."

"Absolutely." She met his gaze and a flash of understanding passed between them. He wanted to check on her—and she wanted him here, wanted him close.

"There's a place in Port Angeles that carries a good supply."

"Oh, I was going to head up there in less than an hour, anyway." She stood up, brushing the seat of her leggings. "Give me the info and I can pick it up myself."

"I want to make sure you get the right kind, and I can get a law enforcement discount." He scuffed the toe of his boot against the carpet. "You can ride with me. I'm not sure that old truck could make it."

A smile tugged at her lips. He didn't have to do any convincing. "That would be great. I just have a few errands to do, so I won't be there all day."

"Hell, we could make an event out of it and have lunch on the water."

"Perfect. Are you ready to go now?"

"I was on my way when I stopped here."

Grabbing handfuls of her baggy T-shirt, she stretched the hem down to her knees. "I just need to change into something warmer, and I'll be right with you."

She nudged one of the boxes with her toe. "Do you have room for a few of these boxes? I'm going to drop them off at a place that lists items on an online auction site, collects payment and ships them out."

"I have my truck. I'll load them up while you change." He waved. "Hey, there, Annie. I like the van."

"Hi, Coop." A broad smile claimed half of Annie's face. "My cousin Scarlett designed it for us."

"Tell her I said it looks great."

Kendall gave Annie a tight smile as she squeezed past her on the way to the back rooms. Did Coop's charm have the same effect on every female within a hundred-mile radius of him?

Not that she had any claim on the sexy sheriff—none at all.

As Coop loaded the last box in his truck bed, the front door of the house closed. He looked up, getting a great view of Kendall's backside as she bent forward to sweep up the freebie newspaper from the ground.

She'd swapped her black leggings for a pair of tight jeans that fit her almost as closely. She'd tucked those jeans into a pair of furry ankle boots, which she probably never wore in Phoenix.

Holding up the newspaper, she called out, "You want this?"

"I have about ten of them in a pile in my house."

She chucked the newspaper onto the porch and strode toward the door he was holding open for her. "Could you fit all the boxes in your truck?"

"With room to spare."

Planting one furry boot on the running board, she hoisted herself up. He grabbed her elbow to steady her.

"Whoa." She turned her face toward him, a laugh bubbling on her lips. "Why do guys like these trucks way up off the ground. I could get a nosebleed up here."

"It makes us feel superior."

"Are you sure you're not compensating for something?"

She winked and a surge of lust thundered through his veins. Her mouth softened and her eyes widened in a sure invitation to a kiss, or maybe her expression was a reaction to his. What did he look like when he wanted a woman so badly, he could already taste her?

He cleared his throat. "Now, what would we be compensating for?"

"I'll think about it, long and hard, and let you know later."

The woman was flirting with him. He slammed the door on her smirk and practically ran to the driver's side.

"Music or conversation?" His hand hovered at the power button for the radio.

"How about a little of both, as long as the music isn't too intrusive."

"I can do unintrusive. My truck came with that satellite radio, so you can find just about anything on there."

"This thing is all tricked out, isn't it?" She tapped the buttons, jumping from station to station, little blips and blurbs of music flashing by in a kaleidoscope of sound.

He gave her a sidelong glance as he pulled into the road. "Are you suggesting more overcompensation on my part?"

"I'm not going to say a word. I know when I've got it good." She pressed two fingers against her luscious lips. "I'd rather ride in comfort for the next hour or so, than in that rattle-trap truck of my aunt's."

They talked easily with a bantering, flirtatious tone that Coop hadn't used for a while, and that he hadn't expected from Kendall. But with each mile they traveled away from Timberline, Kendall's demeanor grew more and more relaxed. Her smile got brighter, her eyes grew clearer and the stiff way she'd held herself eased.

As she laughed, teased and sang snatches of songs from the radio, she spun a web around him with her charm and natural sexiness.

The exit for Port Angeles appeared way too quickly. He could've driven all the way to Alaska in her company.

He rolled his shoulders. "How do you want to do this? I

can drop you off and then go look at the security systems myself, and then pick you up or we can meet at a restaurant by the water for lunch."

"That sounds like a plan." She flipped down the visor and rolled some lipstick across her mouth. "I don't want to bore you with the auction stuff, and my other errand is confidential."

He whistled. "Ooh, confidential."

"It's really not that exciting." She smacked her lips together and smacked the visor back up with the palm of her hand. "I have your number. I'll call when I'm ready. If I'm done earlier than you, I can probably get a bus down to the water."

"Deal." He tipped his chin toward the windshield. "Where am I going now?"

Swiping her index finger across her phone's display, she said, "Let me check the address."

She tapped the screen a few more times and a robotic, female voice started reciting directions from the cell phone.

He followed her orders until the truck was idling in front of a row of one-story shops. "Do you see it?"

"It's the business in the middle with the box on the sign."

"The security place is a few miles away. Do you have any preferences before I buy your system?"

"You're the expert. Just make sure you find me something that's going to stop people from creeping around my property, digging graves." She hopped from the truck.

He met her at the truck bed and unloaded the boxes. "Open the door for me, and I'll carry them in."

She held open the door of the shop, and he stacked the boxes inside.

Putting his lips close to her ear just to breathe in her scent, he whispered. "Don't let them take advantage of you."

He drove the two miles with his mind in a jumble. He needed to back away from Kendall Rush even though every male part of his body urged him forward.

She'd made it clear she had no intention of sticking around Timberline. At least that's one thing Kendall and Steffi had in common—they both hated the Pacific Northwest, or at least this particular town in the Pacific Northwest.

If Kendall planned to hightail it out of here as soon as she settled her aunt's affairs and listed the house, they'd only have time for a superficial quickie—not that he had anything against superficial quickies, especially with a woman like Kendall, but it would be a bad move on his part.

Despite her shell, Kendall had soft, squishy insides. Her dark brown eyes always held a tinge of sadness. The twin who was no longer a twin.

He couldn't take advantage of a woman's vulnerability—not again.

He threw the truck into Park and pushed through the two glass doors of the security shop.

"Can I help you?"

The clerk behind the counter pounced on the only customer in the store.

Coop approached the glass case and dragged his finger across the top of a few of them until he found the security items. "I need to put together a system for a house—motion-sensor lights, cameras, the works."

"We can do that." The clerk launched into an explanation of all the high-tech gadgets and the must-haves.

Coop got into the spirit so much so that the guy must've thought he wanted to protect Fort Knox.

But he wanted to protect something much more precious than gold—he wanted to protect Kendall Rush.

JESSA PATTED THE last box. "I'll send you an email verifying all your prices on the items, and if I see anything of real value I'll recommend a higher price. You know the auction site charges a percentage for listing on top of the percentage I charge for handling the listing?"

"Yeah, I know that. Totally worth it." Kendall picked up a pair of gold lamé boots. "Really?"

"Supposedly they belonged to Elvis." Jessa shrugged.

Kendall snorted. "Right. I'll leave it all in your capable hands, Jessa. I'll be in Timberline for another week or two if you need me to come back."

"I've got all your contact info." She flicked her finger against the computer monitor.

Kendall held her phone up to her face and tapped it for the address of Dr. Jules Shipman. "Can you tell me how far I am from the five-hundred block of Marine Avenue?"

"Marine runs east-west, and I think the five hundreds are east of here." Jessa pointed a finger out the window. "That's left if you keep going up the street."

"Can I walk?"

"It's about a mile, but I can give you a lift. I was just about to go out to the office supply store."

"I don't want to put you to any trouble."

Jessa cupped her hand around her mouth. "Tony, I'm heading out. Can you watch things up here?"

"Got it, babe. Don't forget the shipping tape. We're down to two."

She called back. "On my list."

Jessa grabbed a set of keys from a hook behind her desk, and Kendall followed her out the front door.

She scooted into the passenger seat of Jessa's car, which was emblazoned with ads for her business.

"What's the address?" Jessa pulled away from the curb without even checking her mirrors, and Kendall's fingers curled around the edge of the seat.

"It's 538 Marine."

"Yeah, that's definitely left." Jessa's little car covered the mile faster than Kendall thought possible and when she screeched to a stop in front of a two-story office building, Kendall shot out of the car. "Thanks, Jessa. I'll be in touch about the items."

Jessa waved and squealed away from the curb.

Shaking her head, Kendall walked under the overhang of the building and headed toward the directory behind a glass case on the stucco wall. She'd confirmed Jules's office number on the phone this morning but wanted to verify first.

Murmuring the number, she turned toward the first office—number too high. The one she was looking for must be the office in the front, the door she'd passed on her way to the directory.

When she reached the office of Dr. Jules Shipman, her cell phone buzzed. "Hi, Coop. Are you done already?"

"Almost, give me about ten minutes."

"I'll be about twenty more minutes, so go ahead and find a place for lunch and I'll meet you there."

"I'll look up something on my phone, and I'll swing by and pick you up. I don't mind waiting."

Her gaze wandered to the nameplate on the wall next to the door. There were lots of offices in this building. Coop didn't have to know she was visiting a therapist for Wyatt.

"Okay. I'll try to hurry up." She gave him the address of the building next door and ended the call.

She pocketed her phone and hunched forward, pressing her ear against the office door. That didn't tell her a thing. Turning the handle slowly, she eased open the door, peeking into the empty waiting room.

She let out a breath. Before she could take another step into the room, a dark-haired woman burst from the door on the other side.

"Kendall Rush?"

Kendall let the door swing shut behind her. "Yes, nice to meet you, Dr. Shipman."

The woman tilted her head to one side, and a lock of hair slipped from her messy bun. "You can call me Jules, and you know I'm not a psychiatrist."

"But you're a Ph.D."

"Yeah, but that doctor stuff sounds so pretentious. Do you have your Ph.D.?"

"Nope, just my master's in clinical psych."

"I wish I could tell you the doctorate commands more money, but it doesn't, not in private practice, anyway."

"I had heard that. Thanks for seeing me on such short notice."

"No problem." She swiveled her wrist inward. "My next client's not due for another twenty-five minutes."

"I won't take up too much of your time. As I mentioned on the phone, my friend is having some difficulties dealing with the kidnappings in Timberline because his brother was one of the Timberline Trio. Are you familiar with the case?"

"I didn't grow up here, so I hadn't heard about the case until these recent kidnappings. Horrible. I can't imagine the pain this man feels right now."

Kendall gave a curt nod with no intention of revealing her own connection to the case. "Last night he pleaded with me to help him, but I explained that therapy with me wouldn't work."

"I'd be happy to see him. I'm not quite at full capacity now, and I see a lot of clients from the surrounding smaller towns like Timberline. Do you want to ask me any questions?"

"Just a few." Kendall proceeded to ask Jules about her methods and her practice, and they even commiserated about the pitfalls of the profession.

At the end of their discussion, Kendall had a good feeling about Jules.

"I think you'd be great for Wyatt. Can I have your card? In fact, I'll take a couple."

"They're in my office." She jerked her thumb over her shoulder.

Kendall followed her into the inner sanctum, a soothing environment with low lights, comfy chairs, plants and scenic art on the walls—looked exactly like her own office.

Jules plucked several cards from the holder on her desk. "Here you go. Have Wyatt call me anytime he's ready."

"I'd better make way for your next client." Kendall thrust out her hand. "Thanks so much for meeting with me."

"Absolutely." Jules walked her into the outer office. "I actually have a client who moved to Phoenix recently. I might be able to return the favor and give you a referral."

Kendall slipped out the front door and immediately saw Coop's truck idling at the curb. Damn. She should've given him an address half a block down so he wouldn't see her coming out of Dr. Shipman's office, even though there was no way he could read the nameplate from the street. Hopefully, he'd know not to ask questions.

Tugging her jacket closed, she practically skipped toward the truck. She couldn't wait to sit down with Coop and have lunch. She grabbed the door handle and yanked.

"Sorry to keep you waiting..." Her voice trailed off as she took in Coop's profile, hard as a block of ice and just as cold.

Then he turned toward her and she flinched at the pain in his eyes.

"What kind of sick game are you playing, Kendall?"

Her foot slipped from the running board and her knee banged against the passenger seat. "Wh-what?"

He leveled a finger at her. "Are you going to deny you

were in Jules Shipman's office? Don't even try. I saw you coming out of there."

"I don't understand. What's going on?"

"Did you have your little confidential conversation with Dr. Shipman? Did she tell you she killed my wife?"

Chapter Nine

Kendall jerked back. Whatever she'd expected to come out of Coop's mouth—that wasn't it.

"Killed your wife? What are you talking about? You know Jules Shipman?"

His brows shot up. "Oh, that's how it's gonna be?"

She closed her eyes, took a deep breath and hoisted herself into the truck. They couldn't continue this crazy conversation on the sidewalk. Jules's next client might hear them.

"What is going on, Coop? You need to back up several steps here." She swept her hands across her face as if trying to get a fresh start. "Dr. Shipman didn't mention your wife. I didn't realize you and your wife knew Jules. I saw her on…business."

He peeled one hand from the steering wheel, where he'd been squeezing it with a white-knuckle grip, and covered his mouth. He stared out the window for several seconds. "Are you telling me the truth?"

Okay, he'd almost regained his senses.

"I'm telling you the truth. I never met Dr. Shipman before today. I looked her up, along with a couple of other therapists in town, and she happened to be the only one who was free to talk to me this morning." She held up two fingers. "I swear."

"God, I feel so stupid." He leaned his forehead against the steering wheel. "I'm sorry I went off on you."

She touched his shoulder. "Do you want to tell me about it? If there's something I should know about Dr. Shipman..."

The muscles across his back tensed. "She's a quack."

"What happened with Dr. Shipman, Coop?"

Lifting his bowed head, he rolled his shoulders and put the truck in motion. "We have a reservation at the Pelican's Nest."

Kendall snapped her seat belt and sank against the seat. That lunch she'd been looking forward to had just lost its appeal. The tension in the truck was about as thick as a Washington Peninsula cloud cover, and she didn't dare open her mouth in case it set Coop off again.

He drove down to the port in silence and paid for parking in a public lot. The hostess showed them to their table, one with a beautiful view, but Kendall barely noticed it.

She sat across from Coop and ordered a glass of white wine. She could use about five of them.

Reaching across the table, he took her hand. "I'm sorry, Kendall."

"Look, I don't know what just happened back there, but can we wipe the slate clean and just enjoy our lunch before leaving? Unless you want to leave right now."

A spasm of pain crossed his face. "My wife, Alana, committed suicide."

Her hand twitched beneath his. "I'm so sorry."

"She took a bunch of pills while in the bathtub, although I guess it doesn't matter how she did it."

She ran the pad of her thumb along the knuckles of his hand. Now she understood. Jules had been seeing Alana, and now he blamed the therapist for Alana's death. That was such a common reaction even if it wasn't based in reality.

"Depression?"

"When Alana finally admitted it to me, told me how much she was suffering, I tried to get her help. I tried, but it ended in disaster. Dr. Jules Shipman was a disaster."

Kendall bit her lip, literally and figuratively. If Coop had been putting his faith in Jules to rescue his wife, he was destined for disappointment. Therapists weren't miracle workers.

The waitress arrived, and Coop snatched his hand back as she delivered their drinks and took their orders.

He poured his mineral water into the glass and studied the bubbles for a few seconds. "You're going to defend her, Dr. Shipman, aren't you?"

"I don't know what went on in their sessions, and neither do you, but psychotherapy can only do so much for a depressed patient. Pharmaceuticals play a bigger role in managing depression and suicidal thoughts."

"Have you ever lost a patient…like that?"

She blinked. "Two."

"Did the families blame you?" He cupped her wineglass in his hand and took a sip.

"One did, one didn't. It's not easy for anyone." She shoved the wineglass back toward him. "Have another."

"When I saw you coming out of her office—" he tugged on his earlobe "—I thought…I don't know what I thought."

"That I was spying on you? Gathering intel on you for some nefarious purpose?" She traced her finger around the base of her glass. "Why didn't you tell me your wife committed suicide? Timberline is a small town. You know I would've found out sooner or later, and what difference would it make? It's something I would rather hear from you."

"I knew you'd find out. I just didn't want to be the one to admit my failure."

His admission didn't surprise her. Relatives, especially

spouses, always felt the guilt, and that's why they blamed the mental health professionals.

Crossing his arms over his chest, he leaned back in his chair. "You're not going to jump in and tell me it wasn't my fault? I don't have any reason to feel guilty?"

"No."

A muscle in his jaw ticked and he reached for the wine again. "Once I discovered the way she was feeling, I did everything in my power to help her."

"I believe you."

"Including sending her to see Dr. Shipman." His nostrils flared as he shifted the blame from himself to Jules.

"It feels good to blame someone besides yourself, doesn't it?"

"You think I'm blaming Dr. Shipman because I really blame myself, don't you?"

"You wouldn't be the first."

The waitress approached their table, a plate in each hand. "Fish and chips and the salmon fettucine. Can I get you anything else?"

Coop held up a finger. "Vinegar, please."

"And another glass of chardonnay." Kendall held up her half-empty glass.

When the waitress walked away, Coop's lips twisted. "I promise I won't steal any more of your wine. Therapy session over."

"Just because we talk about more than the weather, doesn't mean I'm playing therapist. I'm playing friend and I care what happens to you and your daughter." She picked up her fork. "I'm just happy you don't believe I was skulking around behind your back."

"What *were* you doing at her office?"

Kendall ran the tip of her finger along the seam of her lips. "Confidential, remember? We don't kiss and tell."

"Right. Sorry." He bit into a piece of fish with a crunch.

"Time to change the subject. I got a good security system for you. If there's time this afternoon, I'll start installing it at the house. I'm back at work tomorrow."

"I can get Lester Jenkins to install it. He's handy with that sort of thing."

"Or I can start on it and Lester can finish it off."

"What time is Steffi done with school? Don't you need to pick her up?"

"She goes home with Genevieve's mom—you met her last night at Sutter's. I never know from week to week what days I'm taking off, so it's just easier and more consistent for her to go to her friend's house." He pointed a French fry at her plate. "Are you eating or talking?"

"Eating." She shoved her fork into the pasta and twirled.

The lunch hadn't gotten off to the best start, but as they both started to relax the food tasted better, the view looked more spectacular and she'd become much more witty.

Maybe that last part had to do with the wine buzzing through her veins. She even had Coop laughing about the gold lamé Elvis boots…and she liked to hear Coop laugh.

They finished lunch on a high note, and she insisted on paying since he'd gotten dinner the night before and he wouldn't take her money for the security system.

The drive back to Timberline proved to be even more relaxing, especially with a glass and a half of wine coursing through her system. She must've dozed off because when the truck hit a bump in the road and her eyelids flew open, they were passing the Quileute Indian Reservation.

She yawned and skimmed her tongue across her teeth. "I wonder if Annie and her crew are done with the house yet."

"You'd already cleaned half of it. I'm sure they are."

Kendall waved to a little girl by the side of the road selling trinkets with her mother. "You know, Annie didn't want to do any cleaning outside."

"They don't do outdoor work. If you need someone, I can find someone for you."

"It wasn't just the work." She trailed her finger down the inside of the window, following a drop of moisture on the outside. "She was afraid to go out there because of the crosses by the creek."

"I'm sure it's gonna affect a lot of people that way. The area is cordoned off, anyway."

"I know I sound like Rebecca, but I hope it doesn't affect the sale of the house. It already has one strike against it because of the crime committed there twenty-five years ago."

"I'm sure outsiders aren't going to care one way or the other. They'll probably come in and tear the whole place down."

"I hope they do."

He gave her a quick look, and then shifted his gaze back to the highway. "You don't have any happy memories of Timberline? Is that why you left and never came back?"

"I have some happy memories, but that one tragedy overshadows everything. It didn't stop with Kayla's kidnapping. My parents never had the most stable marriage to begin with, and losing Kayla put even more stress on them. My parents divorced and my mom slipped into a kind of madness. She's in a rest home in Florida now, and Dad passed away earlier than he should have. Aunt Cass never wanted kids, but she did her best in her own way."

"I'm sorry. Some families never do recover."

"So, I could never be truly happy here. Besides, I hate all the rain."

He chewed on his bottom lip and heaved a sigh. "Steffi hates the rain, too. Do you think..."

"What?"

"After trashing your profession, I feel like a hypocrite asking for your advice."

"Ask away. I don't think you're a hypocrite." He was a man who still blamed himself for his wife's suicide and found some relief in turning his wrath on her therapist.

"Steffi was just a baby when Alana killed herself, nineteen months old to be exact."

Kendall's nose stung with tears. How was Steffi going to feel when she got older and understood what her mother had done?

"That's sad." She sniffled.

"It was raining that day—hard. You know how it gets sometimes? That unrelenting rain that pours from the clouds."

"I remember it well."

"I was working and Alana had dropped Steffi off with a babysitter and never came back to get her. I was overwhelmed when I came home and found Alana in the tub. The babysitter offered to keep Steffi with her for the night." He smacked the steering wheel with the heel of his hand. "I never should've allowed that."

"Wait." She tapped her fingers lightly on his corded forearm. "You can't blame yourself for that. You did the right thing. Police, ambulance, her mother's body. Do you really think Steffi would've felt any sense of security or normalcy about all that?"

"So, her mother dropped her off and Steffi never saw her again, and it rained and rained that day and into the night like it would never stop." His arm tensed beneath her touch. "I think that's why Steffi hates the rain so much. Is that crazy? She was only nineteen months old."

"That's not crazy at all. You're probably right."

He blew out a breath as he made the turn toward Aunt Cass's house. "I'm really sorry. I thought this would be a nice day-trip to Port Angeles to get your mind off of everything going on here, and I brought down the whole mood."

"Life rarely follows a plan."

"Ain't that the truth? But I should've kept my mouth shut when I saw you coming out of Dr. Shipman's office. I snapped. If I'd taken a couple of deep breaths, I'd have realized you had no reason to be checking me out."

She had every reason to check him out—just not the way he meant.

"Sometimes our minds jump to the fastest conclusion, even if it's not the most logical."

He pointed to the Dreamweavers van in the drive. "Looks like Annie and her crew are still here."

"They must be doing a thorough job."

"I'm going to start installing your system before I pick up Steffi, unless you're anxious to get rid of me."

"You don't always have to be the smiling, helpful sheriff, Coop. You're allowed to have emotions."

"How would having a sheriff running around falling apart instill confidence? And you're one to talk. You're kind of tightly wound yourself." He parked his truck behind hers.

"Therapists can't run around falling apart, either."

Turning, he traced a finger along her jaw. "You're not my therapist so any time you need to let go, I'll be there."

Her lashes fluttered, and she almost let go right then and there, confessing her overwhelming attraction to him, even though he hated therapists and his daughter was lukewarm about her.

She coughed. "I'll take you up on that offer...for as long as I'm in Timberline."

"That's what I meant." He threw open the door of the truck. "I'm going to get started."

She slid from the truck and peeked into the house. The antiseptic smell that greeted her made her nose twitch.

Annie poked her head around the entrance to the kitchen. "We're almost done. See anything you'd like us to do before we leave?"

"It smells so clean." Kendall took a deep breath. "I'm sure it's fine."

"Then we'll start packing up our stuff."

Kendall shed her jacket and hung it up in the closet. "Annie, do you know any landscapers who could use a one-time job? Mostly cleaning up and clearing out. I don't want to do anything too fancy since the new owners might do a teardown."

"Quileute?" Annie leaned a mop and two brooms against a stack of boxes in the corner. "Are you looking for someone from the rez?"

"Sure."

Annie shook her head, and then gave one of her workers a little shove. "Take these out to the van, Lucy."

Lucy took her time collecting the cleaning supplies, her gaze darting between Annie and Kendall.

When she banged through the screen door, Annie sighed. "Kendall, no Quileute is ever going to work on this land."

Kendall wedged her hands on her hips. "Because of the buried photos? Is it fear...or something else?"

"It's not just the recent discovery."

"You mean my sister's disappearance." She tapped the toe of her boot, trying to appear nonchalant. "You're here, and Lucy and the others."

"I had to use threats to get them to come." She raised her palms to the ceiling. "And I'm only half joking."

"You're not...superstitious?"

"Is that what you'd call it? Would you call yourself superstitious?"

"No."

"And yet you left this place as soon as you could and never returned, and now that Cass has passed on you can't wait to dump her belongings and get out of town."

"You got me." She smacked her palm against her chest. "What would you call it, then? An aura?"

She snorted. "I call it a job, but you could ask my cousin Scarlett. She's the shaman."

"I remember that. Maybe I will."

"I think you'll be gone before she comes back. She's also a famous artist now and she's down in San Francisco for a show of her work."

"That's great." A shadow passed across the window, and Kendall lifted the curtain to watch Coop lean a ladder against her house. "You don't know anyone who shares your skepticism of the bad aura and needs a few days' work?"

"Most landscapers are pretty busy these days working for the Evergreen families, but you might check with Gary Binder. He's not Quileute, but he's been doing odd jobs since he got out of prison."

"Prison?"

"Drugs—using, selling, manufacturing."

"Doesn't surprise me." She remembered Gary as a morose, moody young man, but he had to be over forty now. "I think I'll pass."

"He's clean and sober, could use the work."

"Is he any good?"

"For what you want? He'll do, and the man needs a break. Everyone needs a break now and then." Annie dipped and grabbed the handle of the plastic bucket at her feet. "Let me know if you want us to come back when you get all the furniture and boxes out of here."

"Will do." Kendall dug into her purse for her wallet and pulled out the cash she'd gotten from the ATM earlier that morning. "Thanks a lot, Annie."

Kendall stood on the porch and waved to the other women. "Thanks, ladies."

When they drove off in the van painted by a famous artist, Kendall crossed her arms and leaned against a white post on the porch. "Did you realize that the Quileute think my house is haunted?"

"Makes sense." He pounded a nail into an eave. "I don't claim to be any expert on the Quileute since I haven't been here that long, but some of the tribe members do seem to have a heightened sensitivity to otherworldly phenomena."

"Is that what you'd call it?"

"I suppose so." He strung a wire between two nails. "I'm setting up the infrastructure for the security system. I can finish it up tomorrow. I can probably get it done faster than Lester."

"That would be great." She scuffed some dirt from her porch with the toe of her boot. "Big plans tonight?"

"As a matter of fact, yes. It's back-to-school night and the principal asked me to give a presentation to the parents about safety."

"That was unheard of in this town until the Timberline Trio went missing. Even a few years after the kidnappings, when the shock had subsided, Timberline had gone back to the good old days. Even I was allowed free reign in the woods and on my bike with the other kids. People slowly started leaving their doors unlocked again."

"Yep. That's the town we moved to when Alana was pregnant with Steffi, and we had almost five solid years of that security." He climbed down from the ladder. "I'm going to return this to the side of the house and put the rest of the system pieces inside. Is that okay?"

"What's a few more boxes in the living room?"

"Are you going to be okay here tonight?"

"Absolutely. I still have my work cut out for me."

Coop folded the aluminum ladder and hitched it beneath one arm. While he carried it around the side of the house, Kendall scooped up the various boxes and pieces of equipment for her security system and carried them inside.

She met Coop at the door. "Do you have everything?"

"Just wish I'd had more time to get the system up and running." He scratched his stubble. "Maybe you can go visit Melissa and Daryl."

"They're on a romantic getaway in Seattle." She tucked her hair behind one ear and gave him a halfhearted smile. "I'll be fine. I'm going to take a look around town at some of the new shops that have gone in since the last time I visited Aunt Cass, which was before Evergreen moved here."

Reaching forward, he cupped her face with one hand. "Be careful, Kendall. Someone has decided to play some sick game with you."

"Not just me."

"What?" He dropped his hand.

She'd just torpedoed any moment they could've had. Maybe her instincts were kicking in to protect her from another sort of danger.

"Wyatt. Someone left a plastic dinosaur for Wyatt. I told him to mention it to you."

"Why didn't he?" His brows collided over his nose. "He's been working at the station. You'd think he would've told me if he told you."

"I'm not sure. I told him you'd want to know."

"Why would he want to keep it from me?"

"You'll have to ask him, but don't say you heard anything from me."

"That might not be possible because I'm going to ask him about it and I'm going to ask him to turn that dinosaur over, although there's probably not much hope of getting any prints now." He smacked the doorjamb. "Take care and call me if you need anything."

With the Dreamweavers and Coop gone, that old silence settled on the house again. What she wouldn't give for a fifty-six-inch flat screen and a hefty dose of reality TV right now.

She had to replace the emptiness with something, so she booted up her laptop and started playing her music library. Humming to the music in the background, she created some signs for the estate sale, exchanged a few emails with Jessa regarding the auction price of her aunt's items and checked her emails and voice mails.

No emergencies from any of her clients, and thank God she didn't have any with suicidal ideation at the moment. Had Coop expected Dr. Shipman to work miracles with his wife? No wonder he was leery of her profession.

She'd almost forgotten the reason she'd visited Dr. Shipman. She reached for her phone and tapped in Wyatt's number. It went straight to voice mail.

"Hi, Wyatt. It's Kendall. I found a therapist for you in Port Angeles. I think she'll be good for you. Her name is Dr. Shipman. I'll give you her number and you can call her when you're comfortable."

She reached into her purse hanging on the back of the chair and pulled out one of Dr. Shipman's cards. She recited the number for Wyatt, and then ended the call.

Stretching her arms over her head, she yawned. She'd better get her second wind because she had no intention of eating alone in this house tonight.

Her heart jumped when the screen at the front creaked open and someone pounded on the front door.

With her phone in one hand, she crept toward the front. Her aunt didn't even have a peephole in the door. She placed a hand on the doorknob and leaned forward. "Who is it?"

"It's Gary Binder, ma'am. Annie Foster said you needed some help clearing the property out here."

She leaned her forehead against the door. Darn that Annie. Couldn't she let her make her own decisions? If she didn't open the door, he'd think she was holding his prison term against him. If she did, he could force his way in here.

And do what? Make her take drugs?

She pulled in a deep breath and swung open the door. She put her poker face into action as she stared into the faded blue eyes of Gary Binder. A long scar from the corner of his eye to just beneath his earlobe emphasized the other deep lines on his face, and he wasn't trying to hide anything as he wore his graying hair cropped close to his head. He was a forty-five-year-old man inhabiting a sixty-five-year-old body.

"Hi, Gary. News spreads fast. I just told Annie about a few hours ago I was looking for someone." Her gaze wandered to the darkening sky behind him. He couldn't wait until morning?

"Annie knows I'm always looking." He ran a hand over the bristle on his head. "I ain't gonna lie to you, ma'am. I've been in and out of the joint and in and outta rehab but I'm clean and sober now and just lookin' to pick up some work here and there."

"I get it." She pointed past his shoulder. "I need the brush cut back here in the front and some general cleanup in the back—just down to the edge of the woods. Do you think you're up to it?"

He spread his lips into a gap-toothed smile. "I may look like hell, ma'am, but I'm strong and wiry. I can do this work, but I don't have a lot of tools of my own."

"I'm sure my aunt Cass has something in the shed by the side of the house."

Gary's face brightened up, making him look ten years younger.

"And I'll tell you what. When you're done with the job, you can keep whatever tools you find in there."

"Instead of pay? I guess I can do that."

"No, no. I'll pay you. I have to clear out all that stuff anyway. You can have it."

"Thank you, ma'am. Just tell me what needs to get done and I'll do it."

"It's a little late, Gary. Can you come back tomorrow? Maybe around ten o'clock…in the morning."

"Sure thing. I just wanted to get a jump on the job in case you were lookin' to hire someone else. Those Quileute? They ain't gonna work here anyway."

"Yeah, Annie told me that." She rubbed her arms as a rash of goose bumps raced across them. "So, tomorrow at ten?"

"Yes, ma'am."

She watched him walk down the drive with a peculiar jerky stride and yank a bicycle off the ground by its handlebars.

When she shut the door, she let out a breath. He wasn't so bad. He looked pretty rough, but she hadn't seen any signs that he was using.

Before any more nocturnal visitors could make their way to her front door, she slipped on her boots, grabbed a jacket and headed out for dinner.

The rain had stopped for the day, but Kendall pulled up her hood anyway as she scuffed through the leaves toward the truck. The first thing Gary could do was rake up all the leaves and needles on the drive. She planned to put most of Aunt Cass's stuff out here for the estate sale so she didn't have people traipsing through the house. The weatherman hadn't forecast any rain for the weekend.

She grabbed the handle of the truck and yanked open the door. It seemed to be creaking even louder than it had been yesterday.

A piece of paper fluttered beneath the windshield wiper. She slid out of the truck and plucked it free.

Squinting, she held the paper toward the light spilling from the truck. The slick paper had housing info printed

on it—looked like one of Rebecca's open house flyers—
but it was just a piece, a half sheet of paper.

She turned it over and drew in a sharp, cold breath.

Someone had left her a note in a spidery black scrawl.
She clambered back inside the truck and punched on the
dome light with her knuckle.

She read the note aloud. "Kendall, meet me at my house
later. I know something about the pink ribbon."

Chuck Rawlings had printed his name in block letters
at the end of the note.

Her gaze shifted to her rearview mirror. When had
Chuck left this note on her truck?

She smoothed her thumb across the shiny paper—dry.
It had to have been after they had come home because she
would've noticed it on the way into the house. Why hadn't
Chuck just come to her door?

Why hadn't he talked to her last night when he'd obviously been following her down the sidewalk?

The hand holding the note trembled and she dropped
the paper onto the passenger seat. Was this some kind of
trick to lure her to his cabin? Not that she was young and
fresh enough to catch his perverted interest. She was no
sixteen-year-old girl to fear his advances.

From the looks of his gaunt appearance last night, she
could probably take him down with a few of the moves
she'd learned in her self-defense class…unless he had a
weapon.

She picked up the note again. If he knew something
about the pink ribbon, maybe he knew something about
the kidnapper even if he didn't realize it.

Turning the key in the ignition, she glanced at the clock
on the dashboard. Coop was still at the open house. Maybe
Rawlings did have some information and didn't want to
bring attention to himself by calling Coop or, worse, the FBI.

If Rawlings could tell her something about the ribbon,

she could help Coop. Then that FBI agent would have to listen to him.

She read the note again. Later? What did he mean by "later"? She peered at the dark sky with a sliver of moon peeking out from behind a cloud. Looked later to her.

It took her ten minutes to drive to Rawlings's cabin. His truck was parked by the side of the property, under a spotlight. Another spotlight illuminated a circle that encompassed his front porch and half of his driveway. Rawlings had his own security system.

For some reason, she closed the door of the truck just enough to kill the interior lights but she didn't slam it shut. She didn't want to alert him to her presence—not that she expected to catch him performing a human sacrifice or anything—she just preferred having the element of surprise.

She crept up to Chuck's house and stalled when the first step to his porch creaked beneath her foot. She straightened her backbone and took the next two steps with purpose. Chuck had asked her here, and she had nothing to fear from him.

Not seeing a doorbell, she rapped her knuckles against the frame of the screen door. She took a step back and laced her hands in front of her, muscles coiled for action.

In her head, she rehearsed the lines she'd say to him. She'd start out friendly, grateful for the info, but he'd better not be toying with her because she planned to get to the bottom of this and she had every intention of relating their conversation to Coop.

But Chuck had to open the door first.

She tugged on the handle of the screen door, and knocked on the heavy wood of the front door. As soon as her knuckles hit the wood, the door inched open.

Leaning toward the crack in the door, she called out. "Mr. Rawlings? Chuck?"

A soft whine answered her, and a furry, gray paw emerged from the bottom of the gap.

"Hey, little guy." She crouched and touched her finger to his velvety, black nose. "Where's your owner?"

The dog mewled and scrabbled for freedom, his claws clicking against the wood.

Kendall tried again. "Mr. Rawlings? Are you there? It's Kendall Rush. I got your note."

This time the dog barked, a high-pitched sound that ended on a little growl.

Pulling her bottom lip between her teeth, Kendall rose. Chuck Rawlings was not a young man and from the looks of him last night, not a particularly healthy one. Maybe the excitement over revealing what he knew about the pink ribbon had gotten the best of him. As far as she knew, he had no relatives in the area to check up on him.

She placed one hand against the door and shuffled her feet close to the opening to keep the dog from bolting. She pushed the door open, moving into the open space to block the dog. "Mr. Rawlings? Are you okay?"

She let the screen door bang behind her, while keeping the front door open.

A fire dying in the grate warmed the room, and a lamp on an end table cast a circular yellow glow that encompassed a pair of slippers dropped haphazardly by the side of the sofa. Their frayed ends indicated that they'd been nibbled on by the little mutt at her feet.

She swallowed hard. Where was Rawlings? Lying in wait in his bedroom or behind the door with an ax?

The little dog pranced around her ankles, and pawed at her jeans. Would an ax murderer have a little precious like this?

Dipping down, she chucked the pooch under the chin. "Did you chew your master's slippers, you naughty pup? And where is your master?"

He licked her fingers and jumped up again, dragging his paws down her shin. The dog's presence calmed her jumpy nerves, and he could be her protection in case Rawlings did come at her.

"You little rascal. Do you want to be my bodyguard?" She cupped her arm beneath his body to swoop him up and noticed several spots he'd left on her jeans. She brushed at the smudges, drawing her brows over her nose at the moist feel of the stain.

She turned her hand over, studying the dark smear on her fingers. She released the squirming mutt and staggered on her knees toward the light, holding her hand in front of her.

Before she could even confirm her suspicions about the substance, her knee bumped a bare foot. Gasping for breath, her heart slamming against her chest, she leaned to the side to see around the corner of the couch.

Chuck Rawlings stared back at her with empty, mannequin eyes.

Chapter Ten

Coop stared out at the sea of pale, worried faces, wishing he could offer more assurances. "Are there any other questions?"

A redhead in the front row raised her hand and started speaking before he could call on her. "What about that pervert, Chuck Rawlings?"

"What about him, ma'am?"

"Have you checked him out? When my husband and I moved here four years ago, we looked at that sex offender database for Washington and he's on it." She folded her arms and fixed Coop with a steely stare.

"We've investigated him thoroughly, ma'am. He's clear."

"And the others in that database? Because we have more than Rawlings in the area now." A big man standing in the back shoved off the wall he'd been leaning against. "When Evergreen moved in here, they brought all their problems with 'em. I have to wait at that damned signal now on the main drag for close to a minute and the mayor won't respond to my emails."

A man in the front wearing a suit cranked his head around. "Yeah, among the problems Evergreen brought were more money for the schools and an increase in your property values. Even those ramshackle cabins near the woods are going for close to a quarter mil."

"Whose place are you calling ramshackle." The man in the back puffed out his chest.

"Stop." Coop held up his hands. "We're not here to discuss those issues. Follow the precautions on the flyer you picked up at the door. Most of the suggestions are common sense. I just wanted to assure you tonight that my department and the FBI are doing all we can right now to find out what happened to those children."

Someone in the crowd snorted and a few others coughed. Coop gritted his teeth.

"If there's nothing else, I'm sure we'd all like to collect our children, hug them tightly and head home."

Before anyone could start the Evergreen argument again, Mrs. Stoker, the principal, started clapping. "Thank you, Sheriff Sloane. We appreciate your presentation tonight. Let's start putting our newfound vigilance to practice. When you pick up your child from his or her classroom, please show the teacher your driver's license or other photo ID. I do realize most of the teachers know you, but let's turn these safety procedures into habits."

As the parents started shuffling out of the room and Coop was thanking Mrs. Stoker, his phone started going off in his pocket.

He held up his finger. "Hold that thought, Meg."

He plunged his hand into his pocket and withdrew his buzzing phone. The display indicated the call was coming from the station and it was the third call within the last minute.

Maybe someone had good news about those kids. "Coop here. What's up?"

"Coop, it's Payton. We have a dead body."

Coop's heart skipped a beat. "Not…"

"Not the kids, no." Payton sucked in a breath. "It's Chuck Rawlings."

"Rawlings? What happened?" Coop turned away from Mrs. Stoker, cupping his hand around his mouth.

"The officers on the scene aren't sure yet. He died from blunt force trauma. Could've been an accident."

"Are you telling me it could be murder?"

"'Fraid so, and that Timberline Trio lady found his body."

This time it felt like his heart had done a full somersault. "Kendall Rush? Kendall found him? Where, for God's sake?"

"In his house."

"Why the hell was Kendall in Rawlings's house?"

Payton paused a couple of beats. "Don't know. Don't know what to tell you, Coop."

Coop ended the call and made a beeline to the classroom where Steffi's age group had gathered during his talk to the parents. Luckily Britt and Rob were still there collecting Genevieve.

Coop tousled Steffi's curls and kissed the top of her head. "I just got an emergency call from the station. Can you take Steffi home with you tonight?"

Genevieve clapped her hands. "Please, Mom."

"Of course, Coop." Rob's gaze shifted to the two girls hugging. "Is it…"

"Something else. I really appreciate it. I'll pick her up when I'm done."

He had his police SUV at the school and drove out to Rawlings's place as if the man could still be saved, but he could spare very few thoughts about Rawlings. What had Kendall been doing in Rawlings's cabin?

He pulled up behind the police cruiser in the driveway. The rotating lights bathing the figures on the porch in red and blue. He squinted at Kendall on the bottom step, clutching something to her chest.

As he drew closer, his boots crunching the gravel on

the driveway, the bundle in Kendall's arms squirmed and yapped. She had Rawlings's mutt in a firm grip as she talked to Officer Stevens.

She lifted her head to watch his approach, and then buried her face in the dog's fur.

Coop reached her in two long strides. "What happened? What were you doing here, Kendall?"

"R-Rawlings wanted to meet me. He left me a note." She rested her chin on top of the dog's head.

"So, you just came out here on your own?"

Out of the corner of his eye, Coop noticed Stevens's round eyes and his mouth hanging slightly ajar.

Coop dragged a hand through his hair and started over. "Did you call the county coroner's office, Stevens?"

"Yes, sir. The van's on its way. Paulson and Unger are inside with the body, taking pictures and checking out the scene."

"What do you think from your initial assessment? Accident or...homicide?"

Kendall's breath hissed between her teeth. "Homicide? Murder? He fell. Didn't he just fall over and hit his head?"

Coop raised an eyebrow at Stevens.

"Sir, he could've fallen and hit his head on the corner of a table."

"You called county Homicide along with the coroner?"

"Yes, sir."

"Stay here. I'm going to go inside and have a look." Coop placed a hand on Kendall's back and the little dog growled at him. "Looks like you have a protector. Where'd you find him?"

"He greeted me at the front door, which was open a crack. H-he had blood on his paws." She scratched the pooch under the chin and the tag on his collar jingled. "His name is Buddy."

"Okay, stay here with Buddy and Officer Stevens. Stevens, you wait for the county boys to get here."

Although he wanted to stay and question Kendall himself, he edged into Rawlings's house and dropped his gaze to the scuffed wood floor. The officers had put tags next to the bloody paw prints and a pair of slippers that looked like they'd been yanked from the deceased's feet—most likely the work of Buddy.

Deputy Unger came from the back room. "Hey, Coop. I was checking out the back windows for any evidence of a break-in."

"Anything?"

"Locked up tight."

"Ms. Rush said the front door was ajar when she got here."

Unger chewed his lip. "He could've been letting in some air, or maybe he felt bad, went to the front door for help, staggered back to the couch and then fell over."

"That's quite a scenario."

"For all we know, the guy had a heart attack and died from that instead of the blow to the head." Unger shrugged.

Coop eyed the blood pooling on the floor beneath Rawlings's head. "Maybe, but that wound was probably enough to kill him."

"I guess we'll find out from the autopsy."

Coop reached across and flicked aside the curtain at the front window. "The county coroner and Homicide just pulled up."

Coop and his officers spent the next hour going over details with the homicide detectives while another detective questioned Kendall. He wanted to be with her during the questioning, but he couldn't swing it.

When the detective finished with Kendall, she poked her head into the cabin. "Is it okay if I leave now?"

The lead detective answered. "Of course, Ms. Rush. We

may call with a few more questions in the next couple of days, and we do have your contact info in Phoenix, right?"

"Yes." Her gaze shifted to Coop, and her eyebrows lifted.

He excused himself from the huddle and drew up beside her, taking her arm. "Are you okay to drive home by yourself?"

"I'm fine. I'm taking Buddy with me. I already put him in the truck. Detective Ross said it was okay."

"Poor little guy doesn't have anywhere else to go except the pound. I should be finished up here in the next ten minutes and then I'm going to drop by your place, okay?"

"I know." She cupped her hand around her mouth and whispered. "We haven't had one minute to talk privately."

His pulse ticked up a notch. Did that mean she had more to tell him? "I'll be at your house as soon as I can."

That happened to be fifteen minutes. The coroner loaded the body and the homicide detectives loaded their baggies of evidence. "We'll keep in touch, Sheriff Sloane." Detective Ross scratched his chin. "Timberline is sure seeing its share of trouble to close out the year."

"Yeah, and we still have three months to go."

He hightailed it to Kendall's place, blowing out a breath when he saw her truck parked in front. He hadn't wanted to let her out of his sight.

She met him at the door with Buddy wrapped in a towel and tucked beneath her arm.

He leveled a finger at the dog. "Did you give him a bath already?"

"He had Rawlings's blood on his paws."

"Did you get it off?"

"Most of it." She swung the door open for him and placed Buddy on the floor. "Coffee?"

"No. I want to know why Rawlings asked you to his place."

"He left a note on my windshield tonight." She spread her hands. "I turned it over to the detective who questioned me."

"Of course. They'll be handling the investigation. We don't have the resources or manpower for what could be a homicide. If it proves to be an accident, we'll close out the case. What did the note say?"

"Rawlings wrote that he knew something about the pink ribbon."

He rubbed his chin. "How easy was that to explain to the detective?"

"Let's just say his eyes started to glaze over after about five minutes into my explanation."

"You should've told me, Kendall. You should've waited for me."

She took his hand. "Let's sit down."

They settled next to each other on the worn-out sofa in front of the cold fireplace.

"I was anxious to find out what Rawlings knew, and I really didn't think he posed any danger to me. I mean, he had sex with two teenage girls thirty years ago."

"That's what we know about, anyway." He stretched his legs out in front of him, his knee brushing hers. "Do you believe him? Do you think he had information?"

"He'd been watching me the night before in town."

"What?" He jerked his head toward her. "You didn't tell me that."

"I forgot. It happened after you and Steffi left the restaurant. I was walking back to my car, and he was sort of tracking me from across the street and then nodded at me right before I got in the truck."

"If he had this information, why didn't he tell you then?"

"I have no idea. Maybe he didn't want other people to see him talking to me. Maybe he thought I'd freak out if he approached me. I mean, he is the town pariah."

"Was. The town will have to find a new pariah."

She clasped her hands between her knees. "Do you think someone killed him to stop him from telling me about the ribbon?"

"It's a possibility, and if that's what happened it's the kidnapper who left you the ribbon and the kidnapper who killed Rawlings. If someone was playing a prank on you with the ribbon, that's not motive enough for murder."

She shivered beside him, and he pressed his shoulder against hers. "It's all speculation, Kendall. It could all be a coincidence that Rawlings died of a heart attack or a stroke or a fall on the very night he invited you over."

"Some coincidence. Looks like the good citizens of Timberline are right—I am some sort of unlucky talisman."

Buddy pawed at her ankles, and Coop patted his head. "Buddy doesn't think so…and neither do I."

Kendall scooped Buddy into her lap and dropped her head to Coop's shoulder. "I'm not sure what I'd do without you here, Coop."

He draped his arm across her shoulders, and Buddy nipped at his fingers dangling close to Kendall's breast.

He laughed. "I think Buddy wants to be your bodyguard and won't stand for any intruders."

She tugged on Buddy's ear. "He saved me as much as I saved him. Having him there gave me something to concentrate on other than Chuck Rawlings's dead body."

Coop twirled a lock of Kendall's dark hair around his finger. "So, we have a kidnapper who snatched two children, taunted two family members from the previous kidnapping case and then murdered a local man who had some information about a pink ribbon."

"My question is why?" Kendall scratched beneath Buddy's chin. "Why not just abduct the children and move on. Why continue to leave possible evidence?"

Coop's phone buzzed and he checked a text message from Britt. "Murderers do taunt law enforcement and don't always act rationally. Sometimes they even want to be caught."

"I hope the FBI can oblige him. And I hope we're dealing with a kidnapper only and not a killer." She hugged the dog to her chest.

Lucky little bastard.

"Where's Steffi tonight?"

"With Britt and Rob. I just got a text. She's already fast asleep."

"How'd the talk go? Were you able to reassure the parents?"

"Not much. It would've been better if Agent Maxfield had given the talk. The FBI is keeping me out of the loop and I didn't have much info to give the parents about those pictures or the progress of the investigation."

"That must be tough. Are you sure you're cut out for small-town policing?"

"Good question. We moved here because we thought a small town would be better for Alana's anxiety and depression. That didn't work, and I told you Steffi isn't happy with all the rain."

Buddy sprang from her lap. Brushing her hands together, she turned to face Coop. "I know I haven't known you long, Coop, but it seems to me you're not happy playing second fiddle to the FBI on the kidnapping case and you're not happy playing second fiddle to the county detectives on a possible homicide."

His lips quirked into a smile. "You haven't known me long, but you know me well."

"I'd better let you go." She stretched her arms over her head. "I need to find a place for Buddy to sleep tonight, and I have someone coming by tomorrow morning to start the yard work."

"You found someone?"

"Annie Foster found someone for me—Gary Binder."

"The ex-con?" A muscle at the corner of his mouth jumped. "You're hiring Gary Binder to clear your weeds?"

"I-it's not like he murdered someone. He was a junkie, and he's off the stuff now."

"Because he told you he was?" He shook his head. "As a therapist, you should know better."

"I seriously doubt he's any kind of danger to me, and he'll be working outside so he's not going to be stealing anything. I already told him he could have Aunt Cass's tools in the shed."

"I'll be around for a while tomorrow finishing up your security system in case he gets any ideas." He pushed up from the sagging sofa and shuffled his feet so he wouldn't step on Buddy. "Was Gary Binder living in Timberline at the time of your sister's kidnapping?"

"He was here. He was in his early twenties, a high school dropout." Folding her arms, she hunched her shoulders. "Are you implying that he could've been involved?"

"Anything's a possibility. I'll check the old case files to see if the FBI ever questioned him."

"It's not like he was in prison for twenty-five years and just got out to do another round of kidnappings. From what I understand, he's been in and out of jail for years."

"If Binder's going to be working around here, it's safer to check him out."

When she got to the front door, she tilted her head to the side. "Security system, personnel background checks. Have you become my private security guard?"

He touched a finger to her bottom lip. "Are you complaining?"

Her lips parted on a sigh. "I can use all the help I can get—for as long as I'm in Timberline."

And just like that, she reminded him that whatever they had between them was fleeting and temporary. She seemed to accept that fact—why couldn't he?

Chapter Eleven

The following morning, Gary Binder showed up at ten o'clock on the dot. Would someone still using be so prompt?

He leaned his bike against a tree trunk and rubbed his hands against the legs of his worn jeans. "I'm ready to get started."

She discussed the scope of the job with him again and his salary. "Deal?"

"Deal." He shook her hand. "Did you hear about old Chuck Rawlings? He fell and cracked his head open—probably plastered."

So, the cops, or someone, was spreading the accident story. "Was he a drinker?"

"Oh, yeah."

Buddy launched himself against the screen door inside and started yapping.

"You have a dog?"

"Actually, he was Chuck's dog."

Gary's eyes bugged out of their sockets like a cartoon character. "How'd you wind up with Chuck's dog?"

"It's a long story." She waved one hand in the air. "I can let him out here so he'll stop barking."

"Don't…please." Two red spots formed on Gary's pale cheeks. "I don't much like dogs, ma'am."

"Oh, okay, as long as you don't mind the barking."

"I'd rather have the barking than the biting."

"I don't think Buddy bites, but I don't know him all that well, so I'll keep him away from you." She pointed toward the shed. "Let's have a look at the tools."

She plucked a key from the large, silver ring that sported many more. "I think this is it. It's the only one small enough for a padlock."

The key fit and she swung open the door of the shed as the rusty hinges squealed. "No lights. Let's get the other door."

Gary reached around inside and lifted the stake that held the second door in place.

With both doors open wide, the daylight streamed into the close quarters, both sides lined with shelves and tools hanging from the walls. A lawn mower and weed whacker took up one corner.

"Looks like enough to get started." Gary hooked his thumbs in his belt loops.

"Not sure there's any gasoline for that lawn mower."

"I can take care of that, ma'am."

"Then I'll leave it in your hands." She pulled some cash and the keys to the truck from her pocket. "Buy what you need and take the truck to get it."

He carefully counted the money before folding it up and putting it in the front pocket of his jeans. "There's eighty bucks there. I'll give you your change and receipts at the end of the day."

"That'll be fine." She almost said something about his need to show his trustworthiness, but it was just that—a need. He had to go through that for his own peace of mind and well-being—probably part of his road to recovery.

A black truck turned into the drive and her heart leaped for a brief minute and then landed with a thud when she saw the driver. Wyatt waved out his window instead of Coop.

He scrambled from the truck and strode toward her, a

big smile splitting his baby face. "How's it going, Kendall?"

She raised her eyebrows. What a difference a couple of days made, or maybe he'd unburdened himself to his new therapist. "It's going. I'm getting ready for the estate sale this weekend and Rebecca already got a couple of bites on the house."

"Really?" Wyatt pushed his baseball cap farther back on his head. "For this old place? Makes me think I should list my folks' place."

"With Evergreen creating more and more jobs, the real estate prices will keep going up."

"I hope so. Did you hear about Rawlings?"

"I did. I'm the one who found him."

"What?"

Wyatt's surprise seemed forced. The word must already be out that she'd discovered Rawlings and Gary just missed the memo.

"I went over there to see him about something—his dog—and I found Chuck on the floor." If Dr. Shipman had Wyatt feeling better about life, she didn't want to bring him down with reminders about the kidnappings—past or present.

"That's not what you want to find when you go to someone's house." Wyatt rubbed his chin. "I heard he was drunk and took a spill."

"That seems to be the general consensus. He was bleeding from the head, but of course he could've had a heart attack and hit his head on the way down."

"That's rough." He pointed to Buddy furiously pawing at the screen door. "I see you got the dog, though."

"Buddy. I'd let him out, but Gary doesn't like dogs."

"I don't like them, either. Gary?"

"Binder." She jerked her thumb over her shoulder. "He's going to be clearing out the weeds and shrubs."

Wyatt dropped his chin to his chest. "Do you think that's a good idea, Kendall? Don't you remember Binder when we were kids and he was the town punk and druggie?"

"Vaguely, but he's clean and sober now."

"That's what they all say. Look at Rawlings."

"I'm not sure Rawlings ever claimed to be clean and sober."

"He went back and forth, like they all do."

Wyatt should know since his father had descended into alcoholism when Stevie went missing, just as her own mother had descended into madness. The kidnappings had created ripples of misery that had gone on for years.

"Well, Annie Foster recommended him and I'm giving him a chance."

He shrugged. "Since she's a fortune-teller or something, I guess she'd know."

Hadn't Wyatt lived among the Quileute long enough to know the shamans didn't consider themselves fortune-tellers? "I think you mean her cousin Scarlett Easton, and she's a shaman, not a fortune-teller."

"Whatever. Too bad Scarlett's not here to find those kids."

"I don't think she does that sort of thing."

Gary dragged a wheelbarrow from the back and she and Wyatt jumped.

Crossing his arms, Wyatt called out, "You know what you're doing here, Binder?"

A twist of anger claimed Gary's face for a second before he retreated back into his obsequious persona. "Yes, sir. It don't take an expert landscaper or an expert *plumber* to clear out some brush."

Wyatt's hands balled into fists against his biceps, and Kendall stepped into the space between the two men as

Gary started whistling an off-key tune. "Can I do something for you, Wyatt?"

"I just wanted to thank you for being a friend, Kendall." He rolled his shoulders and tilted his head from side to side, cracking his neck.

He must've seen Dr. Shipman, who must've told him not to blab about his sessions all over town.

"Anytime, Wyatt. We do have a bond, even though it's one we'd both rather forget."

Another black truck pulled up, and Coop honked his horn twice.

Wyatt squinted at Coop's truck even though not one ray of sunshine had broken through the cloud cover yet. "What's Coop doing here? Is he gonna talk to you about Rawlings?"

"I doubt it, since he called out the homicide detectives from county."

Wyatt's gaze tracked between her and Coop, now getting out of his truck, trying to put two and two together.

She *wished* there was more going on between her and her hunky bodyguard, but she'd have to be satisfied with meaningful looks and accidental skin-on-skin contact. As a single dad, Coop probably didn't go for one-night stands and love 'em and leave 'em hot nights. And she'd be the one doing the loving and leaving, since she had no intention of staying in Timberline for Coop or anyone else.

Coop's boots crunched the gravel as he approached them. "Looks like a regular convention here." He nodded at Gary.

Wyatt gripped the bill of his baseball cap, tugging it down over his forehead. "I just dropped by to see if Kendall was all right after finding Rawlings last night."

"I'm wondering the same thing." Coop quirked an eyebrow at her.

"I'm fine." She shifted her gaze away from Wyatt. So,

he *had* known she was the one who found Rawlings, or he was just covering in front of Coop.

"Good to hear. I gotta go now." Wyatt shook Coop's hand and headed for his truck.

"I have about an hour free." He spread his arms, opening his jacket and indicating his khaki uniform. "I think I can finish installing the security system in that time."

"You're not doing this on your lunch break, are you? And when do those days off start?"

"It's a break. We don't have to call it lunch, and I'll take the time off when I need it."

"The least I can do is get you some lunch. I'll pick up some sandwiches at Dina's Deli." She jerked her chin toward Gary. "Between you and me, he could use some meat on his bones."

Coop tipped his head back and laughed as he marched toward the house. "Beware of stray dogs."

He swung open the screen door before she could warn him about Buddy, and the little dog didn't waste any time escaping. He bounded from the porch and made a beeline toward Gary.

As Gary backed up into a bush, Buddy scampered back and forth in front of him, stopping every few seconds to bark up at him.

"Buddy!" She jogged over and picked up the squirming animal with both hands. "You need some obedience training. Sorry, Gary."

"That's okay." He edged away from her and Buddy. "I got bit by a dog once and never liked 'em since."

"That's understandable." She tucked Buddy under one arm and scolded him all the way to the front door.

Coop looked up from the boxes and wires spread in front of him on the table. "What was all that about?"

"Buddy went nuts on Gary, and Gary doesn't like dogs."

Coop snorted. "Probably had a few run-ins with some

nasty mutts when he was busy breaking into people's homes."

"You and Wyatt just can't cut the guy a break." She picked up a wire and twirled it around. "You don't still suspect he had something to do with the Timberline Trio case, do you?"

"Haven't dismissed the idea yet, but I haven't had time to check him out in the old files, either."

Buddy put two paws on the coffee table where Coop had the parts to the security system laid out and grabbed a piece in his mouth and took off.

"Buddy!"

"You'd better get that piece outta that mutt's mouth." Coop lunged toward the spinning, yapping dog, but Buddy weaved between his legs and scampered toward the hallway.

Kendall followed him into the bedroom where he'd jumped onto the bed, a white piece of plastic between his paws and clamped in his jaws.

"You naughty boy." She slipped her fingers into his mouth and pried the piece from his teeth.

"You got it?" Coop filled the doorway, his hands braced against the doorjamb as if he could block Buddy's exit.

She held up the mangled piece, wet with Buddy's slobber. "Was it important?"

"Just the motion sensor." He ran a hand over his mouth. "I can put everything else in, but I'm going to have to go back to Port Angeles tomorrow to replace this part."

"Perfect." She dropped the piece on her nightstand and wiped her fingers on her jeans. "I have to pay a visit to my online auctioneer. We can go together."

"Do you trust me?" He walked to the bed and swept the sensor from the nightstand and growled at Buddy. "I kinda made a mess of our trip last time."

"I trust you. We'll do it right this time, but I'm just

warning you." She crossed her two index fingers in front of her face. "I'm going to drop in on Dr. Shipman, and it has nothing to do with you. She actually has a referral for me in Phoenix."

He ducked his head. "Don't rub it in. I made a total ass of myself."

"You'll get no argument from me."

"I didn't think I would." He picked up Buddy with one hand and deposited him in her arms. "Now, keep an eye on this nuisance while I wire up your security system."

Holding Buddy, Kendall followed Coop to the front door and watched him lean the ladder against the house.

She put her lips close to Buddy's furry ear and whispered, "You're a good bodyguard, but Coop's even better."

THE FOLLOWING MORNING, Kendall stood on the porch and surveyed Gary's progress.

Sensing her scrutiny, Gary looked up from hoeing a patch of dirt. "Everything okay, ma'am? I thought I'd turn up this area here and then start on the bushes lining the driveway."

"Looks fine. You're doing a good job, Gary. Do you want me to leave you some leftovers for lunch?"

"No, thank you." He indicated a small, soft-sided cooler and a container of water next to his bike. "I brought my own lunch today."

"All right." She waved at Coop pulling up in his truck. "I'm heading to Port Angeles today, but don't worry about Buddy. I penned him up on the patio in the back."

"I'll just take care of business out front."

She nodded and practically skipped to Coop's truck. She and Coop planned to take care of their own business this morning in Port Angeles and try lunch again.

When she hopped in the truck, Coop narrowed his eyes

and stared at Gary. "You sure it's okay to leave Binder here alone?"

"I locked up the house." She snapped her seat belt in place. "He's actually doing a pretty good job. Don't you think so?"

"Looks okay."

"Has he been causing any trouble around here since his last stint in jail?"

"He hasn't been around much since I moved here. The guys in the department told me about him, said his mother still lives in the area and that he comes and goes when he visits her. As far as I can remember, he hasn't had any arrests."

"He'll be fine. Besides, I have Buddy to stand guard, and he's terrified of the dog."

"That mutt is not terrifying, but he is a menace." Coop tapped a box on the console.

"Is the sensor in there?"

"Yeah, and I'm hoping they'll replace it for me at no charge."

"If there is one, I'll cover it." She turned down the radio. "Any news on Rawlings?"

"Not yet. Homicide is running a toxicology report, and the medical examiner is going to do an autopsy. If they can rule out accidental or natural causes, Homicide will step up its investigation."

She shivered and cranked on the heater. "Are they looking into my story about the pink ribbon?"

"They're taking it into consideration, but they're not all that excited about it being a motive for murder."

"Okay, that's it." She pretended to zip her lips. "I'd like to enjoy at least one day when I'm not talking about pranks, kidnappings and murder."

"And since this is officially a day off for me, I'm with you on that."

They kept to their word for the rest of the drive, at least in spirit. Kendall never could quite banish the gloomy thoughts that had dogged her since returning to Timberline. But then, Timberline and gloomy thoughts went hand in hand for her, and that's why she couldn't wait to return to Arizona—except for the thought of leaving this man behind.

As they pulled into town, Coop turned to her. "I'll come with you to the online auction store, and then I think it would be better if we parted ways. I'll drop you off at Dr. Shipman's, and then I'll head to the security shop."

"I think you just want to check out the Elvis boots." She punched him in the arm.

The Elvis boots were gone when they got to the shop, so Coop wandered around looking at the other odds and ends while Kendall went over final pricing with Jessa.

"I guess that's it, Jessa. Thanks for everything."

"No problem. I think this stuff will sell."

Brushing her hands together, she stepped onto the sidewalk with Coop. "Glad that's over with."

When they got back in the truck, Coop gripped the steering wheel with both hands. "You know, when my wife died, I couldn't get rid of her stuff fast enough—clothes, toiletry items, even the foods she liked—I didn't feel guilty until some people started giving me strange looks. But I guess you and I are alike…lose the stuff that causes you pain and move on. Isn't that how you feel about your aunt's things? The collections? The house itself?"

"I do, and it's not like I'm ever going to forget my twin. I will never forget Kayla, but I have my own memories of her in here." She thumped a fist against her chest. "I don't need the stuff that reminds me of the day I lost her forever."

He cranked on the engine. "Exactly."

Coop drove the short distance to Dr. Shipman's office and pulled up to the curb.

Kendall slid from the truck and went around to the driver's side as Coop powered down the window. "Do you want to try the same place for lunch, or would that be bringing back bad memories?"

He chuckled. "I think we can make some new memories there. Give me a call when you're done. I'll head back over here once I get this piece replaced, and I'll wait here if you're not ready."

"Got it." She stepped away from the truck and waved.

She walked toward the office while Coop's truck idled at the curb. She reached for the door, turning the handle, and a crack resounded in the distance. The stucco on the wall next to her shattered. A piece struck her cheek.

Her hand jerked to the sting on her face, and her fingers met moisture. As if in a dream, she stared at the blood on her fingertips.

Coop shouted behind her. "Get down! Get down! Someone's shooting."

She turned her head just in time to see Coop launching his body at her. Another crack split the air and she lost all the breath in her lungs.

Chapter Twelve

Coop landed on top of Kendall, and she grunted with the force of the pressure.

A door opened and a woman screamed. More shouts and screams from outside the office.

"What happened? What are you doing?"

Coop glanced into the face of the woman he blamed for Alana's suicide.

She recoiled and clapped both hands over her mouth, her eyes wide and glassy. "Mr. Sloane!"

Kendall's body jerked beneath his and he rolled off her. His heart slammed against his chest when he saw the blood staining her cheek. Had he reacted too slowly?

"Kendall? Are you all right?" He rose to his knees and shouted at Dr. Shipman. "Call 9-1-1."

"Wh-what happened?"

"Someone was shooting outside."

"Oh, my God."

"Kendall?"

Her eyelids flew open and she panted out jerky words. "What. Happened out. There?"

"Did you get hit?" He ran his hands down her arms. "Your face is bleeding."

"The stucco. The stucco hit me."

A man poked his head in the office door. "Is everyone okay in here?"

"We're fine. Out there?"

"Everyone hit the ground or took cover. Someone saw him on top of the building across the street."

Adrenaline blasted through Coop's system, and he jumped to his feet. "Dr. Shipman, can you help Kendall?"

"Of course, and the police are on the way."

He couldn't wait for the Port Angeles police, not if a killer was on the loose.

He helped Kendall to the love seat in the waiting room and tucked her hair behind her ear. "Stay here with Dr. Shipman."

Gripping his arm, she said, "Be careful, Coop."

With his weapon in his hand, he hit the sidewalk. "Which building?"

His gaze glued to the gun, a man pointed to a white, three-story building across the street.

"I'm a cop. When the Port Angeles police get here, tell them I went after the shooter."

Coop sprinted across the street in case the guy started shooting again. He hugged the side of the building, and then slipped in the front door.

A few people cowered near a potted plant in the corner, and Coop flashed his badge. "I'm a cop. Stay inside. The shooter was spotted on the roof of this building. Did you see anyone coming down and leaving the building?"

They all shook their heads, and one woman pointed to the ceiling. "You can get to the roof from the stairwell around the corner, past the elevators."

He headed for the stairwell and jogged upward, bursting through the door to the rooftop. Crouching, he made his way to the edge of the building that faced the street and Dr. Shipman's office. Sirens wailed, closer and closer.

He studied the gravel on the surface of the roof and noted several disturbances, although they could've been recent or from days or weeks before. He crouched, the gravel shifting beneath his feet, and ran his hand along the edge of the roof—plenty of room to hide and aim a rifle.

His gaze swept the surface, but the shooter must've collected his shell casings before he left. Coop sniffed the air and detected a faint scent of gunpowder. Or was that his imagination?

The door behind him crashed and a female voice shouted. "Place your weapon on the ground and put your hands up."

Coop complied with the officer's orders.

"Turn around, slowly."

He turned with his hands raised in the air. "I'm Sheriff Cooper Sloane from Timberline, ma'am."

"Badge?"

"In my pocket." He dipped his chin toward his chest, indicating the front pocket of his flannel shirt.

Another officer burst onto the roof behind the female cop.

Without shifting her aim, she said, "Says he's Sheriff Sloane from Timberline. Badge is in his front pocket."

The male officer had his weapon trained on Coop, as well. "Take it out of your pocket nice and easy and toss it toward us."

Coop followed his instructions and once they got a look at his badge, they lowered their guns.

"I was across the street when the shooting started and someone said the shots came from up here."

The first cop on the scene answered. "Did you find anything?"

"No, and nobody in the building saw him leave."

"There's a back exit from the stairwell. He may have gone that way." The male officer holstered his weapon. "We have officers combing the area."

"I'll leave you two to canvas the roof. I left my friend down there. One of the shots came close to her head."

They asked him a few more questions and let him leave. By the time he got back to Dr. Shipman's office, the EMTs had Kendall bandaged up and sitting on the back of the ambulance.

"Are you okay? How's the face?" He leaned against the ambulance door.

She touched a fingertip to the edge of the white square on her cheek. "It's okay. I'm fine. You didn't find anything on the roof?"

"I didn't. The Port Angeles police are up there now." He circled his finger in the air. "Did anyone else see anything?"

"Just the few people who'd claimed to see someone on that roof at about the same time the shots were fired. The police already questioned me, but I was useless. I didn't even know what was going on."

"Then I tackled you." He brushed a hand over the smooth hair on the top of her head. "I think I knocked the wind out of you."

She caught his hand. "I think you saved my life."

Giving her fingers a squeeze, he asked, "Were any more shots besides those two fired?"

"The two that were fired at me, you mean?" She shook her head. "I don't think so. All anyone reported hearing were the two shots."

An EMT returned to the back of the ambulance, peeling off a pair of plastic gloves. "All your vitals check out, miss. You're free to leave, but remember to remove your bandage in a few hours to clean your wound."

Coop took Kendall's arm as she hopped off the back of the van. "Do the officers need to question you anymore?"

"They told me I could leave after I gave them my contact info. Like I said, I was no use whatsoever."

"I'm just glad you're okay." He cupped her face in his palms, and her soft hair brushing the backs of his hands made him ache somewhere deep inside. "When I heard that first shot and saw the wall next to you explode, my heart stopped."

"Kendall, how are you feeling?"

Coop raised his eyes above Kendall's head and met the gaze of Dr. Shipman. His gut knotted as he remembered their last encounter, the one before he crashed on her office doorstep on top of Kendall.

Kendall disengaged herself from him and turned to face Dr. Shipman. "I feel okay, Jules, still a little weak in the knees."

"I can't believe that happened here. Must be some very disturbed individual, and I hope the police find him before he has a chance to do it again."

"Do you think he will?" Kendall crossed her arms, hugging her purse to her chest. "He sure gave up quickly. Two shots and done. Isn't that unusual, Coop?"

A sharp pinprick of fear jabbed the base of his skull, and he rubbed the back of his neck. "I don't know what's usual or unusual in these circumstances. He could've gotten spooked when those people turned and pointed at the roof."

"I hope it spooked him enough to scare him out of these parts." Dr. Shipman hunched her shoulders. "Kendall, you're probably too shaken up to discuss that other matter. I can give you a call or we can interface over the computer."

"Of course. Thanks for your help, Jules."

"I'm just glad my office provided you some shelter." She gave Kendall a quick hug. "Have a nice trip back to Phoenix, and I'll be in touch."

"Thanks, Jules."

Dr. Shipman nodded toward Coop. "Sheriff Sloane."

Coop unclenched his jaw. "Thank you, Dr. Shipman."

Kendall blew out a long breath. "Lunch?"

"Are you kidding?"

"Not at all. Remember those two glasses of wine I had the last time we lunched at the Pelican's Nest? Well, I could use a couple more."

"Aren't pelicans supposed to bring bad luck to sailors? Maybe we should change it up."

She pinched his arm. "That's an albatross, as in you don't want one around your neck."

"I don't think I want a pelican around my neck, either."

Kendall started laughing, doubled over and then started snorting.

"Are you getting hysterical?" He rubbed a circle on her back just as a news van pulled up and discharged a reporter and a cameraman.

Coop grabbed Kendall's arm. "Unless you want to be on the six o'clock news, I suggest we head for the Pelican's Nest or even the Albatross's Nest if that keeps you laughing."

She wiped a few tears from the corners of her eyes and matched him step for step back to his truck, which it seems they'd left a lifetime ago.

He started the engine, did a U-turn and drove toward the water.

When they were seated with a couple of drinks in front of them, Coop took Kendall's hand and started toying with her fingers. "Out with it, Kendall. What were you thinking back there at Dr. Shipman's office? What were you thinking about this sniper?"

"I think you know." She took a gulp of wine as if to fortify her courage. "Why shoot at someone about to go into a building? Why two shots only? Why did the shots stop when the first and only victim—" she raised her hand "—was pushed out of range?"

"You think the shots were meant for you." He pinged

his fingernail against his beer bottle and watched a rivulet of moisture run down the glass.

"Are you telling me that thought never crossed your mind?"

"I was too busy going after the shooter to consider it."

"But now that you've had a chance to consider it?" She took another swig of wine from her glass, leaving a pink lipstick print on the rim.

He wanted to ignore the feeling of dread sketching a cold trail in his veins but if Kendall had the guts to face the truth head-on, he owed it to her to come along for the ride. "I know strange things have been happening to you, but I still can't put my finger on a motive. I've turned it over a few times, and haven't come up with a good reason why the kidnapper would want to kill you—unless he's the same man who took your sister and he's afraid you'll remember."

"What would be his motive for any of it? The ribbon? The mannequin? Burying those photos on my property?"

"Maybe he wants you to find the missing children, but it doesn't explain the shots fired"

She buried her chin in her palm. "I don't know, but I'm getting out of here."

His heart dropped with a thud and he made a big deal out of studying the menu. "Are you going to eat lunch first?"

"I'm not leaving right this minute." She flicked a finger at his menu. "But I'm going to get through the yard sale this weekend and then I'm leaving."

"Probably a good idea. Whatever's happening to you is tied to Timberline and those kidnappings. The sooner you get back to Phoenix, the better...for you."

She raised the menu to cover her face and responded in a muffled voice. "I think so, too. Have you heard anything from the FBI about the pictures or any evidence left at the burial sites?"

He held up his hand as the waiter approached, and they ordered their food.

Coop took a sip of his beer, and started picking at the foil label. "The FBI guys are tight-lipped when it comes to local law enforcement."

"It's been almost a month since those kids were taken, hasn't it?"

"Yeah, earlier in September."

"Maybe those pictures mean the kids are still alive. They looked kind of grungy, didn't they?" Kendall's eyebrows rose in a hopeful expression.

"They did, so maybe that's their condition after being held for three weeks." He entwined his fingers with her fidgeting ones. "The FBI is looking at other clues from the pictures, like the lighting, which is harsh and unnatural. They're also investigating where someone would get that newspaper with the Timberline Trio headline."

"That is odd. How would someone get ahold of that? I don't think even Aunt Cass had saved those papers, even though it seems like she saved everything else." She wrinkled her nose. "And actually I thought she had saved a pile of those."

"The FBI hasn't even determined yet if those are original newspapers or printouts or reprints. They could've come from anywhere."

"I guess." She tapped the window. "Have you even noticed the view today?"

He looked into the depths of her dark eyes. "I noticed the view."

A pink tinge touched her cheeks. "I meant the one out the window."

"That, too." His gaze shifted to the grayish-blue water

lapping at the boats in the harbor. "We were going to have a stress-free day."

"Yeah, that lasted until the shooting started."

"The shooting's over and you're safe, so let's try to salvage the afternoon."

The waiter delivered their food as if on cue, and Coop flicked his napkin into his lap. "I'm rebooting the afternoon, starting now."

"I'll drink to that." She touched her wineglass to his bottle. "We'd better pick up the pace here if you're going to pick up Steffi from the Fletchers'."

"I'm only going to see her for a short time tonight. There's a birthday party sleepover, so I'm just there to be her chauffeur and personal assistant to make sure she packs everything."

"It seems like she spends a lot of time with Genevieve's family. Do you think you're using Britt as a substitute maternal figure for Steffi?" She swirled the wine in her glass, holding her breath.

Coop pinched the bridge of his nose. "It's not easy being a single dad to a little girl. Once Steffi started school and saw all the other moms, she seemed to want to spend more time at her friends' homes, homes with moms who had high heels and make-up and clothes for dress-up—and I let her. Does that make me a bad father?"

Kendall swallowed the lump in her throat. "Of course not."

"It wasn't always like that." A small smile played over his lips. "When she was a toddler, it was just the two of us—the zoo, the park, swimming lessons. The shift happened when she started school. Instead of spending time with me, she wanted to be with her friends. I suppose I screwed it all up."

She traced the knuckles of his clenched hand with her

fingertip. "You didn't screw up anything. She'll gravitate back toward you."

"Thanks, Kendall."

"Besides, she seems well-adjusted." She slid her hand from his and then cupped it around a slice of lemon and squeezed it on her fish.

He lifted one shoulder. "Yeah, except for that irrational hatred for the rain—and she's in a bad place for that."

"I wouldn't necessarily call it an irrational hatred." Kendall wiped her hands on a napkin, and then traced a drop of moisture rolling down the window outside with her fingertip.

He stabbed a tomato with his fork. "Most kids don't pay attention to the weather one way or the other. Steffi was born here. You'd think she'd be used to it like all the other kids in Timberline. Did you even notice the weather here until you grew up and moved somewhere else?"

"I used to like the rain—the smell of it, the feel of it on my face, the taste of it on my tongue. I liked it until the cool temperatures and gray skies started getting depressing, and yes, that happened as I hit adolescence and started brooding on my lost twin."

"That had to be painful. I have a sister and as annoying as she is sometimes, I can't imagine losing her even though I don't see her often."

Kendall blinked back her emotions and sawed off a corner of her fish. "Why is that?"

"Her husband works for the State Department, and they live in Spain right now."

"Must be nice." She tilted her head to one side. "Did you have one of those idyllic childhoods with the family of four behind a white picket fence?"

"Guilty." He raised his hand. "That's why I was unprepared for my wife's…darkness."

She snapped her fingers in the air. "No more darkness today."

They finished their lunch, recovering from their rocky beginning just like they had the other day. Kendall was the type of woman he should've been with from the beginning—pragmatic, resilient, strong. The guilt leaped in his chest like a flame. Kendall would probably be the first one to tell him that Alana's depression didn't make her weak, just ill.

Before they left Port Angeles, Coop stopped by the security store and exchanged the damaged sensor for a new one.

On the way home, the sprinkles turned into rain.

Kendall sighed. "I hope it's not raining like this in Timberline. I was hoping Gary could finish the front today so I'd have a cleared-out space for the estate sale."

"We were supposed to have a respite from the rain this weekend, so maybe this will clear up by the time we get back."

He was right. By the time they had pulled into Timberline, the dark clouds had thinned out, but Binder still hadn't finished the work.

"What the heck happened?" Kendall sat forward in her seat. "It doesn't look like he got much further than when I left."

"I'm not going to say I told you so." He parked his truck behind Kendall's. "His bike is gone."

"Damn. I thought the guy was sincere about wanting to get the job done." She jumped from the truck before he turned off the engine.

He joined her as she stood in the middle of the front yard, hands on her hips.

"I can finish it up for you—at least enough so you can put some tables out here for the estate sale."

"You need to finish the security system and, besides,

you've already done enough." She kicked a rock with the toe of her boot. "I'm going to check on Buddy and release him from his prison."

Coop returned to his truck to get the new security sensor.

Then a high-pitched scream pierced the air and he dropped the bag and ran to Kendall.

He rounded the corner to the backyard and tripped to a stop as Kendall, her face ashen and her eyes like two black coals, held out Buddy in front of her.

"He's dead."

Chapter Thirteen

Kendall pressed the limp dog to her chest as a sob broke from her lips. This place. This house. Took everything from her.

Coop crouched beside her and wrapped his arms around her and Buddy. "I'm sorry. What happened to the little guy?"

She lifted her eyes, brimming with tears, to his face. "He was lying on his side in the pen. He had foam bubbling from his mouth."

"Still bubbling?" He took Buddy into his own arms and pressed his ear against the dog's body.

"Yeah." Her gaze scanned the patio within the pen and stumbled across a piece of lunch meat and a dried leaf.

"He's still alive, Kendall. He has a faint heartbeat." Coop sprang to his feet, Buddy in his arms. "If we can get him to Doc Washburn as soon as possible, he might have a chance."

Kendall dashed the tears from her face and staggered to her feet. "What are we waiting for?"

She followed Coop to his truck and slid into the passenger seat, where he transferred his bundle to her. She cradled Buddy in her arms, whispering, "Hang on. Keep fighting, Buddy."

Coop's truck flew across the wet asphalt of the road and screeched to a stop in front of the local vet's office.

Kendall jumped from the truck and ran into the waiting room with Buddy against her shoulder. "We have an emergency. I came home and my dog was unresponsive and foaming at the mouth, but he's still breathing."

The receptionist pressed a button on an intercom attached to the wall. "Emergency in the front."

Within seconds, a tech burst through the swinging doors that led to the examination rooms. As he took Buddy from her arms, Kendall explained the dog's condition.

"Do you know if he ate something? Chewed on something?"

"There was a piece of meat and a leaf in the pen he was in."

Nodding, the tech backed into an examination room and said, "Wait out front. We'll do what we can."

Kendall stumbled back to the waiting room where Coop was on the phone, pacing across the floor.

"Do you need to go to Steffi?"

"It's not time yet. I was just checking up on her. She's at Genevieve's and they're helping Britt frost the birthday cake." He took her hands. "Did Doc Washburn say anything?"

"I didn't see him. A tech took Buddy into an exam room and asked me some questions." She grabbed his wrist. "Coop, there was a piece of bologna or something in the pen. I didn't give Buddy anything like that."

"Did you pick it up? Do you have it with you?"

"No. Should I go get it?" Her gaze darted to the swinging doors. "I don't want to leave him."

"Are you okay here alone? I can drive back and pick it up."

"Would you?" She pressed her lips against his knuckles. What would she do without this man by her side?

"Hang in there. I'll be back as soon as I can."

When Coop left, Kendall wandered around the waiting room picking up and discarding magazines.

After the receptionist assisted a customer with a cat carrier in hand, she turned to Kendall. "Was that your dog you brought in?"

"Yes. Buddy."

The receptionist cocked her head. "Wasn't that Chuck Rawlings's dog?"

"I…uh…adopted him."

"Okay. I thought so. We've seen Buddy before."

"For anything like this?"

"Not that I remember—just routine stuff. Do you know what happened to Chuck?"

"No idea. Heart attack?" Kendall shrugged. She wasn't about to reveal her suspicions to this curious receptionist. It would seem that she brought bad luck everywhere she went, not only to humans but animals.

Another forty minutes ticked by before Coop returned, a small plastic bag in hand. He dangled it from his fingers in the light. "A piece of bologna."

"Where did it come from?"

"It didn't fall from the sky. I wish I'd had the security system hooked up." He pressed the bag into her hand. "Do you want to give this to Washburn?"

She waved the plastic bag at the receptionist. "Buddy was eating this. Do you think Dr. Washburn wants to see it?"

"Absolutely. I'll call Blake up to get it."

She pressed the intercom again and the tech materialized in the waiting room. "Buddy, the dog that just came in? He may have been eating this."

"Okay, great."

"How's he doing? Do you have any news?"

"I'll let Dr. Washburn tell you. He's almost done and it looks like Buddy's going to pull through."

Kendall closed her eyes and covered her face. "Thank you."

Coop pressed a hand against the small of her back. "Sit down. You've been on the edge ever since we found Buddy, and your afternoon wasn't exactly a walk in the park, either."

She allowed him to propel her to a vinyl chair that squeaked when she dropped to the seat. "Someone poisoned him. Someone fed him tainted meat. And what happened to Gary?"

"Do you have his phone number?"

"The guy doesn't have a cell phone."

"He lives with his mother, Raylene Binder. We can call Raylene at home or drop by." Coop ran his knuckles along his stubble.

A pulse throbbed in her throat. "What are you thinking?"

"I'm wondering if Gary dislikes all dogs or just Buddy."

"And why would he just dislike Buddy?" She flicked her tongue across her dry lips, suddenly unable to swallow.

"Because Buddy was there when Binder killed Rawlings."

Kendall sucked in a breath. "I had the same thought."

"And if Binder had a reason to kill Rawlings, it might just have to do with Rawlings's meeting with you." He drummed his fingers on the arm of the chair. "Did you ever check with Annie about whether or not she even talked to Binder? Maybe Annie came up with Binder's name because he approached her to put in a good word for him."

Kendall pressed her fingers to her temples. "This is too much. Do you think Binder took off after poisoning Buddy?"

"Look, this is all supposition at this point, Kendall. I'll need to find Binder first and talk to him."

"Ms. Rush?" Dr. Washburn stepped through the swinging doors, a clipboard tucked under his arm.

She popped up. "Yes?"

"Buddy's going to be fine. He's a little weak from getting his stomach pumped, so he just needs some rest and soft food for a day or two."

"Thank you. Was it poison?"

"Probably rat poison. I recommend using traps instead of poison if you have rats."

Coop placed a hand on her shoulder. "Did you test the piece of lunch meat that we brought in?"

"A preliminary test showed nothing on the meat, but that doesn't mean someone didn't wrap a cold cut around some poison." Dr. Washburn shoved his glasses up the bridge of his nose. "Is that what you think happened?"

"Possibly. Have you had any other cases of pet poisoning?"

"We have not, Sheriff, but as you might remember we had a rash of pet murders a few years back. Someone was shooting dogs and cats with a pellet gun."

Coop nodded. "I remember that. It stopped after about eight months."

"There was a string of those before you came here as sheriff. Those stopped as suddenly as they started, too." Dr. Washburn spread his hands. "Other than that, we haven't had any issues. I hope what happened to Buddy is not the start of another pet killing spree."

"I hope you're right." Kendall pressed a hand against her heart. "Can I take Buddy home now?"

"I think he'd like that."

As she settled the bill at the counter, the tech brought Buddy out, wrapped in a fuzzy blue blanket. His tail hanging out of the end, wagged weakly.

"Buddy!" She took the little dog in her arms and pressed her cheek against his head.

Coop led the way back to the truck. "I'm going to drop off you and Buddy, and then I'm going to pay a visit to Raylene Binder."

"I'm coming with you."

"And Buddy?"

Scratching the dog's ear, she said, "I could tuck him at home."

"I've got an idea. The Fletchers are dog people and I want to see Steffi before she goes to the sleepover, so let's leave Buddy there where he can get lots of attention."

"Great idea."

As Coop drove to the Fletchers' house, Buddy seemed to perk up. Kendall stroked the pup's soft fur and rubbed his belly. "Who could harm a pet?"

"You heard Dr. Washburn. There are a lot of sick people out there."

"As evidenced by the kidnappings."

"Sometimes the same urge that drives someone to harm an animal compels them to harm a human. A lot of serial killers started out practicing their art on pets."

She swallowed. "And they walk among us like normal people."

By the time they reached the Fletchers', Buddy was licking her fingers and thumping his tail. "You're in for a treat. You get to recuperate with kids."

Britt answered the door and squealed when she saw Buddy poke his head from the blanket. "He's adorable."

Steffi and Genevieve were soon crowding in, tugging at the blanket to get a peek at Buddy.

"Sit down, Steffi. I'll put him in your lap."

Coop's daughter plopped down on the sofa, and Kendall placed the dog in her arms.

Steffi touched her nose to his. "He's cute. Is he sick?"

"He's a little weak. Just cuddle with him and keep him company. Can you do that?"

Steffi ignored her question, but Genevieve jumped up and down. "I can. I can."

Coop tweaked one of Steffi's curls. "Be gentle with him. I'm leaving Mrs. Fletcher our key so she can get your stuff for the sleepover. Daddy has some work to do."

Steffi's blue eyes rose from Buddy and flicked between Kendall and Coop. "Okay, Daddy."

Britt walked them to the door. "They'll be fine, but you're picking up Buddy before the party, right? I have a feeling some of the little girls don't like dogs as much as these two do."

"I just need to question someone, Britt. I won't be long."

Britt's eyes widened. "I hope this doesn't mean someone's going to start terrorizing pets again. We lost a cat the last time."

Coop squeezed her shoulder. "I think this one is personal. Thanks again."

On the way to Mrs. Binder's house, Kendall asked, "Do you really think Gary will be there? He could've hit the road already."

"If he has, maybe we can get something out of Raylene."

The truck rolled down the slick asphalt of a street that the Evergreen revival had bypassed. Weeds poked up from cracks in the sidewalk and water swirled around gutters clogged with leaves and debris.

"Baker Street is still an eyesore. Why doesn't the city council do something about the conditions here?"

"The mayor and his pal Jordan Young have bigger, more profitable fish to fry." Coop pulled in front of a gray, clapboard house with a sagging roof and a front yard choked by weeds. He pointed out the window. "Binder's bike."

"I didn't figure he'd hightail it out of Timberline on his ten-speed."

"Raylene's car is here, too, so if he left town he did it on foot."

Coop parked the truck and as Kendall's boots hit the ground, a curtain at the front window twitched. If Gary didn't want to talk to them, he wouldn't open the door.

They walked up the porch and Coop rapped on the crooked screen door. Several seconds later, the front door opened a crack.

"Yes?"

Coop cleared his throat. "Good afternoon, Mrs. Binder, is Gary home?"

"He's home but he's sick."

Kendall ground her back teeth together. "Can we talk to him for a minute?"

"Ma, is that Ms. Rush?" Gary's voice, weak and strained, filtered to the front porch.

Mrs. Binder looked over her shoulder. "And the sheriff."

"Let 'em in."

Gary's mother widened the door and stepped back.

Coop walked in first, as if shielding Kendall, but if he expected some kind of threat from Gary Binder, he'd misjudged the man. Had she?

Gary lay on the couch, huddled beneath a blanket, in front of a cooking show on TV. He muted the sound and struggled to sit up.

"I'm really sorry I didn't get much done today, ma'am. After I ate my lunch, I felt real sick. Too sick to even leave you a note. I did put all the tools away, and I have a receipt for a new line I had to buy for the weed whacker."

"D-did you see Buddy?" She put one hand on her hip.

"Buddy?"

"The dog."

"Oh, Gary don't like dogs." Mrs. Binder flapped her hands in the air. "Ever since he got bit once."

"Quiet, Ma." Gary swung his bare feet to the floor.

Raylene pulled her sweater around her skinny frame. "I'll be outside if you need me."

Gary rolled his eyes. "I didn't see the dog, ma'am. I didn't go out back today."

Coop's eyes met hers and he lifted his brows. "When Kendall and I got back to her place, she found Buddy lying on his side, sick. We took him to Doc Washburn, who said the dog had been poisoned."

"Poisoned?" Gary clutched the blanket around his middle. "I didn't poison no dog. Is that what you think? Is that why you're here?"

Coop took several more steps into the cluttered room and hovered over Gary still sitting on the couch. "That's what we thought. The dog was sick, you were gone."

Gary bounded from the couch and immediately grabbed the back, as he swayed on his feet. "I swear, Sheriff. I don't like dogs, but I wouldn't hurt one. I got sick. I got sick, too, maybe just like that dog."

Kendall folded her arms across her midsection. "What are you saying, Gary?"

He swiped the back of his hand across his mouth and sank to the arm of the couch. "Someone poisoned that dog…and someone poisoned me."

Chapter Fourteen

Coop stepped behind Kendall, who looked as unsteady as Gary. Narrowing his eyes, he studied the pale-faced ex-con. Was this guy on the level?

"Do you know any reason why someone would want to poison you along with a dog?"

Binder chewed on the side of his thumb. "Dunno."

"And yet that's the conclusion you jumped to?"

"Dog's sick, poisoned, and I get sick at the same time." Binder rubbed the back of his neck where he sported a tattoo of a star. "Could be poison. I don't have any insurance to see a doctor."

Kendall had regained her color and took a deep breath. "What did you eat for lunch?"

"A bologna sandwich on white bread and some potato chips. I had one of those chocolate cupcakes, but I didn't get to it. Upchucked everything."

Coop stuffed his hands in his pockets. "Did you say you left Kendall's house today before you got sick?"

"I had to get the lines for the weed whacker." He glanced at Kendall. "I have the receipt."

Coop's pulse picked up a beat. "Did you leave your lunch at the house when you went?"

"Yeah." Binder lurched forward. "And I didn't poison no dog, ma'am. I wouldn't do that."

"Do you know who would?" A muscle ticked at the corner of Coop's mouth.

Binder's eyes widened. "What? How would I know that?"

"Weren't you around these parts a few years ago when pets were turning up dead?"

The screen door banged and Raylene charged into the room reeking of tobacco. "My boy wouldn't hurt no animals. One of your guys questioned him about that and nothin' came of it."

"I believe you, Gary." Kendall put her hand on Gary's arm. "You should go get checked out by a doctor. Go see Dr. Crandall and I'll foot the bill."

Binder's face turned bright red. "That's okay, ma'am. I'm feeling better, and I can finish the job tomorrow."

"I insist. Get checked out before you come by tomorrow morning."

With further pressure from his mother, Binder agreed to make an appointment with Dr. Crandall.

When they got in the truck, Coop turned to her. "You want to find out if Binder was poisoned, right? That's the reason you were so adamant about his appointment with Dr. Crandall."

"I believe him, don't you?"

He started the truck and drove off of Baker Street. Once he turned the corner, he answered. "I can understand why someone might want to kill Buddy if that someone murdered Rawlings, not that we know yet what happened to Rawlings, but why risk killing Binder?"

"Binder's not dead."

"Because in his words, he upchucked everything."

She grimaced. "I just wish that security system was operational."

"You and me both. Every time I try to finish up, something gets in the way." He smacked the steering wheel. "I'm going to finish tonight."

"Since Steffi is at the sleepover, I'll make you dinner and we can both convalesce with Buddy." She stretched her arms over her head. "I feel like I've been run over by a semi today."

He touched the bandage on her cheek. "Someone tried to shoot you and someone poisoned your dog. Can't get much worse than that."

"Oh, I think it can get worse, especially if the person who shot at me and the person who poisoned Buddy is the same guy."

Coop let her suspicion hang in the air, not because he thought Kendall was off track, but because he had no answers for her.

If the present-day kidnapper of Harrison and Cheri was threatening Kendall, Coop may not know why but he'd do everything in his power to stop him and protect her... and this time he wouldn't need a psychologist to help him.

"How's THE PATIENT?" Coop peered around the edge of the screen door, wiping his boots on the mat outside.

Kendall patted the top of a sleeping Buddy's head, as his tail rose and fell in a halfhearted attempt at a wag. "He's fine. Is the security system operational?"

"It is." Leaning against the doorjamb, he pulled off one boot and dropped it on the porch. "I'm going to leave my muddy boots out here. I don't want to spoil Annie's handiwork."

"Good idea, although Dreamweavers is coming back after the estate sale for a final cleanup." She lifted the computer from her lap. "Can you show me how to tap into my security cameras?"

"Let me wash up first." He lifted his nose and sniffed the air. "My stomach just growled. What's cookin'?"

"I have a pot roast in the oven with some potatoes. Do you want a salad with that or some green beans?"

"I'll take the green beans. Do you need any help?"

"Nope." She pointed to the hallway. "You get cleaned up and then show me how to access my security system. The dinner is cooking itself at this point."

He gave her a mock salute and sauntered toward the hallway in stocking feet.

Watching his rolling, rangy gait, she fanned herself. The man didn't even have to get cleaned up to look hot as hell.

How'd she get so lucky? Timberline's sheriff could've been old, potbellied Sheriff Carpenter who'd ruled over the town for most of her time here. Instead she'd gotten washboard abs, or at least she imagined Coop had washboard abs beneath his layers of clothing. Would she have a chance to find out before she left? Did she even want to know what she'd be missing?

Coop emerged from the hallway with his short hair slicked back, his flannel shirt tossed over one shoulder. "Ahh, that's better."

She narrowed her eyes, taking in the way his white T-shirt clung to his muscles—including his six-pack. She hadn't been wrong.

He dangled the shirt from his fingertips. "I'm sorry. Did I get too comfortable? My shirt got wet outside."

"You did all the work. Get as comfortable as you like."

Her mouth watered as he dropped the flannel and stretched, his biceps bunching and the T-shirt clinging to his pecs. Police work in a small town must be more active than she thought.

He dropped beside her on the sofa and she dipped, her shoulder bumping his. "Okay, let's take a look."

He reached across her, and the soap in the bathroom had never smelled as good as it did on his warm skin. He tapped a few keys on the keyboard to bring up the security system. "You can also get this app on your phone."

He led her through the easy steps it took to view the video footage of her house and to check the alerts when they came through.

"You can turn this all over to the new owners when the time comes. Even if they choose to tear the place down and put up a mini mansion, they can reconnect the system."

She sank back against the cushion. "Even if they don't keep it, I feel so much better having it in place, especially after today."

Coop scratched Buddy behind the ear. "If I'd gotten it connected sooner, we would've seen exactly what happened to Buddy today...and Gary."

"Do you believe him?"

"If Gary did poison Buddy for some reason, he's not the one who took a shot at you. Even if he'd taken his mother's car to Port Angeles, I don't think he would've had enough time to get there, set up, escape, come back here and feign an illness, even with Raylene's cooperation."

She shoved her computer from her lap to the cushion next to her. "What if the sniper was a general kook just looking to cause some mayhem? The shooting was all over the news. What if Gary thought he could make friends with Buddy by sharing some of his lunch with him, and that lunch was bad and made them both sick? When he realized what he'd fed Buddy made him sick, he panicked. Gary Binder is all about doing the right thing now."

"I'd like to believe all that, Kendall." He picked up a lock of her hair and twirled it around his finger.

"But you don't."

"That would require too many far-fetched coincidences."

"And in your line of work, you've come to suspect far-fetched coincidences?" She folded her hands in her lap and studied her fingernails. "I don't believe in coincidences, either. But you know what I do believe in?"

"What?" He released her hair and watched it spill against his hand.

"Fate."

"Fate, like destined by the stars or something?"

"Sort of." She took his hand and traced the pad of her thumb over his knuckles. "You saved my life today. You pushed me out of the way of that second shot. If you hadn't been with me, I'd be dead."

"Maybe if I hadn't dragged you into this investigation, you wouldn't have a target on your back." He clenched his hand into a fist beneath her touch.

"You don't really believe that, do you? That pink ribbon showed up in my aunt's cabinet before you ever knocked on my door. Someone was waiting for my return, for whatever reason." A chill skittered up her spine. "Maybe it's the same man who took my sister and kicked me into unconsciousness."

"Usually violent criminals don't stop their activity only to take it up twenty-five years later, unless…"

"Unless they've been in prison. You mentioned that before, but the thought of hapless Gary Binder as some vicious kidnapper is ludicrous."

"Haven't you ever watched the news stories after the capture of some serial killer? All his neighbors go on and on about what a nice guy he was—fixing bikes for the kids, taking in stray dogs—and at night he's going out and slashing hookers' throats."

She dug her fingernails into the back of his hand. "Ugh. Thanks for that visual."

The timer dinged from the kitchen. "That's dinner. Give me a shove so I can get up from this cushion. I don't even think I can sell this sofa."

Coop placed a firm hand on the small of her back, his fingers curling around her hip.

She sprang from the sofa, afraid she'd fall back into his arms where she wanted to be right now.

As she bounded toward the kitchen, Coop followed and hung on the doorjamb. "You know what I'd do if I bought this house?"

"Raze it to the ground?" She grabbed two oven mitts and gripped the handles of the roasting pan.

"I'd knock out the wall between the living room and kitchen, make it one big room with an island or peninsula counter separating the two areas."

"It is kind of old-fashioned having the solid wall between the two rooms and a doorway into the kitchen." The heat rose from the oven, warming her cheeks. She placed the roast on top of the stove and poked at the quartered potatoes in the pan. "Do these look done to you, or do you prefer them crispier?"

He broke off a corner of one potato with a fork and blew on it before popping it into his mouth. He rolled his eyes to the ceiling. "Perfect."

"I know my cooking's not *that* good."

"To a single dad, this is a piece of heaven right here." He waved his fork over the pot roast. "I can't do this. My cooking skills are basic."

"Then your skills are perfectly suited to cutting the green beans into two-inch pieces, washing them and sticking them in the microwave. Then you can toss them with a little lemon juice and parsley."

"Lead me to the green beans."

When they'd set the table and Coop had sliced pieces of meat from the pot roast, Kendall held up a bottle of red wine. "You're still officially on vacation, right?"

"One glass." Pinching the stem of the wineglass, he

held it out to her and she poured the ruby-red liquid almost to the rim. "Whoa. You'd never make it as a sommelier."

"If they're stingy with their wine, then you're right."

She grabbed the back of her chair, but he got there first and pulled it out for her. "After the day you had, I don't know why you were in here cooking up a storm."

"Someone took a couple of shots at me and poisoned my dog." She jerked her shoulders up and down. "What am I supposed to do, assume the fetal position?"

He clinked his glass against hers. "I can never imagine you doing that. Even when you were five years old, you fought back."

She choked on her wine and pressed a napkin to her mouth. "What made you say that?"

"Your sister was sleeping and you kicked the kidnapper in the shins. She was taken. You weren't."

"I tried to save Kayla, too, not just myself." She took a bigger gulp of her wine, and her eyes watered.

"Kendall." Coop crossed his fork and knife on the edge of his plate. "You were five. Knowing you, I'm sure you did more than most five-year-olds would've done in that circumstance. You didn't curl up in a ball then, either."

She blinked. "That's why I became a therapist, you know. I try to save people a little bit every day."

"And I'm sure you do." He covered her hand with his.

She snatched her hand away and sawed into a piece of meat. "I'm not sure you have much faith in psychology."

"I have faith in you." He tapped her plate with his knife.

"I couldn't even protect *him*." She jerked her thumb over her shoulder at Buddy, sleeping in a basket in the corner. "That's why I've always avoided pets...and children."

"You did save Buddy. You checked on him, took him straight to the vet, noticed the piece of poisoned sandwich meat and now he's recuperating nicely."

Coop had completely avoided her statement about kids.

He had to realize by now she and he were completely wrong for each other, even though the air sizzled between them and his touch sent a thrill racing through her blood.

She stabbed a potato with her fork. "He does look pretty darned good, doesn't he?"

They managed to finish their meal without any more deep, dark confessions slipping from her lips. She'd never admitted to anyone except her therapist her reasons for studying psychology and going into private practice. Of course, that private practice didn't include children or families. She didn't think she could handle any failure in that area.

After Coop claimed the last potato, he tossed his napkin onto the table. "I'm going to wash all these dishes, and you're going to have another glass of wine and relax in the other room."

"You did your share of work on the security system today. Just leave the dishes. I'll deal with them tomorrow."

"No way." He started collecting the plates. "My mama taught me never to leave dirty dishes in the sink."

Kendall warmed her wineglass between her palms. "Did your mother come out here and help you? After…?"

"My mother, my sister and my aunt. I got a crash course in housekeeping, not that I was a slouch at it before. My wife…sometimes she couldn't even get out of bed in the morning."

"I'm sorry, Coop." She put her hand on his forearm, tracing the corded muscle with her fingertips.

The faraway look left his blue eyes and he smiled. "I do the best I can for Steffi, and we have a good life."

"You do a great job with your daughter. Don't beat yourself up." She rubbed a circle on his wrist. "Father of the Year."

"And now I'm bucking for Sheriff of the Year." He poured her another glass of wine. "Go. Unwind."

Her eyes met his over the rim of the glass as the fruity wine trickled down her throat. If she unwound any more, she'd end up in a puddle at his feet.

He swallowed and held up the plates. "Dishes."

She pivoted and returned to the living room where she dragged her computer onto her lap. "You do realize there's no TV in here?"

He called above the running water. "I noticed. Steffi wouldn't last five minutes in this house."

Kendall unzipped her boots and propped her feet on top of the coffee table while she accessed her new security system, courtesy of Sheriff of the Year. "All clear."

Coop's head appeared at the kitchen door. "What are you saying in there?"

"Go back to the dishes." She waved her hand.

By the time she'd reviewed every side of the house and the land in the back, Coop returned to the living room with a glass of water.

"Thanks for dinner. It was great. Are you feeling more relaxed now? You've checked your home security, Buddy's snoozing in the kitchen and you're on your second glass of wine."

She raised her half-empty glass. "And I have Timberline's vacationing sheriff by my side."

He took the glass from her and rubbed his thumb across the lipstick smudge on the rim, never losing eye contact with her. "And I'm staying right here."

Kendall swallowed. "Coop, I—I'm not your wife."

He swirled the wine in her glass where it caught the lamplight. "Not by a long shot."

"I mean," she said as she brushed her knuckles across the soft denim encasing his thighs, "I may need rescuing from time to time, but I don't need saving. Does that make sense?"

"Do you think I'm trying to save you?"

"I just don't want there to be any confusion about what this is between us."

"What is it?" He placed the wineglass on the coffee table and laced his fingers with hers.

A tingle of pleasure zigzagged through her body, and her eyelids fluttered as a small breath escaped her lips. "It's...it's not forever. I'm not staying here."

"I tried telling myself that." He kissed her fingertips, and then pressed her hand against his thundering heart. "And I don't need forever, do you? I just need right now."

Curling her fingers against the white cotton of his T-shirt, she whispered, "I'm glad you said it first."

Keeping her hand against his chest, Coop curled his other arm around her shoulders and brought her in for a kiss. His lips moved against hers tentatively as if questioning her commitment to the here and now.

She parted her lips and drew his tongue into her mouth. She felt no hesitation about being with Coop and wanted him to know it.

He cupped the back of her head and deepened the kiss, sealing his mouth over hers. A longing so powerful washed over her, she jerked away from him to gasp for air.

His blue eyes glittered beneath half-mast eyelids as he tilted his head. "Is that a no?"

Even if she lived to regret this night, even if this man made all other men in her future pale by comparison, even if he invaded her dreams on hot, restless, Arizona nights, she couldn't put the brakes on her desire for his touch.

Entwining her arms around his neck, she breathed into his ear. "Yesss."

He buried one hand in her hair, tugging until her head tipped back. He pressed a kiss against the base of her throat, and her pulse throbbed beneath his lips. Or was that his pulse? She'd lost all sense of the boundaries between them.

She bunched his T-shirt in her hands and managed to get out one strangled word. "Bedroom."

He shot up as if on springs, taking her with him. Standing face-to-face, toe-to-toe, they stared into each other's eyes. They must've seen the same thing because she went willingly into his arms at the same time he pulled her closer.

Coop melded every line of his body against hers, and his kiss scorched her lips.

She wiggled away from him to reach beneath his T-shirt and skim her hands across the hard planes of his chest and flat belly. When she tweaked his nipple, he nipped her lip and she smiled beneath his kiss. She finished her exploration by hooking her fingers in the waistband of his jeans.

He sucked in a harsh breath. "I thought we were moving this party to the bedroom."

Sliding her fingers farther into his pants with one hand, she crooked the index finger of her other. "This way, Sheriff."

His stride matched hers but she kept her hold on him anyway, not willing to relinquish the warm feel of his skin against her fingertips.

When they got to the bedroom, he walked her backward to the bed until the back of her knees pressed against the mattress. Wasting no time, he grabbed the bottom of her sweater and pulled it over her head.

He sighed as he ran a finger from the neckline of her camisole to where she'd tucked it into her jeans. "You're wearing too many layers."

"I can fix that." She tugged the camisole out of her pants, but she must've been moving too slowly to satisfy him, because he snatched the thin cotton from her fingers and yanked off the camisole and tossed it over his shoulder.

Hooking his fingers around the straps of her bra, he said, "This better be it."

She giggled like a high school girl in the backseat of the star football player's muscle car.

And with probably as much practice as that star football player, Coop unhooked her bra in the back. He then planted a trail of kisses from her jaw to her shoulder and pulled at the bra strap with his teeth.

With a little cooperation and a lot of impatience from her, the lacy bra fell to the floor.

He cradled her breasts in his large hands, his thumbs toying with her nipples, which peaked and ached beneath his touch. Standing on her tiptoes, she nibbled his ear and flicked his lobe with her tongue.

Craving the full skin-to-skin contact, she lifted his T-shirt. "Talk about layers. Take this off."

He complied and in a nanosecond he had her back in his arms. When chest met chest, bare skin against bare skin, Kendall hissed just to provide the sound effect for their connection—and they had a connection. She could almost see the steam rising from their bodies.

"You feel so good." Coop's ragged voice had her digging her nails into his back to urge him on.

This might just be a one-nighter, but at least it wasn't going to be a quickie. If this was going to be the first, last and only time they indulged their desire, she needed an overdose of Coop to keep her going through those long, lonely nights in Phoenix.

As if sensing her urgency, Coop stripped out of his jeans and boxers with lightning speed. Fully naked, he nudged her onto the bed and, straddling her hips, he pulled her jeans, panties and socks from her in one continuous motion.

He hovered above her and traced a slow line from her chin to her mound with the tip of his finger while she squirmed beneath him. He flashed a grin that would do the devil proud. "Don't be so impatient. I need lots of memories to get me through the cold, rainy nights ahead."

She whispered, trying to keep the sob from her voice, "I was just thinking the same thing."

"Then let's make some memories."

He lowered himself on top of her, his erection throbbing against her thigh. Her skin, flushed with warmth, tingled from the tips of her toes to the top of her head...and everywhere in between.

Stroking her palms across the hard muscle of his buttocks, she hooked one leg around his calf. She wanted him inside her now, but she was willing to humor him and go along with the buildup.

His lips found the nipple of her left breast, and he teased her by sucking on it and then blowing against her moist skin, and all of a sudden, the buildup didn't seem like such a bad idea.

As she explored his body with her hands, he made love to every part of hers with his lips, his tongue, his teeth, setting her nerve endings on fire. When he brought her to climax, it took him just a few flicks of his tongue to send her over the edge.

He entered her as she was still descending from the precipice of her release. She pressed her lips against his collarbone to keep her scream in check as he drove into her.

Sensing her reserve, Coop growled in her ear. "Why are you holding back? Give it to me."

Her head fell to the side and she released a slow moan that had started somewhere in her tummy. As the friction and excitement built up between them, she wrapped her legs around his pumping hips, clamping around him as if she was riding a mechanical bull—but there was nothing mechanical about this bull. Coop was all hot flesh and hotter kisses.

She started to unravel beneath him, the tight coil in

her belly spinning out of control. As her second climax scooped her up onto another wave of desire, Coop shuddered and groaned, a deep guttural sound.

His eyes had been closed, but now his eyelids flew open and he pinned her with a deep blue gaze as he came inside her. She tried focusing on his orgasm, she tried focusing on her own, and then gave up and went along for the delicious ride.

When they were both spent, Coop rolled onto his back and draped one heavy leg over hers. "I knew that was gonna be good."

"Mmm, I had the same suspicion, but you exceeded my expectations."

"I wanted to commit every bit of you to memory." He entwined his fingers with her. "Just in case we don't get another opportunity before you leave."

Her nose stung and she rubbed the tip of it. "You're going to be a busy man once your vacation is over."

A muffled buzzing noise came from the floor at the foot of the bed.

She pinched Coop's thigh. "That must be your phone because mine's in the other room."

He winked at her and scrambled toward the foot of the bed, leaned over and rustled through his jeans. "Got it."

Sitting up, she drew her knees to her chest, a feather of fear drifting across the back of her neck. "Is it the station?"

"No." He drew his brows over his nose as he squinted at the display. "It's Britt. I hope Steffi hasn't gotten sick stuffing herself on popcorn, brownies and soda.

"Hey, Britt, everything okay?"

Kendall clutched the sheet to her chest as all color drained from Coop's face. Everything wasn't okay—not at all.

"Coop? What's wrong?"

His eyes met hers and she flinched at the ferocity in their blue depths.

"He has Steffi."

Chapter Fifteen

Blackness engulfed him from all sides. He couldn't hear Kendall's words even though her mouth was moving and he could no longer hear Britt's wailing over the roaring in his ears.

He couldn't have her. He couldn't have his little girl.

Dropping the phone, he launched from the bed and dragged on his jeans.

Kendall was beside him in an instant, her hand on his arm. "I'll drive you."

His gaze swept over her naked body, still dewy from their lovemaking, and he blinked. That seemed light-years away now.

How could he have let Steffi down like this? He should've never let her out of his sight.

Three children. A trio of children. The Timberline Trio. Two girls and one boy. He should've known the kidnapper would strike again.

Following his gaze, Kendall's cheeks flamed, as if realizing for the first time she was naked, as if he hadn't already explored every intimate detail of her body.

Reaching behind her, she dragged the sheet off the bed and draped it around her shoulders. "Give me a minute to get dressed. You shouldn't be driving."

What did she see? He jerked his head toward the mirror

above the dresser. Except for his heaving chest, he didn't look like a man who had just lost everything in the world.

His hands curled into fists and every muscle in his body coiled into a hard spring. He would do some serious damage to the piece of garbage who'd snatched Steffi—once he got his hands on him. *If* he got his hands on him.

Kendall, now fully dressed, shoved his T-shirt against his chest. "Finish dressing and let's get going. The faster you get all the details, the faster we'll get Steffi back."

He stared at the shirt in his hands as if he'd forgotten what to do with it. "We didn't get Kayla back, did we? Or Harrison? Or Cheri?"

"Stop." She gripped both of his wrists, digging her nails into his flesh. "We're getting her back—all of them. This guy just made a colossal mistake."

He finished dressing, his body ping-ponging back and forth between fright and flight. One moment he felt overwhelmed and close to panic and the next he wanted to smash something...or somebody.

Kendall brought him back to earth, shoving a plastic bottle under his nose. "Have some water and give me your keys."

He dug into his pocket and dragged out his keys. He dropped them into her outstretched palm, her wiggling fingers the only sign of agitation.

She led the way to the truck and climbed behind the wheel.

Putting a hand over hers as she inserted the key in the ignition, he said, "Are you sure you're okay to drive after drinking that wine?"

"I had two glasses, it was a while ago and I...uh...engaged in some physical activity. I'll be fine."

He directed her back to the Fletchers' place where two cruisers were already parked out front, their lights spinning and casting an eerie glow on a nightmarish tableau of parents frantically hugging their crying children and dragging them away from the scene of the crime.

Britt stopped sobbing long enough to rush toward him, babbling apologies and explanations.

Coop enfolded her in a hug. He couldn't blame her. He was at fault. He should've been watching over Steffi instead of...

"Coop, come on inside and I'll give you what we have." Sergeant Payton pulled him away from Britt's death grip. "Agent Maxfield is on the way with the rest of the task force."

"They've had almost a month to find the other two children. I don't have a lot of faith in him or his band of pencil pushers." Reaching back, he grabbed Kendall's hand. She was the only thing keeping him sane right now. "Come with us, Kendall. I need you."

As she trailed after him and Payton to the house, she squeezed his hand. Amid the chaos, he heard her whisper, "I'm here."

When they entered the house, Rob led them to the den and closed the door. "My wife's hysterical. I think it's better that she stay with her sister right now. She's not going to be much use."

Coop paced the room, plowing a hand through his hair. "Britt said the girls were outside. My God, Rob, what were five-year-old girls doing outside?"

Rob covered his face. "They snuck out, just Genevieve, Molly and Steffi. From what we could get out of Genevieve, someone threw pebbles at the window. They thought—" he choked "—they thought it was a wood sprite, like that movie about the fairies and elves. *The Fairies of the Glen.* They're obsessed with that damned movie."

Coop crossed his arms, hunching his shoulders. He knew that movie well. Did the kidnapper know it, too? He had to know how appealing that gesture would've been to a bunch of little girls. But why *his* little girl? Was it just a coincidence, or had he been aiming for the sheriff's daughter?

Payton cleared his throat. "You didn't hear the girls coming downstairs or going out the back door?"

"Britt and I were in the bedroom with the door shut." Rob reddened to the roots of his thinning hair. "We should've left the door open. We were going to check on the girls later, but all seemed quiet at the time."

Judging by his blush, Rob and Britt were probably engaged in the same activity as he and Kendall.

"How are the other girls?" Coop massaged the back of his neck.

"Upset, traumatized." Rob broke into a sob and Kendall covered her eyes with one hand.

God, this had to be hard for her, too—reliving this nightmare she thought she'd escaped.

Coop swallowed. "Did the girls see anything?"

"It was dark. As they crept closer to the edge of the woods, a man, masked, all in black materialized."

Kendall gasped.

"Without saying a word, he snatched Steffi. The girls ran screaming into the house."

A tap on the door broke the tension in the room. "Agent Maxfield here."

Coop rolled his eyes at Payton. "Let him in."

The sergeant got up from behind the desk and opened the door.

The agent charged into the room like he owned it, his minions following closely on his heels. "Sheriff, I'm sorry about your daughter. We're going to nail this SOB. What do we have so far?"

Rob went through his story again and Payton chimed in about the search they were conducting in back of the house.

"I saw the spotlights out there. Good job, Sergeant, but we brought in our own equipment and we'll take it from here."

The agents continued talking about a whole lotta nothing until Coop stopped his pacing and strode to the door. "Less talking and more doing. I want to see where Steffi was snatched. If that bastard left one thread, I'm going to find it and hunt him down."

Payton couldn't do anything but follow him outside, and Rob went to console his wife and the children.

Coop didn't have a wife or a child to console.

He turned to Kendall, still by his side. "You can stay in the house if you like."

She shook her head. "I need the fresh air."

Law enforcement personnel milled around outside along with anxious parents, who had come back after securing their children at home.

Coop led the way around the back of the house and looked up at the window of the room where the girls had been giggling, watching movies and eating popcorn. Hadn't he taught Steffi better? How many more times could he fail his family?

His officers had collected several small rocks on the ground that the kidnapper could've used to pelt the window. But if the guy was wearing gloves, they'd get no prints. Any shoe prints looked like they'd been smoothed over and there were more scuff marks than solid prints.

Coop continued to stare at the ground until his eyes ached, but despite the FBI crowing over an old cigarette butt and a few freshly snapped twigs, nothing of substance materialized.

He rubbed his eyes and looked up, studying the faces of the local crowd that had gathered around the newest focal point of tragedy.

He peered into the darkness, straining his eyes, looking for Kendall. But she was gone, too.

Would everyone of importance in his life disappear?

KENDALL STARED AT the text glowing in the dark.

Do you want another chance, Kendal? Do you want to save Kayla? Walk to the wooded path behind the new house. Come alone and dont say a word or they all die.

He didn't spell her name right and didn't know how to use contractions, but the meaning was clear.

With her heart doing somersaults in her chest, Kendall looked up from her phone. Knots of people huddled together discussing this newest development. Coop was still in the back with the FBI agents and Sergeant Payton.

Nobody was watching her. Could she do this? Could she make a difference? Could she save Coop's daughter?

The kidnapper had wanted to involve her all along. Maybe it was the same man from twenty-five years ago, maybe not, but she had a chance here.

She'd given Coop the keys to his truck after she'd parked it. Should she chance leaving him a note on the windshield? She scanned the crowd of looky-loos. Was the kidnapper watching her now? She couldn't chance leaving a note for Coop—too much at stake.

Looking both ways, she scurried down the wet sidewalk recently installed in front of this new development of homes. As she made her way to the new house, the only one yet to sell, she replied to the text message but it bounced back. He'd blocked her number.

The noise and lights in front of the Fletchers' house faded as the dark night enclosed around her. She picked her way across the unlandscaped front lawn and headed to the woods behind the house.

Realtors like Rebecca used that stretch of forest behind these houses as a selling point, but they might have to re-think their strategy after this night.

Her boots stuck in the mud and she had to pull them free with each step. She called out with one breathless word. "Hello?"

Her muscles froze. Was that a twig snapping?

She edged closer to the tree line, walking on the balls of her feet, adrenaline coursing through her veins.

A whoosh of air at her back had her making a half turn, but it was too late. The rough cloth, soaked with chloroform closed over her nose and mouth. She shoved her tongue against the gag. She twisted in her captor's grip. She reached behind her to claw at him. But none of it did any good.

And the night got darker.

Chapter Sixteen

A sticky finger prodded her cheek. "Wake up."

Kendall squeezed her eyes shut, trying to wring out the pain throbbing against her temples. She peeled her tongue from the roof of her dry mouth and ran it across her teeth.

"Open your eyes." Her tormentor poked her in the back. "You need to wake up."

Kendall moaned and rolled onto her back. A sweet taste lingered in her mouth and she tried to spit it out, but her mouth was like a desert. A wisp of hair tickled her cheek and she focused on moving her hand to brush it away.

Drugged. She felt drugged, groggy.

A jolt of fear zapped her body and her eyelids clicked open like a doll's. Chloroform. Someone had drugged her, incapacitated her with chloroform.

A heart-shaped face curtained by long, blond ringlets hovered over her. "Finally."

"Steffi?" Kendall struggled to sit up. Was this a dream? Small hands pulled at her arms, and her head fell to the side.

A dark-haired boy tugged on her arm again. "Are you okay?"

A sob bubbled up in her throat and she choked. "Harrison? Are you Harrison Keaton?"

He cocked his head, his dirty, stringy hair brushing his shoulder. "Uh-huh. How'd you know that?"

Steffi, kneeling beside Kendall, put a hand on her hip. "Everyone knows you, Harrison. You're kidnapped."

Blinking her eyes to focus in the dark, Kendall dragged herself to a sitting position and leaned against one rough stone wall of their prison. "Cheri? Is Cheri here?"

"She's sleeping." Steffi pointed to a dark form curled up on a straw mat.

Kendall spread out her arms and enfolded both children into a giant bear hug. "Oh, my God. I am so happy to see all of you. Are you all right?"

"I'm hungry." Harrison kicked at a crumpled, white bag. "All he ever gives us is fast food. My mom's says I'm not allowed to eat fast food."

"I hope you've been eating, Harrison." Kendall rubbed her thumb across a smudge on the boy's dirty face. You've been missing for almost a month. Have you been here the whole time?"

"I dunno." He shrugged his shoulders.

Kendall looked around, running her hand across the rock at her back. "Where is here? It looks like we're in some kind of cave. Steffi, were you awake when he brought you here?"

"No." She rubbed a hand across her lips. "He put stuff on my mouth and I went to sleep."

"Did you see him? Did you see his face?"

Steffi shook her head. "He had a mask on and gloves."

Harrison chimed in. "He always does. When he brings food and stuff. I can't see him."

"Where's the entrance?" Kendall staggered to her feet, tipping her head back.

"It's up there." Harrison pointed to the ceiling of the cave, which looked like an abandoned mine, clearly left over from Timberline's silver mining days.

She found a foothold in the cave wall and hoisted herself up to get a clearer view of the entrance. "Have you tried climbing up here?"

"I have." Harrison punched the wall with a small fist. "But there's a door or something blocking everything."

Kendall squinted into the gloom. No light appeared from the area at the top of the mine. Had he rolled a boulder over the entrance?

She hopped back to the ground, her gaze tracking over the two children in front of her—Steffi surprisingly calm after her ordeal and Harrison matter-of-fact and filthy.

Putting a hand on Harrison's shoulder, she asked, "Does he ever come down here? Does he ever talk to you or... touch you?"

The boy shook his head, his scraggly hair whipping across his face. "He never comes down here. Probably afraid of my ninja skills."

"Probably." Kendall smiled but drew her brows over her nose at the same time. What did he want? Was he involved in some kind of child trafficking and just waiting for his contact? Had he been waiting for an opportunity to snatch a third child?

And what did he want with *her*? Could it really be the same man who'd kidnapped Kayla all those years ago?

Steffi sniffled. "Kendall?"

"Yes, sweetie?" She ruffled the girl's baby-soft hair.

"Is my daddy going to find us?"

Kendall swallowed the lump in her throat. "Maybe. There sure are a lot of people looking for you right now."

A big tear rolled down Steffi's face. "I don't want to be here. It's dark. What if it rains?"

"It rains all the time." Harrison scuffed the toe of his shoe against the dirt. "Big deal."

"Does it come in here? Does the rain fill up the cave?" Steffi's eyes grew big and round, fear shining from their depths.

The tone of Steffi's voice clearly rattling him, Harrison peered at the ceiling. "I—I don't think so."

Steffi started to shake, and Kendall put an arm around her and led her back to the cave wall. She crouched down and straightened out a beach towel on the ground. "Let's sit down. Harrison, you too."

Kendall sank to the ground, shrugging off her jacket. She patted the towel next to her. "Sit, Steffi. Harrison, are you cold?"

"Nah." He plopped down next to her while Steffi lowered herself on Kendall's other side.

She wrapped her jacket around Steffi's trembling form and pulled her close. Steffi dropped her head on Kendall's shoulder.

"I wanna go home."

"I know, sweetie. When the man comes back, I'll talk to him. I'll find out what he wants us to do to get out of here."

The sleeping girl mumbled and sat up, rubbing her eyes. She yelped when she spotted Kendall.

"Cheri?"

She pressed herself against the wall of the cave and started crying.

Kendall's heart broke in two. She gestured with her hand. "Come on over here, Cheri. I'm Kendall. I'm not going to hurt you. We're going to keep warm together."

Harrison said to Cheri, "She was kidnapped, too, and she's gonna get us out."

Kendall bit her lip. Had she been kidnapped? What did her abductor have in store for her? Did he want to tie up the loose end that he'd left twenty-five years ago?

And could she get the children out?

Cheri crawled toward her, dragging a towel behind her. "Are you okay, Cheri? You're not hurt, are you?"

She shoved her finger in her mouth, a regressive gesture for a six-year-old. Then she curled up next to Kendall and rested her head in her lap.

"Now that we're all together, do you want to play a game?"

"Ninja warriors?" Harrison looked up hopefully.

Kendall tugged on his ear. "How about I Spy?"

Steffi hiccupped through her tears. "It's dark. We can't spy anything."

"This is going to be imaginary I spy. You're going to tell me what you *think* you see in the dark and we can turn this cave into anyplace you want."

Cheri popped her thumb from her mouth. "The fairies in the glen?"

"Not the fairies in the glen." Steffi's bottom lip trembled. "That's for babies."

Harrison started first, his voice echoing in the cave. "I spy a green dragon."

They all took turns, filling the cave with animals—real and mythical, cupcakes, swimming pools, one particular boy band and lots of food.

Kendall giggled so much, her sides hurt, and at the end of the game, Harrison yawned and said, "I'm glad you were kidnapped, too, Kendall."

"Me, too." Cheri burrowed her head against Kendall's lap.

And then Steffi whispered, "Me, too, Kendall."

As the children fell asleep around her, Kendall's mind raced. Maybe her nemesis from twenty-five years ago had done all this for her. Maybe he'd wanted her all along. He'd taken the wrong twin. Would he take her and leave the children? He hadn't harmed them...yet.

She brushed Harrison's cheek with her thumb and smoothed Steffi's hair back from her forehead. He wouldn't harm them as long as she stood guard over them. She'd give her life to protect these children, Coop's daughter.

And maybe that's what this pig wanted.

COOP BANGED ON Kendall's door and Buddy whimpered and scratched at the wood inside. "Kendall?"

Stooping forward, he cupped his hand on the window and peeked through a gap in the drapes. Buddy jumped on the window, his claws scrabbling at the glass.

The squeak of a wheel had Coop spinning around and his gaze clashed with Binder's, as the ex-con rode up on his bike.

"Have you seen Kendall?"

"Just got here." Binder leaned his bike against a tree and scratched his beard. "I heard about your little girl, Sheriff. I'm sorry."

Coop narrowed his eyes and the man started fidgeting. "Did you ever go to the doctor?"

"Nope." He pulled the bill of his cap lower over his eyes. "My ma made me some soup and I drunk a bunch of sports drinks. I feel okay now. I wanna finish the job I started yesterday."

"Kendall's not home."

"I can still work. I got the tools around back."

Where had Kendall gone last night? She'd left his truck at the Fletchers'. Did she walk home? Catch a ride with someone there?

He'd taken a quick look for her before following Agent Maxfield to the task force war room and had tried calling her later, but her phone had been turned off. Was it time to triangulate that cell or was he overreacting?

He waited for Binder to come to the front of the house, lugging his gardening tools. Then Coop slipped around to the back, made a sharp tap on the window of the kitchen door to break it and let himself into Kendall's house. At least she had a security system to tell her who'd broken into her place.

Hearing his entry, Buddy ran into the kitchen, his paws skidding across the linoleum until he crashed into his ankles. "Easy, Buddy. Where's your mistress?"

He tucked the dog under one arm as he surveyed the kitchen. The dishes he'd washed last night after dinner were still stacked in the dish drainer on the counter. No coffee had been made, no breakfast dishes were piled in the sink.

Buddy whimpered, so he set him down. The dog trotted to his empty water dish and Coop's heart stuttered. No way would Kendall leave Buddy without any water.

He barreled into the living room, taking in the empty wineglass from last night sitting on the coffee table. He continued onto the bedroom. He pounded on the doorjamb when he saw the tousled covers of Kendall's bed—just the way they'd left them after making love.

Why hadn't she come home? Where was she? His mind wouldn't work. He'd been up all night scouring the area for Steffi, leading a search team, just as they'd done for the other two children—with the same results.

In a state of numbness, he let Buddy out into the backyard and filled his dishes with fresh water and some puppy kibble. He called Agent Maxfield to check for any updates and let him know that Kendall Rush seemed to be missing.

"Any signs of foul play?"

Coop's gaze darted around the living room, exactly the way they'd left it last night. "I can't tell, but she hasn't been home."

"She's an attractive woman. Maybe she has a boyfriend in town."

"She…" Coop snapped his mouth shut. What was the point? "Any other news?"

"We'll let you know as soon as we have something. We're doing our best, Sheriff."

Coop ended the call and shoved the phone into his pocket. The FBI's best wasn't good enough.

He secured Buddy in his pen on the back patio since he had no idea when Kendall would be coming back. Where could she have gone and why wasn't she returning his calls?

Memories of the shots ringing out in Port Angeles yesterday caused him to clench his jaw, already aching with tension and fear. Had Kendall gone looking for Steffi herself and gotten into trouble?

If the trouble included a run-of-the-mill car accident or sprained ankle in the woods, he would've heard something by now. Did the battery on her phone die because she hadn't been home to charge it? Had she turned it off to save it? Or was there a more sinister reason why her phone was offline?

He chucked Buddy under the chin. "Don't worry, pooch. I'll make sure you have water and food."

Rising from the ground, Coop brushed off the knees of his jeans and strode to the front of the house.

Binder had stopped working and was leaning against that rickety old bike of his, hands open in front of him, a water bottle on the ground at his feet.

His head jerked up at Coop's approach, his eyes wide in his gaunt face. He spun toward his bike and buried his hands in the saddlebag strapped to the handlebars of the bike.

Coop had been a cop long enough to recognize suspicious behavior, and he changed direction in midstride. "Whatcha got there, Binder?"

"Nothin'." Stooping over, he plucked his water bottle from the ground. "Just getting my water."

"What did you have in your hands?"

Binder peered at his empty hand as if it belonged to someone else. "Nothin'."

"Didn't you just put something in your satchel?"

"No." Binder grabbed the handlebars of his bike, the water bottle falling from his hand.

Coop launched forward and pushed Binder away from the bike. He flipped back the lid on the satchel and plunged his hands inside. His fingers curled around all of the items he could grab, and he yanked them out of the bag.

He opened his hands. His breath hitched in his throat as the plastic dinosaur tottered in his palm and the pink ribbon fluttered in the breeze.

"I—I didn't…I—I don't know." Binder put his hands in front of him in a defensive position.

Coop dropped the items, so indelibly linked to the kidnappings, and drew his fist back to smash into Binder's sickly face.

Chapter Seventeen

Kendall rubbed her eyes and shivered. She cuddled the kids closer to her body. How had these poor babies been keeping warm with just beach towels to cover them?

At least Wyatt and Cheri had been kidnapped wearing their jackets. Steffi just had her pink, flannel pajamas to protect her from the elements.

Kendall pulled her jacket more tightly beneath Steffi's chin and rubbed her arms.

Had Coop figured out yet that she'd gone missing? He was probably much too concerned about his daughter and not some woman he'd been having a one-night stand with when Steffi had been kidnapped. Was he blaming himself?

She should've texted him, left him a note on his truck, but she'd been afraid the kidnapper would see her and harm the children.

She sucked in her bottom lip and closed her eyes. What kind of therapist was she? She couldn't even be honest with herself. She'd wanted to save Steffi for Coop. She'd wanted to save all of the kids for herself, to make herself feel better after failing to protect Kayla.

When she opened her eyes, her gaze clashed with Steffi's. "You're awake."

"I'm not afraid, anymore." Steffi blinked her blue eyes, so like her father's. "I'm not afraid 'cuz you're here and it's daytime. My daddy will find us during the day, won't he?"

"It'll be easier during the daylight hours." She gestured around the mine. "This place can't be too far from town, from the road. He must've carried me here."

Harrison mumbled. "I'm hungry."

Kendall surveyed the little nest the children had cobbled together. "Does he leave you any extra food?"

"We had cereal and granola bars." Harrison yawned. "But those are gone."

"Maybe he'll bring us some food this morning, and I can talk to him." She had every intention of bargaining with this monster to free the children. The kids couldn't harm him. They hadn't seen him or heard him talk.

A scraping noise echoed from above, and Harrison grabbed her arm. "It's him."

"Cheri, wake up." She shook the little girl, who rolled over, instantly awake.

Kendall staggered to her feet, her head tilted back. "Hey! Hey, you! Let us out of here."

"Kendall? Kendall, is that you?" There was more scraping and a shaft of light skewered the floor.

Relief washed over her, and she braced a hand against the rock as her knees wobbled. "Wyatt?"

"Oh, my God, Kendall. What are you doing down there? Are those kids down there, too?"

Cheri started crying, Steffi stood up, clutching Kendall's hand and Harrison jumped up and down beside her. "I'm here! I'm here!"

"Yes. We're all here, Wyatt. Me, Harrison, Cheri and Steffi."

"Thank God I found you." He grunted and released a breath. "I can't move this boulder. I need some help."

"Oh, God. Please don't leave us here, Wyatt. He might come back."

"Who? Who put you here?"

"I have no idea. I didn't see him. The kids didn't see

him." She put her arm around Cheri. "Please don't go away."

"I'm not going anywhere. I have cell phone reception out here. I'm going to call 9-1-1 and get some help moving this rock."

"Make sure they call the FBI and Coop. Please call Coop."

"I'm just going to step away where I can make the call. Hang on. It's gonna be okay."

Kendall made the kids come in for a group hug and Harrison chattered about all things he was going to do when he got out.

Wyatt interrupted their celebration. "I made the call. They're on their way. I can't really see you through the space. Is everyone okay?"

"The kids are fine. Everyone's fine." She wiped a tear from her face. "How'd you find us?"

"I saw something last night but it was too dark. Came back this morning."

Before he could go any further into detail, sirens called out in the distance and Kendall had never heard such a lovely sound.

Within minutes, even though it had seemed longer, the first responders above had rolled the rock from the opening and light flooded the cave.

The rescue began in earnest. The cheers Kendall heard above as each child was released warmed her heart and brought a big smile to her face. She was the last to come up and before the fireman could even unbuckle her from the harness, Coop had his arms around her.

"I was so worried about you." He kissed the side of her head. "Thank you. Thank you."

She pointed to Wyatt, surrounded by members of the FBI task force. "You should be thanking Wyatt."

"I did, believe me, but Steffi told me how you kept it

all together down there, how you made them all feel better, not so scared."

Through misty eyes she watched Harrison and Cheri in their parents' arms, holding on like they'd never let go again. Then her gaze shifted to Steffi, sitting on the back of the ambulance. Their eyes met and Steffi waved.

"They're all incredible kids—brave, strong, fearless."

When the harness dropped from her body, Coop curled his arm around her neck and pulled her close. "You did it, Kendall. You made Kayla proud today."

As the FBI ushered Wyatt out of the forest, he turned to Kendall and gave her a thumbs-up. "Wyatt made Stevie proud, too."

A FEW DAYS LATER, Kendall boxed some of Aunt Cass's items that didn't sell during the daylong estate sale.

Wyatt had come late and was perusing a table littered with books and old record albums.

"You can help yourself, Wyatt."

"I'll pay. I wouldn't feel right otherwise."

"C'mon, you're the man of the hour. The mayor is going to declare Wyatt Carson day and give you the keys to the city."

He snorted, but his cheeks reddened with pleasure.

Coop pulled up in his truck and poked his head out the window. "Do you want me to haul the rest of this stuff to a donation center?"

Wyatt waved at Coop and then winked at Kendall. "I'll take this box in the house for you. Is Buddy still penned up in the back?"

"Yes." She turned away and rolled her eyes. How two grown men could be so afraid of a little dog, she'd never get.

Her heart skipped a beat, and she pressed her hand to

her chest. But then one of those men may have had reason to fear Buddy.

Coop hopped from the truck and swooped in for a kiss. "How'd it go today?"

"Sold a lot of stuff." She spread her arms wide. "Even most of the furniture."

"Maybe the house isn't cursed anymore."

She shoved her fingers into her back pockets, palms outward. "Does the FBI really believe Gary Binder had something to do with the Timberline Trio kidnappings, too?"

"Maybe, but they still don't have enough evidence to tie him to the current ones. Raylene is giving him alibi after alibi."

"She would, right?" Kendall hunched her shoulders. She was torn between wanting to believe Gary was the kidnapper so the community could feel safe again, and disbelieving the polite, obsequious ex-con could've pulled it off.

"I think Raylene would do anything to protect her boy, even though her boy is a forty-five-year-old man with a past." He hugged her close and mumbled into her hair. "I can't wait to get out to Phoenix to see you."

"I can't wait, either." She curled her arms around his waist. "Even if Phoenix PD isn't hiring, there are other departments and agencies."

"I'm not worried. I'll find something." He jerked his thumb over his shoulder. "Do you want me to help you box up the rest of this stuff?"

"I'm good. Wyatt can help after he finishes picking through the leftovers." She smacked his behind. "Besides, you have to get back to work. Vacation over, Sheriff."

"Yeah, and what a vacation." He nibbled her ear. "Can you smack my backside again? It kind of turned me on."

She giggled. "We'll continue this in Phoenix."

"Can't wait." He pressed a kiss against her lips. "And don't forget. Dinner with me and Steffi tonight before I take you to the airport tomorrow morning, and don't forget to bring Buddy. We'll take care of him until we can reunite the two of you in Phoenix."

"I won't forget Buddy. How's Steffi doing?"

"She's fine. Having you there spared her an even greater trauma. You helped all the kids, and even Harrison and Cheri seem to be recovering. Harrison's parents are taking him to Disneyland, and Cheri's mom is taking her to Seattle to visit family."

"I'm glad. Now get back to work, so you can afford my dinner tonight."

They kissed again, long and lingering, since it would be their last time together alone until he dropped her off at the airport.

He held his hand out the window of the truck as he pulled out, and she blew him a kiss.

When Coop's truck disappeared, Kendall gathered up the remaining odds and ends from the estate sale and put them in two boxes. She carried the first one into the house, and Wyatt dropped an album cover he'd been studying to hold the screen door open for her.

"There's one more if you wouldn't mind bringing that in."

"Sure." He jogged down the steps and returned with the box in his arms, whistling a tune. "On the floor?"

"Yeah." She scrunched up her nose. "What's that song you're whistling? It's catchy."

"It's from that popular kids' movie, something about fairies."

A little chill touched her heart. That had been Steffi's favorite movie. "I didn't peg you as a fan of kids' animated films."

He chuckled. "I was doing a plumbing job for the Kendrick family and those kids must've watched that DVD twenty times while I was there."

She rubbed the gooseflesh on her arms. "If you want to take this box, you can, or I can have Rebecca Geist, my Realtor, drop it off for me tomorrow at a donation center."

"You're flying out tomorrow morning?"

"Yep. Back to Phoenix." She pointed to the box he'd been going through, anxious for him to be on his way so she could finish packing, get ready for dinner and most of all bring poor Buddy inside. "You can just take it all, Wyatt. Whatever you don't want, you can donate or sell at your next yard sale."

"I wouldn't feel right just taking it for free."

She patted him on the back. "You deserve it—hero."

He ducked his head. "I did it for Stevie. It felt good. You know, like we'd come full circle."

"Yeah, it did." Her nose stung and she sniffled.

"I'll tell you what." He pulled his wallet from his pocket by the chain attached to his belt. "I'll give you twenty bucks for the whole box."

"If you insist." She walked into the kitchen to wash her hands, and Wyatt followed her, peering into his wallet.

"Personal check okay? I only have a few bucks."

"Whatever you want to do, Wyatt." She probably wouldn't cash it anyway. She tugged a dish towel from the handle on the oven door and wiped her hands as Wyatt wrote out a check on the counter.

"Here you go." He slid the check across to her.

"Buddy, settle down." When they'd walked into the kitchen, the little dog had gone nuts, yapping and jumping against the wire mesh of his pen. "Sorry."

Wyatt shrugged, but his hand trembled when he put down the pen.

With one finger, she scooted the check toward her and glanced down at it. "Oh, you spelled my name…"

She froze.

He'd made it out to Kendal Rush. She stared at the

spelling of her name. Kendall with one *l*, just like the text from the kidnapper—the text the FBI couldn't trace, the text they were having a hard time tying to Gary because Gary didn't own a cell phone and so far they'd turned up no records that he'd bought one.

The words on the check blurred in front of her eyes. *The Fairies of the Glen* was a new movie out in theaters. The kids couldn't be watching that movie on a DVD at home.

Wyatt made a small noise in the back of his throat.

Slowly, she raised her eyes to his, pasting a fake smile on her face. "Okay, well, thanks for the check and…everything."

He shook his head. "It won't do, Kendall. It won't do at all."

Chapter Eighteen

"Buckle your seat belt." Coop glanced at his daughter in the rearview mirror and an overwhelming urge to climb into the backseat and give her a big hug overcame him. God, he'd been so close to losing her.

When he'd left Kendall's, he'd decided to pick up Steffi from the Fletchers' house early instead of heading right back to work. She was practically jumping in her seat at the prospect of having Kendall over for dinner. Kendall had made quite an impression on his daughter.

Raindrops began to pelt his windshield, and he gave Steffi a reassuring smile. "There won't be much rain in Arizona, at least not like this—cold and gray."

"Good." She had her forehead pressed against the window and was breathing onto the glass to create a misty patch. She started wiggling her finger through the condensation. "Daddy?"

"What, Tiger Lily." Steffi had recently become a big fan of Peter Pan.

"Who's Stevie?"

"Stevie?" He made the next turn, pumping his brakes. "I don't know a Stevie. Is that someone new in class?"

"No, the man said Stevie."

His pulse sped up. "What man?"

"You know. The man."

"The man who took you?"

"Uh-huh."

"I thought you said you didn't hear him speak. He didn't talk to you."

"Not really to me. It was when I was falling asleep, after he put the stuff on my mouth."

"What did he say, Steffi? What did he say about Stevie?" His heart banged against his rib cage, and he had to pull the truck over.

"He said like in a whisper, 'It was always you, Stevie. Everything was about Stevie.'" She rubbed her fist across the window. "Who's Stevie?"

Coop swallowed hard. Stevie Carson, Wyatt's brother, kidnapped with Kendall's sister and the other little girl, Heather Brice.

Wyatt, afraid of Buddy. Wyatt, a hunter. Wyatt, the hero who knew just where to find the kids. Wyatt, alone with Kendall at her house.

Cranking the wheel, he made a U-turn in the middle of the street. "I forgot something at work, Steffi. Do you mind hanging out with Genevieve for a little while longer before dinner?"

"No, but who's Stevie? You never said who Stevie was."

"He was a little boy, Steffi. A little boy who lived here a long time ago."

"Did he hate the rain, too?"

"Yeah, I think he did."

Coop dropped Steffi back at the Fletchers', trying to keep a poker face. The anxious looks in their eyes told him he'd failed.

He raced back to Kendall's house but parked his truck down the block. His chest almost exploded with relief when he spied Wyatt's plumbing truck and Aunt Cass's old jalopy in the driveway.

Maybe he was way off base here. Maybe Steffi was mistaken, or maybe the kidnapper, Binder, was obsessed with the Timberline Trio. He didn't know, but he couldn't take any chances.

He'd missed all the warning signs of his wife's condition and he had no intention of ignoring his gut now.

He crept around the side of the house where Buddy's yelps assaulted his ears. As he stepped around the back, he spotted the dog practically doing flips in the pen.

Buddy stopped barking when he noticed Coop, and he mumbled a curse under his breath. Would Buddy's silence draw Wyatt's attention?

Coop sidled along the wall of the house to the back door, cardboard covering the window he'd broken two days ago to get into Kendall's house.

Voices wafted from the dining area off the kitchen, and Coop peeled back a corner of the cardboard.

Hot rage blinded his vision for a split second when he got a look at Kendall bound to a kitchen chair with the silver electrical tape she'd been using to pack up boxes. Wyatt stood in front of her wielding a knife, talking.

Coop withdrew his .45 and took aim.

Wyatt moved out of range, but Coop could still hear his voice.

"You remember how it was, don't you, Kendall? Kayla and Stevie, Kayla and Stevie, oh, and Heather. That's all we heard about. Their pictures were in the paper. People tied ribbons on trees for them. My parents looked at me like they wished I had been kidnapped instead of Stevie." He stepped into view again for a moment as he shook the knife in Kendall's face. "Don't tell me your parents didn't do the same. I mean, your mom even went nuts."

"They were kidnapped, Wyatt. You almost sound jealous."

"I was…for a while, and then we got some attention, didn't we? The siblings that were left behind. So it got better."

"Got better? It never got better."

"For a while it did, and then all the excitement died down. They were never found and Heather's family moved away and you became the popular girl in school and I became nothing."

"You're not nothing, Wyatt. Y-you're a good man."

He laughed and the edge of madness in the sound made Coop clench his teeth.

"I wasn't really, Kendall. I pretended. I played the game." He lunged at her and drew back again. "I killed those animals, you know. I don't hate animals, except Buddy, but I do like to watch them die. Hunting's not good enough for that."

"So, why did you do it? Why'd you kidnap Harrison and Cheri and Steffi?"

"To create another Timberline Trio. I was interviewed when Harrison went missing. Did you see me on TV?"

"I missed that."

C'mon, you son of a bitch. Give me one shot.

"It was good. I didn't want to kill the kids, though, not really. It was different from killing an animal. So then I got a better idea. I'd kidnap one more and then rush in and save them all. And it worked, too."

"I don't think it would've worked in the end, Wyatt. The case against Gary is already starting to fall apart."

Wyatt swore. "That druggie ex-con."

"Why'd you drag me into it? Why the ribbon, the mannequin, the photos buried on my property?"

Wyatt came close to Kendall's chair again and Coop raised his weapon. Then, like prey sensing a predator, Wyatt shuffled back again.

"It made the story more exciting. I was doing you a favor, Kendall. Everyone in town was talking about you. It even got you hooked up with the sheriff." He laughed. "You should be thanking me."

"But you shot at me. You tried to kill me in Port Angeles. Are you going to tell me that wasn't you?"

"Guilty. That wasn't part of my original plan, but I went to see that woman you recommended, Dr. Shipman. I don't know. She put a spell on me or something. I started telling her about how Stevie's kidnapping made me feel. I told her about the animals. When you went out to see her that day, I thought she was going to tell you everything."

"She wouldn't. Everything is confidential."

"I read all about therapy. It's not confidential when someone's committed a crime."

"Did you tell her you kidnapped those children?"

"No, but I could tell by her face she knew something." Wyatt tapped on the wall. "Just like I could tell by your face that you knew once you saw that damned check. Who knew you spelled your name with two *l*'s?"

"And Chuck Rawlings? What happened to him?"

"That was just an accident. He saw me with the pink ribbon, and then I noticed him following you that night in town. I was afraid he was going to talk to you then, so I faked that panic attack for you. Dumbest move ever...except for writing that check."

"You never got a dinosaur."

"Nope, but I had to make sure Rawlings didn't talk to you. I knew he wouldn't go to your house to see you. Creepy perv."

Takes one to know one. Coop tightened his finger on the trigger.

"So, I went to his house, and we had an argument. I might've grabbed him, and then he pulled away and fell. I got the hell out of there, but that stupid dog knew me. I should've taken him out before I left."

"Wyatt, just stop now. You're not going to get away with any of this, and if Rawlings's death was an accident, you haven't killed anyone. You didn't harm the kids. I could testify on your behalf. We could get you some help. Y-you'd even get a lot of attention and publicity."

Coop nodded. Smart girl.

"You didn't mean to kill Gary, did you? You were just thinking of framing him for the kidnappings."

"Naw, the little bit of poison I slipped into his sandwich when he left for the hardware store did just what it was supposed to do—make him sick and make him take off— in case someone wanted to pin the Port Angeles shooting on him. Not that the guy could hit a barn door with a water hose."

"How'd you get to Port Angeles so fast after poisoning Gary's sandwich?"

"The old shortcut, Kendall. It's rough, but it's fast."

"You haven't killed anyone, Wyatt. You can get out of this. It's totally understandable what you did. You're suffering from post-traumatic stress disorder due to Stevie's kidnapping. I can help you."

"It's too late Kendall with two *l*'s. Now that I'm a hero, that's even better than regular attention. I'm a hero. The town's gonna throw me a parade."

"You won't get away with it, Wyatt."

"I think I will, but there's one problem."

"What's that?"

"Like you said, I haven't killed anyone yet and it's too hard doing it up close like this."

"Because you're not a killer. Let's stop this right now."

"Sorry, Kendall. We're just gonna do this a little differently. You see, I can hunt just fine. I can kill when my human target isn't right under my nose—and that's how I'm gonna kill you. I'm gonna hunt you on Aunt Cass's property."

Kendall gasped and choked. "Stop, Wyatt. You can't do this."

"Sure, I can. I have my hunting rifle in my truck. Same

one I used on you in Port Angeles. I would've had you that day except for Coop."

"He'll never let you get away with this. It's broad daylight. Your truck's parked in front of my house."

"There's nobody around. I'll make it work. I can even destroy that security setup you have."

Finally, he moved into Coop's range. As Wyatt leaned forward to secure the tape binding Kendall, Coop took his shot.

Kendall screamed and Wyatt clutched his side, spinning around.

Coop ripped the rest of the cardboard from the window and took aim again. "Drop the knife, Wyatt."

Instead of taking his advice, Wyatt raised his knife and turned toward Kendall.

Coop shot him in the chest and Wyatt dropped to the floor, his knife clattering on the linoleum.

Kendall raised shocked eyes to his, and he reached through the door and unlocked it. He was at her side in seconds, wrapping her in his arms as he used his own knife to slice through the electrical tape.

When he freed her, she jumped from the chair, knocking it over, and launched herself at his chest. She sobbed against his shoulder. "I knew you'd come back."

Stroking her hair, he kissed her tears that fell like raindrops on her face.

She glanced down at Wyatt's still form. "I guess he'll get what he always wanted—fame."

Coop corrected her. "Infamy."

Epilogue

Holding a glass of lemonade in each hand, Kendall nudged open the screen door with her hip and her flip-flops smacked against the patio. She sat on the edge of the chaise lounge where Coop sprawled, one leg hanging off the side.

She set down the glasses and rubbed one hand across his warm chest. "You're going to be a bronzed god in no time."

"You have cold hands." He captured her wrist and kissed her palm. "But a warm, warm heart."

"Is Gary doing okay?"

"Speaking of your warm heart." He took a sip of lemonade and puckered his lips. "Binder's doing fine. He started a little landscaping business with the truck and tools you gave him."

"Do that thing again with your lips." She puckered her own and he beat her to the kiss.

She took a sip of lemonade to cool down. "The new owners are going to tear down Aunt Cass's house, aren't they?"

"They are." He brushed one knuckle across her cheek. "Are you happy about that?"

"Yes—too much tragedy. Although I should consider myself lucky that I didn't go off the deep end like Wyatt."

"You don't think he was already twisted and his brother's kidnapping was the final straw?"

"I'm not sure, but I don't think he was killing animals before the Timberline Trio kidnappings and, of course, he was too young to have had anything to do with those kidnappings."

He squeezed her knee. "I'm just happy Steffi remembered what Wyatt had said about Stevie."

"I am, too. I helped her and she helped me. I think we have the beginning of a great relationship." She crowded onto the chaise lounge next to him, dropping her head to his shoulder. "Is she excited about moving to Arizona when your new job starts?"

"She's sad about leaving her friends, but she can't wait." He tangled his fingers through her hair. "And neither can I."

"I think we're right to have separate places at first, don't you?" Her tongue darted from her mouth to taste his salty skin.

He growled in her ear. "When you do stuff like that to me, I think it's the dumbest idea on the planet to have separate places, but for Steffi's sake, I think we're doing the right thing. We'll do it right—wedding in a year, a sibling in a year."

She snuggled in closer, hooking her leg around his. "Or two or three."

"Siblings?"

"Years."

"You haven't changed your mind about having kids, have you?" He tugged a lock of her hair. "I know kids weren't always in your game plan."

"My game plan started to change the day I met you."

After several long kisses, they came up for air and Coop sucked down the rest of his lemonade. "You know, we never got any closer to figuring out what happened to the Timberline Trio."

Kendall squinted at the sun glinting off the water in the

pool and stretched her arms toward the warmth. "I'll leave that mystery for someone else to solve. I know in my heart that five-year-old Kendall did everything she could to save her twin. And grownup Kendall has nothing to prove."

"Not so fast, grownup Kendall." Coop trailed a hand down her back. "This is my last night in Phoenix before I go back to cold, rainy Timberline, and you still have a few things to prove to me."

She pushed up from the chaise lounge and grabbed his hands. "Then what are we waiting for?"

* * * * *

MILLS & BOON®

INTRIGUE
Romantic Suspense

A SEDUCTIVE COMBINATION OF DANGER AND DESIRE

A sneak peek at next month's titles...

In stores from 11th August 2016:

- **Laying Down the Law** – Delores Fossen *and*
  Dark Whispers – Debra Webb
- **Delivering Justice** – Barb Han *and*
  Sudden Second Chance – Carol Ericson
- **Hostage Negotiation** – Lena Diaz *and*
  Suspicious Activities – Tyler Anne Snell

Romantic Suspense

- **Conard County Marine** – Rachel Lee
- **High-Stakes Colton** – Karen Anders

Available at WHSmith, Tesco, Asda, Eason, Amazon and Apple

Just can't wait?
Buy our books online a month before they hit the shops!
visit www.millsandboon.co.uk

These books are also available in eBook format!

MILLS & BOON®

The Regency Collection – Part 1

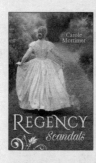

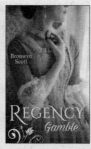

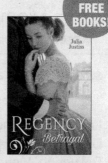

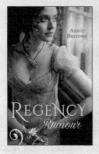

Let these roguish rakes sweep you off to the Regency period in part 1 of our collection!

Order yours at **www.millsandboon.co.uk/regency1**

 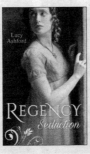 
 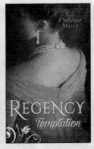 

MILLS & BOON®

The Gold Collection!

You'll love these bestselling stories
from some of our most popular authors!

Order yours at **www.millsandboon.co.uk/gold**